ENCOUNTER WITH A COMMANDING OFFICER

BY
CHARLOTTE HAWKES

REBEL DOC ON HER DOORSTEP

BY
LUCY RYDER

MILLS & BOON

Born and raised on the Wirral Peninsula, England, **Charlotte Hawkes** is mum to two intrepid boys who love her to play building block games with them and who object loudly to the amount of time she spends on the computer. When she isn't writing—or building with blocks—she is company director for a small Anglo/French construction company. Charlotte loves to hear from readers, and you can contact her at her website: charlottehawkes.com.

With two beautiful daughters, **Lucy Ryder** has had to curb her adventurous spirit and settle down. But because she's easily bored by routine she's turned to writing as a creative outlet, and to romances because—'What else is there other than chocolate?' Characterised by friends and family as a romantic cynic, Lucy can't write serious stuff to save her life. She loves creating characters who are funny, romantic, and just a little cynical.

ENCOUNTER WITH A COMMANDING OFFICER

BY
CHARLOTTE HAWKES

Published in Great Britain 2017
By Mills & Boon, an imprint of HarperCollins*Publishers*
1 London Bridge Street, London, SE1 9GF

© 2017 Charlotte Hawkes

ISBN: 978-0-263-92663-7

Printed and bound in Spain
by CPI, Barcelona

Dear Reader,

This is my first story set in and around the fictional Military Camp Razorwire, in the middle of nowhere, thousands of miles from home—and I'm enjoying writing several more.

I am a great supporter of our armed forces, and am often humbled by the heroic stories of soldiers—both from history and the present day, male and female—who have made that split-second decision to put someone else's life ahead of their own and then dismiss it as '*something anyone would have done*'.

Both my hero—a dedicated Infantry soldier—and my heroine—an army trauma doctor on the helicopter emergency response—are dedicated to their careers, and both are trying to make up for unhappy childhoods, if for different reasons. Working together proves a distraction neither of them appreciates, and yet ultimately neither of them can hold out.

I have had great fun writing about the push and pull of heroes and heroines who are committed to their careers only to meet—and strive in vain to resist—the one person who can get under their skin. The one person who can make them forget everything they had hitherto held as important.

I do so hope you enjoy reading Fliss and Ash's story as much as I did writing it.

Charlotte x

To Flo,
Thank you for all your understanding and patience
this past difficult year.
x

Books by Charlotte Hawkes

Mills & Boon Medical Romance

The Army Doc's Secret Wife
The Surgeon's Baby Surprise

Visit the Author Profile page at millsandboon.co.uk.

**Praise for
Charlotte Hawkes**

'…well-written, well thought-out and one of
greatness…definitely one to pick up for an amazing
story.'

—*Harlequin Junkie* on
The Surgeon's Baby Surprise

CHAPTER ONE

'So, I TAKE it you've never had the pleasure of meeting Colonel Man Candy either?'

Fliss paused in her half-hearted attempt to cut up her breakfast with the flimsy plastic knife and fork, and stared at her friend incredulously. Then, given the din of the several hundred men in the Army mess tent, assumed she must have misheard. Clearly the latest forty-eight-hour shift had messed with her imagination.

'Say again? For a minute there I thought you said Colonel Man Candy.'

'Yeah, I did.' Her friend grinned wickedly. 'But it gets better. Apparently up until a few months ago he was Major Man Candy.'

Fliss snorted. '*Major* Man Candy? Seriously, Elle?'

'Seriously.'

'People *actually* call him that?'

'They actually do.' Her friend shrugged. 'To the extent that I have no idea what his real name is. But I *can* tell you that a good portion of the camp is buzzing about his arrival, male and female as it happens, though for different reasons. Apparently, he's also something of a maverick who has risked his life for his men on multiple occasions.'

Unconvinced, Fliss wrinkled her nose.

'I haven't heard any *buzz*. Not even a single *z*.'

'No, well, you wouldn't—you don't indulge in gossip and anyone who knows you knows better than to engage with you unless it's strictly Army related, preferably medical.'

'I do…gossip.' Fliss nodded uncertainly, biting back the fact she'd been about to comment that it would be inappropriate for any colonel, Man Candy or otherwise, to have any kind of relationship with most of the camp.

Her friend's snort said it all.

'Fliss, you *cannot* gossip for the life of you. And certainly not about fellow military colleagues.'

'I don't agree. For a start *this,* what we're doing right now, is gossip.'

'No, this is *me* gossiping and *you* listening, about to say something like, *Well, interpersonal relationships between ranks aren't appropriate because they compromise the integrity of a unit.'*

Caught red-handed, Fliss could only flush as her friend laughed fondly. She lifted her head.

'Well…it *is* true.'

'Fliss, you know that I love you. In fact, if you were a stick of rock you'd have *Army Rules and Regulations* stamped through and through.'

Fliss blew out a deep breath, a familiar ripple of uncertainty and frustration lapping somewhere inside her before settling back down again. She'd always been known as *serious* Fliss, *nerdy* Fliss, *prim and proper* Fliss; she couldn't help it, it was ingrained in her. The result, no doubt, of having being raised from the age of eight by an uncle who was a military man through and through, believing in the extremely high reputation of the British Army with its strong sense of discipline, values and ethics.

And he'd drilled it into her. Not that she was complaining—her highly principled uncle had been her one saviour, her rock, throughout her life. The one person who hadn't seen her as a burden, but as a bright though shy girl with potential. The one person who hadn't rejected her. Her uncle had spent twenty-five years supporting her and encouraging her. He'd been so proud of her when she'd finally achieved her dream of becoming an Army trauma doctor, just as she was immensely proud that he was now one of the most highly decorated generals in the army, and that she could call herself his niece.

Spearing a lump of scrambled egg, Fliss popped it into her mouth, but her throat was a little too tight to swallow. Not for the first time, she wished she could forget the baggage and lessons of her past. Just once it would be nice to know what it felt like not to be the solid, dependable Fliss who immediately assessed the ramifications of any given situation, but to be more like her friend, Elle, who was always able to have a carefree laugh and whose sunny disposition and kind-hearted openness made her popular wherever she went.

'Go on, then—' Fliss plastered a cheery smile onto her face '—tell me more about Major Man Candy.'

She didn't miss the flash of suspicion on her friend's face but, to her credit, Elle didn't question it.

'Okay, so it seems he's been infantry major on the front line in warzones, doing several back-to-back tours of duty over the last few years, and, like I said, he has a reputation as being quite the maverick, the kind of guy they make Hollywood films about. Plus, Man Candy has the kind of military commendation record which would leave even the most decorated generals or admirals envious.'

'And now he's a colonel in a non-combat zone?' Fliss looked dubious. 'Stuck within the confines of a place like Camp Razorwire and meant to work behind a desk all day instead of out in the field. He isn't going to like that, is he?'

She could still remember the year when her uncle had been promoted from a field-based officer to one who spent most of his time in barracks. He'd found the transition hard and Fliss had hated to see his frustration.

'Well, if half the single female contingent I've heard chatting about him get their way, I think he's going to be too busy dealing with ambushes and bombardments of a more sexual nature to miss being on the front line in the middle of the action.'

'You make it seem like they're all highly sex-charged.' Fliss frowned, aware she was being prudish but unable to help herself. 'They *are* professional soldiers.'

'And they're also women,' Elle pointed out airily, accustomed to Fliss's more steadfast opinions. '*Single* women. Out here for six months at a time. They're entitled to a bit of harmless flirtation in their downtime.'

'Until it all goes wrong,' Fliss shot back, but a hint of niggling doubt had already set in. Elle's argument was all starting to sound a little too pointed.

'For example, if two officers—let's say like you and oh, I don't know, a certain new colonel—were to… As long as you were discreet, what harm could it cause?'

'I knew it,' exclaimed Fliss, dropping her plastic cutlery on the paper plate. 'Forget it, Elle. That's just not my style.'

'Why not? Because you've never done it before? So what? Maybe this is your one time to do something crazy. Especially now that idiot ex of yours is out of the picture.'

A heaviness pressed on Fliss's chest. Not sadness exactly, but a sense of…failure. She strived to ignore it.

'Because he doesn't sound like the kind of guy I'd go for. And please don't mention Robert—you were always more than honest with me about your feelings about him.'

'All right.' Elle chuckled fondly. 'But, from what I've heard, Man Candy is everyone's type.'

'He doesn't sound like mine.'

In fact, he sounded the complete opposite. Robert had been solid, steady, dependable. The pressure increased on her chest. She'd been attracted to the fact that, like her, he was dedicated to his career, driven to achieve. She'd thought they were a perfect match. A logical couple. A practical choice.

Look where that had got her.

'Well, if anyone would be immune to the Man Candy Effect it would be you,' Elle teased, oblivious. 'You're probably the most highly principled person even *I* know.'

'Yeah, yeah, Fusty Fliss.' The old nickname slipped out before Fliss had time to think about it. 'I remember.'

'Where did *that* come from?' Elle exclaimed, setting her plastic cutlery down in surprise. 'I haven't heard anyone call you that since first year of uni.'

Colour heated Fliss's cheeks. She hadn't meant for Elle to realise she'd been feeling a little vulnerable lately. It was a weakness Fliss wasn't proud of, and didn't want to reveal. Even to her best friend.

'Brody Gordon,' Fliss mumbled. 'And you're right, the guy was an idiot. I don't know why I even said it. Just forget it, okay?'

Ducking her head, she resumed her breakfast but her appetite was waning. She might have known her friend wouldn't let it drop.

'Is this about Buttoned-Down Bob?' Elle demanded. Too close to the bone for Fliss's liking.

'Don't call him that.' She kept her voice soft, trying to play the topic down. But Elle was like the proverbial dog once it had a juicy bone in its sights. 'He's a respected surgeon. A good man.'

Elle wasn't having any of it.

'He's also as boring as they come. Everything he did was so painfully predictable.'

'Breaking up with me via a *Dear John* letter whilst I was stuck out here, at Camp Razorwire, in the middle of vast nothingness was hardly predictable,' Fliss pointed out.

'All right, but, that aside, he was so numbingly characterless. And, before you tell me I'm wrong, tell me that losing him has broken your heart.'

A restlessness rolled around her chest, along with something else when she thought about Robert—something she didn't want to identify.

'Don't be so melodramatic.'

'You're side-stepping,' Elle said, not unkindly. 'Tell me your heart broke when you read his words. Tell me you rushed to the phone to find some way to communicate with him and find out what went wrong.'

'You know I didn't,' Fliss muttered, the restless rolling increasing like the rumble of thunder before a flash of lightning.

'Then tell me you love him, you miss him, you don't know how you're going to get by without him.'

She knew what Elle was trying to say but it wasn't as simple as that.

'Just because I'm not racked with despair doesn't mean I didn't love Robert in my own way. It doesn't mean I wasn't hurt.'

Yet she couldn't explain it to her friend. No, theirs hadn't been a great romance like Elle had with her own fiancé and childhood sweetheart, but it had been comfortable. He hadn't looked at her with shame like her grandparents had, and he'd never raged at her like her mother had. Life with him *had* been predictable, yes. But Fliss had appreciated that. She'd thought they both had.

It had hurt to read his letter and find out that even Robert needed more from a relationship, to see in black and white that even *he* found her too emotionally distant. The worst of it was that she knew he was right. The heaviness in her chest felt like a rising reservoir of water, its swirling dark depths drawing her closer to the edge. She'd chosen Robert because she'd thought they had the same life goals, and because she'd thought she couldn't be hurt. But his letter had felt like a painful echo of her childhood rejection.

'I did care for Robert,' she told her friend quietly. 'But I was never *in love* with him. It isn't his fault that I couldn't give him more. It's mine. I don't have that capacity in me, Elle. I don't do passion and emotion and intense love.'

'Bull,' Elle snorted. 'You just haven't met the right guy. Trust me, when you do, you'll forget all these daft rules and fears of yours. When you find *the one*, you'll know it.'

'Like you and Stevie?' Fliss said softly.

A shadow skittered unexpectedly over her best friend's face and Elle suddenly looked a million miles away— or, more likely, three thousand miles. Concern flooded through Fliss as she placed her hand on her friend's to draw Elle's focus.

'Elle, is everything okay?'

Elle blinked, the instantly over-bright smile not fooling Fliss at all.

'Of course I am. I'm just trying to help you move on from Buttoned— Sorry, Robert. And maybe have a bit of fun in the process. And, since Man Candy is off-limits to me, I have to live vicariously through you.'

Fliss bit back the questions tumbling around her head. The Army dining hall was hardly the best place to grill her best friend but she knew she had to talk to Elle the first chance they got.

'Just promise me you'll think about it? One crazy fling.

There's no better time than now and, by the sounds of it, there's no better choice than Man Candy.'

'You realise, of course, that even if I did fall over on my way out of here today, bump my head, change my personality and decide that hot sex is indeed going to sort out all my problems, then there's still the issue that he's an infantry colonel and therefore nothing to do with our medical unit and, with around eight thousand of us out here in Razorwire, we're hardly likely to cross paths.'

'So, you are at least open to the mere possibility of it?'

Fliss rolled her eyes.

'If that's what you want to take from what I said, then fine.'

'Good.' Elle nodded, swiping half a round of uneaten toast from Fliss's plate. 'By the way, did I mention that Simon wants to see you for an oh-eight-hundred briefing?'

Fliss groaned. Colonel Simon Johnson was the Commanding Officer of their medical unit. A brilliant surgeon and, like a high proportion of the medical team, a civilian volunteer. This was his second tour to Razorwire and Fliss both respected and liked him, but right now, after a forty-eight-hour shift, all she'd been looking forward to was eating her scram and then heading for the Army cot-bed which was calling to her from the shipping container she and Elle shared.

It was because of her tiredness that it took her a moment too long to register Elle's affected air of innocence.

'Wait, I have a briefing? What for?'

'Hmm? Oh, the new infantry Commanding Officer replacing Colonel Waterson is arriving.'

'Ah.'

Both women fell into a few seconds of respectful silence. They'd only met him once, but Colonel Waterson's death had been a shock. Razorwire was in a non-combat environment, its task to help local communities rebuild and improve. But the former infantry colonel hadn't been content to stay behind a desk and had flown out, on a spurious task, to a danger zone some six hundred miles away. His death had knocked the rest of the camp, not to mention rocked his own unit who were now being dragged into an internal investigation which, though standard, had the effect of further dragging down their already low morale.

Fliss could only hope that the arrival of their new Commanding Officer would help the infantry unit to heal. Not least because that particular infantry unit provided the protection units, or Quick Reaction Forces, for any other teams travelling outside of the camp, from logistics to her own medical team.

'Anyway—' Elle broke the silence firmly, both women knowing that, especially out here, far from home, it didn't pay to dwell '—since the new colonel's men form the four-man QRF teams we work with on a daily basis, Simon felt we should meet him.'

Fliss narrowed her eyes at her friend. She should have seen the set-up coming from the start.

'And this CO, is he by any chance the all-singing, all-dancing Colonel *Man Candy*?'

'Why, now you mention it—' grinned Elle '—I do believe he is. Though I think you should wait for Simon to introduce you. I don't know how the new colonel would react to you actually calling him *Man Candy* to his face.'

Fliss could only shake her head as her friend chortled with laughter. At the end of the day, she reasoned to herself, it was only a bit of fun between two friends. Man Candy was hardly going to make her go weak at the knees. The things she'd heard other women talk about had never happened to her; it just wasn't who she was.

'You're a sneaky sod, do you know that? And anyway,

if you really think someone who's as allegedly dynamic as Man Candy is going to fall for an uptight wallflower like me, then maybe you're the one who took a knock on the head.'

'Piffle,' Elle sputtered.

'Piffle?'

'You heard. You've never appreciated how attractive you are; everywhere you go there are guys just clamouring for attention but you never notice. You're intelligent and wittier than you give yourself credit for, and definitely not a wallflower.'

Gratitude bloomed in Fliss like a thousand flowers suddenly opening their petals. What would she do without her uncle or Elle? They were the only two people she would ever trust. The only two people to whom she mattered. She didn't need men like Robert; they didn't offer her anything more than she already had.

'You're a good friend, Elle,' Fliss said, suddenly serious.

'That is true.' Elle consulted her chunky sports watch. 'You'd better go; briefing is in ten. Don't forget what I said. Open mind, yes? What harm can it do?'

'Fine.' Fliss shoved her chair back and stood up, lodging an apple between her teeth as she picked up her tray to take to the clearing section. 'But don't hold your breath.'

Man Candy or not, she was never going to believe in love at first sight. It just wasn't who she was.

'Ah, you're here.' The medical Commanding Officer beamed with something approaching relief as Fliss was ushered in by the adjutant.

By the look on Simon's face, the new colonel wasn't quite as sweet as his nickname suggested. Stepping into the office, she turned to greet the new infantry colonel for the first time.

It was as if time caught a breath; everything happened in slow motion. Even the air felt as thick and sticky as the sweet honey she'd spread over her toast at breakfast. All Fliss could do was suck in a long breath and stare, her mind suddenly empty of anything but the man standing, *dominating* the space.

So this was Colonel Man Candy?

The nickname simply didn't do him justice. It suggested sugar-coated and frivolous. This man was anything but.

He was tall, powerful and all hard edges more lethal than a bayonet on the end of a rifle. His uniform—sharp and crisp with that edge to it that seemed to mark infantrymen out over all other soldiers—did little to conceal the physique beneath. If anything, it enhanced it. The perfectly folded up shirtsleeves which clung lovingly to impressive biceps revealed equally strong, tanned forearms. But it wasn't merely his forearms, more something about his demeanour which suggested to Fliss that he was a soldier who was used to physical exertion in the field. Certainly not the kind of man to relish being stuck behind a desk. He exuded a commanding air. Rough. Dangerous.

He was definitely more suited to an adrenalin-fuelled life on the front line than being stuck here in the safe confines of a place like Razorwire.

Abruptly, Fliss realised that even as she was assessing the Colonel, he was appraising her too. Narrowed eyes, the colour of mountain shale and just as inhospitable, slid over her. And everywhere they travelled, they left a scorching sensation on her skin. She wanted to move, to say something. Instead she stood rooted to the spot, her throat tight and her heart pounding out a military tattoo in her chest.

Something unfurled in the pit of Fliss's stomach. Something which she didn't recognise at all but which made her feel the need to regroup. Something which scared her, yet was also perhaps a little thrilling. And then it was gone, so fast that she wondered if she hadn't simply imagined it.

Slowly, she became aware of Simon speaking with a forced cheerfulness, as though he could sense the undertones but couldn't compute them.

'Colonel, this is Major Felicity Delaunay, the trauma doctor who leads one of our primary MERT crews,' Simon introduced her, referring to the Medical Emergency Response Team which flew out from the camp in helicopters to retrieve casualties from outside the wire.

'Major, let me introduce Colonel Asher Stirling, the new CO replacing the late Colonel Waterson.'

'Colonel,' Fliss choked out, finally finding her voice as she proffered her hand, relieved to see that it wasn't shaking.

The new Colonel didn't take it. Instead, he folded his arms across his chest in a very deliberate move.

'Major Delaunay,' he bit out. 'So you're the doc who thinks she's so important she's risking the safety of my men, not to mention the rest of her own crew.'

His hostile glower pinned her in place. She wanted to snatch her own gaze away but found she couldn't. He was too mesmerising.

Still, a defiant flame flickered into life inside her.

'Would you care to elaborate, *sir*?'

She made a point of emphasising the acknowledgement of his superior rank. She didn't like what he was suggesting, but she had no intention of being accused of insubordination as well.

'I'm saying your position is on the helicopter, receiving incoming casualties and staying where my men can protect you.'

His voice was deep, his tone peremptory. And Fliss didn't just hear the words, she *felt* them too. Compression waves coursed through her whole being. He didn't just have the rank of a colonel, he *oozed* it. Authoritative and all-consuming. She had never reacted so innately to anyone—to any *man*—before. She hadn't even known it was possible to do so.

She was vaguely aware of Simon attempting to interject but it felt as though there were only the two of them in the room. The CO soon faded out, making some spurious excuse and dashing for the door.

'Is this about the incident last week when I had to leave the heli to attend a casualty?'

'As I understand it, not just last week, no,' the new Colonel continued coldly. 'My men are there to protect you…'

'They're there to protect the helicopter, the asset,' she cut in.

Waves of tightly controlled fury bounced off him.

'They are *tasked* to protect you, but I understand you make that impossible for them on a regular basis. Yet if anything were to happen to you, my men would be responsible.'

'Your *men*…'

She stopped and bit her lip, her sense of self-preservation finally kicking in. He clearly only had half the story and if he thought she was just going to stand there without setting the record straight then he could think again. But as much as this dressing-down galled her, she refused to speak badly of his men. They'd been through enough.

Straightening her spine, she jutted her chin out to give the impression she wasn't intimidated. Instead, it only reminded her just how close to each other they were standing. White heat snaked through her. She had a feeling that when this man spoke, people listened. But Fliss forced herself to push it to the side, forced herself to wonder if he was equally capable of listening.

She was about to find out.

'Your men are feeling understandably uptight right now, and I appreciate that you're only looking out for your new unit, but there *are* two sides to this story, Colonel.'

'And you're about to enlighten me?'

It was phrased as a question but the gravelly sound resonated through her, pulling her stomach impossibly taut. *This was it.* She'd challenged him and now she was going to have to back it up. Either that, or he would dismiss her as weak for ever.

She gritted her teeth but refused to back down. That wasn't what her uncle had ever taught her. And, besides, a terrible part of her desperately wanted this man's respect. His esteem.

'I understand that you've recently been promoted to colonel, and that you were a major on the front line before that, so this is a new unit for you, and these are men that you don't know well yet. I appreciate that you're only looking out for them after what happened with Colonel Waterson. He was *their* CO and it was a shock to them. But it was a shock to us all. Razorwire isn't in a warzone; we have a different mission to whatever we've had before. Whatever *you've* had before, on the front line.'

'And your point, Major?' he demanded impatiently.

'My point, Colonel, is that your men—*my* QRF—are jumpy at the moment. I know why—a helicopter is a big target for anyone on the ground with rocket launchers, and the QRF don't want us to hang around too long. But we're not in a warzone, Colonel. We're on a Hearts and Minds mission and I think your men have forgotten that in the wake of Colonel Waterson's death. They never had a problem with my getting off the heli before, and they won't again in a few weeks. And the reason I jump off is because the casualties who can't get to the heli in time might not make it if we just abandon them.'

There it was, she noted triumphantly.

The flash in his eyes suggested her words had hit home. She'd suspected that, of all people, this new Colonel wasn't the type to leave a fallen man behind. And she was right; he'd reacted as soon as she'd said the word *abandon*.

Still, he clearly wasn't about to give in that easily. And that didn't surprise her.

'My men informed me that the casualties weren't in immediate danger.'

'With all due respect, sir, your men aren't trauma doctors. I am. Just because there are no bombs out here, no IEDs, with fatalities and casualties requiring multiple amputations, doesn't mean there aren't urgent cases.'

'I am well aware of that, Major,' he ground out, his eyes drilling into her. 'I've carried a fair few men to a MERT over the years.'

'Yes, but usually from the front line, I understand. Out here, we have non-combat injuries to deal with, from Road Traffic Accidents to local kids in gas bottle explosions around their home, from peace-keeping troops with appendicitis to local women in labour requiring emergency medical intervention. It might not always look fatal to your battle-hardened troops but fatality comes in less obvious guises. And I made a judgement call each time.'

And she'd been right each time too, not that she was about to offer that information up. It would have far greater impact when the Colonel found that out for himself. And she knew without a doubt that he would.

'Indeed?' The Colonel raised his eyebrows at her.

His mind was not entirely swayed but he was clearly considering her position. She suppressed a thrill of pleasure. It was a victory of sorts. And all the sweeter because, for a second there, she'd almost lost herself to a side of her character she had never before known existed. A side which wasn't immune—as she had so long believed—to the tedious and feeble vagaries of an instant physical attraction.

But she had fought it, and she had won. Hopefully she'd managed to convince the new Colonel to get his men to back off for the last few weeks of her tour of duty and, with him being infantry and her being medical, there was no reason she'd have to see him again.

Relief mingled with something else which Fliss didn't care to identify.

It was all short-lived.

He stepped in closer, almost menacingly so, and instinctively her eyes widened a fraction, her breath growing shallower.

He picked up on it immediately, but it was only when his eyes dropped instantly to her rapidly rising and falling chest, his nostrils flaring as she heard his sharp intake of breath, that Fliss realised he was as affected by her as she was by him.

Her? The girl Brody Gordon had referred to as Fusty Fliss? Attracting a guy as utterly masculine as the Colonel? It hardly seemed possible.

And then she realised what this uncharacteristic moment of weakness was all about for her. It wasn't some incredible, irresistible attraction at all. It was merely the fact that Robert's rejection had exposed unhealed wounds from her past which she had scarcely buried beneath the surface. Old rejections and feelings of inadequacy that her mother, her grandparents and boys like Brody Gordon had cruelly instigated.

She wanted to pull away from the Colonel now, use the revelation to her advantage. But it seemed that even knowing the truth wasn't helping her to resist him. He pinned her down, his eyes locked with hers, inching forward until they were toe to toe and her head was tilted right up to hold the stare. For several long seconds Fliss was sure she stopped breathing.

And then, finally, he broke the spell.

'I must say, *Major*, my interest is piqued.' The fierce expression had lifted from his rough-hewn face to be replaced by a look which was simultaneously wicked and challenging. White heat licked low in her belly.

'I understand your next forty-eight-hour shift begins at oh-six-hundred tomorrow?'

'That's right,' she acknowledged carefully, a sense of foreboding brewing in the tiny office.

'Good. Then I'll accompany you for the first twenty-four hours and we'll see what we discover, shall we?'

Her whole body shivered.

'You can't do that; you don't have the authority. You're not my commanding officer. You're not even medical.'

'No—' he seemed unfazed '—but I *am* the CO of the infantry unit which provides your protection unit and, since they are my guys, I *do* have a reason to be on that heli. I hardly think your buddy Simon is going to object when I run it by him. Do you?'

'It's *my* heli, *my* run. I could tell my CO it wouldn't be appropriate.'

She was grasping at straws and they both knew it. The wicked smile cranked up a notch, and so did the fire burning low in her core. He dropped his voice to a husky rasp which seemed to graze her body as surely as if he'd run callused fingers over the sensitive skin of her belly.

'And on what grounds exactly are you going to object?'

He had a point; she could hardly tell Simon that she didn't want to be in close confinement on a heli with the new infantry CO because there was an inexplicable chemistry between them that, when she was around him, made her body heat up and her brain shut down.

She was trapped and they both knew it. Worse, Fliss was left with the distinct impression that a tiny part of her actually *liked* it.

Clenching her fists and spinning around as Simon finally bustled back into the room, Fliss studiously ignored the terrifying voice which whispered that the truth was, she just might have experienced her very first *lust* at first sight.

CHAPTER TWO

CROUCHED IN THE corner of the cramped, sweltering, noisy Chinook—kitted out as a full airborne emergency room, its engines the only thing one could smell or hear—Ash fought down the nausea which was threatening to overwhelm him.

He'd seen the MERT in action too many times to count during his seven tours of duty over the last decade, several back to back. He had an incredible respect for the doctors and medics who ran what was, essentially, an airborne operating room. Many of his men, his *friends*, were still alive today because of the swift, skilled actions of MERT teams. But although he'd carried many casualties to the heli as part of the infantry team on the ground, the only time he'd actually been on board had been when he himself had been seriously injured.

Ash kept his eyes firmly open. If he closed them, the sounds were too brutally familiar. If he closed them, the scents, the turbulence, transported him right back to that day. If he closed them, he could almost feeling his life ebbing away.

Instead, he studiously watched the attractive blonde major who was running this flying operating room with impressive command and focus. Even now she was diligently prepping any last pieces of equipment. He could imagine her as the focused, methodical doctor, but he still couldn't imagine her ever breaking the rules to save a soldier, the way his new unit had claimed she'd done on more than one occasion.

But that wasn't the reason he was here, was it?

From the minute she'd walked into that room yesterday, she'd somehow slipped under his skin and he'd found himself reacting to her in a way that made him feel out of control. And for Ash it was all about being in control. About not allowing himself to feel. Because feeling meant being at the mercy of emotions. And that wasn't something he permitted.

He'd kept an iron grip on his emotions for two decades now. They were a liability he couldn't afford. Not since the beatings, the push and pull from the miserable care home to the squalor of foster homes, to his dad, who'd somehow convinced the authorities he'd stopped the drinking, right up until the cycle had started all over again. Only Rosie and Wilf had shown him another way. They'd been the only foster parents able to take on that angry, out-of-control kid that he'd been and show him love, and hope, and a way out.

A darkness unfurled in him, snaking its devious way up to constrict his chest painfully until he found it hard even to breathe. Controlling his emotions, keeping people at arm's length, had been an important lesson growing up and it was even more important now. Out here on a tour of duty and waiting, at any time, for a phone call to tell him the inevitable had happened, that Rosie had finally lost her fight and he would have to fly home for what was likely to be the worst funeral of his life.

Perhaps it was no wonder, then, that he'd reacted as he had done when the Major had strode into that office yesterday. Even now, at the mere memory, awareness crackled through his body, dancing over the darkness which had filled him a moment ago as though it was nothing. As though that forbidding fear couldn't compete with the light-hearted lust which toyed playfully with him. As though it knew that once, *just this once,* he could be tempted to cross the line and consider a hot…fling with someone like the Major, just because it offered him the promise of distraction, a release from the tension of waiting. Of not knowing.

That's not going to happen.

Furiously, he shoved the idea aside. He *never* mixed personal relationships with his career. Not out here. Not within the Army. It had too much potential to become…messy.

Yet his eyes slid inexorably across the heli to the commanding Major. She made him react to her in the basest of ways. Yet she also challenged him mentally. He hadn't intended to give her the dressing-down that he had, anticipating instead that he'd voice his concerns and find out what she had to say before making a judgement. Instead, he'd allowed his attraction to her to override his usual common sense.

But, instead of meekly surrendering, she'd looked him in the eye and refuted every one of his statements clearly and confidently. And that had piqued an interest in Ash. Before he'd known where he was, he'd bagged himself a ringside seat to all the shouts her MERT would respond to over the next twenty-four hours.

This wasn't helping.

He dragged his attention away from her and concentrated on the four-man QRF team made up from his new infantry unit. The Major had been right about them too. It hadn't taken him long yesterday to find out that his new unit *was* particularly wound up about the incident which had claimed the life of Colonel Waterson. He would do well to boost their morale and he had no doubt that, given half a chance, the Major would happily instruct him on that too.

And now he was back to her. Again.

But now, for the first time he could ever recall, his iron grip, honed over the last two decades, was slipping. His focus threatened. And all because of this one woman.

His gaze slipped back to the by-the-book Major as he tried to work out what was so different about her. So prim and proper, she was certainly attractive with those barbed Nordic blue eyes and blonde hair pulled into such an eye-wateringly severe yet generous bun that his fingers had actually itched to reach up and release. To slide his fingers through the silk curtain and soften the strait-laced doctor, even a fraction.

What the heck was wrong with him?

It was the last thing Ash needed. Not just because she was General Delaunay's niece but because this was the first role Ash had taken behind the wire, in the relative safety of Camp Razorwire. He certainly felt on edge at the prospect of facing the next few years behind a desk instead of out in the field. Out where he belonged. Barely a month ago he'd been a major himself, on the front line and leading his company as he risked his own life alongside his men. Now he was a colonel, in charge of a battalion and destined—maybe not on this tour of duty, but on a future one—not to lead his men but to *send* them into potential danger zones.

How the hell was he supposed to get used to that?

Behind a desk wasn't where he functioned best. All his career he had experienced the adrenalin kick, the fear, the buzz, and he'd been in control.

Now, as galling as it was to admit, he felt lost.

Suddenly, the heli filled with dust as it dropped, the rotor blades churning up the ground covering and drawing it into the back on the air currents, blinding them all. Ash buried his nose into his combat jacket like a filter so that he could breathe. And then they landed, rough and abrupt, and the dust was sucked quickly instantly out, leaving the aircraft clear again.

It took everything Ash had to fight his instinct to jump out of the back ahead of his QRF to help secure the area around the heli, safe zone or not. As two of his men secured the rear, where soldiers were already running across the open ground carrying a litter-bound casualty, the other two men leapt up to man the ramp-mounted and side-mounted machine guns respectively. They were smooth and slick and Ash nodded to himself in satisfaction. It was what he'd expected, but still, it was good to see.

'RTA on the Main Supply Route,' the young team medic for the soldiers' unit rushed ahead to the heli to brief the MERT, yelling over the din. 'Local guy driving a flatbed truck across the bridge running perpendicular above us when he suffered a tyre blow out and lost control. Nothing he could do, his truck jack-knifed and he crashed through the barrier and landed on our convoy. We've got three casualties.'

Even as he finished, the soldiers had already reached them with the first casualty and the Major and her team efficiently hauled the litter on board and began their medical care. Just behind, two soldiers were helping the injured local man to hobble to the heli, an open fracture to one arm and clearly shaken. Walking wounded, that was always preferable. The teams would settle him in a seat and then pass him on to the camp hospital for care. But, even from across the helicopter, Ash could see that the first victim had significant crush injuries. He wasn't a doctor but Ash had enough experience to know. All vital signs were absent and, to all intents and purposes, the soldier was gone. But it wasn't the MERT's place to call time of death; they didn't have the authority. That could only be done when they returned to Camp Razorwire and a team from the hospital came out.

Not that you'd know it from the Major's poker face; there was no sign of defeat in her expression, nothing to knock the morale of the soldiers on the ground, who wanted her to save the life of their buddy. Instead the MERT were doing their job and starting care, the Major already checking the casualty's airway and giving oxygen as the team began cardiopulmonary resuscitation. It meant a lot out here, in the middle of vast nothingness. Back on the front line, it would have been exactly the kind of mental boost the guys would need. A reluctant admiration sparked in Ash.

Suddenly, a movement in his peripheral caught Ash's attention. A third team carrying a casualty, stretcher-bound like the first, was rounding the bend approximately one hundred metres away. Even from that distance there was evidence of heavy blood loss but what worried Ash more was the long metal rod protruding from the casualty's abdomen. There was no way they would be able to get the soldier onto the heli like that.

In an instant, Ash had sprung out from his corner and jumped off the ramp to dart, body low against the downdraught of the rotors, across the open ground. There was definitely a sandstorm coming in; he'd spent enough time out in the field to be able to sense it before almost anyone else. Reaching the litter, he was relieved to find the casualty on his side, delirious but mercifully still alive.

'Set him down gently, lads,' Ash commanded quietly but firmly enough to counter their resistance out of loyalty to their friend. 'He's not going to get on board like that.'

Ash watched as, for a split second, understandable desperation to get their buddy to the heli warred with following a senior officer's instruction. It was only when he heard the voice over his shoulder that he realised the Major had followed right behind him carrying an emergency kit bag.

'The Colonel's right, lads. I need to check your buddy out first and we'll go from there.'

Pushing briskly through, the Major settled next to the litter and pushed lightly to encourage the soldiers to set it down on the level ground.

'What's his name?' she asked.

'Hollings.'

'Corporal Hollings.'

'Okay—' she nodded, checking the lad's vital signs '—and his first name?'

'Oh, right. It's Andy.'

'Andy, can you hear me? You've got the MERT here now; we're just going to get you ready for transport, okay?'

Ash watched as she began to administer oxygen, all the while calming the other soldiers and creating some space around them.

'We're going to need to cut the rod down to a more manageable size prior to transport.' She lifted her head to look directly at him. They both knew the MERT wouldn't be able to wait.

Quickly, Ash dropped down until they were close enough to murmur without broadcasting. 'There's a sandstorm coming in.'

'We need to get him out of here as quickly as we can.'

'I'll handle it. How long do you need?'

'Longer than we've got,' she muttered grimly. 'Radial pulse is weak, thready. He's not moving air around and there's pressure in the pleural space. I can carry out a needle decompression but it's only a temporary measure. All the good kit is on the heli. Because of the location of the rod I can't get him into a supine position. And that's without knowing for sure what damage he might have caused internally.'

With a curt nod, Ash raced back to the heli to relay the information, telling them to leave now but to call in the other MERT. At least that way it would have the wait time. The Major had better be able to do what was necessary in that window. Once the storm closed in the helis wouldn't be able to fly and travelling by road would take too long.

He had to admit, though, that he'd seen a lot of good trauma doctors in his time, but the Major had something extra about her, an edge, which he couldn't help but respect.

'Any sheltered locations around here?' Ash demanded as he ran back to the casualty, which the Major had already moved further back in anticipation of the dust cloud the departing helicopter would raise.

'There's a couple of abandoned buildings about half a click away, but they're boarded up. We'll have to bust a way in.'

With any luck the MERT would be back before the sandstorm hit. But if they were unlucky, they were going to need a decent place to wait it out, especially with the casualty.

'Grab any kit we might need and show me,' Ash commanded one of the soldiers.

'Okay, when we cut the rod the vibration could cause more internal damage, so you and you hold it absolutely steady,' she was instructing firmly, calmly, ensuring everyone knew their role whilst still efficiently moving along the task. 'And you cut right here, understand?'

'Ma'am.'

Ash was quickly getting the impression that, once this was all over, he was going to owe the Major something of an apology.

CHAPTER THREE

'MAJOR.' ASH STEPPED to one side in the corridor as the team filed out of the briefing room several hours later. 'A word.'

'Colonel?'

'I wanted to say that was nice work this morning.'

She eyed him carefully, the corners of her mouth twitching before glancing around to ensure everyone had left.

'Is that your idea of an apology?'

She was teasing him?

Something wound around Ash's gut. Hot, raw. It pulled tight.

He fought it. Drew in a sharp breath.

'No, it's my idea of an acknowledgement. If you hadn't leapt off the heli like that, prepared to be left in the middle of nowhere, Corporal Hollings would probably never have made it back here alive. Good work.'

'He also might not have made it if you hadn't secured that compound the way you did. We all played a part in that success,' she breathed.

'Well…' His voice was huskier than usual and Ash consoled himself with the fact that she didn't know him well enough to know that.

He silenced the voice that whispered it was a shame she didn't know him well enough to know that.

'So is that really what you stopped me out here to tell me?'

She held his gaze unwaveringly, drawing him inexorably down into those seductive and all too perceptive depths. He couldn't recall if he'd ever wanted any woman quite as much as he wanted her. He kept trying to tell himself that it was just the shared experience out there which had bonded them in a way which wouldn't otherwise have happened. It was hardly surprising. A few hours in such a hostile environment allowed you to see facets of a person it might otherwise take years to unearth.

He knew it was more than that. The chemistry had been palpable from the moment they'd met. It was what had caused him react so strongly back in her CO's office. Had he really thought that attacking her the way he had instead of getting her side of the story would prove that he hadn't been standing there imagining what it would be like to have been in that office alone and claimed her as though they were teenagers behind the back of the school gym, instead of professional, responsible army officers?

'I did want to mention it. But no, it isn't all I wanted to say, *Major*.' The emphasis of her rank was more to remind himself than her. 'You were right about the men in my new unit. They are finding it difficult to assimilate replacements and, as you identified, because Camp Razorwire isn't a warzone the previous CO may not have paid enough attention to it.'

The tilt of her head, the light in her expression, even the increased respect in her eyes all played to his basic male pride. Ash knew it yet was powerless against it, the raw sexual appeal too strong.

'I'm glad you can see it too.' She nodded sincerely. 'They're good lads; they just need someone who can talk to them in their language, someone who understands what it's like out there on the front line, someone who can take them in hand.'

It was clear to Ash what she was being careful *not* to say. That Colonel Waterson had been on the front line a little too long before he'd got his commission and hadn't handled the transition to flying a desk well. It was the same unsettling battle Ash himself was now facing, but seeing how failure to get the balance right had led to some poor decisions on the former Colonel's part, with tragic consequences, Ash knew it was imperative that he found a way to accept the monumental change his promotion had brought.

'Actually, I was hoping for your help in that,' he announced, firmly quashing any doubts that, if he wasn't yet playing with fire, he was most certainly toying with a full box of matches.

He didn't blame her for her suspicious frown but he had to clench his fist to stop himself from reaching out to smooth it away. Her skin looked silky-soft.

What would it be like to touch his lips to her, taste her?

'You want *my* help?'

'You were the one who noticed the men were beginning to close ranks, view others as outsiders.' He shrugged. 'You work with them on a daily basis and you clearly care deeply about your fellow soldiers. Why *wouldn't* I want your help?'

He could practically see her mind whirling, trying to decide whether he was serious. Whether she should acknowledge the sparks which, even now, arced between the two of them. They made his stomach pull taut, his chest swell; she made him feel like a horny kid again, but he was determined that if he ignored it long enough it would pass. It had to. He'd never allowed himself to be distracted from his Army career before and he wasn't about to start now.

His rank and reputation were all he had left.

Rosie might not be dead yet, but realistically he'd lost the only mother he remembered a long time ago. Pain seared through him but he thrust it viciously away. Waiting for the phone call to confirm it felt like losing her all over again. It was just another version of hell.

He would control it. Just as he always controlled his emotions these days.

Dragging himself back to reality, he was just in time to see Fliss peering crossly at his right shoulder. He resisted the urge to twist away, knowing it was too late.

'What's that?' she demanded.

He gritted his teeth. 'It's nothing.'

'There's a dark stain discolouring the fabric and it looks suspiciously like blood,' she accused. 'Did you think that just because it's called *multi-terrain camouflage pattern* I wouldn't spot it?'

'It's probably Corporal Hollings's blood.'

The dark look she cast him actually made him ache. It was as though she actually...*cared.*

Something inside him cracked. The faintest hairline fracture, but it was there all the same.

'What, *after* you've grabbed a shower and changed? Anyway, the line's too neat for that. It looks as though someone's tried to patch it up and it has seeped through the sides of a bandage,' she said pointedly.

'I advise you to lower your voice,' murmured Ash, equally pointedly.

Her head jerked up sharply. He couldn't blame her; she'd hardly been shouting but he had no idea who else might be around. She cast him a disappointed gaze.

'Are you going to pretend you're fine? Because I can tell you now that the macho soldier doesn't impress me.'

'So you think I'm trying to impress you? Do I need to remind you that I may not be your CO, but I am still *a* CO?'

She flushed but stood her ground. It was a trait he'd got to know very quickly. And one he liked. A lot.

'As you wish, *Colonel.* But do I need to remind you that,

CO or not, when it comes to medical issues I have ultimate authority, even over you?'

She was so damned sexy when she was being combative. As though she couldn't bear to relinquish control any more than he could.

'That doesn't change the fact that I'm not discussing this here.'

'So it *is* macho pride?' She shot him another disappointed gaze. 'I was beginning to think better of you. But, either way, you *will* show me that wound, *Colonel.*'

Unexpectedly, she marched up the corridor, unlocked a supply room door and held it open with a jerk of her hand to command him inside.

'Or do I have to physically manhandle you in here?' she muttered.

He'd like to see her try. He swallowed down a wicked grin. Scratch that, he *wouldn't* like to see her try. He was barely controlling the impulse to pull her closer and kiss that defiant glower right off her delectable mouth as it was. Having her touch him, in any capacity, would be like striking the damn match.

He hesitated, then consented to enter the room, his voice low but clear.

'It's not about *macho pride*, as you call it. As you pointed out so succinctly yesterday, my men have already lost one colonel and morale is low. I don't want it sinking even further because they caught wind of some rumour that their new CO had also been injured.'

A pretty flush spread up and over her neck as she realised the truth of his words. Ash wasn't sure what was cuter, the Major mad at him or the Major embarrassed by him. Still, she recovered quickly enough. Or at least that was what she wanted him to think.

'What's more, injured on your first sortie,' she pointed out shakily.

He couldn't keep the wry tone out of his voice. 'Indeed.'

Checking the corridor, she closed the door behind them and gestured to him to join her beside a clear countertop.

'Take your shirt off, and whatever layers you're wearing underneath, and let me see that wound properly.'

So clipped, so professional, but Ash thought he heard the faintest quiver beneath. For a moment he debated the wisdom of being in this claustrophobic room, half-naked and alone with a woman he couldn't seem to keep his hands off, at least in the privacy of his own head.

And what about the scars?

He'd never worried about his scars before. He was an infantry soldier; other men who'd seen them knew better than to ask, and women who'd seen them had swallowed whatever superficial story he'd thrown at them.

But the Major?

Ash had a feeling she would be able to see right through him.

He locked his jaw irritably. Since when did it matter to him what she—what anyone—thought? Hooking his fingers under the layers, he pulled them over his head in one smooth movement before folding his arms, seemingly casually, over his chest.

With something approaching satisfaction, he heard the air *whoosh* out of her lungs, saw her pupils dilating as she backed up further. She was fighting it, this attraction. And yet, even as she did so, her eyes didn't stop raking over him, with the results as real as if she'd actually raked her fingernails across his skin instead. His body burned up with desire.

They just had to get through this before he gave in to his baser instincts and, for the first time in his career on an active tour of duty, mixed his Army life with his personal one.

Every time he thought he was back in control, she slipped beneath the surface and unravelled all his iron-clad control like a kitten would toy with a ball of yarn. Suddenly, he didn't want to fight it any more. He wanted to know how it would feel to give in—just this once—and steal one perfect kiss from those plump, quivering lips.

One kiss.

No, he'd survived ambushes, engaged in fifty-hour fire-fights and fought with the enemy in hand-to-hand combat. He'd pick any one of those over letting this woman get close enough to sneak behind his armour.

Just one kiss.

It was a constant battle between his baser instincts and his brain. *Only an animal couldn't control their baser instincts,* he warned himself contemptuously. Besides, this woman could hurt him more than any enemy could.

But just one kiss.

The man was magnificent.

Her heart couldn't work out whether to race or to miss beats, her eyes seemed riveted on the well-honed physique to which even her imagination hadn't done justice and her nostrils filled with a fresh, citrusy shower gel scent mingled with the undertones of leather. Ever since she'd mentioned the shower, standing back in that corridor, she hadn't been able to stop mentally placing him under the hot flow of water as it cascaded over those broad shoulders and down that all too sculpted physique. His proximity was so damned consuming.

'Can you see it from there, or are you going to come a little closer?' Deep and sensual, his voice reverberated through her, body-slamming her and sending heat pooling between her legs.

'I need supplies first,' she hedged.

Another eyebrow quirk. 'Without inspecting the wound?'

She felt decidedly rattled. Whatever had happened to 'stick of rock' Fliss, with Army Rules and Regulations stamped right through her? She scrambled for an excuse not to step closer until she was sure she wouldn't do something as improper as running her hands over him.

But what would it be like to feel those beautiful muscles bunching beneath her palms? Those callused fingers grazing her soft skin?

'I can tell from here it's going to need suturing,' she lied, coughing to clear her throat.

In all her years within the military she had never— not once—fantasised about a fellow soldier. Fliss stopped abruptly.

Come to think of it, she had never in her life fantasised about anyone.

She hadn't been able to see what purpose a fantasy served. No one before had ever set her pulse racing or filled her with such a raw need that her whole body actually trembled at the thought of their touch.

And then the Colonel had come along and she'd stood in that tent and felt as though she'd been hit by an armoured tank. Being in the field with him and seeing him in action, working with him in such harmony as though they'd known each other for years, had only intensified the attraction.

She'd seen a fair few heroes in her role as an army trauma doctor, but the Colonel was the stuff of action films. And he had something more, something harder, some inner drive. She'd been given a taste of what he was capable of, how loyal he was, and the physical attraction had expanded into something more.

It frightened her even as it excited her.

He's just a man.

She tried to push the tumultuous emotions from her brain but, even now, he dominated the space, his backside resting on the countertop, his long, powerful legs stretched out in front of him, one ankle crossed casually over the other. Her heart hammered so fast she was surprised he couldn't hear it. She wanted to look away but she couldn't tear her eyes from his body. The tiny room practically pulsed with his dark, powerful energy, sliding under her skin and into her veins to flutter wildly at her neck. His eyes slid to her pulse as if he could read her thoughts, swiftly followed up with his lips thinning as if in distaste.

It was a rejection she recognised all too well.

Hurt cut through her. Enough to kick-start her sense of self-preservation. What was she thinking, imagining a guy like him could really be interested in someone like her?

Focus, Fliss.

'Right, let me inspect the wound,' she bit out, shaking back hair which wasn't there and advancing as confidently as she could, hands outstretched.

He braced himself. Only a fraction of a second but she didn't miss it. Heat suffused her cheeks. He could read her silly schoolgirl crush and was embarrassed on her behalf. It was all she could do not to turn and flee.

Hauling her eyes to his shoulder, she saw where he'd tried to bandage the seeping wound, not wanting anyone to know about the injury. But, as neat a job as he'd managed, the damage beneath was clearly too deep. Carefully, she reached out and peeled away the dressing. At least her hands were steady, which was more than could be said for the rest of her.

'Jeez, what did you do?' she cried out, her eyes darting to his in horror.

'What does it look like? I tried to suture it.'

'Yourself? Without anaesthetic?'

He shrugged, ignoring the second question.

'I'm usually right-handed.'

'Yeah, because *that's* why it's bleeding.'

She stared into those shale-hued eyes and felt herself teetering *oh-so-close* to the edge. With a supreme effort she pulled herself back.

'I've had worse.'

She didn't doubt it.

'How did you get it?'

'Sliced it on some rusty metal when we were breaking down the door to that compound.'

She clucked her tongue, relieved at the banality of the exchange. At least it was keeping her mind distracted whilst they were so dangerously close to each other. She prattled on quickly to stop her voice, and hands, from shaking.

'So you're going to need stitches *and* a tetanus, but you weren't intending to come to me. What are you, some kind of idiot?'

'Careful, Major.' His low voice rumbled through her. 'I've let a lot slide because you're kind of sexy when you're bossy. But don't push it.'

He was right; it was no way to speak to a superior. Certainly no way Fliss would ever have previously dreamt of speaking to one. But nothing about him had her acting like normal and, despite her best efforts, he disconcerted her, leaving her jangling nerves needing an outlet.

Wait... He thought she was sexy?

Belatedly, her eyes snapped to his, her tongue flicking out to moisten her parched lips. His gaze pulled down to the movement.

'And that doesn't help.'

'What doesn't?'

Was that breathy sound really her voice?

They had inched closer. She hadn't noticed it, but they had. Now the soft caresses of his shallow breaths tickled her cheek.

'Tell me how it is that you don't have a boyfriend or partner somewhere, worrying about you?'

Pain sliced through her more than she'd have wished. But, like every time before, it was about the sense of rejection rather than losing Robert himself.

What was so very wrong with her that the people who were supposed to care about her didn't think she was special enough for them to stay?

She took a step back from Ash, as though putting physical distance between them might ease the feelings of inadequacy. What if she told him and it caused him to think less of her as a woman?

'Who says I don't have someone?' She'd meant it to sound nonchalant but it just came out brittle, cold.

'If you did have someone, you wouldn't be here now,' Ash pointed out, unperturbed. 'You certainly wouldn't have allowed yourself to respond to me the way you do. However strong the attraction, you'd have shut it down back in your CO's office the other day.'

He was right; she would have.

'Fine,' she snapped. 'There's no one.'

'But there was?' he pushed, perceptively.

'It's none of your business.'

'Fair enough.'

'What about Simon?'

'Simon?' Fliss stopped her inspection and shot him an incredulous look.

'Your CO.'

'Yes, I know who he is.' She shook her head. 'There's nothing…like that going on.'

'He wouldn't mind if there was.'

'You're crazy,' Fliss snorted, wondering where that had come from. 'Besides, I don't do that.'

Before she could think anything else, however, Ash had slipped one arm around her waist, the other hand closing around her wrist, his legs parting as he pulled her in between them. She was far enough away that there was a clear gap between his body and hers, but so close she could almost feel him.

'Good to know,' he muttered.

She should push away. But she didn't. She couldn't resist him. Her body literally ached with the need to press against him. But, if she did, she was afraid she might forget all her principles entirely.

'I… I just said. I don't do this,' she choked out.

'Do what? *This?*'

His thumb pads stroked the inside of her wrists, causing her pulse to lurch yet again, and Fliss wondered if he could feel it. The silence hung between them, his heartbeat drumming steadily, strongly, beneath her palm as invisible threads seemed to wrap around them.

She was frozen. She knew she should pull away but she couldn't.

Someone was going to get hurt and she knew exactly who. But, even as she struggled to pull away, eyes the hue of mountain shale bound her tight, as entrancing and as perilous as a fathomless mine shaft. If she got too close to the edge she would tumble, and there would be no climbing out.

And still she didn't move away.

Slowly her hand lifted involuntarily to rest on his chest.

Another inch closer and his breath rippled over her lips, sending electricity *zinging* around her body. He was going to kiss her and she wasn't going to do anything to stop him.

So very close.

Fliss fought to harness her galloping heart as one hand still held her wrist as the other brushed up her body to cup her ribcage, his thumb grazing the underside of her breast whilst only barely touching.

And then, leaning forward, he brushed her lips with his own.

A small squeak escaped her lips.

'Oh.'

She was pretty sure she'd never squeaked in her life.

The heady mix of citrus and leather intensified and Fliss couldn't stop herself from wondering what his skin might taste like, how it would feel to graze her body against his. Her breasts felt strangely heavy, aching at the idea. But that was nothing compared to the flames licking around other parts of her body. It was like nothing she recognised.

Sex before had always been pleasant but perfunctory. She had a feeling *pleasant* was the last adjective a woman would use when describing sex with the Colonel. Her body shivered suddenly at all the adjectives she *could* imagine.

'What are you doing?' she murmured.

'I've no idea,' he admitted, running his thumb over her bottom lip, and then chasing it with his tongue. 'I just know I keep trying to resist you but then I find myself crossing the line I've always drawn in my head.'

Molten heat bubbled up inside her. The idea of pushing a man as virile as this over any line was exhilarating. Could he really want her that badly? It offered an odd sense of power. Almost a validation as a woman. And right now that was something she was sorely lacking.

Frightened of talking herself out of it, Fliss abruptly closed the gap between them. His evident arousal let her know in no uncertain terms just how badly he wanted her. Fire whipped through her and she shifted against him, hearing the moan in the back of his throat as he lifted his hand to cradle the back of her neck, his other hand cupping her backside as he pressed her even more tightly against him.

Instinctively, she parted her legs slightly, rocking against him, revelling in his low groans and her own soft sighs. And then he slipped his lips from hers, kissing along her jawline to the dip beneath her ear as his hand dropped from her neck to her breast, cupping it in one solid palm as he raked a thumb over the nipple. Even through her uniform it sent another hot stab rushing to her core. But she wanted so much more.

'Colonel…'

'Given the circumstances,' he murmured, his words trailing over her lips, 'I think calling me Ash might be more appropriate.'

'Ash…' She rolled the name around her tongue, liking the way it felt on her lips.

Finally slipping her wrist out of his grasp, she flattened her palm on his shoulder, careful to avoid the wound she hadn't even got around to dealing with yet, and let her palm graze down over his body.

It was even more incredible beneath her touch. Muscles bunched and tensed as she teased him, and he got his delicious revenge by dropping white-hot kisses into the hollow of her neck. She traced lower and lower, until she felt the edges of scars.

They went on for ever.

Surprised, she pushed back from him, her legs staying where they were but enough to dip her head to see. His whole body had tensed, his grip that little bit tighter on her body.

'What happened?'

'Grenade,' he answered simply.

So that was how he wanted to play it?

'Must have been some grenade.'

'I'm still alive,' he bit out. 'Body armour took the brunt of it.'

She could tell that wasn't exactly true and, in any case, body armour caused problems of a different kind. But Fliss said nothing; instead she traced the scars, the damaged tissue, the skin grafts. Up to his pectoral muscles, across his abs towards the line of hairs to his belly button, down over his lower abs until it dipped down beneath his waistband, where she couldn't trace it any further. Then her hands skimmed over to the insides of his forearms.

Small, circular scars, too regular in shape. She'd seen it before, but on a guy like *this*?

She snapped her head up to make direct eye contact.

'And these?'

Ash thrust her away from him so fast she almost stumbled backwards. He made no move to catch her, only folded his arms across his chest, those biceps bulging all the more, and glowered at her.

'Just get the suture kit and do your damned job, *Major*, if you can keep your hands to yourself for that long. Then we can both get the hell out of here.'

CHAPTER FOUR

'WHAT HAVE WE GOT?' Fliss jumped off the heli to speak to the medic on the ground as her team hauled the casualty on board.

'Fusilier Bowman, nineteen, was playing football with the local lads when two of them had a collision and Bowman fell on his shoulder and broke his clavicle.'

Already she could see her team checking the airway, breathing, and circulation, one of her crew moving behind the casualty to examine the clavicle itself, including any signs of deformity.

'Oscillate and percuss the lung fields to exclude pneumothorax and carry out a neurovascular examination, particularly for upper limb pulses, decreased perfusion and muscle power,' she called out. 'Okay, let's see the other lad involved.'

A brief check confirmed the other player had got off lightly. More than likely the break had occurred on impact with the ground rather than with the other player. Still, Fliss wanted to rule out the possibility of a head injury.

Satisfied, she was on her way back to the heli when a voice halted her.

'Ma'am?'

Fliss stopped, turning to the trio of soldiers eagerly approaching.

'We heard Colonel Stirling is in Razorwire now; he was on a MERT shout yesterday?' one of them asked.

Fliss nodded, wishing her whole body didn't react at the mere mention of his name.

'Are you likely to see him, ma'am?'

She plastered a pleasant smile on her lips. 'Doubtful, gents. Sorry.'

'Oh.'

The lads looked disappointed, and before she knew it she was being drawn in.

'Why?'

'It's just that... Would you just tell him...?'

'That it's a bit quiet here without him,' the second lad interjected.

Fliss pressed her lips together. It wasn't what the lads were saying so much as what they *weren't* saying. This was the closest these guys got to saying they missed someone. It said a lot about the Colonel. Her expression softened.

'He was your company commander?'

'No, ma'am.' The second lad shook his head. 'He was only a captain when we knew him, our recce platoon commander. Before he got himself blown up.'

Her heart bounded around her ribcage.

'The grenade? You were there?'

They looked like kids.

'Yeah, of course. Six years ago. The boss saved our lives,' the first lad announced proudly. 'Mick, Jonesy and me, ma'am. And some others who are going to be mad they aren't here now.'

'I see,' she acknowledged. 'I knew the Colonel had been involved in a grenade incident but I'm afraid I don't know the details.'

'Let me guess, the boss doesn't like to talk about it,

ma'am? Claims it was no big deal and he was just doing his job? That sounds about right.'

'You don't agree, gentlemen?'

'No, ma'am, we don't,' the second lad declared. 'A bunch of us wouldn't be here without him.'

Their pride and admiration was infectious and Fliss couldn't help herself. She could pretend it was professional interest. She knew better.

A few days ago she wouldn't have even considered discussing Ash's injury but, after what had happened in the supply room, she couldn't shake the part of her which was desperate to know more.

'I understand the injury is extensive; the blast got under the body armour.'

'Yeah. We'd been ambushed, ma'am, pinned down in a small courtyard. He had about six seconds between the grenade rolling in and it going off to make a decision. If he'd told us to make a run for it we'd have all got caught by the blast or the shrapnel. But the boss being the boss, he grabbed a small daysack, threw it on the grenade and threw himself on top of that.'

'He was in pretty bad shape, ma'am,' another confirmed. 'Aside from the blast injuries themselves, he had some twenty fractures or breaks from the body armour. We didn't think he was going to make it.'

'He got transferred out and I think he was recovering for about a year, ma'am, before they placed him with a new unit and made him fly a desk for three years. I think he hated every second of it.'

Fliss absorbed all the information. It certainly explained why he was finding it so hard to work in the new role as colonel, as well as why he had such an impressive reputation. But, before she could answer, one of the QRF ran over to her.

'Reports coming in of another shout,' he yelled, as Fliss had already started running alongside him back to the heli.

'A series of explosions involving gas canisters used by the local school for cooking. Multiple casualties, they're sending both MERTs out. Kids were caught in the first blast and locals and soldiers there as rescuers in the second blast.'

'Fine,' she yelled as she leaped back on board. 'We'll take this casualty back to camp and head straight back out.'

All she could do was hope against hope that it wasn't as bad as it sounded.

Ash spotted her the moment he reached the rooftop, her hunched up shape silhouetted against the horizon as she sat in solitude watching the last of the sunset over the desert.

'They said you'd be up here.'

If she heard his voice, she didn't react.

He inched along the concrete terrace, ducking low until he reached her. Her shoulders stiffened awkwardly as she finally turned, discreetly brushing at her cheeks as though they were damp and wiped a finger under each eye. Something twisted inside him to see her in distress.

'Mind if I sit down?'

There was a moment of hesitation before she inclined her head, but they both knew he'd have sat anyway.

'Want to talk about it?'

Another hesitation and this time she shook her head.

'Okay,' he acknowledged, folding his arms and allowing them both to lapse back into silence.

But at least now she wasn't alone.

He'd heard about the incident and could well imagine the grim scenario. He knew that was why she was up here alone, to vent some emotion in private without bringing down the morale of the rest of the camp. The other members of her team could console each other but he knew Fliss would feel that, as their major and leader, she had to stray strong. She could be there for them, but not the other way around.

An ingrained sense of responsibility and duty. Just like her uncle, the General. Just like *him*. He should respect that. He should just tell her the little sliver of good news he had and then he should leave.

He didn't get involved, he reminded himself brutally.

'Anyway—' Ash broke the silence '—I came up here to tell you about Corporal Hollings—the soldier from the RTA yesterday?'

'I remember who Corporal Hollings is.' She nodded quietly. 'Andy Hollings.'

Ash wasn't surprised. He had a feeling she remembered every single soldier she rescued. All her casualties mattered to her. Not that he hadn't met plenty of trauma doctors who cared before now, but there was something...*more* about Major Felicity Delaunay.

'I figured it must be pretty unpleasant sometimes, being on the MERT. You see those who don't make it, but you never get to find out what happens to those soldiers you keep alive long enough to get to the hospital.'

'Yeah, sometimes,' she agreed jerkily. 'The rush of saving a life is the greatest feeling and I love my job, I wouldn't change it for the world. But sometimes...'

'Yeah, so I thought you'd like to know that Hollings' operation went well yesterday. He'll be stable enough to be leaving on a plane back to the UK hospital within the next twelve hours. He's still alive, thanks to you.'

'And you. If you hadn't got us into that shelter...'

'We made a good team.'

He didn't realise how intimate that would sound until

the words were out. Yet with anyone else it wouldn't have held any deeper significance. By the loaded silence, Fliss thought the same.

'Thanks,' she managed at last. 'I mean, for coming to tell me.'

'No problem.'

Another silence pressed in on them. He ought to leave. He straightened his legs, ready to get up.

'Wait.'

He paused. Stopped.

'How did you know about Andy Hollings?'

Ash didn't know how best to answer her.

'It's not as though you're around the hospital much.'

'I just happened to be there,' he offered.

Her shrewd look seemed to pierce through him, boring into his armour, creating cracks where none should be.

'Do you mean you went in there specifically to check on the lad's progress? You couldn't just leave it, could you? You hoped he had pulled through the operation.'

'It isn't a big deal.'

She clicked her tongue. 'They *really* were right about you.'

'Don't read so much into it,' he warned uneasily. 'Who was right?'

'No one, forget it.'

Ash clenched his jaw. The problem was that her looks, her words, her touch, all chipped away at the guise he had painstakingly built up over the years. She was getting behind it and reaching for the man in there and he was finding it harder and harder to resist.

But he had to resist. He was having enough trouble resisting the physical attraction as it was, without her throwing in the dangerous complication of emotions.

He should leave. He'd said what he'd come up to say. Ash tried to make a move but a heaviness had set in, bone-deep, and he stayed exactly where he was.

'I've never seen the sunset from this height before,' he commented, his tone deliberately casual. 'It's impressive.'

'It's beautiful,' she muttered. 'I've taken several photos over the last few months. And this is one of several safe rooftops around camp—at least for now. Back when I was still in training, I used to have to go to a FIBUA training area back home, near where I lived. We had exercises where the soldiers would be practising their Fighting in Built-Up Areas skills, and doing casualty evacuation scenarios, and I would play out treating the casualty. I…didn't have the best childhood so I've always found it hard to talk to people. But there was a rooftop similar to this—different view, of course—which was deserted after hours so it always seemed such a peaceful place to go in order to think, to process.'

He couldn't help it. Instantly, Ash wondered what had happened in her childhood. He could bet it hadn't been anything like his. A kid like her, with a general for an uncle and Army blood running through her veins, always destined to be a commissioned officer, wouldn't know what a bad childhood was. Not the way he did. Not the way a huge number of the infantry soldiers, still kids themselves, did. He waited for the habitual bristle of resentment which always seemed to get to him when people who'd had it relatively easy thought they'd had it bad.

But for once it didn't come. Instead, he found himself trying to empathise with her. Trying to see that it was all relative and, from her point of view, it *might* have felt like a difficult time growing up.

'You come up here to process events like today,' he repeated carefully. 'I understand that.'

She hunched her shoulders, neither confirmation nor rebuttal.

'It's more than that. One day at the FIBUA an over-eager soldier fell out of a second-storey window during a routine house clearance. I ended up treating a casualty for real and performed my first emergency tracheotomy. I saved my first life and I didn't freeze, I didn't panic. The adrenalin was pumping, yes, but other than that it just came naturally. It was the moment I realised I could really do it, I could be an army trauma doctor—I could be a *great* army trauma doctor. The rooftop was where I finally let go of the past and embraced a new, positive future.'

'So you come up here after bad days like today to try to recapture that sense of victory,' he realised.

'Yes,' she whispered. 'To remember what it feels like to get it right. Saving a life is a rush like no other; it's an unbeatable feeling. But losing one is devastating. And the nature of the MERT means that sometimes you lose more than you win.'

Yes, he could certainly understand that, just as he understood her need to come up here and have her moment of weakness out of sight of the others, her reluctance to shed a tear in front of her team. He understood her sense of propriety that, as their team leader and a major, she should stay strong for them.

It was a degree of staying in control he recognised all too well.

So why was he still up here instead of leaving her alone?

Because he felt as if he could help her, Ash realised. Some part of him *needed* to help her. It wasn't about this inexplicable chemistry between them, although that had probably been the catalyst. It was about the way they had *clicked,* working in the field together the previous day. In all his experience, he had never fallen into such harmonious synchronicity with someone in such a short time, almost pre-empting each other's needs as they'd worked towards the common goal of saving that corporal's life.

'Felicity, you know you did everything you could today. You…'

'We lost them all,' she choked out, interrupting him. '*All* of them. It wasn't enough.'

'And you aren't to blame,' he stated firmly.

She didn't answer immediately, simply stared angrily out over the sunset. When she did finally speak, her voice was little more than a whisper.

'It's bad enough when it's a warzone. When there are IEDs and enemies. I've been to enough of them; I've dealt with explosions, and fatalities, and soldiers requiring multiple amputations. And all I can do, every shout, is know that I've done my utmost to get them back as much in one piece as I can.'

'I know,' he murmured reassuringly.

Her voice was choked and he knew she was close to the edge. He had no idea why, but he found himself putting his arm around her shoulders and drawing her in. She stiffened at first, resisting him, and then allowed herself to be shifted, still fighting to hold back her sense of failure.

'But here we're not in a warzone. It was an avoidable accident and it killed so many. And there was no one I could help. Not a single person. Not even one child.'

Before he could stop himself, or tell himself that this wasn't keeping control of his emotions around her, Ash twisted her around to cradle her. It was more than a colonel being there for another soldier, it was personal, and inappropriate, and dangerous.

He rubbed his hand up and down her back to soothe her. And for several long minutes she let him.

Finally, as the tears subsided and she fought to regain control, she shifted away from him as he reluctantly let her go. A dark shadow he didn't care to identify stole over his chest, pulling a tourniquet around his guts and clenching his fist.

He rubbed a hand over his face. For two people who valued their self-control, neither of them seemed to have been doing particularly well since they'd met.

What was it about this woman that was so different to anyone else?

For years he'd succeeded in keeping people at arm's length, maintaining a barrier between himself and the rest of the world. Only Rosie and Wilf had been the exception. He'd known that the only sure-fire way never to lose control of his emotions, the way his father had, was to ensure he didn't let people close enough to generate those emotions in the first instance.

Yet here he was, on the roof with a woman he'd met barely seventy-two hours earlier, wondering what it might be like to have someone like this in his life. To have a bond with her that was more than the one they'd forged out there in the field the previous day.

She turned to him, then returned her gaze to the front. He twisted again to study her elegant profile—the long neck whose sweet scent he could still recall if he closed his eyes.

'So are you here as Colonel Stirling, CO of the QRF team? Or Ash, the man who nearly kissed me in that supply room yesterday?' she managed hoarsely, still not turning to face him again.

'Whichever you'd prefer.' Ash kept his voice low and

even, blocking out the fact that the same question was tumbling around his own head.

Why had he felt so compelled to seek her out?

Part of him wondered if it had anything to do with the news he'd received today about his foster mother. Something threatened to bubble up inside him, and Ash swiftly closed it down to concentrate on Fliss. Willing her to give him the answer he shouldn't want to hear.

The silence felt like an eternity.

'Tell me about the grenade scar,' she said quietly, by way of response.

He stuffed down the black storm which immediately began to batter the lid of the box he kept it in. Only this time it didn't seem to rage with quite the power it had in the past.

'I told you, it was nothing.'

'So you say, but I ran into some of your old platoon in the field, and they didn't seem to think it was nothing.'

Ash frowned. 'My old platoon?'

'Mick, Jonesy and another guy…they called him Donald but I don't think that was his name.'

The names rushed through his head, leaving a trail of memories in their wake.

'Donaldson,' Ash said quietly. 'His younger brother had died in an ambush a couple of months earlier.'

'I'm sorry; I didn't know.'

'How could you have?'

'They told me you saved their lives, throwing yourself on a grenade.'

He stared at the sun, now so low behind the horizon that it was becoming quite dark up on the roof.

'I happened to be closest.' Ash shrugged. 'Any one of them would have done the same.'

'They said you'd say that.'

'Because they know it's true.' Ash brushed it off easily.

Fliss flashed him a sudden, genuine smile, and it was as though the sun had sprung back up into the sky again. It dazzled him, flowed into him, and filled him with light which chased down to even the darkest corners.

'Maybe,' she said. 'What about the other scars?'

The flooding light inside him pulled up sharply and began to recede. They both knew which scars she meant. He'd never told anyone about them before—except for the army doctor, of course—and he didn't particularly want to now. He'd faced the enemy and been hopelessly outnumbered on countless occasions in his career. He'd been cornered in the most brutal firefights and he'd had to escape and evade in the most hostile of environments.

But he'd take any one of those situations over facing down this resilient woman any day.

Except that Fliss was asking him to trust her, and he had an inexplicable urge to keep being honest with her. He liked the way it made her look at him, the way she responded to him. She was challenging him to open up—the one thing he couldn't afford to do. It would make him vulnerable, and he never wanted to be that again.

He pulled his lips into a tight line, determined to quell the storm inside him so that when he stood up to bid her farewell he wouldn't betray himself. He wouldn't reveal the quagmire of emotions raging within.

But before he could speak, Fliss did.

'Tell me about the cigarette burns, Ash.'

His world stopped.

And then started spinning. Wildly. Frighteningly. Out of control.

'If you already know what they are, then what's to tell?' he bit out.

But still he didn't stand up. He didn't leave.

She sucked in a breath. 'Who did that to you?'

He glowered into the night.

'Please Ash, talk to me.'

He shouldn't. But the compulsion to answer her, the *need* to answer her, was too strong.

'Foster mother.'

She didn't gasp; she didn't need to. Her shock and distaste radiated from her.

'How long were you in foster care?' she asked at last.

In the distance the flash of a headlight rounded a hillside, a local vehicle crawling along the dirt road. It provided him with a welcome distraction but no real relief.

'I was shuttled between care homes, foster homes and my old man from the age of about seven.'

He heard the steel edge in his voice, felt the way she flinched on his behalf, as though it had cut her personally. He didn't know what to think. To feel. So he did what he did best and he shut down the side of himself which held the awful memories and just focused on the basic facts themselves.

It was the only way to avoid losing control.

'What about the stab wound?'

'That one was a wallboard saw.'

'A what? Your foster mother again?'

'No. Foster father. Different family. Earlier time.'

'What happened?'

Ash shrugged before realising she probably couldn't see him. And still he kept his voice as neutral as possible.

'He was a gambler. And a heavy boozer. Probably lost at the former and so didn't have enough money for the latter. I was late in from my paper round—I used to do two but he didn't know about the second—and he was waiting for my weekly pay so he could go to the pub.'

'How many foster families?'

Ash could hear the horror in her voice. He steeled himself but still he was finding it harder and harder to stay detached. He could hear the incredulity in her voice and something twisted inside him. Why had he told her? The last thing he wanted was for her to look down on him. As people had looked down on him when he was a kid.

'Too many to remember, but they weren't all like that.'

'Still…'

He cut her off, not wanting to hear it since he couldn't change it.

'We can't all come from army blood and boarding schools.'

He actually felt her flinch beside him.

'It wasn't like that,' she bit out.

'But your parents never hurt you.'

It was a statement rather than a question, and he could almost hear the unspoken accusation in his tone.

Why was he getting angry with her?

It wasn't her fault his life didn't match hers. Ash shook his head. For over a decade he'd had a chip on his shoulder the size of a surface-to-air missile launcher, but he thought he'd managed to get rid of it over the years, as he'd progressed through the ranks and begun to accept himself for who he was. Somewhere along the line he'd realised his own worth.

Yet this one woman made him re-evaluate himself, and where his life was heading.

'I don't know who my father is and whilst my mother never physically hurt me the way you were hurt, she wasn't…kind.'

The words were uttered so quietly, he almost missed them at first. But the bleakness cut into him.

'But your uncle, the General?' People rarely caught Ash out.

He didn't like the feeling. When your life depended on judging people and situations quickly and accurately, it was a skill you learned to hone early on.

'My uncle tracked us down when I was eight and told my mother it was no place for a kid.' The admission was grudging; she clearly felt her past was her own business. 'He gave her an ultimatum. Either she came home to my grandparents with me, or my uncle would take me away.'

'So you and your mother ended up living with your grandparents.'

'No. She told him to take me. The next time I saw her was when I was eleven and she needed money. Anyway, this isn't about me. This is about you. Or is this what you do? Turn a conversation around any time it gets too close for comfort?'

Ash opened his mouth then closed it again, fighting back the overwhelming need to know more about Fliss. To understand her better. She was nothing like the picture he'd built in his head, and he was suddenly desperate to uncover the real woman behind the Major.

But she was right. Normally, turning the conversation onto the other person was *exactly* how he dealt with this kind of scenario. Instead, he fought the impulse. This conversation had started with her asking about him. If he wasn't willing to open up to her then how could he expect her to trust him?

'What do you want to know?' he heard himself asking.

She hesitated for a moment. 'I asked how many foster families you lived with.'

Ash sucked in a silent breath. 'Quite a few. I was seven when I first went into care and stayed there for about nine years, on and off.'

'Why? What about your family?'

He thought he'd hardened himself to all these memories a long time ago. Now, he was beginning to realise he'd buried them only just below the surface and a couple of questions from Fliss threatened everything.

'Until I was six, home life was good. Great. My parents were good, kind. They worked hard, were proud of our home and every bit of family time we had was spent doing something together, from playing football in the park to teaching me how to build a homemade telescope.'

'My uncle did that once.' He could hear the soft smile in her tone.

'When I was six, my mum was diagnosed with advanced ovarian cancer and that year she died. My dad couldn't handle it. He didn't deal with her death; he didn't even talk about her after that day. He was too proud to ask for help. He lost his job, couldn't pay the bills, forgot to buy food or clothing, or even soap. He did, however, discover alcohol. By the time I was seven, we had lost our home and social services took me away. I got my first taste of foster care after that.'

'I thought there were many good foster families out there. I used to dream of being taken in…before my uncle finally rescued me.'

'Oh, don't get me wrong.' Ash hunched his shoulders. 'I had several placements which were okay. And there *are* lots of kind families. Some are even exceptional. But there simply aren't enough foster carers and the better they are, the more valuable they are in dealing with troubled kids. I wasn't considered in that category at first.'

'At first?'

'Every so often my dad would get his act together and I'd go back to him. But I don't know whether it was because I was too sharp a reminder of my mother or what, but at some point or other he'd slide back down and the cycle would start over. By the time I was thirteen I'd had a couple of bad homes and I'd fallen in with the wrong crowd in school—not that we were ever in school. At fourteen I was completely off the rails. That was when I got busted by the cops for boosting a car.'

Fliss was actually facing him now, her body turned to his, intent on what he had to say. Her compassion was palpable. Somewhere, deep inside his being, something in Ash twisted and broke away.

'That was when I got sent to my last foster family. They were in their sixties and they were…*different*.'

'Different?'

He could hear the suspicion in her voice. Almost as though she *cared*. His chest pulled tight.

'Rosie and Wilfred saved my life,' Ash clarified simply. 'Figuratively and literally. They pushed me, challenged me, refused to give up on me. Both of them, but especially Rosie. She made me take a long look at where my life was heading and whether I really wanted to be going in that direction. And then she helped me find a way to turn things around. I owe her—I owe them both—everything.'

Even in the darkness he could sense the questions which jostled on her lips. It felt unexpectedly good to have someone pushing him to talk.

'But that was over two decades ago. Ten years ago Rosie started suffering from Alzheimer's and ten months ago she was diagnosed with pancreatic cancer. A week ago they sent her home to…be with family.'

'Oh, Ash, I'm so sorry.'

'It is what it is.' He shrugged, grimly holding back the emotions which threatened to rush him. Especially at the empathy in her tone. 'I was never meant to be out here; I was to take up the post of CO once the battalion returned from Razorwire. But then Colonel Waterson's accident left them without a colonel and I came out for the men, for their last ten days.'

'They couldn't let you be home with her?' Fliss asked, aghast. 'Surely, if they'd known? The Army have contingencies for circumstances like these.'

'It makes no difference,' Ash cut in. 'I'm no use there anyway. Because of the Alzheimer's she doesn't know who I am. And I'm better out here. It's the right choice all round.'

'I really am sorry.'

Her concern, so obviously genuine, slammed into Ash, hard. He had never told anyone any of that, preferring to compartmentalise his emotions so that he could do the job he needed to do when he was on the front line. But here, in Razorwire, everything seemed to have a slightly softer focus to it, from the camp to the people. And especially Major Felicity Delaunay.

She seemed to have a habit of getting under his skin and chipping away at the armour he'd spent so many years hammering into place.

She threatened the separation of his two worlds, all endless legs and lithe body as she danced in and out of his thoughts on a daily basis, especially when he was stuck behind that desk trying to get to grips with his new job.

He had never, in fifteen years, lost control as he had that day in the supply room. She made his body thrum with desire simply by standing a couple of feet away. And if he didn't want to lose control again, then Ash knew there was only one thing he had to do.

Stay well away from Major Felicity Delaunay.

CHAPTER FIVE

Fliss shifted on the cot-bed—which was currently doubling up as a rickety sunbed—in the quiet nook she and Elle had discovered shortly after arriving at Razorwire. Tucked away between the accommodation shipping containers and the wall of a compound, it was one of the few wonderfully secluded areas on Camp. At least, one that wasn't on a rooftop.

Usually she revelled in the searing kiss of the sun on her skin, coursing through her body to heat her very bones. Today it just made her feel restless. It wasn't the sun's kiss she wanted on her. Despite the heat, goosebumps spread over her torso, her breathing catching at the memory.

Why couldn't she get Ash out of her head?

It didn't seem to matter how many times she reminded herself that Ash wasn't the uncomplicated, steadfast guy she needed, nothing seemed to settle her body's ache to feel his touch again.

More importantly, it didn't matter how many times she reminded herself that *she* wasn't what *Ash* wanted, that he had rejected her, it didn't diminish her attraction to him. And that knowledge caused a perpetual maelstrom to rage in her mind. Because, of all people, she knew how utterly painful it was to be rejected over and over again. Even now she kept hoping each sporadic visit from her mother would be different. And each time it wasn't she suffered a fresh rejection, and the black void in Fliss's heart grew that little bit deeper.

So why was she still even entertaining thoughts about Ash after he'd pushed her away so categorically in the supply room barely a week ago?

She shifted on the sunbed, finding it impossible to get comfortable. She already knew the answer to her own question; she just didn't want to acknowledge it. Doing so would only raise twice as many issues again. But she couldn't shut her mind off.

The truth was that she didn't *feel* rejected. If anything, it had felt more about *his* baggage than hers. He'd been the one trying to protect himself when she'd asked about the burn scars. Hadn't he come up on that roof to seek her out? Hadn't he told her about the scars? Hadn't he opened up to her?

The fact that he hadn't tried anything on was a good thing. It meant he truly had trusted her without it being a ploy to get her into bed.

Right?

She couldn't even talk to Elle, who had headed back home for a two-week R&R, and without her friend Fliss felt lost. She tried to recreate the conversation in her head, but she wasn't sure she would even have told her best friend about the encounter with Ash.

It was like a little secret that only she knew, and she hugged it to herself as though sharing it would make it pop and disappear like an ethereal bubble in the air. It felt special and fragile, but if she wanted it to have the chance of any more substance then she was going to have to do something about it. In two days' time she would be gone and the decision would have been made for her.

She sat bolt upright on the sunbed, perturbed at the

thought. It seemed like such a waste. Such a squandered opportunity. So what was the alternative? Breaking every rule she had by seeking Ash out to give in to a moment of temptation which would hold no promises, and no future? A fortnight ago she would have scorned the very idea, but now even one night together seemed almost worth it. If only she could find some way to ring-fence her heart.

She reached for the bottle of sunscreen, applying it as though it could do more than protect merely her skin.

If only it was that easy.

Lost in her thoughts, Fliss missed the soft footfalls of a jogger approaching until the figure stopped abruptly, casting a long shadow over her torso and legs. She squinted, lifting one ineffectual hand against the bright sun, even though its glare was too bright for her to see. But she didn't need her eyes to tell her who it was. Her body seemed to know, every delicately fine hair on her body prickling in awareness.

Flustered, she stood up so quickly that she almost toppled. But, unlike in the supply room, this time strong arms steadied her in an instant. She reached out instinctively to brace herself, her hands connecting with one very hot, solid, familiar bare chest.

'Ooomph!'

'Easy, you'll cause yourself injury,' Ash murmured as Fliss's entire body seemed to tingle beneath his unabashed, and unmistakably male, appraisal.

And all her courage seemed to float into the air above their heads like a bunch of bobbing balloons and disappear before she could snatch it back.

She snapped her arms across her chest, all too conscious of the revealing, fire-engine-red bikini Elle had loaned her when they'd first discovered the quiet sunbathing spot. The barely-there two-piece, though perfect for her friend's lean, athletic B-cup body shape, felt entirely too scant on her own more curvaceous D-cup figure. She tugged at the material but that only seemed to make the problem worse.

'What are you doing here, Colonel?' she blurted out. 'First the rooftop, now here? Are you following me?'

It was a daft accusation, a defence mechanism to try to hide her embarrassment, and she wanted to swallow it back the moment it left her lips. But, far from goading him, he actually looked amused.

'No one's around, Felicity; have you forgotten my first name?'

Despite herself, a delicious shiver rippled through her. She tugged again at the material.

'And you might want to stop doing that.'

His voice rasped across her belly, carnal lust heating between her legs and making her nipples harden until they were almost painful. When she looked at him, it was clear he hadn't missed her body's reaction to him and his shale-coloured eyes were almost black with desire.

'Why?' She swallowed.

'Because you're clearly fighting a losing battle and if you continue then those flimsy straps of yours are going to give way entirely. Those two pathetic triangles of cloth are no match for such...*generous* contents. It's a matter of physics.'

With anyone else, Fliss knew she would have prayed for the dusty ground to open up and swallow her. Her mother had told her that they were unattractively oversized, unsuitable for a dancer, and made her look fat. But the gravelly lust in Ash's tone, raw and unrestrained, suggested a different story. No man had ever spoken to her in quite that tone. It made her feel attractive, glamorous, even sexy.

Something ignited deep inside Fliss. It was like a sign. In two days' she'd be out of here. Tonight was her last

chance to do something utterly out of character with the
only man who had ever dislodged her professional mask.

*If she didn't stop jiggling those incredible breasts around,
he was seriously going to lose it.*

Ash shifted as discreetly as he could—he was so
aroused it was a kind of torture—and he had never been
more grateful for his slightly baggy cargo running shorts
as he stood, his hands still seared to her bare flesh. Surely
no red-blooded male could watch that provocative show
without having such a primal reaction? And what made
it all the more arousing was the fact that such a stunning
woman could be so wholly unaware of just how incred-
ibly sensual she was.

He would stake his life that the bikini didn't belong to
Fliss. From the colour to the cut, it just didn't seem like
something she would choose for herself. But she looked
absolutely sensational in it. Then again, she looked equally
stunning in even the most unflattering army uniform, complete with dusty body armour. All of which would be con-
siderably harder to divest her of than those three scraps
of siren temptation which wouldn't even stand up to the
briefest run-in with his teeth.

A ferocious need pounded inside him. An urge to touch
her, taste her, every last hot, slick inch of her. So much
for his promise to himself that he would avoid her for the
couple of days until the end of her tour. With a supreme
effort, Ash dropped his grip and stepped away from her
as casually as he could.

It was a mistake.

Instead of lowering the sexual tension, it only seemed to
increase it as he was treated to the full head-to-toe effect of
Fliss's body. She had the softest, most feminine curves he

thought he'd ever seen. Not to mention a backside that was so perfect he ached to cup it as he pulled her against him.

What the heck was wrong with him?

She swallowed hard before speaking, her voice loaded with intent.

'Going somewhere?'

Ash could only cock an eyebrow in response. Had any other woman ever had quite this overpowering effect on him?

'Be very careful, Felicity,' he warned.

'Why do you say that?'

She took a step towards him but the slight quiver behind the seductive tone only confirmed his suspicion.

'Because I can't offer what you want.'

'I think you can.'

Another step. His body tightened further but he valiantly ignored it.

'I can't give you more than sex.'

'Who says I want more than that?'

'You did. When you told me you didn't do *this*, remember? But I don't go for meaningful relationships, I don't do intimacy. I *just* do sex.'

Fliss closed the gap between them, so close they could have touched if either of them had raised their arms.

'I know,' she murmured. 'Because sex is what you use as a defence against intimacy.'

Her gentle observation sliced right through him, hitting its mark. It certainly wasn't the first time he'd been accused of that. Just as he'd been accused of using his career and tours of duty to keep from putting down roots back home.

He could still recall every stage of his father's cycle of self-destruction when his mother had died. His father had lost all control, all reason, and he hadn't cared who he hurt in the process. Even a six-year-old boy who was trying to cope with the loss of his mother.

Ash couldn't remember how old he'd been when he'd sworn to himself that, whatever happened to him for the rest of his miserable life, he refused to become like his father. He would never let anyone close enough to be so torn apart by their loss. That way, he'd never be in so much pain that he'd hurt anyone, and he'd never, *ever* lose control.

'I don't want to have to think about someone else,' he lied, the proximity without contact only cranking up the sexual tension another intolerable notch. 'I'm an infantry-man; my life is too dangerous to inflict on a girlfriend or a wife, and certainly not a family.'

'Rubbish,' Fliss retorted evenly, her hands finally raising to his chest, her fingers running gently over the contours of his body, tracing the ridges of the shameful circular scars as though she saw none of the ugliness behind them.

'You protect yourself because you had an appalling childhood and you got hurt. But I'm not asking you for more than you're willing to give, Ash. I'm accepting it will only ever be this moment between us.'

He needed to shut this down now. Keeping things as just sex would be one heck of a task. It would be so easy to fall for a woman as unique as Major Felicity Delaunay.

He moved to step away from her but instead Ash found himself placing his hands on her hips and drawing her close, her skin decadently smooth beneath his fingers. Then he hooked two fingers beneath her chin, tilting her head up to his as he lowered his mouth to finally claim hers the way he had back in that supply room what felt like an eternity ago.

Her lips parted for him with a soft sigh, her eyelids seeming to grow heavy as they fluttered closed and her body moulded to his, skin to skin but for her insubstantial bikini and his shorts. For now he resisted the urge to peel either away; he was barely holding onto his self-control with his fingertips as it was, and he could already feel Fliss's nipples through the material as her chest rose and fell with shallow breaths. Ash rubbed his thumb along her jawline before tugging the hair elastic from her ponytail and slipping his fingers into the silky curtain as it tumbled down, even richer and more luxuriant than he'd imagined it would be.

'So beautiful,' he marvelled, not merely referring to her hair.

The clipped sound she made was accompanied by her dragging his mouth back to hers and Ash indulged in the kiss without reservation, tasting every millimetre of her lips, her mouth, as her tongue danced with his in perfect synchronicity. She was clinging to him as if all the strength had gone from her legs, and it only made her feel all the more delicate in his arms.

Tantalisingly slowly, he allowed his hand to trace a line back to her chin, gliding slowly down her neck to the fluttering pulse, the smooth collarbone and the generous swell of breasts he ached to touch, to lick, to tease. With deliberate precision, he glided his hand down to cup one full breast and let his thumb sneak beneath the red triangle to graze over one straining peak.

Fliss trembled beneath his touch as she breathed his name with such bliss that he couldn't help himself. He lowered his head and took one peak in his mouth, his hand caressing the other. As she rocked her lower body against his there was no mistaking the heat emanating through the thin layers of material from her very core.

'Ash...please.'

White-hot need tore through Ash, infinitely hotter than the sun beating down on their bodies. It would be so easy to tear off what remained of their clothes, wrap those endless legs of hers around his hips and thrust inside her. But if this was the one chance they were going to get then he owed it to both of them to make sure they didn't rush it.

He didn't hear his pager when it first went off, the sound slowly permeating through the hunger of their exploration. For a split second he was tempted to ignore it.

'You know I have to get that, don't you?' he managed hoarsely.

Reluctantly, Fliss released her grip and he eased her back, struggling to retrieve the pager, given her position and his arousal.

He shot her a rueful glance then checked his pager.

His blood ran cold, nausea surging and churning. When he finally spoke he didn't even recognise his own voice.

'I have to go.'

The message he'd been dreading had finally arrived.

CHAPTER SIX

FLISS SANK INTO the metal chair in frustration.

Delays weren't uncommon—especially during Relief in Place—with the sheer volume of air traffic, thanks to the change of troops at the beginning and the end of tours of duty, but she still didn't relish the prospect of being stuck at the Air Force base for the next thirty-six hours, waiting for a new part that had to be flown in for the aircraft.

At last they were finally out of the overheating tin can on the runway. Seven hours stuck out there in the blistering sun, after what was supposed to have been a brief, routine refuelling stop-over, had been quite enough.

But it wasn't just about where they were. Or the delay. It was the fact that Ash Stirling was still in her head. A dark bleakness stabbed at her. He hadn't sought her out the previous day. He hadn't summoned her. He hadn't even got a message to her. Something, anything, it wouldn't have mattered.

Logically, Fliss knew the way tasks were at Camp Razorwire; they had a habit of swallowing up days before you even noticed it. But she couldn't shake the rejection and it attacked her more violently than it had in many, many years. It was over. Done. She needed to relegate to the past an imperfect experiment. But if she closed her eyes she could still feel the sheen of moisture on that impossibly hard body, take in the citrus and leather scent, hear the sensual huskiness of his voice.

Dragging herself back to reality as she exhaled a deep breath, Fliss pulled her bergen in between her legs and began to untie it to grab a couple of items packed closest to the top.

Regrets were useless; the situation had been taken out of their hands. She needed to straighten her head out. Starting with accommodation. Cot-beds had been set up in the neighbouring hangar and if she was quick enough she might even bag one of the choicest locations in the quietest corner.

'Ah, Colonel Stirling, your driver is ready to take you.' A voice from behind snagged her attention. 'You have a seat on the first direct commercial flight out of the main airport in the morning. Unfortunately, the airport hotel was already fully booked but I took the liberty of booking you into a hotel in the nearby tourist resort.'

'That sounds fine, Sergeant.'

If merely hearing his name had set the hairs bristling on the back of her arms, pausing in the action of retrieving her wash-bag, the sound of that rich, steady tone was enough to make her heart falter before galloping off.

What was he doing on a flight out of here too?

His infantry battalion wasn't due to leave for another week, which could only mean something bad. Without stopping to second-guess herself, Fliss stuffed the items haphazardly into the top of her rucksack, snatching at the closing ties and dragging it onto her shoulder as she sped across the floor.

'Colonel?'

There were too many soldiers around to risk using his first name but she trusted that he would see beyond the clipped tone. However, he didn't stop, striding confidently away from her and towards the main doors so that Fliss was forced to call again, barely concealing the note of panic in her tone.

To her relief he stopped, turning slowly, aviator-style glasses in his hand and an expression she didn't recognise cloaking his handsome face. She stopped abruptly, thrown. He looked like hell.

'Major?'

He was the very definition of poker-faced. She swallowed nervously. How was she supposed to do this with people all around them?

'I'm in a hurry,' he bit out. 'Walk with me.'

Without waiting for an answer, he turned and walked out of the doors, the wall of heat from outside hitting her despite the air-conditioning within the hangar. She stared after him, then her legs acted for the rest of her body, carrying her right along behind him. He'd walked to the end of the path to the road where the car was waiting for him. They'd moved out of the line of sight from the glass doors and no one was around.

'Is everything okay, Ash?'

Something flickered over his face, perhaps pleasure at seeing her, but then it changed to something she couldn't identify, and it was gone as quickly as it had arrived.

'I'm sorry I didn't get a chance to speak to you.' His clipped tone gave nothing away.

She waved it away as though it hadn't mattered.

'But are *you* okay?'

'Of course.' He hesitated a fraction too long. 'But I have some…loose ends to tie up in the UK. My promotion was never meant to take place until the battalion had returned from Razorwire; it just got accelerated after Colonel Waterson's accident.'

'You're booked on a commercial flight?'

'It's time sensitive.' He shrugged.

If she was overstepping, he didn't show it. In fact he showed no emotion at all. Unease rippled through her.

'Should I...would you like me to come with you?'

It had taken Fliss a lot to make the offer. The look he cast her was flat, expressionless. Her stomach pitched.

'Why would you do that?'

'Just to talk? Or...to finish the other day, if you like?'

Flat eyes stared at her. Then, all of a sudden, Ash's gaze turned hard and demandingly hot. It raked over her, as though virtually stripping her right down on the concrete. She could barely breathe, let alone move.

'You want to do that?' he demanded harshly.

'I want to,' she confirmed.

'All right, Major.' She hoped his use of her rank was because someone was approaching—his driver, perhaps. 'You can share my ride. Inform the duty sergeant and ask him to book you a flight and a hotel room.'

Had he misunderstood?

'Wait—' she lowered her voice '—I meant...'

Without warning, he pivoted, advancing on her so quickly they were almost toe to toe and she had to tip her head right back to look up at him. Every nerve-ending sizzled.

'I know exactly what you meant, Felicity,' he muttered under his breath. 'But if you want to keep the illusion of propriety, you'll want the duty sergeant to book you your own room with your own bed. Understood?'

'Understood,' she murmured in response.

He was so close she could feel his breath on her skin and the effect on her body was an immediate pooling of need between her legs. No man had *ever* affected her the way Ash did.

'Good. Then I suggest when I step away you look as though I have just given you a bit of a rollicking.'

'Right.'

Allowing him to step away, Fliss ducked her head and looked respectably contrite.

'Understood, Colonel, I'll deal with it right away.'

She turned to return to the duty sergeant at the desk.

'Leave your bergen here, Major.' He softened his voice just a fraction but it was enough to quell some of the fluttering in her chest. 'I'll get the Corporal to load it into the car while you make the arrangements. We don't have all day.'

'Major?'

Ash peered over his shoulder, not expecting to see Fliss's soundly sleeping form. He paused, catching his breath. She looked even more breathtaking in slumber than she did when she was awake, as though she didn't have a single care. Thick, dark lashes rested gently on her smooth cheek. Her breathing was slow and steady, for once not waiting to jerk awake at any unexpected disturbance.

Anger punched at his gut.

He shouldn't have agreed to this. He'd been in shock for the last two days, working on autopilot and remembering none of it. He'd only consented to her coming because the moment she'd stepped up to him in the hangar, the bright energy spilling from her had seemed like the very thing he needed to help him keep the darkness at bay. Without her, he knew it would engulf him and he didn't know if he'd ever make it back ashore.

Dragging her with him now was selfish and cruel. He was using her.

But if he made damn sure it was the best night of her life, then did it matter?

'Major—' he increased his voice whilst keeping it deliberately cool. 'Time to wake up; we're here.'

She finally stirred and offered a decidedly feline stretch, and as the seat belt running down the valley between her breasts grew taut, so did Ash's body.

It was ridiculous, the effect she had on him.

But it was also exactly what he needed.

The last time he'd experienced such unrestrained lust he'd been sixteen and still discovering the thrill of sex. Unsophisticated but exhilarating. He'd soon unlocked the skill and perfected the sophistication. But Fliss brought back that youthful excitement—the innocence.

She peered out of the window then gazed back at him through sleepy, lowered lashes, which did little to calm his racing pulse.

'Already?' She looked shocked.

Second thoughts, perhaps?

Ash waited until the Corporal had climbed out of the four-by-four and was headed around to the back to collect their bergens before speaking urgently.

'If you've changed your mind, you can always go back.'

She could also stay in the room that the desk sergeant had booked for her, but he didn't want her to feel under any kind of misplaced obligation.

'I haven't changed my mind.' The gaze she shot him was both loaded with promise and a little nervous. 'I just expected the drive to feel a little awkward.'

So had he.

As the Corporal opened the back door, they both climbed out of the vehicle.

'Do I remember passing though somewhere and seeing a lot of floats, or did I dream that up?' she asked the young lad politely.

'It's Summer Festival time, ma'am,' the Corporal offered. 'Towns up and down the island celebrate in different ways. There's a parade with floats and live music and dancing not far from here tonight.'

'Really? It all looked beautiful.' She nodded. 'I've never been to a festival.'

'Never, Major?' Ash asked curiously, the suddenly pained expression in her eyes twisting at his gut, helping him to compartmentalise his own worries.

Already he was feeling more at peace than he'd felt in the last forty-eight hours.

'No.' She shrugged lightly, swiftly covering the moment.

He might tell himself it was none of his business but his mind kept asking questions.

Wordlessly, Ash reached for the rucksacks, passing Fliss hers as he hoisted his own onto his shoulder before thanking the young NCO and wishing him a safe return, then striding ahead into the cool hotel lobby to begin check-in. He couldn't even stop to see if Fliss was accompanying him. In uniform, and with the Corporal around, there was no place for chivalry.

Moments later he heard her greet the other receptionist at the far end of the four-metre-long desk and begin to confirm the booking the desk sergeant had made back at the airport base.

'I'm sorry you weren't able to get onto the six a.m. flight tomorrow morning with your colleague,' Ash heard the clerk saying.

'It's fine; don't worry.' Fliss's soothing smile carried in her tone. 'I was more than happy to get the early evening flight.'

'Still, the hotel would like to offer you a complimentary massage treatment in our spa, as well as use of our facilities even after the midday check-out.'

'Gosh, that's really kind of you,' she enthused in typical Fliss fashion. 'Thank you; I'd appreciate that.'

Images of Fliss's luscious body instantly flooded Ash's brain and he burned all over again, suppressing a grin. Yep, there was no denying that something about the woman transported him back to his teenage years.

His eyes slid across to hers for a fraction of an instant before she bowed her head with a flush. But not before he'd caught the sparkle of delight at his unrestrained interest.

Ash marvelled at the fact that neither Fliss herself, nor her fellow soldiers, appeared to be able to see past their perception of a prim, uptight, rigid rule-following major. There was so much more to the woman, so much raw passion, which bubbled away barely beneath the surface. She was like one of those papier-mâché volcanos Wilfred had taught him to make in their little man shed at the bottom of the garden. But instead of adding white vinegar to the bicarb mix to make it erupt, all Fliss would need would be a little love and the emotion would spill out of her.

Where the hell had that come from?

It was just another reminder that he should stop this now.

Instead, as though an invisible thread bound them, Ash concluded his check-in and moved along the desk to stand by her, his arm deliberately touching hers as he rested it on the granite surface. Unremarkable to any onlooker, but as his skin seared at the contact and goosebumps sprung up over Fliss's arm Ash experienced a renewed sense of satisfaction.

'I understand it's the Summer Festival across the island at the moment; we saw some floats on the way here?' He deliberately faced the clerk rather than Fliss.

'That's right, Colonel,' the young man agreed. 'There's a parade tonight. I could book you a taxi if you like; it's only about a ten-minute drive away.'

'What do you think, Major; shall we give it a go?'

'I…well… I thought this was about…?' With a subtle side-step she broke the physical contact and took a breath. 'If that's what you want, then we'll go.'

Relieved to occupy his mind, Ash narrowed his gaze at Fliss. Whatever made Fliss uncertain about going tonight, it wasn't just about wanting to finish what he'd started with her the other day. She was avoiding something.

The question was, what?

He'd spotted a moment of sheer longing in her regard when she'd mentioned the floats. As if it was something she wanted to see but couldn't bring herself to do.

He turned back to the young desk clerk. 'A taxi sounds fine.'

'Very good, sir. And will you be dining in the hotel restaurant?'

Beside him Fliss stiffened; evidently she preferred the structure of a known location. Yet another reason to change things up and see if he could get past those prickly defences of hers.

'No,' Ash decided. 'Thank you but I think we'll wing it and enjoy the festival atmosphere. Major, I'll be over by the lifts when you've concluded here.'

Before she could object to the change in evening plans he hoisted up the rucksacks, ignoring her attempts at a protest and leaving her with only a smaller one for appearance' sake. Then, making his way to the seating area, he watched her ramrod-straight back as she controlled her frustration, instead maintaining her charming smile for the clerk whilst she concluded her check-in.

By the time she finished and marched over he was already holding a lift for her and she stepped inside and pivoted stiffly around, opening her mouth.

'Which floor, Major?' he enquired politely, effectively cutting her off.

'Oh.' She halted, flipping the keycard over to check her room number. 'Fifth. Please.'

She waited for the lift doors to close before turning on him.

'Why did you do that?'

'Do what?' he asked innocently.

'Decide we should go to the parade?'

'Don't *you* want to?' He kept his voice deliberately even. 'It sounded like a bit of fun after the last six months you've had out there. Is there any reason you wouldn't want to go?'

She hesitated a fraction too long. 'No.'

'Okay.' He smiled carefully. 'So, what's the issue?'

Fliss lowered her bergen, clearly buying herself time. 'I thought tonight was about…' She flushed. 'I don't *know* what it's about. Talking, or…sex, I guess.'

He deliberately didn't react. He couldn't say the same for his body.

'You weren't planning to eat?'

'I…obviously.'

She didn't fool him; she clearly hadn't considered food at all. He suspected she'd been so caught up in doing something out of character that she'd only geared herself up for the moment itself, without thinking around it.

In a sense it was flattering.

'You just thought we'd go to the room and get down to it?' he continued, not unkindly.

'Well…no.'

'How exactly did you think the evening would pan out, Fliss?'

'I don't know but I…we were going to…sleep together… the other day,' she croaked eventually.

'For the record, there wasn't going to be any sleeping going on.' He arched his eyebrows.

She shivered in appreciation. 'No.'

'But at least then it would have been spontaneous. Natural,' he pointed out. 'This isn't the same. I just thought it would be nice to go for a meal together, chat a little, let things develop at their own pace.'

She paused. He was throwing her off, one minute firing her up and the next trying to relax her. She wasn't sure if it was deliberate, or if Ash himself was having trouble deciding which he'd rather do.

'That does sound…nice. But why go out? The restaurant has a good reputation.'

'And it's also too close to the bedrooms. Do you really think you'd be able to relax? I felt it would help to get right away from here for a few hours, release the pressure valve and just get to know each other a little.'

Not entirely a lie.

'Is that what you usually do? Get to know your one-night stands?'

'I've told you before, you shouldn't go on reputation alone. Yes, I like to know a little about a woman I might choose to have sex with. And, even if I didn't, I'd like to know a little about *you*.'

He let her digest that for a moment, wondering if it would frighten her off. He already knew enough to know that talking about herself was the last thing she enjoyed doing.

She sucked in a steadying breath, her words slow and thoughtful.

'You're talking about a meal and an evening out?'

'Yes.'

'Kind of like a date?'

'Exactly like a date.'

'Okay, then.' Fliss offered him a weak smile just as the lift stopped and the doors *pinged* open.

Rucksacks in hand, they walked along the corridor together.

'Fine, then how about I meet you in the lobby, say around nineteen-hundred hours?'

'Nineteen-hundred hours.' She nodded as she stopped at a bedroom door. 'This is me.'

Obligingly, he set her kit down and as he stood outside her door he debated the wisdom of his decision to wait. It took a dignified effort to continue along the corridor.

A linen closet separated his room from hers.

Slipping his keycard out of his pocket, Ash deftly passed it through the lock, opening the door before he could change his mind. But in his peripheral vision he could see Fliss still stuck at her own door, stabbing the card into the reader. He watched it flash red a couple of times. Pushing his door open, he dropped his bergens inside and strode back down the corridor to take the keycard gently from her fingers.

'Don't be so rushed,' he murmured, sliding it gracefully through the lock and seeing the green light. Like some kind of sign. 'Take it slowly.'

'Slowly,' she echoed shakily. 'Got it.'

They both knew they were talking about more than the lock.

'You're sure you're not coming in?' Tentatively, she raised one hand to touch his lapel with her palm.

He knew it was her attempt to avoid having to go to the carnival, but it still had an effect. He groaned. His self-control was barely intact as it was.

'Fliss, I'm trying to do the gentlemanly thing here.'

'I never asked for that,' she whispered. 'It wasn't the gentle side of you which attracted me in the first place.'

'You wouldn't like the other side of me,' he growled.

'How do you know?'

They stood, unmoving and silent, until she snatched back her hand, yanked at the door handle and stumbled over the threshold.

'Never mind. You're right. I'm not exactly the kind of woman who elicits impulsive tendencies.'

He followed her in swiftly, catching her shoulders and spinning her back around as he drew her close.

'That's where you're wrong.'

His hands cupping her face, he pinned her back against the wall and lowered his mouth to hers. She tasted every bit as sweet as he recalled, but this time it was laced with a hint of ferocity, as though heightened by the frustration of their last encounter. He caught her lower lip in his as her hands inched up his arms to rest on his shoulders, her body moulding itself to his despite the uniforms in the way.

This needed to stop. It wasn't the way he wanted things to go between them.

She flicked her tongue over his.

With another groan Ash deepened the kiss, so long and deep that his only thought was that he could drown in her kisses and never want to come up for air. Heat licking over him, his hands glided up her body to rest at the underside of her breasts. He wanted to touch every incredible inch of her body, and have her touch every single inch of his.

As abruptly as he'd started it, Ash drew away, his voice rasping. '*Now* do you see that you're the kind of woman who can drive a man wild with longing?'

Without another word, he hauled open the door and marched to his own room before temptation undermined him.

Closing the door, he leaned heavily on it.

This was no longer just a matter of a distraction from the

blackness inside him. Or about getting past Fliss's prickly armour. It was more than that. It had become a matter of exerting his own self-control. He wanted her with a need that actually scared him.

He couldn't allow his emotions to rule him like that. If he could control the course of the evening, rein in his hunger for Fliss long enough to get through a date, then enjoy one incredible night with the woman before walking away and never looking back, then maybe he could indulge in his desire for her without losing his prized self-control.

He had to. If he didn't, then stirring *any* emotions tonight could bring the whole lot crashing down.

CHAPTER SEVEN

FLISS SCREWED CLOSED the lid of her new mascara bottle with shaking hands as she checked her reflection in the mirror with a hesitant smile and tried to quell the rolling in her lower abdomen. An orchestra of crickets might as well have decamped in there. She rarely wore make-up, certainly never at work, but she'd found a few perfect supplies at the local market—not too much, but enough to enhance her sun-kissed glow—and couldn't help wondering if Ash would like what he saw.

Logically, it shouldn't matter; she'd learned a long time ago not to care what anyone thought. But nothing about Ash was what she was used to. Logic seemed to fly out of the window when he was around, as did practicality. She should have refused the moment he'd raised the idea of seeing the carnival. After the last couple of emotional weeks, it threatened to unearth things best left forgotten. Instead, she'd let Ash talk her into it.

She was acting on pure lust and complete gut instinct. It was absurd and it was terrifying.

And it was also intoxicating.

She couldn't even remember when she'd last been excited about going on a date, let alone excited about getting *ready* to go on a date. She'd heard girls giggling about it over the years, but she'd never understood it. Until now. It was why she'd actually enjoyed spending a portion of her afternoon, when she would otherwise have preferred to be sleeping, going down to the local tourist market and un-covering unexpected treasures like the tiny pot of powder and brush, the subtly sparkling lipgloss and the wand of mascara. She'd even managed to squeeze in an appointment at the hotel's hair salon. Elle would never have recognised her, but she could hear her friend's approving voice in her ear, urging Fliss to just have fun for once.

Well, she definitely intended to do that.

Satisfied, she reached for her keycard and new clutch bag and then for the door handle.

It was ten to seven and she was going to be early—dat-ing rules probably dictated that she shouldn't be, but Fliss couldn't help that. Punctuality was ingrained in her. She couldn't change that now.

Taking every last ounce of confidence in her hands, she stepped out of the door and made her way to the lift. The last person she expected to see standing there was Ash, a crisp shirt doing little to conceal those broad shoulders or honed physique which had already marked him out as an eligible male within a contingent of the females down here. Somehow he managed to appear even more power-ful and commanding than he did in his military uniform.

A hint of possessiveness shot through her, mingled with a pinch of smugness that *she* was the woman he was wait-ing for. But then her heart plummeted; he didn't exactly look pleased to see her hurrying straight over to his corner.

Served her right for her hubris.

'You're early too.' She nervously smoothed down her black jersey trousers to hide her unease.

The trousers might have been old but they were also comfy, flowing prettily around her legs. The perfect foil to her new, uncharacteristically sexy, cleavage-revealing halter-top, which she was suddenly thinking might be a little too nightclub for her.

'Felicity—' he looked genuinely thrown '—you look… incredible.'

With a start, Fliss realised that he hadn't immediately recognised her, but now he had he treated her to a full, very heated appraisal, darkened eyes taking in the visual of head to toe, and *everything* in between.

Her confidence bounced back a little. He clearly liked what he saw but, when he hadn't appreciated it was her, he hadn't been about to flirt with the stranger heading in his direction. The crackle of crickets leapt around Fliss even more madly.

'Your hair,' he managed.

Self-consciously, she flicked at the cascade of gold, expertly volumised so that she felt like some kind of glamorous shampoo model.

'New clothes?'

Her confidence rose a little higher again. He was having a hard time lifting his eyes from her cleavage. But, rather than feeling self-conscious, or condemning Ash for his primal reaction, an unexpected sliver of sensual power rippled through her. She felt bold and sexy, and proudly feminine. She chose not to answer the question.

'Shall we see if the taxi is here?'

He stepped close to her by way of response, sliding a strong palm to the dip of her back as they moved through the foyer. It was such a small but intimate gesture, he might as well have seared its impression into her skin.

'Are you hungry?' he murmured into her hair.

Stay calm.

'Famished.'

'Good.' He guided her out of the doors and to the waiting taxi. 'Then let's go.'

* * *

The drive was fortunately short—being so close to Ash on the back seat was having a woeful effect on her ability to breathe, let alone to construct coherent sentences. She tried to move her thigh from his, the solid, muscular length playing havoc on her senses, but he simply closed the gap again and all she could think about was what was going to happen later that evening back in the hotel room.

Arriving at their destination was both a relief and a disappointment and Fliss tried to concentrate on the carnival sounds to distract herself. The evening had barely started and she was already hung up on what was to come. She was beginning to be grateful to Ash for starting the evening far away from the hotel.

The driver had already warned them that the main town was closed to traffic for the parade so they would have to continue the rest of the way on foot. They trailed along cobbled streets with old buildings built with yellow and cream stone and red-tiled roofs. Flowers and streamers hung from windows of various homes and shops.

Yet, even as they got closer to the central square, and the sounds of music and laughter grew louder, Fliss still wasn't prepared for turning the corner into the main parade street.

It swept her away in an instant.

More flowers, flags, streamers and lanterns adorned the wide road in their hundreds—as far as the eye could see. Laughing couples and families thronged the place, and live music played as people danced in the street. Now and then, incredible cooking smells wafted to her nostrils, making her stomach rumble in appreciation.

Ash turned his head to look at her and she grinned, unabashed. Then, his arm firmly around her shoulders and her body melded to his, he led her into the crowds.

'Where are we heading?' she said, laughing.

He smiled, shaking his head to indicate he hadn't heard her over the bustling street.

'Say again?'

'Where are we heading?'

'Anywhere we want.' Ash placed his lips to her ear, so close his breath tickled her. 'Stop me if you see anywhere which takes your fancy.'

She didn't want to draw comparisons. What good would it do? Still, it felt heady to be so impromptu. Dates in previous relationships had been so planned, so rigid—everything she'd thought she wanted. She was beginning to realise that predictability could be dull and uninspiring.

Except this wasn't really a date and it certainly wasn't the start of a relationship. She needed to remember that.

'Here.' She stopped Ash abruptly.

A small but pretty restaurant had caught her eye. Unlike some of the other places, with tables spilling out into the road and smiling servers running around a multitude of tourists, this place looked smaller, more family-run. And there looked to be several locals enjoying a meal, which was always a good sign in Fliss's book.

'Good choice,' Ash agreed, threading his way to a table for two and holding her chair out for her to sit down, before seating himself at ninety degrees.

It was nicer than sitting opposite him, Fliss thought with surprise, and it allowed them both to watch the festival without the pressure to make conversation. He was making everything so easy; if only she could convince her over-excited body to agree.

With a concerted effort, Fliss pushed her nerves about the later part of the evening to the back of her mind and focused on the carnival around them. The bands had taken a break and the dancing had stopped but she could still hear plenty of buzz, and music in the distance. Craning her neck eagerly, she realised that the parade had begun and the first troubadours and baton-twirlers were moving energetically down the streets, leading the most breathtaking floats Fliss had ever seen.

She clapped her hands along with the crowd, their appreciation evident. This wasn't going to be such a tense evening, after all.

It was an hour before the last of the floats passed by, the music slowly drifting away, the lanterns now casting a warm glow over the darkening sky. Ash watched as Fliss turned back, her whole body more relaxed than he'd seen all evening. Possibly ever.

She glanced at her empty place setting.

'The meal's gone?'

'You finished it.' He chuckled softly. 'You don't remember?'

She offered a rueful smile. 'I know I'm full, and I know the food was beautiful.' She glanced at the bottle of red wine. 'Ah, well, that isn't why I'm feeling so chilled out; it's only half empty.'

He didn't have the heart to tell her it was their second bottle and she'd drank two-thirds of that one.

They fell into an easy silence, the street scene still offering plenty of entertainment.

'So you enjoyed the parade?' Ash asked, once the waiter had brought them a round of coffees.

'I loved it.' She nodded, her eyes sparkling happily. 'It was almost magical. And now all the lanterns are so pretty; it's like being in a fairy tale.'

'I'm glad you had fun.' He was careful to keep his tone upbeat. 'I still can't believe you've never been to a festival.'

He watched Fliss's mind ticking over, wondering how best to respond. But then the server chose that moment to clear the dishes from their table and by the time they were alone again Ash feared she might have composed herself enough to brush him off. He was surprised when she answered hesitantly.

'It wasn't somewhere my uncle wanted to take me.'

'He didn't want to, or you didn't want to?'

She slowly stirred her coffee, her eyes trained on the mini-vortex.

'A bit of both, probably.'

He waited quietly in the hope she would offer more of her own volition, but she didn't, and that ate away at Ash. He wanted to know her better, to understand her, but she was shutting him out. He couldn't explain why that bothered him so much.

Then again, she wasn't shooting him down either. It could mean part of her wanted to talk, if he could just coax it out of her without scaring her off.

'You said your uncle raised you?'

She paused, then nodded. 'From the age of eight.'

'You mentioned your mother wasn't kind to you.'

Perhaps by reminding her of things she'd already told him, it would help her to feel she'd already trusted him once. At least partially.

A brittle sound escaped her. 'I represented the end of all her dreams. And she never let me forget it.'

He'd seen that often enough, with other kids in care.

'She was an aspiring ballerina.' Fliss bunched her shoulders.

Ah. Not that it excused it, but it gave him a better understanding of what Fliss had dealt with.

'Would she have made it?'

'I honestly don't think she would.' Fliss met his gaze, not spiteful but factual. 'My uncle said she was good, but there are thousands of *good* ballerinas. She wasn't great, certainly not stand-out. But she could never accept that. She always had to have someone to blame. Never herself. Before I came along she blamed her parents for not supporting her enough. Then when she fell pregnant and neither of my two potential fathers wanted to know, that was their fault. And finally, when I came along, I was the excuse she needed to explain why she'd given up dancing altogether. She could be…cruel.'

'Is that why you're so responsible? So rule-abiding? Except for when you're leaping off helicopters to save injured soldiers, that is.'

'I don't know.' Fliss looked surprised. 'I've never really thought about it, I guess. I just know I vowed to myself I'd never be like my mother.'

'And yet your uncle, the General, he's one of the most responsible, straight-down-the-line men I know.'

'Yes.' A fond smile leapt to her lips. 'He was the typically duty-bound older brother. He had a younger brother who died as a baby—cot death, I think. When my mother came along within the year—another new baby and a girl to boot—I think my grandparents were overly protective.'

'So, as she grew up, your mother got away with a lot?'

'If you listen to her then no; her father was a military man too, and she bemoans the fact they were suffocating in their strictness. But if you ask my uncle, he'll say she was given a lot of leeway. Yet the more she got, the more she demanded. She became known as a bit of a whinger, whilst my uncle was always expected to be the big brother and pick up the slack. He carried that with him when he followed in my grandfather's footsteps into the Army. It's what's made him the General, I suppose.'

'And you're like him. Always striving to do the right thing,' Ash mused.

He was certainly beginning to understand her better. He and Fliss had more in common than he would have believed.

'But it doesn't make you boring, or dull.'

'I just think I was looking for someone I could trust. A man with the same qualities I see in my uncle. But I couldn't love them the way they deserved to be loved. That isn't me. I confused solid and reliable with boring and disconnected.'

'Why? Why are you so afraid to let go, Fliss?'

She offered a helpless shrug. 'I don't want to be like my mother. She only thought about herself, about what *she* wanted. Did I tell you that we didn't start off alone? That she only dragged me away from my grandparents' house when I was four? And that was because she wanted to push me into all the dancing lessons she wished that she had taken, but her parents hadn't allowed her to?'

Ash shook his head. 'Did you like dancing?'

'I *hated* dancing. But she said I was being selfish. That I owed her that much. I'd taken away her dream of dancing, so the least I could do was try to be half the dancer she felt she had been. It took my uncle four years to track us down. We were squatting in a house with about twenty others. We had no heating, no food because all the money she had went on sparkling new dresses so she could push me onto the circuit.'

He'd seen and heard a little about pageants over the years.

'They can be quite cut-throat, can't they.'

'That's an understatement.'

He could virtually see the nausea, the fear rising in her.

'So you loathed it,' he confirmed.

She bounced her head, unable to answer him for a moment. 'Every single second of the humiliation. My mother would scream and bawl at me for missing a pivot or split.

I was five, Ash. *Five.* I should have been playing on the swings, or being taught how to ride a bike. Having fun, laughing. Being loved.'

His throat constricted. He knew exactly how that felt. The loneliness, the despair, the rejection.

'My uncle found us backstage after one of those competitions. I was on the floor, sobbing over something or other, when he walked in and I thought he looked like the biggest, bravest, most heroic man I'd ever seen.'

'That was when he gave her the ultimatum.' Ash drew his lips into a thin line.

She stopped abruptly, dropping her eyes from his, but he could see that, even now, her pain was still as intense.

'Fliss?'

'When my mother refused to leave with him—' her voice dropped to a whisper '—she told him I was useless anyway and that she was better off without me. Then she dragged me off the floor and threw me across the room to him. She told him if he wanted to look after a worthless baby like me, then he could have me. Finally she walked out.'

Anger rushed up inside of Ash, along with something else. A fierce protectiveness. A need to ensure that no one hurt her or made her feel so worthless ever again.

He knew it wasn't his place to feel that way but he couldn't curb it; it refused to be pushed aside.

'Ash, I don't want to talk about this any more.'

Nodding grimly, Ash pulled his wallet out and thrust a generous pile of notes at the delighted server and pulled Fliss gently from her chair. Right now, she needed to be reminded of the better side of life. And he was determined to be the one to do that for her.

'Come on, Fliss. Time to get out of here.'

CHAPTER EIGHT

'WHERE ARE WE GOING?' Fliss cried as he clasped her hand, holding her tightly as he weaved his way through the crowds, the music and dancing starting up once again to their left as they were jostled and bumped by revellers.

Holding on as though he never wanted to let her go, Ash maintained the pace and, although she was initially reluctant, Fliss discovered the further they got from the restaurant, the more she felt as though she was leaving the conversation—and her past—behind.

The only time Ash stopped was when they passed a street vendor selling popcorn. He halted abruptly but, instead of buying a cone of hot buttered puffs, he asked for a small bag of kernels.

'What are they for?' she asked curiously.

Dropping them inside his shirt pocket, he patted the outside, his expression giving nothing away.

'Secret.'

And then, before she had a chance to say anything more, he set off again, her hand still tightly in his, and resumed their determined pace. By the time he pulled them both left into a side street that was decidedly less packed than the main route, Fliss had forgotten her earlier unease and felt a renewed sense of adventure. She marvelled at the effect. How easy Ash made it for her.

'According to our server, there's a path up the hillside here which offers a view out over the town. Apparently it's well worth a look.'

'I never even heard you ask.'

He shot her an indulgent smile which lifted her spirits even further.

'That's because you were too entranced by the floats. So, are you up for it?'

She glanced up at the cobbled path, infrequent lanterns offering pinpoints of light, lending it an almost romantic air.

'Sure, why not?'

As they headed along the narrowing streets, she couldn't suppress the rush of pleasure that, even though they were no longer pushing through crowds, he still enveloped her hand in his as though he wasn't ready to let her go.

As they left the last of the bars and restaurants, souvenir shops and revellers behind, the night closed around them like their own personal cloak. The path climbed steadily, a stone wall protecting them from the ever-increasing drop on one side whilst higgledy-piggledy stone buildings lined the other.

As the space between the festival lanterns stretched longer and longer, they began to pass the occasional couple, kissing passionately as they leaned on the wall or up against the buildings, cocooned in their own little world and oblivious to Ash and Fliss approaching. Yet another reminder of a typical carefree youth which Fliss had never allowed herself to experience.

Partly because she was afraid of becoming her mother and having a baby, only to make the child's life the same misery Fliss herself had endured. But also partly, Fliss was loathed to admit, because she was so prickly that no boy had ever wanted her enough—or, at least, made her *feel* wanted enough—to let go of her tightly held reins to try.

'This must be it.' Ash broke into her musings. 'So, what do you make of it?'

Peering around his shoulder as they turned to their left, Fliss took in the view and gasped.

The town beneath them seemed to be dotted by a thousand pretty fairy lights, the floats strategically sited around the streets for festival-goers to enjoy. It was prettier than she could have imagined. She moved to the parapet and stood transfixed, unable to articulate how she felt.

'You seem tense. It was all those couples kissing, wasn't it?' he asked, coming to stand next to her but deliberately giving her a little space.

She turned to look at him, confused.

'I'm not uncomfortable. If anything, I confess I might have felt a little…envious. Fusty Fliss, too uptight for anything like that.'

She snapped her mouth shut, wishing she hadn't said that. She certainly wasn't about to tell him where it had come from.

'*Fusty?* Is that so?' Ash muttered, angling his body so he was now facing her, looking straight into her eyes as though he could see every last worry etched in her face. 'Only *I* don't think that's entirely true.'

Ash lifted his hands to her shoulders, compelling her to turn her body, only to pull it against his, unbelievably hard and unyielding. Her insides turned to molten liquid.

She wanted him with an ache so fierce it should have frightened her.

He dipped his head to skim her lips with his own. He drew a lazy line across her bottom lip with his tongue. He slid his tongue in just enough to tease her. And all the while she could only cling to him, unable to tell whether he was the one thing stopping her from going under or the one thing pulling her beneath the sensual waves. Finally, Ash lifted her arms to hook them around his neck, allowing him greater access to the rest of her body, and she didn't stop him. She couldn't.

His hands explored her body, tracing every contour, firing every nerve-ending. Fliss opened her mouth to invite him further inside and he complied. Tasting her, teasing her. She pressed her body harder against his, the solid length of his erection unmistakable between them. It was a turn-on to know just how much he wanted her and instinctively she rocked against him.

He made a low, guttural sound in the back of his throat. Nerves and boldness mingled and Fliss rocked against him again.

'Be careful,' he warned her.

'What if I don't want to be?' she whispered back shakily.

He stilled, pulling back from her so he could look her in the eye. 'Don't you?'

She hesitated before offering a helpless shrug. 'I don't know.'

She wanted to do something out of character, go a little crazy. But she'd been trapped by her own set of unbending rules for so long that she didn't know how to break free.

'Do you trust me?' he demanded gruffly.

She thought back to the soldier she'd spoken to out in the field. The way every man who had worked with Ash only had good things to say about him.

'Yes,' she murmured.

He gave a curt, almost imperceptible nod, then leaned in to resume their kissing. But this time it was different. So intense and passionate her toes actually curled with pleasure. She ran her hands languidly over his body, exploring the taut, bunched muscles of his shoulders, his back, his obliques. Every inch of him was honed and uncompromising, without an inch of soft skin. And for tonight it was all hers. She only wished she knew exactly what to do with him.

It had never been like this in the past. The physical side of her limited relationships had been pleasant enough, if a little perfunctory. But nothing about Ash was *pleasant*. He was powerful, thrilling, dangerous. Fliss could imagine sex with him wouldn't be any less so. She just needed to convince him that she was ready for him to stop holding back. She let her hands drop to his backside, slipping her fingers in the pockets and hesitantly pulling him tighter against her.

As if reading her thoughts, Ash pressed her against the wall. With one knee, he nudged her legs apart and slid a steel-like thigh against the heat there. His lips blazed a sizzling trail all the way down the sensitive cord of her neck so that she couldn't help but dip her head to the side with a soft sigh, her hands barely holding onto his body as weakness trickled into her limbs.

Every part of her body was coming alive under his touch. He made her feel wanted. Needed. She arched her body towards him in subconscious invitation.

Dropping a hand lazily over her breasts, over nipples aching to be touched, Ash circled her ribcage, his strong hands and fingers splayed over her skin making her feel dainty and feminine. Then he flicked a thumb up and over the aching bud, his kisses dipping into the hollow at the base of her neck. Gasping, Fliss snapped her head back up.

'Ash…'

She didn't want him to stop but she couldn't help her reaction. Her well-worn shackles of propriety had reasserted themselves, making her feel constrained and awkward.

They were so much more exposed up here than they had been in the camp—in more ways than one.

'Shh, I promise you that no one's around,' he murmured. 'No one can see us, or hear us.'

She wished she didn't care. They were only kissing, for pity's sake. Why couldn't she be caught up in their little bubble, just as those few couples they had passed on the way up had been?

'You didn't seem this uncomfortable between the shipping containers and tents back at camp,' he pointed out gently.

'I was more comfortable there,' she hedged. 'It was familiar. Elle and I sunbathed there a few times—in rare moments of down-time, that is—and no one had ever stumbled on us before. Plus, it happened so fast, I didn't have time to second-guess myself.'

'Do you want to stop?'

There was no censure in his tone, no accusation, just a simple question. He wasn't trying to push her faster than she was prepared to go, although Fliss could tell how passionately he wanted her. A shiver of delight cascaded through her.

'I don't want to stop,' she realised aloud. She just needed reassurance.

'Shh, listen,' he told her. 'Close your eyes and listen.'

Obediently, she did.

'What am I listening for?' she asked after a moment, opening her eyes again. 'Aside from the faint sounds of the parade below, I can't hear anything.'

It was still and silent and, with the last lanterns much further down the path, the only light was the glow from the stars, and their eyes had long since adjusted to that.

'Precisely.'

She could hear the smile in his voice.

Feeling more secure, Fliss looped her arms around Ash's neck and pressed her lips to his. They both knew he could have made her forget all her concerns with that clever mouth of his. The fact that he'd chosen to be patient and let her feel comfortable in her own time spoke volumes.

'Happier?' he murmured against her mouth in amusement.

'Much.' She smiled at him, still not lifting her lips from his.

They kissed as he reached up to take one of her hands in his, strong fingers curling around hers. They kissed as he held both their hands to her chest, as though they might be slow dancing. They kissed as she felt her heart beating rhythmically against her fingers. Her body hummed with contentment but, more importantly in that instant, her heart did too. It felt so right, and so natural.

Breathing in, Fliss allowed herself to imagine what it would be like to have this kind of lust and excitement every day. It wasn't what this one night was about with Ash, she knew that, but it made her think that maybe the life she'd been trying to create for herself had never worked out because it wasn't right. She imagined what it might be like to stop trying to convince herself that she was in love with men like Robert, and just allowed herself to fall for a man like Ash. She imagined that could be such a very easy thing to do.

And then Fliss stopped imagining altogether. Finally giving in to what her body was trying to tell her, and losing herself in the magic Ash was conjuring throughout her body.

She dropped her hand down between their bodies and let her knuckles graze the hard length of his erection through the fabric of his trousers. His reaction was immediate, and unmistakable.

'Fliss,' he groaned, 'I can only resist so much.'

'So don't resist,' she whispered, loving the way his voice sounded so torn. So raw.

For a fraction of a second he hesitated, and then he acted. His hand skimmed over her ribcage, the bare sliver of skin of her lower abdomen, the loose waistband of her pants. She sucked in a breath, anticipating his next move, longing for it. Finally, he dipped his fingers beneath the material.

He hadn't planned on anything happening out here. Certainly not like this. He'd genuinely brought her up here because he'd thought it would be pretty and romantic. But then she'd told him how envious she was of the uninhibited displays of the few young couples in love who they'd passed on the way up, and he'd wanted to release that dormant side of her, the passion he knew lurked so close to the surface but which she didn't believe existed.

Now he found himself consumed with his own lust, and a need to see her come undone in his arms.

She was like a drug to him. He wanted her with an intensity which shook him, had done ever since that moment in the supply room in camp. He wanted her with a ferocity he didn't recognise. Driven, as if he was on some kind of mission.

Tonight was his one night to sate this insatiable hunger he seemed to have for Fliss.

Not for the first time, Ash slammed away the question of whether one night would ever be enough with this woman. He couldn't afford to think that way. One night would *have* to be enough; it was all they had. And then it would be back to their careers, heads down and eyes in, that they had both worked at for so long. Neither of them could afford to let anyone else close, to create distractions, to get hurt.

He almost held his breath as he grazed his fingers lower,

deliciously hot and damp through the flimsiest scrap of lacy fabric. She moaned and moved against his hand, urging him on, and Ash barely clung onto his self-control. He drew his body back so that he could see her in the starlight. She met his gaze, her eyes wide and dark, biting her lip as she waited for him to touch her just where she needed him. Her expression was pure, instinctual desire and he revelled in the proud sensation of being the one to put it there.

His eyes never leaving her face, he slid his finger under the lace. She made a small sound, clearly fighting to keep her gaze locked with his as she opened her legs a fraction wider. It was all the invitation Ash needed.

He let her move her hands back up his body before dipping his head to kiss her neck the way she'd loved earlier, all the while moving his fingers back and forth, unhurried at first, grazing their mark with deliberate precision. Her fingers bit into his shoulders as she tried to shift against his hand but he moved it away, only returning it when she stopped.

'Wicked,' she breathed into the night air and his slow smile curved into her skin as he sought out the nub of her sex, her gasp only tightening his own body all the more.

He moved quicker this time, the slickness of her threatening every inch of his willpower just as much as her soft sounds and low moans. At last, he slipped his finger inside her tightness, her body arching in response.

'So damned wet,' he growled, his teeth nipping gently at her neck.

Fliss moved her head to bury it into his shoulder but he reached up with his other hand and cupped her chin.

'Don't hide your head,' he commanded huskily. 'I want to watch you come.'

She trembled against him and Ash flicked his thumb over her entrance as his fingers moved inside her, the pressure making her squirm. She was so very tight and he could only imagine how she would feel around him later tonight. His movements became faster, more concentrated, watching as her eyelids grew hooded. She was close, and he wanted it to be perfect for her. Needed it to be.

She gripped his shoulders tighter, her eyes closed now, her head dropping slightly forward, and he kept moving, feeling the tension mount in her body. And then, with a low cry, she climaxed, squeezing down around his fingers then releasing, and finally pulsing around them in waves of pleasure. He waited, careful not to move his hand until she was ready for him to, all the while dropping light kisses onto her bowed head so that she felt safe.

He understood just how much it had taken for her to confide in him the way she had this evening. In a sense, the fact that they'd both had a difficult childhood had created an additional closeness Ash hadn't been prepared for.

But this closeness is transient, he reminded himself sharply. It would be wrong of him to allow either of them to confuse a temporary moment of bonding for anything more—not to mention unfair on Fliss—just because his head was a bit of an emotional wreck right now with the funeral looming.

He needed to find the right moment to remind her—remind himself—that it was still just sex.

He was still lost in his thoughts when Fliss eventually lifted her head.

'Ash?'

He turned his head, the sight of her soothing his jostling thoughts.

Tell her now.

'You look annoyed.' She peered at him nervously, her initial euphoria seeming to disappear before his eyes.

He hesitated. He *was* annoyed, but at himself, not at Fliss. It wouldn't be fair to burst her bubble when *she* wasn't the one apparently having difficulty remembering it was just about sex. It was *him*. But giving herself to him with such abandon was so out of character for Fliss, Ash hated that her happiness was so fragile. He hated that he could be the one to hurt her when suddenly all he wanted to do was protect her. Always.

Ridiculous. Just sex. Right?

'I'm not remotely annoyed,' he reassured her, forcing a rueful smile to his lips as he searched for a plausible distraction for his reaction. 'Frustrated, maybe.'

She flushed prettily, the way he'd become accustomed to her doing when she was feeling self-conscious. She lowered her hand down his body which, despite everything, kicked in primal need.

Just sex.

'Not here,' he growled, catching her wrist. 'I want to strip you down and taste every last inch of you before I finally slide inside you.'

'Then shall we go back to the hotel?' Her delighted smile was shy and seductive at the same time. 'We only have five hours before you have to leave for your flight.'

Deep inside Ash, something came apart. This was the confirmation he needed that he'd been imagining it when he'd thought Fliss was opening up to him as though there was more between them than just a one-night stand.

So why didn't that please him more?

'Let's go,' he answered grimly, shoving the reservations from his head.

Placing his arm protectively around her shoulders, they headed back down the hillside, her body nestling against his, a perfect fit.

Just sex.

He was finally beginning to convince himself. Still, it was going to be a painfully long taxi ride all the way back, so perhaps it was also the chance he needed to sort his head out.

CHAPTER NINE

SOMETHING WAS DIFFERENT.

Fliss's heart was beating so madly that it felt as though a jackhammer was assaulting her chest the entire journey to the hotel.

His arm might still be around her shoulders, his hard body almost glued to hers on the hot car seats, but mentally Ash was pulling away from her. And she had a fair idea why.

She'd broken their agreement.

She hadn't intended to. But there it was. She'd forgotten the *just sex* part of it and was at serious risk of falling for Ash. And he must know it. It explained why he was trying to distance himself emotionally.

She wanted to put it down to her inexperience with casual flings, but deep down she was afraid it was more than that. It wasn't the unfamiliar act of a one-night stand which was confusing her, but more the unique man sitting tantalisingly close to her. The one who had made her forget her surroundings back up on that hillside, who had made her forget all her usual rules and codes, and forget herself. When he'd played her body with such skill and finesse that it had thrummed with pleasure. When he'd peeled away the armour she'd spent decades melding for herself, and shown her how to live in that one breathtaking moment.

And when he'd laced his fingers through hers and dropped a kiss on her soft knuckles as if he really cared about her.

She'd forgotten all her rules and she'd let herself imagine something more with him. But when she came back down to earth she would remember that neither of them had room in their lives for that. If she was going to salvage tonight then she needed to convince him he had misunderstood, that she wasn't really thinking with her heart instead of her head. She needed to convince him that it was only about the sex for her too.

Because the alternative was that Ash would call it a night now rather than risk any unwanted further entanglement. And Fliss suddenly suspected that no other man was ever going to get under her skin the way Ash had, and if she didn't indulge in this one night of wanton abandon with him then she would regret it for the rest of her life.

Somehow, she had to make Ash believe that she *did* actually know what she was doing.

Even if she didn't.

Suppressing her nerves, Fliss twisted her body around to his and forced herself to sound confident as she leaned in to whisper in his ear. 'This journey is taking way too long.'

'We'll be back soon.'

Ash pulled his lips into a tight line, but Fliss was determined not to be dismissed. She dipped her head so that her lips were skimming the soft dip by his ear.

'Not soon enough,' she murmured, deliberately letting one hand drop onto his thigh. High enough that her desire was clear, but low enough so that it would pique his interest.

At least, she hoped it would. This was about heightening the sexual intensity, but they both knew she wasn't about to do anything else in the back seat of a taxi. Fliss suddenly wished she was a little more skilled in the bedroom department. She walked her fingers a torturously slow inch higher, her voice still a whisper.

'I can hardly wait to touch you properly.'

He caught her wrist in his strong fingers, just as he had on the hilltop, stopping it from moving any higher. But at least he didn't cast her away. In fact, the wall between them was beginning to crumble again. Fliss felt a punch of triumph. She'd convinced Ash that she was only thinking about the sex. And the funny thing about it was that, in the process, she'd started to convince herself that she felt that way too.

'I'm not made of stone, Felicity,' he warned. His voice was a low, strained rumble which seemed to burrow into her lower abdomen. She swallowed.

'I'm not asking you to be.'

Trusting her to keep her hand where it was, he let go and cupped her jaw, forcing her to look at him. For several long moments they held each other's eyes wordlessly. Her stomach flip-flopped. Ash's gaze was so intense it was almost black with desire, allaying any fears that he didn't want her any more. The realisation boosted her confidence more than any words could have.

Closing the gap between them, Fliss pressed her lips to his, so demanding and urgent she barely recognised herself. But she liked it. She liked the boldness Ash brought out in her, and she loved the way his resistance barely lasted a second before he was kissing her back with such heat she could hardly breathe.

She couldn't stop herself any longer. She cupped him through his trousers and he reacted instantly. Lust shot through her and her body arched towards his as liquid desire pooled at her core. If it hadn't been for the driver she didn't think she could have stopped herself from taking it further.

Her. Felicity Delaunay.

'I need more,' she moaned softly.

He pulled at her lower lip with his teeth, gently teasing her, his thumb grazing up and down her jawline.

'Soon,' Ash muttered, without lifting his head. 'I promise.'

Every last drop of their mutual desire was expressed in that kiss. Constrained to that kiss. First shallow and fast, then deepening and slowing. His mouth explored hers just as he had before, yet every stroke of his tongue and pass of his lips ignited new flames throughout Fliss's body as she revelled in the intoxicating feel of his mouth.

It was almost a relief when the taxi finally drew up outside the hotel and they tumbled out, barely able to conceal their hurry. Fliss felt momentarily bereft as Ash paused to pay the driver, but then he snaked his arm around her waist as he swept them inside the hotel lobby and across to the lifts. The wait felt interminably long.

Finally they ducked inside and stood, eyes fixed ahead, just waiting for the doors to close so that they could resume the kiss where they'd left off in the taxi. Her self-control was in tatters and her body throbbed. Finally, mercifully, the doors began to slide closed and Fliss was just imagining Ash hauling her up against the walls of the lift when a walking stick was jammed through the rapidly closing gap.

She felt Ash tug her gently to the side as the doors *pinged* open and an elderly couple shuffled inside, smiling kindly at them.

'Lovely evening.'

'Lovely,' Ash agreed, his voice admirably clear. 'Which floor?'

Her own throat tight, Fliss tried to force a smile to her lips instead. For years she'd wondered what it must feel like when other kids had lamented sneaking a boyfriend to their bedroom only for a parent to walk in. She suspected it felt a little like she was feeling now.

'Fifth floor, please.'

The same as theirs.

Fliss didn't dare glance at Ash. She felt as though she was trapped in some kind of farce and she'd never felt so overwhelmed by frustrated longing before. Just another tiny detail which set the night apart from any other she'd ever experienced.

The lift sped upwards. The silence almost cloying, though no one else appeared to notice.

'Have you been enjoying yourselves?'

A gurgle of laughter bubbled up inside Fliss. Only Ash's arm, offering her silent support, allowed her to control it.

'Very pleasant, thank you,' he responded politely. 'The carnival in the local town was particularly impressive. Have you seen it?'

Smooth and polite, she was impressed. Her own brain was barely functioning it was so overcome with lust. As the couple enthused about the carnival, Fliss fought to regain some semblance of self-control. It was only when the lift reached their floor and the couple stepped out at a snail's pace that the giggle bubbled up again.

Her shoulders shook with smothered laughter as she and Ash kept back. Even his unruffled air didn't help her. How could he be so unconcerned when she felt so on edge? It didn't help that she didn't know what they were supposed to do now. Go to his room? Go to hers? Each go to their own?

It was only when the elderly pair stopped next to her room, fumbling with the keycard with only a fraction less dexterity than Fliss herself had displayed earlier, that Ash broke contact with her to go to their aid, unlocking their door with ease and shrugging off their gushing thanks as he held the door open whilst they shuffled inside.

Uncertain of herself, Fliss lurched to her own bedroom door and tried to retrieve her card from her purse, her fumbling hands hampering her efforts.

'My room,' Ash muttered, startling her as he grabbed her hand and tugged her past the linen cupboard and to his own door, deftly opening it and hauling her inside. 'Your headboard backs right onto their wall.'

As the door closed behind them, Fliss finally let go of the mildly hysterical laugh she'd been suppressing. It took her a few moments before she realised, to her surprise, that Ash was laughing too. Their eyes locked for a moment, only making them laugh all the more. As he sank onto the edge of the bed, Fliss leaned on the wall, letting the moment of humour release some pent-up tension.

'We couldn't have timed that any worse,' Ash joked, eventually sobering up.

'I know.' She shook her head. 'But I didn't think you were bothered.'

'Are you kidding? I felt like a frustrated teenager all over again.'

She bit her lip in disbelief. 'I thought it was just me.'

He shot her an arch look.

'It definitely wasn't just you. I'm just glad I have more self-control than I had as a teenager.'

'Well, you certainly have that.'

'Barely, where you're concerned.' His husky voice fired her body up in a flash. The earlier heat couldn't course through her veins fast enough, and then he reached out a hand to her.

'Come here.'

She was only too happy to comply as he hooked his fingers into her waistband and pulled her to him. His fingers skimmed up her body and, before she realised what was happening, he had undone the tie at the back of her

neck and the halter-neck had dropped down to reveal her
bare breasts.

'Perfect,' he breathed reverently, cupping them with his
hands. 'Just as I imagined.'

She gasped as he leaned forward to draw one taut peak
into his mouth. Exquisite torture. Her entire body felt as if
it were on fire for him. But there was something else too.
The moment of levity had created another thread between
them, and they both knew it.

Just sex, remember? Fliss berated herself as she wound
her fingers through his hair, instinctively letting her head
fall back as she pushed her aching nipple against his skil-
ful tongue.

Her heart gave another kick as he settled her on his lap,
one leg either side, her knees resting on the bed. He was
nestled perfectly between her legs, his erection straining
against the fabric towards her, making her feel sexy and
powerful. Suddenly, she was gripped by the impulse to take
charge. To pleasure him. To make Ash spin out of control
for her, the same way she had for him back on the hillside.

'You've had your fun,' she croaked. 'Now I'm having
some.'

Catching him off guard, she pushed him back on the bed
and concentrated on divesting Ash of his shirt.

'You're telling me you weren't already?' he challenged
smugly.

Her heart raced. Feeling all fingers and thumbs, she
grappled awkwardly with the buttons. She needed to distract him before he noticed.

'A different kind of fun.' She used her best seductive
tone before leaning down to brush her lips against his,
deliberately grazing his shirt-clad chest with her nipples.

Ash's eyes dilated with desire and she felt another kick

of adrenalin. She doubted he let many women take charge over him.

Finally, to her relief, the last fastening slid from its soft anchorage and she pushed the garment off his broad shoulders, which she'd hungered to touch like this ever since that day in the supply room. Fliss lowered her body again to taste his mouth with hers, revelling in the sensation of her nipples grazing over the smattering of hair on his bare chest. His erection twitched against her again, almost making her forget her plan.

Almost.

She rained tiny kisses down on his lips, his neck, his chest, following the trail her fingers blazed, his sharp intake of breath like a silent cheer to carry on. But she couldn't shake the feeling that Ash wasn't completely relaxed; he was only letting her take the lead for so long. She forced herself to take her time, inhaling the woodsy, leathery scent, gradually moving lower. *Lower.* Sliding down his body an inch at a time, over abs, his belly button, the muscular definition of his lower abdomen before it dipped below the waistband of his trousers. And all the while she traced the grenade scar with her fingers and her tongue, revelling in the fact that he didn't stop her.

She was relieved when her fingers unbuckled his belt and lowered his zip with far more ease than she'd managed his shirt. His erection strained against the soft fabric of his boxers. Hooking her fingers over the waistband, she pulled the material down and lowered her lips to kiss the silky tip, then to the side where the grenade wound had stopped mercifully short.

She'd seen enough wounded soldiers to know that the genital area was one of the least protected areas, with no body armour to shield it.

Before Fliss knew what was happening, he had scooped

her onto the bed and flipped her over onto her back, sliding the rest of her clothes off with slick efficiency. She frowned uncertainly.

'Why did you stop me?'

'Because that's not how it's going to play out,' he growled fiercely.

'Why not?' Disappointment welled inside her. 'You can't relinquish control for a moment, can you?'

No, he couldn't relinquish control. Not to Fliss. Not like that.

No one had ever had a hold over him the way she seemed to. Even her hurt and disappointment gnawed at him. But even that one simple question revealed that she understood him in a way hardly anyone had ever done. And if he let her do what she'd intended to do, let her make him forget everything, then he was afraid she would pull away the last of his defences and leave him vulnerable.

Just as he had been as a young child, pushed from care home to foster home and back again. Totally out of his control.

'I'll make it up to you.' He shrugged, pushing away the guilt.

She looked dubious, half sitting up to reach for him again.

'How?'

'Like this,' he muttered, dropping to his knees and parting her legs to lick her in one strong stroke.

She cried out, falling back to the bed, her hips lifting up instinctively even as she called out in panic.

'Ash, this isn't… I don't…'

'You do now.'

He heard the primitive growl in his voice moments

before he buried his head in her heat. Her hips bucked against him.

Hot. Sweet. *His.*

He wanted to be the only man who had ever been able to satisfy her the way he did. Ash fought the feeling of possessiveness which stabbed through him at the idea of her with anyone else. This wasn't about anything lasting; why was he still finding it so hard to remember that?

Sliding a hand beneath her bottom to lock her in place, he raised his hand to caress one swollen breast and lowered his head again, feeling her fingers locking into his own hair as he kissed, and licked, and sucked. Her increasing moans and gasps urged him on, the way she cried out his name stoking the primal need inside him.

She was so close. He could feel her on his tongue. He slipped a finger inside, then another, marvelling at the way she stretched against him, and then he sucked on that sensitive core and pitched her over into nothingness. Her orgasm shattered over her again and again as he never let up for an instant. Her shudders finally slowed and her breathing began to even out again.

'You should have stopped,' she accused softly, only half regretfully. 'I wanted to feel you inside me.'

'Be patient,' he murmured darkly, knowing he wanted that too. Almost too much. He'd had to prove to himself he could control that searing need.

Rocking back on his heels Ash stood up, shucking off the rest of his clothes even as he reached for a condom from the bedside drawer and rolled it quickly down his length. Then he returned his mouth to where he'd left off, hearing her objection give way to a squeak of surprise as he smoothly brought her body back to simmering point.

Only then did he cover her body with his own, her breasts pillowed against his chest, her hard nipples raking his skin. She wrapped her legs instinctively around his hips, her arms snaking around his neck. He tried to hold off but she pulled him down, his tip brushing against her wet heat, intending only to ease in part way until she became accustomed to him. Without warning, she tilted her hips and tightened her legs, drawing him slickly inside with a sensual murmur.

A guttural groan filled the air and Ash didn't immediately recognise his own voice, so thick was it with desire.

'God, Fliss, I don't know how long I can last,' he warned her.

She nodded, heavy-lidded eyes fighting to open and look at him, her hands gripping his shoulders. She was already closer than he'd realised, and the knowledge pushed him perilously closer to own completion.

Think of something else. Anything.

Bracing his arms on either side of her, he forced a gap between them, allowing him to pull out of her before driving back in. Long, slow, deliberate strokes which Fliss threatened to undo when she lifted her hips and matched him, in perfect sync, all the while skimming her fingernails down his back to his buttocks, which she grasped.

'Faster,' she whispered urgently.

He wanted to take more time. He couldn't. She was driving the pace now, meeting him stroke for stroke, and he could barely restrain himself any longer. Their combined breathing became shallower, quicker, her moans louder, her hands clutching him. He changed the angle slightly to graze her just right and immediately her body shattered around him, clamping over him then pulsing as she shuddered in his arms.

And Ash could finally let go too. He drove into her one final time as his own climax overtook him. A climax like no other before. He couldn't tell where he ended and she began. He only knew his body was exploding into hers and she was riding against him on another orgasm of her own. He heard himself call out her name and then he tipped them both over the edge.

His last thought was whether he'd ever be able to get enough of this woman.

It was only later, much later, after he'd claimed her again and again, just before the first rays of the new day started to creep over the horizon, when he realised their time was almost up and he had to leave, that Ash heard himself telling her that he was returning home for a funeral. Just those words, nothing more.

'Whose?' she asked, the concern seeping through her voice, though she was clearly trying to keep her tone even.

Just like back in the supply room, when she'd first seen the blood on his shoulder and wondered how he'd injured himself.

And, just like then, another hairline fracture cracked through his core.

'Rosie's.'

Fliss looked aghast, an angry flush discolouring her skin.

'Ash, I'm so sorry. God, how obvious. You *told* me about your foster mother; I should have remembered. I should have realised when I saw you in the hangar.'

'Don't,' he ordered, taking her hands in his and making her look him in the eye.

'You asked if I was okay and I said I was. I didn't want to talk about it. I didn't want to think about it.'

'You wanted to forget,' she realised. 'I was a distraction.'

He could lie to her. But he didn't want to; she deserved better.

'Yes.'

Instead of looking hurt or offended, however, she nodded at him with understanding. Then she fixed him with those magnificent, expressive eyes of blue and asked him if he wanted her to accompany him. Simply. Sincerely.

Another hairline crack ran through him.

He was tempted. And then he declined.

'I'm going to the funeral to show my respect, but I lost the Rosie I knew, the mother figure, years ago, and I said my goodbyes then.'

She frowned.

'I know you think that now,' she offered softly. 'But it might not feel that way when you get there. As a doctor, I've seen it a lot. Even if you've said your goodbyes, you still might not be truly prepared for the funeral.'

'I'm prepared.'

Darkness swirled and he fought against it.

'Ash, I know you have this self-control which you feel you can't let go of—' she swallowed '—even in bed with me. But you need to give yourself permission to feel any emotions which happen on the day.'

'I understand what you're saying.' He gritted his teeth. 'But I know what I'm doing. That's why I bought the popcorn.'

'Sorry?'

He had no idea why he was telling her. Part of him wanted to make her understand that he was still thinking straight, still remembering his promises to Rosie, and that grief hadn't messed up his head. Another part of him suspected he needed to tell someone. To tell *her*.

'Part of what Rosie and Wilf did was have Family Night. Movie nights, where all the foster kids would join them in the den, watch a film together and eat burgers and popcorn; games nights where we'd gather around the kitchen and play board games; baking nights, which was actually where I first learned to cook something other than baked beans. When I first arrived I refused to join them; I'd spent every night on the streets and I thought I was cool.'

'I bet they soon disabused you of that notion.' Fliss smiled softly.

Warmth and light flowed over him and Ash suddenly found himself laughing fondly.

'You got that right. Movie nights quickly became my favourite and Rosie and I used to love to sit together on the couch and eat popcorn. I even kept going around when I'd left foster care.'

'I remember you saying. I thought that was a lovely thing to do.'

'One night we were watching a film and just when some character was being buried the popcorn went off in the kitchen. Immediately she joked that when she was cremated, she wanted to have popcorn kernels in with her so that she could go out with a bang. For some reason we couldn't stop laughing and somehow it became a running joke, so when I saw that popcorn seller tonight it felt like it…meant something.'

'You're not really going to put the kernels in the coffin?' Her face looked so concerned, so caring that he thought his heart was in a vice.

So much for keeping control of his emotions. For never letting anyone get too close to hurt him. He'd let Fliss in and when he hadn't been looking she'd begun to tear down his defences.

'Of course I'm not going to put them in the coffin.' He shook his head gently at her. 'But having them with me, it makes me feel like I haven't forgotten how close we were.'

'I get it, Ash. I do.'

Her quiet assurance somehow soothed his soul.

'But if you change your mind,' she offered. 'If you need anything. *Anything*, Ash.'

'I won't,' he told her quietly.

And then he took her again, both knowing it was for the last time. They stared at each other as he slid inside her. Until they were both driving it onwards, urgently, greedily, until she arched her whole body and called out as she tumbled into the abyss. And he cried her name and followed her.

Finally, he held her, dropping soft kisses on her body as her breathing eventually slowed and deepened and slumber overtook her. By the time he slipped silently from the bed, got dressed and left the room, Ash knew he had never found it harder to do the right thing.

The morning sun was streaming through the window by the time Fliss awoke again. Exquisitely sore, deliciously sated and inexplicably sad.

She rolled over, away from the empty space in the bed, and the dent on the pillow where Ash's head had rested only a few hours earlier. Picking up her phone, she checked the time.

Oh-eight-hundred hours. Ash's plane would be in the air and almost halfway home already.

The thought didn't help her churning stomach.

Last night had been everything she'd expected it would be and more. She'd been fooling herself if she thought she could manage a one-night stand with anyone, but certainly not with a man like Ash. He had made her feel alive in a way she'd never dreamed possible. Her entire body ached, from her breasts which he'd grazed with his stubble, to her neck which he'd grazed with his teeth, and between her legs which had experienced such delicious torture.

But the part which ached the most was deep inside her

heart and she feared it would never heal. Her only consolation was that at least she'd got out now, before she'd fallen for Ash Stirling, head over heels.

Impulsively, she picked up her mobile and dialled the only person she could.

'Elle?' Sinking on the bed with relief at the sound of her friend's voice, she wondered how best to phrase her request, given that Elle only had two weeks of R&R with her fiancé before returning to Razorwire.

'I'm so sorry, but I could really use a chat right now…'

She tailed off, shutting down the part of her brain that was screaming, *I think I may have actually fallen for Ash.*

'Any chance I could call in to yours for an hour once I get back to the UK?'

'You could—' she heard Elle's hesitant voice crackle over the phone '—but I'm not there.'

A frown deepened on Fliss's face as she listened to her friend talk. Her explanation was so flimsy it could barely support its own weight. And the monotone voice was so different from Elle's habitually jovial tone as they agreed a time and place.

So just what the heck was Elle doing on her own in an airport hotel room about an hour out of the RAF base on the outskirts of Oxford, when she should have been a hundred miles away enjoying her last two days of R&R with her fiancé, Stevie?

Fliss eyed Elle curiously, wondering what had happened in the thirty hours since their phone call to bring about the change in her friend.

'Are you pregnant?' she accused. 'You're positively glowing, your eyes are all sparkly…'

'And my coat is shiny?' Elle cut across her, laughing. 'I'm sorry if I sounded…*off* during that conversation.

You've no idea how relieved I was that you called; I really needed someone to talk to.'

'You and Stevie had a fight? Was it about the wedding plans again?'

She was trying to be sympathetic but all she really wanted to do was pour the whole story out to Elle.

'I walked in on him having sex in *our* bed, with some *groupie.*'

'*Elle!*' Her problems forgotten in an instant, Fliss was aghast.

"And that's not the first time."

Watching Elle's face colour with embarrassment, Fliss couldn't decide whether she was more upset for her friend, or angry on her behalf.

'How dare he do that to you.'

Elle must be devastated, Stevie was the only man she'd ever even kissed. Only the funny thing was, she didn't look devastated. To Fliss, her friend looked the way she herself had felt when she'd received the *Dear John* letter from Robert.

Relieved.

She couldn't help herself. Before she could stop it, she imagined what it would be like to have received a letter like that from Ash. Or to walk in on Ash that way.

It was like a physical body blow. Pain seared through her as Fliss grasped the edges of the chair, trying to steady herself and struggling to catch a breath.

That answered that question then, she realised in horror. So much for Ash being just a one-night fling.

'Are you okay?' She concentrated on her friend.

'Surprisingly, yes. I… I've been feeling Stevie and I were out of step for a while now.'

'I know.' Fliss was tentative. 'Maybe even years, looking back?'

'Maybe.'

They'd both been so indifferent about their respective fiancés, but Fliss had put it down to their careers.

'Now I understand why you sounded so deflated the other day on the phone. But now you look so buoyed?'

Fliss didn't add that it was the same way she felt after her night with Ash. The idea of one-man Elle having a fling was disorientating. But maybe it would be the best thing her friend could do.

After all, hadn't her own fling with Ash stirred more emotions in her in four days than Robert ever had in four years? So where did that leave her?

'So much has happened since then,' Elle started, before stopping abruptly.

'Tell me about it!' Fliss attempted to roll her eyes light-heartedly; Elle would think she was crazy.

But for once Elle was too lost in her own thoughts to notice. Fliss could practically see the tussle on her friend's face as her friend debated whether or not to spill her story. Eventually, Elle shook her head in determination.

'No, *you* called *me*, Fliss. Which means this time *you* have to go first.'

'Since when do you and I stand on ceremony?'

She eyed her friend suspiciously and Elle offered a sheepish smile.

'Sorry, you're right. But I just need a bit more time to process. You go first.'

Fliss suppressed a groan, schooling herself to appear as normal as she could.

'I've no idea where to begin, either.'

'Okay.' Elle grinned suddenly. 'Remember what we did at uni? First animal to pop into your head. Don't think. Just say.'

'Dog.' Fliss floundered, thinking how unoriginal her answers had always been.

'Favourite colour?'

'Purple.'

'What's the big news?'

'I kissed Man Candy.'

A stunned silence filled the room, so loud Fliss could hear it thrumming in her ears. She willed Elle to say something. *Anything.*

'Are you serious?'

Fliss's heart flip-flopped. She hadn't realised how much she really wanted to hear Elle's approval.

'Serious.' She nodded. 'Well, more than just kissed, actually. We slept together. In a hotel. On the way home.'

It sounded so emotionless when she said the words, but nothing could be further from the truth.

'Are you shocked and appalled?'

'Shocked, yes. Appalled, no,' Elle marvelled. 'I know I suggested it, but I never really thought you'd go in for a fling. I'm so pleased; I think it's just what you needed after Robert.'

'You're right, of course,' Fliss began hesitantly. 'Only it wasn't just about having a fling; it was about finding the person who made me want to have a fling.'

'Oh, no.' Elle peered at her. 'You've fallen for him, haven't you?'

Fliss attempted to look horrified. 'No. No, of course not. Well, not *fallen* for, exactly. Okay…maybe a bit.' She puffed up her cheeks and blew out. 'I need your help, Elle. What am I supposed to do now?'

'Don't ask me.' Elle shrugged, feigning nonchalance. 'Following our phone conversation I decided that I wasn't going to spend last night moping in my room, and so I went to some Latin-dance club. After fifteen years having only ever slept with one person, I have now slept with two.'

'You had a one-night stand?' Fliss gaped.

The coincidence of it was striking. Both she and Elle had always been so career-focused, so conservative in their personal lives, yet within twenty-four hours of meeting each other, they'd both had the first, and probably only, one-night stand of their lives.

'So you want to tell me how I'm supposed to do this, because I seem to have got the *fling-then-forget* bit a little messed up? What do we do now?' Fliss joked weakly.

'Don't ask me.' Elle shrugged. 'Only I think I may have fallen a little for my guy too. Not that he is even my guy. So I think that makes you and I a right pair of one-night-stand failures.'

She rolled her eyes and Fliss laughed.

'I think you're right. But hey, at least we can now say that we tried it.'

'Right. But now we just try to figure something out, and forget them.'

She looked about as dubious as Fliss felt and an image of Ash popped, unbidden, into her mind. The way he'd worked so in sync with her that first day. The way he'd come to that rooftop to tell her that Corporal Hollings was stable enough to be flown home. The way he'd listened to her at the table as she'd told him things she'd never told anyone before.

And then other images. The way he'd kissed her back at camp. The way he'd made her forget everything but him as he'd touched her so skilfully on that hillside over the carnival. The way he'd claimed her again and again, making her feel as though no man had ever understood her body, her needs, as he did.

White-hot flames licked at her insides, setting every inch of her skin on fire just at the memories. How was any man going to ever match up to Colonel Asher Stirling?

CHAPTER TEN

ASH STALLED AT the crematorium doors. For a moment he was seven again, and beyond the door wasn't his foster mum Rosie, but his mum.

Part of him wanted to turn and run but that wasn't in his nature. More concerning was the fact that another part of him wished that he hadn't been too proud to accept Fliss's offer to accompany him. If he had, she might be here now, standing right next to him.

But needing anyone wasn't in his nature either.

His nature was to push people away. To keep them at arm's length so they didn't see that weak part of him he'd never been able to fully eradicate. And in protecting himself he often ended up hurting others. Just as he had hurt Rosie. And Wilf. He hadn't intended to hurt them. And if he let Fliss in, he'd end up doing the same.

A hot pain stabbed through him at the idea of anyone ever hurting Fliss.

In one night she'd ignited such emotions in him. Passion, protectiveness, even possessiveness. He shook his head as if that would dislodge the memories of their night together. Memories which played on permanent loop in his brain.

Ironic, really.

He'd intended that night to be the distraction he needed from thinking about the funeral. Now he found he needed a distraction from thinking about that one night. Sex with Fliss was supposed to have been *just sex*. In the past it had always been *just sex*. Hot sex, wild sex, intense sex or lazy sex. It never mattered; the result had always been the same.

He'd tried to deny it but it had been different with Fliss, even from the start. And even when he'd walked out of the door, the memories had taken up residency in his head and refused to be evicted.

'Going inside, mate?'

The unfamiliar voice caught him unawares, snapping him out of his thoughts and reminding Ash why he was here.

The funeral.

He turned with something approaching relief. The expression on the stranger's face was instantly recognisable. A couple of years older than Ash but unmistakably another foster kid Rosie had helped. They nodded at each other in unspoken acknowledgement as Ash gestured for the other man to go ahead.

Stepping through the door, he stood just off to the side and straightened his service dress uniform and black arm band. The other man had made his way up the aisle to where Wilfred stood by the coffin.

Pain tightened Ash's chest.

His foster father looked old. So much older than Ash remembered. Where was the man mountain of Ash's childhood? It had only been, what? He calculated the last couple of tours. *Four years.* Four years since he'd last seen Wilf and Rosie—not that she'd recognised him—yet the frail old man in front of him could have been a decade and a half older. No doubt evidence of the toll Rosie's illness had taken on him.

Wilf greeted the other man with a handshake and a brief embrace, exchanging a few words before the man went to sit down. Emotions rushed Ash. He doubted his foster father would be as pleased to see *him*. He should have come back years ago. But he couldn't leave now, even if Wilf asked him to. He owed it to Rosie to be here.

Alone again, the old man resumed his stance, trying to straighten his back and steel himself against the emotions which were clearly flowing just beneath the surface. Typically stoic Wilfred. He would stay strong for everyone else even though Ash imagined he was crumbling inside.

Then there were no more excuses. Ash forced himself to take his first step to the aisle, placing one foot in front of the other, until his foster father finally looked up and saw him.

'Asher.'

To Ash's shock the old man practically stumbled down the aisle towards him, gratitude and fondness in the watery eyes which were paler than he remembered. He hauled Ash into the tightest bear hug before suddenly appearing to lose all strength, the thin body slumping against his own as Wilf clung on in silence, only his frail, shaking body, betraying himself to his former foster son. And then Ash finally allowed himself to feel. He wrapped his arms around the man who had helped to save his life and they hugged each other for several long moments.

By the time Wilf patted his arms, standing up again and looking him in the eye, the old man's face was slightly wet.

'Thank you. She'd be so happy you came.' He exhaled deeply. '*I'm* so happy you came. And in your uniform. Rosie always loved to see you dressed like that. She was so proud of you. We both were.'

He stopped, choked up, filled with the love Ash recalled so well. Remorse flooded his entire body.

He'd been such a fool and now it was too late.

'I'm sorry.' He shook his head. 'I'm so sorry.'

'You have nothing to be sorry for, son. Nothing. You hear me?'

Something clogged in Ash's throat and he swallowed painfully. 'I should have come a long time ago.'

Bony fingers clutched his arm.

'You were fighting for your country. Hell, you nearly made the ultimate sacrifice when that grenade went off.' He led Ash up to the coffin, resuming his former position next to it, but this time facing Ash. 'And you never dealt with losing your own mum. I understand why you couldn't deal with losing Rosie too.'

'I should never have left it so damn long,' Ash bit out, his voice cracking.

'Rosie didn't know any different. Not by then. She didn't even know me. She wouldn't have known you and you'd have put yourself through hell for no good reason.'

'I let you down.' The words came out by themselves.

Wilf cast him a ferocious stare. 'You most certainly did not. You were there when she needed you. You made her prouder than you know, as an army officer but, more importantly, as an honourable man. You have no idea how proud I was when I heard you'd become a colonel.'

Even after everything, Wilf had been following his career?

Guilt flooded through Ash, making him feel sick.

'I should sit down,' he managed thickly. 'People will want to…speak to you.'

He couldn't say the words.

'Stand with me?' the old man asked suddenly. 'Please?'

It felt like an honour he didn't deserve.

'I…shouldn't.'

A hopeful light danced momentarily in Wilf's eyes as he peered around the building.

'You came with someone?'

'No.' Ash hated snuffing out that light.

'Still haven't met *the one*? You will.' Wilf nodded firmly. 'Rosie always said that one day you'd meet the woman who would complete you and you'd stop fighting the idea of opening your life to someone.'

It took everything Ash had to shut out images of the other night. He'd spent thirty hours trying to convince himself it was *just sex,* but deep down he knew he was going to have to face up to the connection they'd forged when he hadn't been looking. Maybe it had been when they'd worked together so fluidly out in the field, or maybe on that rooftop when he'd told her about the scars, or maybe when she'd opened up to him at the carnival about her past.

At some point he was going to have to admit that it wasn't *just sex* at all.

And once he accepted it, perhaps he could finally put it behind him.

'That's not for me. My career…isn't conducive to a relationship.'

Wilf snorted. 'When you meet your one, everything else will fall into place.'

Before he could answer, more people arrived and made their way to Wilf to express their condolences, and Ash was left alone with his thoughts.

It was no use. He was helpless against the memories of Fliss which assaulted him on multiple levels. From the sweet sound of her laughter and the silky-soft cascade of that blonde hair, to the intoxicating scent of her hot core and the honey taste of her climax on his tongue.

And now he craved more.

But neither he nor Fliss could afford more. They were both dedicated to their Army careers, and the reason they were both so successful was because they didn't have distractions. He knew so many soldiers who left their 'family head' at RAF Lyneham and put on their 'Army head' when they went on operations. But, even then, the smallest thing could throw them, whether news from home or just missing a loved one that day.

Avoiding being tied down meant he never had to worry about that, and Fliss was the same. Which was why they could each focus on their respective tasks and know they would always give everything they had.

He needed to forget Fliss. Get back to life as he'd known it a month ago.

'You're a good boy,' Wilf said softly as they were left alone again. 'You deserve love. But, like my Rosie always said, you just need to let go. You're the only one standing in the way of your own happiness.'

Ash stood firm. 'I'm happy,' he lied. 'Anyway, what can I do for you, Wilf?'

'You're here. That's all I need.'

'Okay.'

Standing together in companionable silence, Ash forced a polite smile to his lips as each new arrival came up to Wilf. Rosie had a good send-off. He wasn't surprised. She'd been an incredible woman.

It felt like an eternity before the two men had to take their own seats. But, just as they were about to move, Wilf placed a hand on Ash's arm, his grip surprisingly strong and his eyes suddenly sharp.

'Did you bring anything with you?' he demanded urgently.

Sheepishly, as if he were fourteen again, Ash reached into his pocket and took out a handful of popcorn kernels.

The grin split Wilf's face in two even as a tear tipped over and rolled down his cheek.

'Me too. I already threw mine in,' he chuckled. 'We'll send our Rosie off with the bang she always wanted.'

* * *

'Ash?'

When Fliss opened her front door at such an ungodly hour, he was the last person she expected to see.

Ever since she'd awoken in that hotel room alone, she hadn't been able to shake the hope that she might see him again. It wasn't just about the sex, but if that was all he was offering then, so help her, she'd take it.

He was exhausted and devastated, and looking dishevelled in his service dress. Her heart vaulted around her chest, questions piling in on her. But, before she could ask a single one, he stepped through the door, tugged apart the tie of her dressing gown and scooped her up, encouraging her to wrap her legs around his hips as he pinned her against the hallway wall. Fliss was vaguely aware of the front door slamming behind him.

'Bedroom?' he ground out hoarsely, abandoning her mouth for a brief moment.

She was barely able to think straight, let alone speak.

'Left, right, right,' she managed.

It never crossed her mind to stop him. But she wanted him too much. Wanted *this* too much. They'd have to deal with the fallout later.

He laid her on the bed, stripping her down so that she felt the cool morning air on her body, sending goosebumps skittering over her skin and hardening her nipples. Ash noticed too, studying her whole body reverently before covering each breast with a large hand and taking both brown peaks between a finger and his thumbs so that sparks shot through her body.

But he wasn't here at this hour for foreplay. Moments later, they were both naked and he was covering her pliant body with his own solid one, holding himself above her, his eyes locked with hers, not a word more spoken.

Neither of them needed words. And then Ash claimed her as his, quickly bringing her to orgasm moments before he exploded inside her.

It was only when their shudders had subsided that he slipped out of her, still caressing her spine as he would a lover, until finally his breathing slowed and he drifted into the first sleep Fliss suspected he'd had since leaving the hotel the other day.

When she woke several hours later the bed was cold, like some pathetic déjà-vu. Only this time, she realised, something felt different. Throwing on an old T-shirt and yoga pants, she padded along the corridor, following the scent of coffee and warm bread. He was dressed in gym gear that she imagined he'd retrieved from a gym bag he kept in the boot of his car, just as she did.

Then her eyes widened in surprise. 'Homemade bread?'

'Rosie taught me,' he answered simply.

She took it for the hedged invitation that it was. Moving gingerly into the room, she slid onto a barstool across the kitchen worktop, as though any sudden moves might startle him.

He watched her, his gaze unwavering. 'I'm sorry about this morning. That wasn't what I intended when I drove here.'

'It wasn't?' She attempted to tease him in an effort to conceal her nerves, but she knew it sounded a little stiff, a little awkward.

The truth was that she didn't want to hear the words. She didn't want him to say it had been a mistake.

Instead, he offered a wry smile. 'Okay, it was. But not like that. I wanted to talk first.'

Something pulled in her chest but she schooled her features, scared to give too much away.

'Oh?'

He raked his hand through his hair, clearly trying to work out where to start. Her heart paused for a beat. The apprehensive gesture was so unlike the man she had come to know.

'I'm sorry.' He blew out a sharp breath. 'I seem to be saying that word a lot recently. But I don't know where to start.'

She had to be careful here. 'How did the funeral go?'

Another pause.

'It was harrowing,' he confessed at last, then frowned. 'Yet somehow...soothing.'

'You got some closure,' she observed.

He rolled his eyes. 'Is that the quack term for it?'

Ah, that flash of macho pride she recognised from too many soldiers, the stigma that still, to some degree, shrouded talking about personal issues.

'Don't knock it,' she warned patiently. 'Or underestimate its significance.'

'Fine. Then I guess I got *closure*.' He bunched his shoulders. 'And I *am* sorry. I was out of line when I told you to mind your own business in the hotel that night. You were right; I wasn't mentally prepared for the funeral. I *did* need to say goodbye and I *did* need permission to feel those emotions. I'm grateful to you for saying all you did; it made me open my mind up subconsciously so it wasn't such a shock when I got there.'

'And your foster father?'

'Yeah,' he admitted. 'You were right too. Wilf welcomed me straight away. Hugged me. Told me he was glad I was there.'

'Good,' she offered softly, relieved she had judged it right.

Nonetheless, it was clear from Ash's changing expression that there was more to it than he was saying. She could practically hear the cogs clicking over in his head, and as he brooded she could feel something building. At first, she couldn't put a name to it. She just needed to give him space to find the right words for whatever it was he wanted to tell her.

'I felt I'd let him down. And Rosie.'

He raked his hand through his hair, short as it was. The helplessness of the gesture tugged at her.

'You're not the kind of person to let people down,' she protested. 'I spoke to your men. Remember?'

His jaw locked, the tiny pulse flickering. Finally, she could pinpoint the source of the tension building inside him. *Guilt and anger.*

'It's not the same,' he growled.

'Why not?' she ventured.

He crossed his arms defensively over his chest, subconsciously pushing her away. She could tell he wished the conversation was over but he felt obliged to answer. She was putting herself in his sights. She didn't know why she was even doing it. She didn't have to. They weren't even a couple.

He turned his back, busying himself with emptying the now cold cafetière and boiling the kettle for a fresh one. She knew he was buying time. Silently she watched, waiting for him to continue.

All at once, a realisation detonated in her brain.

You're going to get hurt because you've let yourself care about him, you stupid girl.

Before she had a chance to regroup, Ash started speaking and inexorably she was drawn back in.

'I told you how Wilf and Rosie turned my life around? Pretty much saved me?'

'You told me they did, yes. Though not how.'

'Well, when I got busted for stealing the car, no one else

was prepared to take me on. Except for them. They were tough, but fair. They told me that they were my last chance saloon. That they could see I had the potential for more but they weren't prepared to take chance after chance on me. That this was my opportunity to lose.'

'They were tough but fair,' she acknowledged.

'Right. They told me what they were prepared to do for me, and also what they expected from me in return. Not least that every hour of my day was going to be accounted for so that I had no time to pick back up with my so-called mates.'

'Was that hard?' she asked curiously.

Even now, the relief in his expression was evident.

'No. It was the excuse I needed to change my life. I knew those guys were no good for me but they were all I had. I never believed Rosie and Wilf would be there for me when it really came down to it, but I was prepared to use them to get out of the cruddy life I had.'

'But they *were* there for you, right?'

'Yes. They were. It took time, but I finally began to see that the more I gave, the more they gave. Rosie tutored me to get my grades back up—no one had ever given a damn about my grades before. Then, when I succeeded there, Wilf found me a job in his garage as a mechanic to earn a bit of money. *My* money, which I could spend however I wanted to.'

'Unlike the foster father who beat you when you were late from a paper round because he'd been waiting for his drinking money,' Fliss recalled.

The memory of him telling her that still punched a hole in her stomach.

'Right. And I responded to the discipline. I respected them for being honourable and fair. Within the year they'd turned me around and got me into the Army Cadet Force. I never looked back.'

He was making it sound easier than it clearly had been. She could only imagine the effort Ash must have made too, to turn his life around.

'I managed to get sponsorship for my engineering degree, an Army Undergraduate Bursary, but I still couldn't afford to go. And then Rosie and Wilf came forward with the money.'

Fliss gasped. 'They can't have afforded to do that for all their foster kids.'

'They couldn't. I hadn't even lived with them for a couple of years, but we'd stayed in contact. They'd made sure of it. Everything I've achieved—my career, being a colonel—is all down to the opportunity they gave me. I could never have dreamed of this life if not for Rosie and Wilf.'

His humility was striking. She wanted to point out that they never would have offered him that support if he hadn't been worthy of it. If he hadn't been Ash. But he wouldn't thank her for it; he was still battling demons for some perceived failing and this was a rare glimpse at the vulnerable side of Colonel Asher Stirling. A side no one else ever got to see. As sad as she was for Ash, she couldn't help feel special that he trusted her in this way.

Fliss bit her tongue.

'Rosie and Wilf were my guests when I had my passing out parade at Sandhurst. They were the family I brought to any officer balls, or garden parties. They were the people I called first every time I got a promotion. I visited them once or twice a year. More, if I wasn't on a tour of duty.'

'You stayed close,' Fliss said softly. 'There's nothing wrong in that.'

In fact it made her wonder, when he had such a support network like them, why he'd become so closed off. So afraid to let other people in.

'And then Rosie started showing the first signs of Alzheimer's. Small things at first, forgetting people's names, telling the same story a few times over the course of a weekend, and it was gradual. But, because I was away so much, every time I went back there was something new.'

Silently, Fliss listened to him.

'She started forgetting medication, eating through a whole box of twenty ice-creams in an hour because she couldn't remember having had one, running out into the street screaming with fear because Wilf had left her alone for five minutes to go and buy a pint of milk. By the time a few years had gone by it had got to the point where she couldn't recognise anyone. Sometimes not even Wilf.'

'That must have been hard.'

The silence hung between them. She held her breath, the urge to touch him, comfort him almost overwhelming, but she didn't dare to. They were getting to the root of the issue but if she said anything, if she pushed him, he could shut her out entirely. She sat immobile, hardly even breathing, willing him to trust her enough to continue.

'Frankly, I didn't handle it well,' Ash stated simply.

For a man who liked to stay in control as much as Ash did, she could only imagine how painful that was for him to admit.

'I returned from a tour four years ago and she didn't know who I was at all. When I tried to tell her, she became hysterical, screaming that I was lying and that the real Ash was only a kid. She warned me not to go anywhere near Ash because he was doing well and she didn't want me pulling him back down the wrong path.'

'She thought she was looking out for the fourteen-year-old Ash again,' Fliss realised.

'Right. And she had no idea that *I* was Ash.' His expression was flat but there was no missing the pain behind those shale-hued eyes. 'I was away so much with the Army and my sporadic presence was only stressing her out, so Wilf and I agreed that it would be better if I didn't see her.'

It must have been like losing his mother all over again, Fliss realised abruptly. Feeling rejected all over again, feeling as if it was him against everyone all over again.

Of all people, she should know how deep that rejection cut. It would be like losing her uncle, the only person who had believed in her.

'But how did you handle it badly? You did nothing wrong,' Fliss pointed out carefully. 'You stayed away because it was the kindest thing to do.'

'I left Wilf to cope all alone. I might not have been able to see Rosie, but I could have pretended to be someone else. I could have been there for Wilf instead of just dumping him in it.'

'Ash, you were off fighting for your country. You're a colonel. You were a major then. The career path we've chosen isn't like other jobs. There are sacrifices. Wilf and Rosie understood, even before the Alzheimer's. With the best will in the world, you couldn't have been there.'

'I should have found a way. I should have taken fewer postings away, fewer tours of duty.'

'But no way would you have ever made colonel. At your level that would have been your career over.'

'I should have made that sacrifice for Rosie. And for Wilf.'

It was the grief talking, she knew that. His mind grappling with an impossible situation. In time he would see that, but for now all she could do was tell him what she thought he needed to hear.

'I don't believe she would ever have wanted you to do

that. From what you've told me about them, I don't think either of them would have thanked you for it. They didn't make those sacrifices to send you to Cadets, to fund you through university for you to walk away from it. You could never have gone back.'

'I should have done it anyway. I could have found a job in Civvy Street, moved in next door. Even if I couldn't have been there to help care for Rosie, I could have been there for Wilf whilst *he* cared for her.'

'That's a hell of a thing to ask of anyone.' Fliss shook her head. 'I know you like to think of yourself as super-human, Ash, and I know your men see you as their hero, but guess what? You *are* only human. You have emotions and you were in pain. I don't believe Wilf thinks you abandoned him.'

'It's not about what Wilf thinks. He can tell me there was no other choice all he likes,' he bit out angrily. But she knew it was anger directed at himself, not at her. 'It's about what *I* know. And I know I could have done more. *Should* have done more. I should have found a way.'

A tight hand was squeezing Fliss's heart inside her chest. His pain was palpable. He'd lost one of the only two people who had cared for him, loved him. And he was alienating himself from the other person because he couldn't shake a sense of guilt which he shouldn't be feeling.

No wonder he kept with short-term relationships, never opening himself up to more hurt. Just like her. They were two of a kind.

So maybe they could help each other? The thought stole into Fliss's brain so softly that she didn't realise it was there at first. She brushed it away and calmed her fluttering heart.

It was a ridiculous idea.

'Thanks,' he said suddenly. 'For listening. This wasn't what you bargained for when we agreed to this one-off fling.'

She managed a nervous laugh. 'It's not a problem. Besides, I told you I didn't usually do one-night stands. Now I can say I definitely have had one. And I'm glad—one night wasn't enough.'

She just about succeeded in not clapping her hand over her mouth at her *faux-pas*, but, rather than distrust, the look Ash shot her was so brooding, so licentious, her body shivered under its intensity.

'One night was most definitely *not* enough.'

She couldn't speak; she could only jerk her head.

He stood up abruptly, pacing her tiny kitchen as though deciding whether or not to say anything more.

'We have two weeks' R&R, Fliss. Aside from a one-day course, which is in this neck of the woods anyway, and a rugby match with my former battalion, I'm not expected anywhere.'

'Okay.'

'What about you?'

'Nowhere,' she confirmed, feeling as though she was trapped in some kind of suspension.

She was almost afraid to think he was suggesting what she wanted with every fibre of her being. Afraid to say it and be wrong and experience rejection on a level she had never known possible.

'What are you saying, Ash?' she breathed.

'I'm saying, to hell with it. We have two weeks and no one else with demands on our time. Let's spend it together.'

Fliss felt as though she were burning up inside, consumed by the need to say *yes,* but her brain told her *no.* If she'd fallen for him this hard after one night, then how far gone would she be after another fourteen nights? And what about the feeling of rejection, of loss at the end of it? Logically, she knew Ash couldn't reject her if they had agreed the terms to start with. But man, she was going to have to keep reminding herself of that.

'Two weeks?' she whispered.

'Two weeks,' he confirmed.

Two weeks to slake this all-consuming hunger they had for each other? She doubted two lifetimes would even be enough. But deep down she knew she'd take two minutes if that was all that was on offer.

'Fine.' She nodded as he strode over to capture her face in his hands and drop a kiss onto her lips. 'Two weeks it is.'

CHAPTER ELEVEN

'OKAY, SO FORGET the golden hour, gentlemen, this is the platinum ten minutes.' Fliss cast her eyes around the bunch of primarily green-gilled young soldiers in front of her and wondered how many of them would be out on the front line within months.

This was a taster day before the main pre-mob training which would take place down the line but, to Fliss, every opportunity to teach these guys how to help save lives gave her a greater window when she was back with her MERT.

'With battlefield injuries, statistics have shown that the majority of fatalities occur within the first ten minutes of the wounding, so every second counts. The MERT can't get to you in that time, however fast you call it in. So it's down to you and the unit medics on the ground at the time.'

Her skin prickled, telling her that Ash had entered the outdoor teaching area behind her. In the last ten days together she seemed to have developed a heightened awareness of his presence, and she was dreading what it would be like when the two weeks finally drew to an end. Far from slaking their desire, each passing day had only seemed to stoke it even higher.

She had no idea where they stood.

They'd never discussed a time frame after that first day,

but the fact that Ash had found her a last-minute teaching spot on the course he was running—just so that they didn't have to spend one of their precious days apart—only made her all the more confused.

All she could do was ride it out, enjoy it and accept the inevitable. And doing the best damned job she could on the course today should help to remind her of the career she loved, and ease her into life post-Ash as seamlessly as possible.

'We've been seeing remarkable numbers of soldiers surviving when they might previously have died from their injuries and that's in no small part down to you guys. Where there are penetrating wounds, whether from rounds, knives, shrapnel or injuries requiring multiple amputation, blood loss at the scene can mean the casualty is dead before we can get in that heli and get to you. So one of your priorities is learning to staunch severe bleeding and applying tourniquets correctly.'

She thought of Ash and the extent of his grenade scar, something unidentifiable tearing through her. If he hadn't had good buddies fighting to save him before that MERT had arrived, she wouldn't have even known he existed.

She would never have had these last two weeks. Never have known what *alive* could feel like.

The truth hit her hard.

She was going to tell him how she felt.

Tonight. She would lay it all out there. And if he rejected her, then so what? She stomped down the ugly fear which threatened to weaken her resolve. At least she would know. It couldn't be any worse than wondering what might have happened if she'd only had the courage to try.

'Right, so *you*, come over here and be my casualty and *you*, bring your kit up; you're about to learn how to save your buddy's life.'

* * *

Ash barely noticed the return drive home, slipping easily through the gears as they sped down the quiet streets, the late night traffic at a minimum.

Even the lights seemed to be in his favour, turning green as he approached as though cheering him on.

He had to tell her.

In three days, their time together would be over. At least, their self-imposed two-week time limit would be up. But Ash already knew he didn't want to give Fliss up, *couldn't* give her up. She felt the same way, he knew it. From the way she looked at him, talked with him, making the most mundane things sound compelling when they were uttered by her lips, to the way she clung to him, crying out his name as she gave herself up to him so completely when they made love.

He had no idea how or when she'd peeled away every last piece of his defences, he just knew that it had started from the minute she'd walked into that tent at Razorwire, all lithe body, long legs and flashing eyes. And it hadn't stopped since.

The time limit had only served to highlight to Ash how precious time was. He needed Fliss in his arms, his bed, his life, for as long as they both drew breath.

And tonight he realised he had to tell her that. He didn't want to wait any longer for them to begin building a different future. Together.

'Whose car is that?' He glowered as they finally rounded the corner to her street and he saw the unfamiliar vehicle in the drive.

His first guess would have been her uncle, but it was far too beaten-up and pranged to be the General's car.

'Stop here!' Her abrupt cry caught him off-guard.

Assuming she'd seen a cat or a fox, he executed an

emergency stop in the dark street, glancing around for
the culprit, but nothing moved except for a breeze through
the trees.

'Wait, what are you doing?'

Beside him, Fliss was scrabbling to release her seat belt.
Ash caught her hand to still her, but she wrenched it free
with a force he didn't recognise. He said her name, then
shouted it but she didn't even seem aware he was still there.

'Fliss? Fliss! Look at me.'

Taking her chin firmly in his hand, it took Ash two attempts to persuade her to look at him. When she did, she
finally seemed to take a breath, although the fearful expression didn't diminish.

'Relax. Breathe. What's going on?'

'It's my mother,' she mumbled eventually.

Her eyes, so uncharacteristically dull, fearful and something else he couldn't quite read, knocked the breath from
him. A blast even more lethal than the grenade which had
almost taken his life. It commanded every defensive, protective emotion in him.

'In your house?'

'She's my mother. She pops round from time to time.'

'Define *time to time*.'

She glared at him. He didn't know whether to celebrate
the fact that the dullness had disappeared, or object to the
fact that any rage appeared to be directed at him.

'Once or twice a year.'

'And she has a key?'

'She's my mother.'

'A title, by all accounts, which she doesn't deserve.'
He slammed his palm on the steering wheel, desperate to
make her see sense. 'For pity's sake, Fliss, you're better
than this. You *deserve* better than this.'

'Any relationship with her is better than nothing.' Her

defensive tone had the same unidentifiable edge to it that her eyes had and Ash couldn't shake the feeling he was missing something, but he had no idea what. He filed it away for later.

'No, it isn't. Not when it causes you to react like *this* at the sight of her car.' He raked his hand through his hair, his feelings for Fliss all jumbling around in his chest. 'How do I make you see this isn't normal, it isn't right? I thought you said she used to rage at you, anyway?'

'Sometimes.' He could tell she wished she'd never told him anything at all. 'But sometimes things are…nice.'

'Why?' He was instantly suspicious. 'Does she want something?'

Glowering at him, Fliss refused to answer.

The answer was obvious to him. *Money.* Inevitably, it would be about money. He wanted to say more, wanted to make Fliss see. But he could feel her slipping away from him already. They hadn't had long enough together for her to trust him. As far as she was concerned, in a few days he would be gone, and her uncle, and sporadic visits from her needy mother, would be all she had.

He should have told her he was falling in love with her before. And he should never have put some stupid time limit on their relationship. Now, all that would have to wait. For now he would have to change tack and wait it out.

'She can't hurt you,' he told her. 'Not unless *you* let her. I'll be here to support you.'

'No!' The cry almost shook the car. 'No, you can't come in.'

Ash gritted his teeth. 'Try to stop me.'

'I don't know what mood she'll be in, but either way she won't like it. It will just make things worse.'

Ash heard her desperation, and realised he'd do anything to erase it. Anything to hear her jaunty, sing-song voice right now.

'We won't let her.'

'We?'

'It's going to be okay,' he soothed, re-buckling her seat belt and turning in his seat to drive the car down the road and into a parking space outside the house. It didn't escape his notice that Fliss's mother had taken the single drive-way space she must have known her daughter would use.

'Take as long as you need,' Ash said quietly as he turned the engine off and made no move to rush Fliss. 'We'll only go in when you're ready.'

This wasn't how she wanted to spend tonight, Fliss realised as she finally swung herself out of the car and forced leaden legs to carry her to the front door.

Her whole life, she'd dropped everything any time her mother had deigned to visit. Tonight was the first time she'd resented the intrusion.

Because there, beneath the flurry of fear and niggle of resentment, sat the ever-present embers of hope. Maybe, just maybe, this time would be different. Especially with Ash by her side.

Warily, Fliss slotted her key in the lock and turned it, a heaviness pressing in on her as she stepped through the door.

'Darling, you're back. I was afraid I might have missed you.'

So it was money she needed. Still, the embers of hope flickered. It meant it was going to be one of her more pleasant visits, as long as Fliss read her mum's signals and found the perfect opportunity to offer the funds without it looking like charity.

Not for the first time, Fliss felt a niggle of uncertainty.

It might be *darling* now, but on another occasion it could be any number of unrepeatable words.

What was she doing?

She hadn't needed Ash to tell her it was a toxic relationship, but she'd always clung on to it anyway. She'd never had the courage in the past to consider walking away. But with Ash here beside her...who knew?

'Mum.'

Fliss allowed herself to be swept up in the wide embrace, then stepped aside as her mother spotted Ash. An undisguised look of shock clouded her face before she greeted him with a decidedly coquettish air, and Fliss didn't miss the way he held her slightly away from his body as he shot Fliss a pointed look.

The fact that he held his opinions in check for her sake bolstered her confidence all the more.

'So this is your famous surgeon fiancé, darling? No wonder she's kept you hidden from me all these years, Robert dear. I have to say you're not what I expected. I didn't think you had it in you, Flissy.'

The needling comment found its mark perfectly as Fliss covered her chest as though to protect herself. The meaning, to Fliss, was clear—what was he doing with her? She only hoped Ash couldn't read it as clearly. Obviously her mother was piqued at the thought her daughter had done so well in her choice of partner.

'Ash Stirling,' Ash corrected her politely.

'Robert and I broke up.' Fliss didn't know why she avoided eye contact with Ash. She had no reason to feel guilt, but it suffused her body anyway. As though her mother's comments negated the fact that Fliss had told Ash that there had been someone before they'd met.

'Oh, I'm so sorry to hear that, but I suppose it was inevitable when you consider how successful a surgeon he was.' She swung back to Ash with a beam. 'And of course I can see you're a colonel. So you work together?'

'Ash is infantry, Mum. We were just running a course together today and Ash ran me home.'

'How thrillingly clandestine for you, Flissy darling.'

As if aware of what she was doing, Ash stepped forward and placed his arm very pointedly around her shoulder. In that moment, she would have given anything to turn in to him and have him hold her. Hold her until her mother finally went away.

Years of barbed comments, nasty digs and cruel undermining—and her mother hadn't even got started so far tonight. And for what?

'Actually, *Fliss* and I were about to go out for a romantic meal,' Ash emphasised. 'But, of course, if you'd like to join us…?'

'Sounds fabulous. I'll grab my purse.' As she passed Fliss she poked a finger into her chest which was just a little too aggressive for fun. 'You do love to punch above your weight, don't you, darling? I've got to give you that much.'

Rage burned through Ash, as it had done for the last few hours since they'd walked into Fliss's home and met her mother.

Rage and an interminable disquiet that, over the course of the evening, the snipes and derisory comments had destroyed the Fliss he knew. The Fliss he had begun to fall in love with. Right now, his fiery, loving, spirited Fliss was barely a shell of herself. Ash could easily see how her mother, in one of her less amiable moods, would have raged at her daughter, whether Fliss was four or forty.

It had taken every last ounce of his self-control not to retaliate on Fliss's behalf. But now they were back at the house and finally alone in the kitchen, he found that he couldn't smother his ire any longer.

'You can't keep doing this, Fliss.' He swung her round, taking the cafetière from her shaking fingers and placing his hands on her shoulders. 'You need to say something.'

Misery emanated from her as she dropped her head to her chest in defeat, but still she managed to shake it weakly from one side to the other.

'You have to,' he growled. 'If you don't, I will.'

'You can't,' she gasped, her head jerking up painfully fast.

'Someone has to.'

'But not you,' she whispered fiercely, shaking his hands away.

The fight was there. He could see it; he just didn't know how to bring it out of her.

'Can't you see what she does to you?' His voice softened. 'Even now? The Fliss I know—the courageous, loyal, passionate woman, the skilled, dedicated, driven trauma doctor—has gone and this…this sullen, irascible teenager is in her place. It isn't healthy.'

'I know that.' He had to strain to hear the words she mumbled so quietly. 'But I can't. I can't do it.'

'Yes, you can. I know you can.'

'I keep hoping.'

'For a different outcome?' He barely managed to disguise the contempt in his voice. 'Don't bother. She'll never change, I know the type.'

'She might.'

'She won't.' He put his hands back on her shoulders. 'You need to do this. And I need you to do this.'

The tiny light which usually sparked so brightly in her eyes flickered faintly back into life; its significance left Ash winded.

'Why?'

'Because I love you.'

He'd thought saying the words would be difficult. He was wrong.

'I love you,' he repeated, the words practically singing in his ears. They sounded good. They sounded natural. They sounded *right*.

She stared at him incredulously and then shook her head.

'No, you don't. You can't.'

'I love you,' he said firmly. 'But you're right. I love the bright, animated, confident Major Felicity Delaunay, who leaps off helis and stands up to arrogant colonels who she's only just met. I don't love this husk-like version of you.'

'We're the same person, Ash.'

'No, you aren't. And I can't be around that version. To-night, your mother has stripped out every last bit of character and confidence and essence of *Fliss,* and you let her. I can't watch you let someone do that to you, year in and year out.'

His voice was thick with emotion; he hadn't felt so utterly trapped and powerless in a long time. He'd sworn as a kid he'd never go through that again and he knew, for his own sanity, that he couldn't afford to break that oath.

He could only hope to make Fliss understand, because she was the one who held the power to save them both.

'I've spent the entire evening barely able to keep a grip on my self-control. That isn't something I can keep doing, Fliss. It's destructive and I won't let myself go down that road. You *have* to put an end to this madness.'

'You're asking me to choose between you and my mother?'

The look she cast him was one of pure anguish that sought to rend his very soul.

'No. I'm asking you to choose between *you* and your mother. You need to cut all ties with her because, until you do, nothing is ever going to change and you're worth more than…*this*. A poor carbon copy of the Fliss I know.'

The slow, mocking clap behind him made them both start.

'Well, that was very touching, *darling*. But you can't honestly expect my daughter to choose a temporary fling like you over her own mother?'

'Fliss,' he said quietly.

Ash willed her to speak out with every fibre of his being. He could do it for her, he had no issue with that, but ultimately it wouldn't mean anything. This was something Fliss had to do for herself.

'You can do this.'

She didn't speak, didn't move.

'I rather think you have your answer.'

The triumphant tone was unmistakable but Ash didn't care. His only concern was the woman he now knew for certain that he loved. The question was whether she loved him enough to come back to him now.

The silence seemed to smother him.

He *did* have her answer.

But it wasn't an answer he could live with. For his own sake, he had to walk away.

Wordlessly, Ash strode into the bedroom, shoved his belongings into his overnight bag, all the while straining to hear Fliss. His gear packed, he slung the bag over his shoulder and headed back out into the hallway. Fliss hadn't even moved from her spot in the kitchen.

Something inside finally shattered into a million pieces as Ash left without a backward glance.

He couldn't afford one.

CHAPTER TWELVE

'I WOULDN'T WORRY about it, darling; it's for the best. You were never going to be able to hold onto a man like that, anyway.'

Fliss turned, the exultation in her mother's expression like a slap on the face. But she was already reeling from everything Ash had said.

He loved her?

He loved her?

It had sounded too incredible to be true. The ground had pitched and shifted beneath her feet and all she'd been able to focus on had been staying upright as she'd tried to work out how her entire world had now changed.

He'd told her she was *worth more*. Told her that she *deserved more*. And she'd thought talk was cheap, but he'd proved it to her by telling her he loved her. It had been like watching a fireworks display—the Army kind her uncle had taken her to where they'd used up all the end-of-year pyrotechnics for a display that surpassed anything in the civilian world. Just like being with Ash surpassed any other relationship she'd ever known in her life.

She understood why he'd said he couldn't be around her if she couldn't even stand up for herself. She'd known all evening that his iron control was slipping but she hadn't been able to help him, because that would have meant helping herself. And she hadn't thought she was good enough for that.

Ash had proved to her she was, and she'd been so stunned that she hadn't reacted fast enough.

And now she'd lost him.

But he'd still left her with a choice of her own. To accept her life as it was, her relationships as they were, or to finally stand up for herself. The least she could do was ensure that losing him wasn't for nothing.

She turned to her mother, determined to find out whether the chasm between them had ever stood a chance of being bridged or whether Ash was right, and her mother would never change.

'Do you really hate me that much?'

She could feel the chill hit the room.

'Don't start believing your little lover's words now,' her mother warned, her voice so sharp that it could have cut through Fliss deeper than any physical wound.

And it would have. Before Ash.

'*Do* you hate me?' She advanced on her mother, a tiny sliver of her old self returning with each step.

In an instant, her mother's face twisted into a smile that was too ugly to be anything but loathing.

'You ruined my only chance at happiness the day you were born.'

'You knew your dancing was over when you realised you were pregnant.' Fliss wasn't trying to antagonise, but it was something she'd always wondered about and never understood.

'Why didn't you get rid of me if you felt that strongly? Why have a child only to put it through such utter hell?'

'You think that isn't what I tried to do?' her mother spat, the truth embedding itself into Fliss's very being.

'Why did you change your mind?' she whispered.

There was no regret, no empathy, no love in her mother's reply. The scornful tone like applying heat to a burn.

'I didn't change my mind. I was more than happy to go through with it. But then your grandfather turned up, stormed in and frog-marched me out. White gown and all. There was no way he and your grandmother were ever going to allow me to do something that would shame them even more than they already were by my pregnancy.'

Rushing blood roared in her ears as she clawed at the edge of nothingness with her fingernails, just to try to find a purchase.

'I'd made a mistake, yes, I'd got pregnant. But the obvious solution to get rid of it wasn't even a consideration for them. That would be letting me off too lightly; in their eyes I was going to have to live with the consequences.'

'So because they'd trapped you into a miserable life, you made mine even worse?' Fliss cried.

'I tried to get out of there, I took you with me so that you wouldn't be brought up with the same restrictions I'd had. But the first chance you got, you went running back to them. You chose them over me,' her mother raged, her face inches away from Fliss's.

'I was eight!'

'You threw everything I did for you back in my face.'

'You did *nothing* for me,' Fliss argued, standing up to her mother for the first time in her life. 'Except make my life more wretched than it needed to be.'

It was almost too much to take in. Feeling for a chair, Fliss backed up and sat down. Ash had been right. Nothing she could say or do would make a difference to her mother. She was craving affection which was never going to come.

Repeating the cycle would only hurt more people. She'd been hurting herself, and she'd definitely been hurting Ash. They deserved better than that.

Maybe it wasn't too late.

Standing up on shaky legs, Fliss fixed her mother with a calm, firm stare. Her major's stare.

'I think it's time you left.'

Her mother snorted, deliberately turning her back.

Fliss inched her way to the door, fumbling with the catch as she hauled it open. It felt heavy, almost too heavy, but she gritted her teeth. 'I said, it's time you left.'

Her mother gave a bark of laughter. 'I don't think so, Felicity.' She didn't sound as sure of herself as usual.

'I'm asking you nicely. Don't make me do this the other way.'

The words were out before she could stop them. And, to her disbelief, they sounded strong, confident, forceful.

Enough that her mother bit back the retort which was on her lips.

For several long moments the two women faced off against each other. It took everything she had, but Fliss refused to back down. Not this time.

'You will regret this.'

'No.' Fliss shook her head. 'The only thing I regret is not doing this sooner.'

Perhaps then she wouldn't have lost someone as special as Ash from her life.

Ash had no idea where he was heading. He'd been driving in circles for the last two hours without seeing anything. He'd left Fliss's house intent on driving back home, sorting his kit out and leaving early for the next posting. Anything to get his mind off Fliss. But his heart had known what his head hadn't yet been ready to accept.

However hard he tried, he couldn't shake her from his head. Her desperate, ravaged face, or her defeated stance. Everything about her marked her as a different person to

the Major he'd been instantly attracted to. The woman he'd
fallen in love with. It killed him to see her allowing herself
to be pulled down as she had tonight, but he couldn't have
stayed. He'd tried to help her see the truth but she hadn't
wanted to listen.

Pressing his foot on the accelerator, Ash tried to ignore the voice in the back of his head. But, however fast
he drove, he wasn't going to outrun it.

The control he'd kept tonight, not for himself but for
Fliss, told him how far *he* had come in less than a month.
And that was down to her. If he loved her the way he
claimed to, shouldn't he be prepared to fight for her?
Shouldn't he try for longer than one evening, to help her
to fight for herself?

And he *did* love her. He loved her intelligence, her focus,
her dry sense of humour, her hidden sense of adventure,
as much as he loved her lips, her body, the way she always
broke apart in his arms.

Checking the road around him, Ash felt a rush of adrenalin surge through his system and it had nothing what-
soever to do with the slick, if illegal, U-turn he had just
executed in the last turning lane of the dual carriageway.

By the time he got back to her house it was bathed
in darkness.

CHAPTER THIRTEEN

ASH SPOTTED FLISS the instant she stepped out of the car with the General. Ash stopped dead on the field where he was supposed to be warming up with his team, his chest constricting. The inter-battalion rugby match was the last place he'd expected to see her, and he couldn't help wondering if she was sending him a message.

He watched her nervously smooth down her dress, barely even noticing the garment itself, and then, as though sensing his eyes upon her, lifted her head and looked right at him.

For a moment he thought he saw a hint of a smile but, before he could respond, a bellow pulled him up sharply.

'Heads up!'

Split second reactions served him well as he caught the well-placed throw of a teammate, pulling the ball into his gut and taking off down the field for thirty or so metres before lobbing the ball to another team-mate to do the same back up the pitch.

By the time he looked up again, Fliss was already disappearing into the marquee set up for family and friends.

He should play it cool.

Instead, he found himself yelling an excuse across the field before striding over the grounds and into the tent. He marched straight up to her, the people milling around only cranking the tension up further, making the need for formality all the more crucial.

'Major.'

'Colonel.'

'Colonel.' The deep voice of Fliss's uncle had Ash swinging around. He hadn't even noticed the old man there.

'General—' Ash greeted him as protocol demanded '—it's very good of you to take time out to attend our rugby match.'

'I hope it's going to be a good match; I want to see that trophy returned to its rightful place.'

'The lads are all geared up, sir. We fully intend to have that trophy in your hands by the end of the day.'

It was like some kind of unending torture. With no notion that Ash was actually there to talk to Fliss, the General was likely to keep the conversation pleasant for a while. It was something of a relief when the older man was pulled away by his aide-de-camp in order to greet a VIP.

He turned back to Fliss. The air between them crackled with unspoken questions. The situation was impossible. Suddenly, Ash didn't care any more.

'Walk with me,' he ordered.

'I...now?' She panicked, dropping her voice to a low tone. 'People will wonder.'

'It wasn't a request.' He didn't bother lowering his voice.

Nor did he worry about the curious eyes on them as he took her elbow and steered her out of the tent.

'Are you okay?'

She swivelled her head to look at him. 'I thought you didn't want any more to do with me?'

Ash didn't even bother to hide his disapproval. 'That isn't exactly what I said.'

'No,' she acknowledged after a moment. 'It isn't. I'm

sorry, I'm just nervous. I wanted to tell you I stood up to my mother.'

Surprise swept through him, followed by the whisper of a promise.

'Why are you here?' he demanded abruptly.

Her gaze didn't waver although he could read the nerves behind those insanely blue eyes.

'Because you said you were playing in the match and I wanted to tell you. To thank you, I suppose.'

'I came to the house.'

This time it was her turn to be surprised.

'That night—' he shrugged '—all the lights were off. Your car was gone. I figured you were out.'

'I went to my uncle's…' She faltered. 'Once I'd asked my mother to leave I didn't want to stay there alone until I'd had the locks changed. Not that she'd do anything. Just… I needed the company.'

'What did your uncle say?'

'He told me that he was glad I'd finally stood up to her. He'd also like to shake *your* hand, not that he knows it was you, of course. But he wanted to thank whoever it was who finally made me see her for what she is.'

'That must have been difficult to hear,' he murmured. He could read Fliss only too well.

'Yeah—' she swallowed '—it was. But it was time. Anyway, you still haven't told me what you came back for.'

'I couldn't leave it the way I did. I had to try again. I needed to make you see what she was doing to you. Or, rather, what *you* were letting happen to you.'

'So you really came back?'

'Yes.'

He could see the pleasure in her expression and couldn't stop himself from wanting to make it shine all the brighter.

'In the boot of my car right now is a fresh overnight bag.

I thought I'd try again straight after the matches. I didn't expect to see you here.'

'I came because you said you were playing today. I wanted to see you,' she blurted out. 'I asked my uncle to bring me along as his guest; given the number of functions he's asked me to accompany him to over the years, I didn't think he'd mind.'

'I'd have thought that would arouse his suspicions.'

'Maybe.' She shrugged as though she truly didn't care. 'Especially after that little performance you put on, man-handling me back there.'

'Hardly,' he scorned before realising she was trying, in her own way, to tease him.

He wanted to know more, wanted to sort it out with her. But he forced himself to hang back. He was sure of his feelings but he needed to be sure of hers. It was testing his self-restraint to the limits. He felt as though an elastic band were pulled tight around his chest, holding a plethora of emotions in check until he knew she was ready for them. Ready for him.

He had to know what stage of their relationship—or not—she had reached. Without anything from him colouring it or pushing her along faster than she was prepared to go.

'Tell me what's in your head. This isn't going to work if you believe I said I didn't want anything more to do with you.'

Her pupils skittered from his left eye to his right eye.

'I said I was sorry about that,' she choked out.

'I know that.' He took her hands in his, both to soothe and to reassure, not even thinking about who might see them. 'I'm not asking for an apology. I'm asking you if you can trust me *now*? Can you talk to me, Fliss? Because until you feel comfortable enough to tell me, I can't help. Right now, the ball's in your court.'

'This isn't easy, you know.'

'I do know,' he vowed. 'But I can't just have part of you, Fliss. It would never be enough. I need you. Body, heart *and* mind.'

She swallowed hard but said nothing. After what seemed like an age she pulled her hands out of his, glancing around nervously. Then, dropping them to her sides, she turned away from him, walking further up the field.

Ash fell into step alongside her, forcing himself to be patient, to give her space, resisting the impulse to simply drag her into his arms and kiss her so thoroughly that she'd realise she couldn't be without him either.

But whether he won her or not, Ash finally acknowledged that he would rather have known this love with Fliss only to lose her, than the alternative. Never having had Fliss in his life, in his heart, would have been worse than any pain he might suffer now if she walked away from him.

They walked in silence. Going up the field, along the field at the top and back down to the pitches. Just when he thought it was going to all start falling down around him, she stopped as abruptly as she had started.

'I want to talk to you, Ash.' She turned to face him, an urgency in her tone. 'I came here *to* talk to you. But now that you're standing here I can't find the words to explain. Especially with practically the whole battalion and their partners wondering what we're doing out here.'

Which meant the General would be wondering what the two of them were doing out here. He hadn't thought that out properly when he'd steered Fliss by the elbow before.

'Meet me tomorrow,' he told her as he began jogging backwards, back towards his team.

'Not later?' She frowned uncertainly, but Ash couldn't help that.

'No. I've got something critical I can't afford to put off.' And a match trophy he couldn't afford not to bring home.

CHAPTER FOURTEEN

'COLONEL, GOOD TO see you again.'

'Captain Wyland.' Ash greeted the eager young officer warmly.

'I believe I have you to thank for my appointment as ADC. So thank you, sir. It meant a lot.'

The lad had been a second lieutenant in one of Ash's units when Ash had marked him out as a potential highflyer, and a possible aide-de-camp for a general. It was satisfying to see his instincts had been right. Not that he was about to say that to the Captain.

'You were the one who put the extra effort in, so you don't need to thank me,' Ash replied firmly. 'You worked for this promotion and you deserved it.'

'Still, thank you, Colonel.'

Ash dipped his head in concession.

'Anyway, General Delaunay is just finishing up on the phone,' the Captain apologised. 'We're running a little late, I'm afraid.'

'Right,' he offered grimly.

Just about refraining from pacing the office, Ash considered his approach. He'd already pulled a considerable number of strings to get an audience with the General without the added complication of time constraints. He knew the man well enough on a professional basis, but turning up without an appointment to ask the General for his niece's hand in marriage was a completely different thing.

Not that it mattered—whether the older man approved or not wouldn't change Ash's feelings for Fliss. But, for her sake, he knew she'd prefer to have her uncle's blessing.

'You can go straight in now, sir.'

The Captain's voice permeated his thoughts as Ash straightened his hat, black with its red band, having swapped his usual combat attire for semi-formal dress for the meeting. Satisfied, Ash marched into the office, coming to attention in front of the General's desk, where he saluted and stayed at attention.

He hadn't done an Army meeting like this in a long time. And he hadn't met a girl's parents, *ever*. It seemed that Fliss's effect on him was more far-reaching than even he had realised. He suppressed a grin, knowing the General wouldn't be too impressed.

'Colonel Stirling, twice in as many days?' He quirked an eyebrow. 'I have to admit I was rather surprised to see your name in my diary for today. Please, take a seat.'

Removing his hat in surprise, Ash sat in the indicated chair as the General called through to his ADC, 'Captain, we'll have that coffee now, please. And you may close the door as you leave.'

Ash couldn't resist. 'Is this because we brought the trophy home yesterday, General? I'm afraid this meeting is of a more personal nature.'

'I rather thought it might be.' The General nodded. 'You're dating my niece.'

Dating? Ash thought as the Captain came back in with the coffee. That was one word for it. Still at least that was one thing he could improve on.

'I'd like to marry her.'

'I see.'

A hush blanketed the room for several minutes as both men fell silent, punctuated only by the sound of the tea being poured and the clink of the spoons against the china cups.

'Thank you.' Ash came to, taking the proffered item.

The General crossed the room again, unhurried, deliberate, picking up his own cup and returning to sit down opposite Ash.

'So, you want to marry Felicity?'

'I do.' Ash wasn't intimidated. He'd held his own enough not to worry about a general, but he did respect the man. 'I love Fliss. And I know that your blessing would mean a lot to her.'

'And I've always had you pegged as an Army man through and through.' The General's voice was careful, as though he was holding back.

Unable to put his finger on it, Ash decided not to over-analyse and instead offered a rueful shrug. '*I* always had me pegged as an Army man through and through, General. But then I met Fliss.'

'Do you think she loves you?'

Placing his cup and saucer down on the coffee table, the General rested his elbows on the arms of his chair and steepled his fingers in front of his face. A silent invitation.

With anyone else Ash might have felt riled. He might have decided to leave. But the General was a man he respected and, more than that, he was Fliss's uncle. Ash was determined to do this right.

'I know she does,' Ash answered simply.

Another moment of silence.

'I'd be inclined to agree with you.'

'Sir?'

'I heard about what happened with her mother, and that

Felicity finally stood up to her. I can only assume that's in no small part down to you.'

'I just told her what I thought.'

'Indeed. And I'm grateful. But that doesn't mean I think you're the right choice for my niece.'

The words swiped Ash's legs out from under him.

'Then you're wrong,' Ash asserted calmly. 'I'm exactly the right choice for Fliss. Not some surgeon who's more interested in advancing his own career than in Fliss advancing hers.'

'Of course not,' the General scoffed. 'The man was a Muppet. But that doesn't make *you* a good match for her.'

'Is that so, General?' Cool, direct, Ash fought to control the icy fury threatening his own sanity.

'I'm sorry. I know you as a selfless, loyal, courageous soldier, an inspiring leader of men and an honourable individual. You're someone I would be proud to fight alongside. But you and I both know, Colonel, that those qualities don't necessarily translate to being a good husband, or dependable family man.'

'I would have thought they were definitely transposable,' Ash refuted steadily.

'Colonel... *Ash*...' The General softened his words, looking almost apologetic. 'You're a maverick; you're known for it. Look at the sacrifice you were prepared to make when that grenade was thrown at your men. And that's only one of many. Sometimes I feel you seem to go *seeking* the most dangerous route. So what happens when you aren't a single man any more? If you make the ultimate sacrifice and leave behind a devastated wife. Maybe even a baby one day.'

'It's called the ultimate sacrifice for a reason,' Ash pointed out, flattening his palm against his knee to stop himself from clenching his fist in frustration, his mind seeking a way to pull the conversation back. Things weren't going at all as he had envisaged.

'Then you'll understand me when I say you're exactly the kind of soldier I want as a commanding officer, but you're not the kind of husband I want for my niece. Felicity will marry you whatever I say, if that's what she wants. But, as you said before, neither of you actually need my permission, and I wouldn't dream of standing in your way. In fact, I'm happy you love each other that much. I just can't, in all good conscience, tell her I'm happy that it's an infantryman she's chosen.'

Despite his conviction, the older man sounded as though he was genuinely sorry. But still, Ash had to school himself not to react. Even though he had considered all of this himself, it was still difficult to hear.

He sucked in a breath, his chest tight.

'I *do* understand what you're saying, General. Which is why I've already applied for a transfer. Give me a role in your headquarters and I'll take myself off the front line.'

The words hung there between them, heavy and ominous. The General eyed him with concern.

'I don't think you've thought this through. I'm not trying to give you an ultimatum, Asher, I'm trying to help you. And Felicity. In the only way I know how.'

'General—' Ash cut across him '—I *have* thought this through. Ever since I realised I was in love with Fliss. I do understand why you're concerned about your niece marrying a front line soldier. We both know how close I came to the end the day that grenade was tossed through that window, and we both know what can happen in a firefight out there. We also both know that I've been offered some great postings based back home in the past, but I've never wanted to take them.'

'And now you do?' The General shook his head. 'That's

commendable, Asher, it really is. But it's also naive. What happens in a year? Five years? When you miss being in the action, the adrenalin rush, the feeling of victory? However well-intentioned you are now in giving it up for Felicity, ultimately you'll start to resent what you had to give up. You'll start to resent *her*.'

'You haven't,' Ash pointed out calmly.

'Say again?'

'You were a formidable major on the front line, General. I've heard the stories about you, sir. Who hasn't? But you gave it up for Felicity, partly because she was your niece and you love her but also partly out of familial obligation.'

'And I've never once regretted that.' The General's tone changed, became short and clipped, but Ash had never been easily intimidated.

'Exactly my point. Now *I'm* prepared to give up a job I used to loved because I'm *in love* with Felicity. Not out of obligation but because I want to be with her. And not because it's a grand gesture, but because since your niece swept into my life like some kind of blonde-haired, blue-eyed tornado, I've felt more settled and content than I ever have before. Because the job I loved up until a month ago no longer holds the same draw, not since Fliss showed me a different life. So this is my way of proving to her how much she's changed me.'

'I rather think, Asher,' the General mused, 'that you have changed yourself.'

Ash suppressed a rueful smile. The more time he spent with the General, the more he sounded like Rosie and Wilf.

'Then it's with the right person nudging me.' He smiled wryly.

'Indeed.' The General rose slowly to his feet. 'Well, I

think you've made your argument very successfully, Ash.'
He outstretched his hand. 'Welcome to our little family.'

'Thank you.' Ash nodded. 'Now, there's just one thing
I'd like to ask you to do.'

CHAPTER FIFTEEN

'WHAT ARE WE doing here?' Fliss glanced around the Army camp as her uncle's vehicle drove slowly through the gates.

'You'll soon find out.'

Fliss snapped her head back in surprise, unaccustomed to her uncle's tone. He sounded almost...*mischievous?* It had been this way for the last hour, when he'd arrived at her home and asked her to come for a ride with him. She'd been intrigued—she was used to his commanding air, his empathetic side, and his quietly contained fury, but she couldn't remember her uncle ever having such an uncharacteristic air of mystery about him.

Slowly the four-by-four pulled over into the old FIBUA she remembered telling Ash about back in Camp Razorwire and her heartbeat began to pick up a steady rhythm.

Had he remembered?

She spun around in her seat, wondering how her uncle factored into it.

'Wait—why did you really bring me here?'

'Someone asked me to. And I liked what he had to say, so here you are. The rest, Felicity my dear, is up to you.'

An eagerness spiked low in her abdomen. The mock-up town, peppered as it was with bullet holes and crumbled sections of pretend housing, held so many fond memories for Fliss. The place had long since been abandoned by the military in favour of a bigger, newly built urban training area and now, bathed in a warm sunset, the place almost looked beautiful with grass growing through the dusty ground and small trees sprouting up through concrete floors. Like nature reclaiming an abandoned civilisation, the cycle of life.

Her uncle's vehicle departed, slowly so as not to leave dust in its wake, and Fliss became aware of a figure walking towards her.

Ash.

Her heart felt as though it was hammering against her ribs, fervently trying to escape its cage.

'Quite a man, your uncle,' Ash said evenly as he approached. 'Even when he isn't busy being a general.'

'I can't believe you went to speak to him,' she said softly. 'And I can't believe you remembered what I told you about this place.'

'I hoped you'd like it. I'm not good at this romance thing.'

'This is perfect,' she assured him. 'This is where I trained when I was doing my medical degree. All those long hours, learning to treat casualties under fire. Learning how to be an army combat doctor. Learning the skills which had finally given me the confidence that, even if my private life—my family life—was a complete mess, then I was still skilled and infinitely competent when I came here.'

He held his arm out to her and she obliged, linking with his as she let him lead her around the old mock-town.

'This is where you put most of your past behind you and looked forward to a bright future?' Ash guessed.

His ability to read her made her feel even more comfortable and relaxed.

'Do you know I saved my first life here?'

'Tell me about it.'

'It started as a routine house-clearing training exercise. But then turned potentially fatal when one of the younger recruits become too over-eager and leapt out of the second-storey window. I ended up performing an emergency tracheotomy amongst other things.'

How long ago that felt now. But it was the moment she'd first felt like a real doctor.

'This place holds some really special memories for me,' she whispered, marvelling at how good it felt to share them with Ash and know that he understood where she was coming from.

She stopped so suddenly she jerked his arm.

'I really need to say this. Thank you, for what you said to my mother, and for what you said to me *about* her. I needed to hear that, even if I didn't exactly process it well at the time. But, most of all, thank you for what you said about me. About me deserving more and being worth more. I think I'd forgotten that.'

'You had where your mother was concerned.' He reached out to cup her jaw and her body fired into life. She barely resisted the impulse to tilt her head into his palm.

'I talked to her, you know,' Fliss told him. 'That night, I asked her all the questions which had been swirling around my head since I was a kid. I think it helped me to understand her better.'

'You need to cut her out completely, not try to understand her.'

His obvious protectiveness was touching and Fliss rose up on her tiptoes to press a quick kiss to his lips.

'I just mean that I guess, as odd as it probably sounds, in her own twisted way she thought she *was* doing something good for me by taking me from my grandparents' home with her. She hated the stifling life with its never-ending rules and boundaries. I think maybe she thought she was doing me a favour by not leaving me there.'

'That's one way to look at it.' Ash didn't look convinced but, instead of shutting herself off to him, Fliss found herself wanting to help him to understand.

'She was still a kid herself. And an immature one at that. She was wrong to make me responsible for her happiness when her own dreams died, but she wasn't the only one at fault. My grandparents weren't exactly perfect themselves.

'I grew up feeling culpable and worthless, and all the other cruel jibes she threw at me on a daily basis. And it went on for so long that even when my uncle tracked us down and took me home I realised that most of what she had told me was right. My grandparents took me in because they felt it was their duty. They were obliged to care for their daughter's fatherless child.'

Ash frowned at her.

'I thought you loved your life once your uncle took you home? I thought he saved you.'

'He did—he was fantastic,' Fliss cried, panicking that she might be portraying her incredible uncle—her rock—in anything other than glowing terms when she thought of all he had done for her. 'He has always been fantastic.'

'But your grandparents weren't?'

She drew in a deep breath, unsure how to explain this to a man who had been physically hurt and wounded as a child.

'They were never unkind to me,' she said slowly. 'They gave me a home, schooling, clothing, everything a child needs physically. But they never showed me any love. My uncle was away a lot with the Army so it was usually just me with them. I worked hard; my grades were outstanding because I thought it was about their fear of me making the same mistakes as my mother. I thought if I worked hard I could show them that I wasn't like that, that I would earn their love.'

'But it didn't work,' he guessed.

She supposed he knew enough about that. If the love wasn't there naturally from the start, then she was hardly going to earn it.

'No,' she confirmed. 'It didn't. I suppose it turned out for all of us to be my way of repaying them for taking me in. My success was confirmation they were meeting my needs. But it didn't change who I was or what I was. Behind the perfunctory *well done*s they never stopped looking at me as the family's shameful little secret.'

Raking his hand over his forehead, Ash closed the gap between them but he still wasn't touching her. She inhaled deeply, the familiar scent both soothing her troubled mind and stimulating her body.

Oh, so stimulating.

'I don't want to talk about it any more,' she said gently. 'I've told you now. And it's done and it's my past. *All* of it.'

She licked her lips, hoping she hadn't misread the signals.

'So how about we focus on the future? One with both of us in it?' She hesitated for a moment. 'You told me you loved me. There is still an *us*, isn't there?'

He'd told her he loved her, but that was before. She had no idea if he still felt the same way.

'Is it really what you want?' He stepped forward, his fingers lacing through hers. He tipped his forehead against hers until she thought the pressure in her chest would compact her.

'Are you all in, Fliss?'

'I'm all in,' she murmured. 'You changed everything for me. You make me feel stronger than I've ever felt. More sure of who I am and what I want. And you give me a sense of belonging.'

Lifting her hands to his mouth, Ash dropped kisses on her knuckles.

'Want to see something incredible?'

She barely hesitated before accepting his hand, allowing him to lead her in companionable silence through the FIBUA towards where, now she was looking, a faint glow appeared to be coming from one of the rooftops. She shivered with anticipation, and it was nothing to do with the cooling evening air. Still, she was glad of the trainers and warm jumper her uncle had told her to wear.

'You know, I don't know whether to be impressed or concerned at the thought of you and my uncle conspiring against me.'

'Whichever you prefer.'

She could hear the smile in his voice.

Together, they made their way past the deserted buildings until the source of the glow became more apparent. She detected the woody scent of a burn, tasting it faintly on the air even before the flickering firelight spilled from the roof of the building in front of her. The crackle of it carried in the still air, making it feel romantic, Fliss thought as they crossed the road and headed up the stone steps which led to the roof.

Her breath lodged in her throat like a tiny bird fluttering its wings, unable to get out of its cage. The old concrete roof was covered with a large rug, a picnic basket and two fold-out chairs on top. A fire pit threw out heat from the front whilst military glow sticks lined the three sides of the perimeter like an Army version of fairy lights. For an instant it evoked memories of being on the viewing point with Ash when they'd watched the carnival floats and something twisted inside Fliss. Hot, red, sensual.

But it was only when she turned around that the full extent of Ash's military make-over became apparent. The fourth perimeter wall which formed the back of the building was two metres high and—right now—it was covered in a mural. The most stunning graffiti art Fliss had ever seen and there was no doubt that it was a faithful representation of the view from the rooftop of the MERT compound back at Camp Razorwire.

'It's stunning,' she breathed, spinning slowly to look at Ash. 'But how…?'

'You remember Corporal Hollings? Andy Hollings?' Ash prompted.

How could she forget the soldier she and Ash had first worked together to save? The reason Ash had come up onto that rooftop back at camp, to tell her the lad had been deemed stable enough to fly back to hospital in the UK.

'Of course I remember.'

'Well, his brother does this for a living; commercial businesses and local councils commission him to paint the gable walls of buildings, under bridge arches—you name it.'

'How do you know that?' She shook her head incredulously.

'He had an unusual tattoo so I asked him about it during that period where he was slipping in and out and you were trying to keep him awake.'

Fliss nodded slowly. 'I remember, but I never heard what he said.'

'He told me it was based on his brother's first piece of work. When I thought about doing this for you—for us—I thought it would be a nice touch. I had a photo from that rooftop so…'

He shrugged, tailing off, but Fliss was still waiting for her heart to start beating.

'So there is an *us*?' The grin spread through her body like warm honey.

Smiling, Ash led her to the chairs, helping her sit down in one whilst he sat in the other; they leaned into each other, his fingers still laced with hers. She didn't even bother trying to drag her eyes from his until he answered.

'There is, without a doubt, an us.'

The heat of the fire was much more apparent here but Fliss suspected it wasn't what was causing the warmth to seep through her body, through her very bones, right now.

'You're strong, Fliss. And you're driven. You have so many incredible qualities, from your empathy and loyalty to your passion and dedication. And I have to tell you, you're damn sexy too. You affect me in a way I can't control.'

'I'm glad,' she murmured.

'And I love that about you.'

The words slid through her. So subtly she wasn't sure if she was hearing things.

'You still love me?'

She swallowed. Hard. It seemed almost too perfect. Too unreal.

'I love everything about you, Fliss. You turn my heart inside out.'

'I do?' she breathed, marvelling at the man facing her. The same one she'd challenged in that office, in the supply room, in the hotel room. And yet a completely different, more open person.

But only open to her, which somehow made it all the more incredible.

'I love the doctor you are, Fliss, I love the Major you are, and the person you are. Most of all I love the woman you are. The way you make *me* want to be a better soldier, better leader, better person. I love the way you make me feel, the way you get under my skin like no one else, the way you challenge me and don't let up. And, for the record, I love the sexy way you bite your lip like that.'

'You love me,' Fliss repeated, the confusion of emotions that had been jostling in her brain finally settling down enough for her to understand his declaration.

It was more than she had dreamed of. A passionate, heartfelt, amazing declaration of love she had never thought anyone would ever say to her. It made her feel part of something special. It made her feel they were something special. Not practical, logical, or sensible. But unrestrained, emotional, intense.

'I love you too.' She stumbled over the words in her haste to say them. To hear what they sounded like when accompanied with all these sensations tumbling around her heart.

They sounded magical. Unparalleled. Perfect.

The feeling started in her curling toes and permeated up through her legs, her body, her chest, fixing an outrageous grin on her mouth as it continued right up to the top of her head. She felt as though together they could face anything.

Together.

She started as Ash slid off his chair in front of her, simultaneously retrieving a neat green leather box from beneath her fold-out chair.

'Marry me, Major.' He grinned. 'It isn't practical or logical but I don't want to do the practical thing and wait until we've dated for a while, because it won't change anything. No other woman could match you. No other woman could affect me the way you do. There will never be another one for me. So I don't want us to wait.'

Fliss could scarcely breathe. It was as though he'd read every last emotion written in her heart and he was rewriting her future even as he did so, throwing out her old rule-book and giving her more freedom. A future with Ash sparkled in a way she'd never dreamed possible.

'I don't want to wait either,' she breathed as he slid the ring onto her finger, then cupped her jaw and drew her into the sweetest yet most intense kiss.

It seemed to last an eternity, drawing her down into its aching longing and beauty. She wrapped her arms around Ash's neck and held herself as close to his body as she could, as if to convince herself that it truly was real and not one of those bubbles about to pop any moment.

By the time they eventually came up for air, Fliss felt more at peace with herself than she ever had.

A sliver of mischief slipped into her head. Sliding off the chair, she pushed Ash's shoulders until he was on his back on the rug, then she moved astride him.

'What, exactly, are you doing?' Ash demanded, the cocked eyebrow suggesting he knew exactly what was on her mind.

Leaning forward, she dropped a kiss to his lips as she shushed him.

'Last time we were outdoors like this, back at the carnival, you taught me something I'd never done before. But when I tried to do something for you, you wouldn't relinquish the reins.' Reaching down, she began to unbuckle his belt, thrilling in the sensation of him finally allowing her to take control.

'I think it's time I repaid that favour.'

His body, already hard against hers, now reacted even further under her touch, making Fliss feel more powerful than ever before.

'Fine,' he managed through gritted teeth. 'But, just so you know, I intend us to spend a lifetime learning new things about each other. And for us to repay each other so many favours that we lose track of whose turn it is, and we won't even care.'

'I can't wait,' Fliss managed, as Ash shifted deliberately beneath her.

And then she resumed her own task, feeling him give himself up to her the way she always did for him. The way she would for him later that night. The way she knew they both would for the rest of their lives.

Because sometimes it was good to lose control.

* * * * *

If you enjoyed this story, check out these other great reads from Charlotte Hawkes

THE SURGEON'S BABY SURPRISE
THE ARMY DOC'S SECRET WIFE

Available now!

REBEL DOC
ON HER DOORSTEP

BY
LUCY RYDER

Published in Great Britain 2017
By Mills & Boon, an imprint of HarperCollins*Publishers*
1 London Bridge Street, London, SE1 9GF

© 2017 Bev Riley

ISBN: 978-0-263-92663-7

Printed and bound in Spain
by CPI, Barcelona

Dear Reader,

I just love writing about quirky characters—and my heroine, Paige Carlyle, is as quirky as they come! Growing up in a houseful of alpha males, she quickly learned it was stand up for herself or get stuck doing sweaty sports-guy laundry for ever. And Paige is no one's fool. She's smart, independent, and prepared to take down intruders faerie-commando-style, totally surprising Dr Tyler Reese, who's returned to the Olympic Peninsula to reconnect with his father and recuperate from an accident that threatens his surgical career.

Frankly, a feisty, quirky woman is exactly what this handsome surgeon needs to jolt him out of his funk. Maybe she didn't quite mean to knock him unconscious—but, hey, for a girl who's spent most of her adult life with her nose buried in medical textbooks, having a hunk fall at her feet is the biggest thrill of the decade.

Despite himself Ty finds himself falling—in an entirely *new* way—for his very distracting neighbour. Of course he tries to deny his feelings—*silly man!*— but he's a smart guy, and finally admits to himself that Paige is as perfect for him as he is for her.

I hope you find yourself falling for Paige and Ty's story too.

Happy reading,

Lucy

This book is dedicated to my great-niece Coral-Mae, who was born during a screaming deadline. Excellent timing, kiddo, but you've brought such joy to us all. We really look forward to all those weekly photos.

And also to my nephew, Jason, who has just graduated cum laude. Congrats to our very own Dr Jay Bass.

Books by Lucy Ryder

Mills & Boon Medical Romance

Resisting Her Rebel Hero
Tamed by Her Army Doc's Touch
Falling at the Surgeon's Feet
Caught in a Storm of Passion

Visit the Author Profile page
at millsandboon.co.uk for more titles.

**Praise for
Lucy Ryder**

'*Resisting Her Rebel Hero* is an absolute delight to read…the sexy writing and refreshing characters leave their mark on every page.'

—*Harlequin Junkie*

CHAPTER ONE

DR. PAIGE CARLYLE jolted awake from her first decent sleep in over a week. One minute she was dreaming about lying on the deck of a sleek boat while a hot captain rubbed oil all over her body, the next…nightmare city.

Frozen with fright, Paige strained for the noise that had awakened her. Vaguely aware that her heart was pounding like that of an overexcited kid pigging out on Halloween candy, she held her breath until… *There,* she thought when the sound came again. *There it is.* A heavy thud followed by…cursing?

In the darkness her eyes widened and her heart rate doubled, banging against her ribs like it was practicing for a world heavyweight title.

You have got to be kidding me!

An intruder?

What the heck had happened to the Chamber of Commerce's pledge that crime was non-existent in Port St. John's? What about her landlord's blithe assurances that she could sleep with her doors unlocked?

Yeah, right, she snorted. Try telling that to her intruder.

A large *male* intruder by the sounds of it.

Had she locked the front door? The sliding French doors leading to the deck? *Dammit*, she couldn't remember. But she'd been in the seaside town eight months and hadn't developed any reckless habits of leaving everything un-locked, so she was almost certain she had.

But "almost" wasn't certain enough, she told herself frantically. Not when a woman's worst nightmare was about to unfold. *Oh, God.* Not when she didn't have a weapon to defend herself with.

Why hadn't she just stayed in the city where everyone locked themselves behind thick doors and deadbolts? Yeah, and while she was at it, why hadn't she just robbed a bank to pay for med school instead of signing her life away on a scholarship?

If she had she wouldn't be here now. Instead of paying off her debt, she'd be working as a pediatrician. Probably from behind bars but, what the heck, at least she wouldn't be—

Black dots began to appear in her vision and she real-ized she was still holding her breath. Expelling it on a quiet rush, Paige tossed back the covers and eased to the edge of the bed, searching in the dark for her cellphone.

It wasn't there and for one panicked moment she couldn't remember where she'd left it… Instead, her hand came into contact with a heavy flashlight she'd used a few nights ear-lier when they'd had a blackout.

Okay. Weapon? Check.

Nerve? Oh, boy.

With the heavy weight in her hand, her head cleared enough to recall the brotherly advice she'd received over the years. But actually doing it was a far cry from prac-ticing on three hulking males who thought it hysterically funny to simply put a big hand on her head and hold her an arm's length away while she "practiced" taking them down.

Bolstered by the fact that she knew a few badass moves and could totally defend herself—she hoped—Paige breathed in and out a few times then headed for the door.

She carefully poked her head into the passage, swallow-ing a squeak of terror when she heard a crash and another round of inventive cursing.

Gulping, she slapped a hand over her galloping heart before it crashed right through her ribs and went tearing off down the stairs, probably to escape out the front door.

Oh, yeah. She was totally kicking this badass thing.

But that was okay, she thought, lifting the flashlight like a baseball bat and giving it a practice swing. The flashlight could probably crush a skull or break a kneecap. Maybe. Probably…in the hands of someone weighing more than one twenty-five soaking wet…but it was all she had.

Tiptoeing to the landing, Paige peered over the railing where light from a nearby streetlamp shone through the stained-glass door inset, illuminating the entrance like a church. She hoped it wasn't a sign that she was about to sing with the angels.

Squaring her shoulders, Paige descended the stairs, bare feet silent on the treads, muscles tensed in preparation for a quick getaway through the front door, and…rolled her eyes.

Look at her, all brave and fierce.

If her brothers could see her now they'd probably die laughing. Or disown her.

There was another loud thud and a couple of beats later a round of pithy curses. Huffing out a breath that disturbed tendrils of wild bed hair, Paige tightened her grip on the flashlight and reached for the landline phone mounted on the wall. She heard the voice of the 911 operator in her ear asking about her emergency and it took a few seconds to realize the intruder was moving again.

Towards her.

Eek.

She caught a brief glimpse of a huge black shadow, arm outstretched like the walking dead, and before she could stop herself she opened her mouth and let rip with a scream worthy of a B-grade slasher flick.

The hulk stopped, swayed for a second before shoving out a hand to steady himself against the wall. A deep voice snarled, "What the—? Who the hell are you?"

She let out another shriek and reacted by heaving the heavy flashlight at him. She heard it connect solidly, he gave a soft grunt, and the next second toppled. Just like a giant redwood. *Whomp!* Landing hard enough to shake the earth.

For several long moments he didn't move and neither did Paige as the flashlight spun in crazy circles on the wooden floor. The impact must have switched it on and with each rotation its beam briefly illuminated the man lying face down on her entrance floor.

Just like a corpse on TV.

When he remained motionless, Paige grabbed the flashlight mid-spin and trained the beam on him, ready to whack him if he so much as twitched.

Beam wobbling in her sweaty grasp, she edged closer and gingerly stretched out a leg to poke him with her foot. He gave a low groan and she jumped back, a strangled squeak catching in her throat.

After a minute of nothing but Paige's ragged breathing, she prodded him a bit harder. Okay, so it was more of a kick but she needed to make sure he wasn't lulling her into a false sense of security before grabbing her and giving her a coronary before she turned thirty.

When he didn't move or make any more creepy sounds, she leaned a little closer…and… *Holy cow*…sucked in a shocked breath.

He was gorgeous.

At least what she could see of him under all the scrapes

and bruises. She didn't know what she'd expected an intruder to look like, but *yeesh*, gorgeous wasn't it.

Damn. What a waste of man candy.

Had she...?

Her heart skipped a couple of beats until she saw that
his right hand and arm was encased in a cast. Exhaling
in a gusty whoosh, she decided that no way had she done
all that. Besides, she was five-five and he was...over six
feet...and solid looking. Big enough to squash her like a
bug if she hadn't panicked and thrown the flashlight at him.

He was all hard angles and masculine power, with the
face of a warrior angel...fierce and awesome male beauty
relaxed in...

Paige gulped.

Oh gosh, she thought a little hysterically, had she just
killed the hottest guy in the northern hemisphere? A guy
who looked like he'd gone a couple of rounds with the
Exterminator and survived. Only to be felled by a...a—

Reality finally hit her and she sagged against the wall,
a shaky laugh escaping. It was filled with more than a little hysteria because... *Wow.* She'd done it. She'd totally
taken out the bad guy.

In her head she did a little victory dance. She was *awesome*! *Who's the girl? Who's the—?*

From down a long tunnel she heard a tinny voice telling
her to remain calm, that the police were on their way. Baffled, Paige looked around and noticed the receiver hanging from the wall unit by a long spiral cord. And blinked.

Oh. Right—911.

Eyes locked on the hot guy, she fumbled the receiver
with shaking hands and lifted it to her ear, managing to
whack herself on the cheek in the process.

"Ouch."

"Hello, ma'am. Ma'am, can you hear me? The police are on their way. Are you hurt?"

Blinking back tears that were most likely from fear and the massive doses of adrenaline still pumping through her system, Paige managed to croak out, "N-no, I'm n-not hurt. But I'm p-pretty sure I just k-k-killed the hot guy."

Her breath escaped in a loud *whoosh*. A seriously hot guy came willingly into her house and what did she do? She killed him, that's what, she thought with a splutter of hysterical laughter. Frankie was going to disown her.

Dr. Tyler Reese swam up through thick layers of consciousness aware of a vicious pounding in his head. Having recently become familiar with the sensation, he let out a rough groan, thinking he was back in the ER after his accident.

A low husky voice ordered him not to move but he disregarded it and lifted a hand to his head before recalling that his arm was encased in a cast from elbow to knuckles. And the move had him sucking in a sharp breath of agony that had nothing to do with his headache.

"I told you not to move," the voice said, sounding a little exasperated. "And use the other hand before you give yourself another bruise. But I warn you. Try anything funny, and it's lights out."

His head pounded harder and a burning pain radiated out from his shoulder. He knew without being told he'd dislocated it—especially as the pain was accompanied by the almost overwhelming urge to toss his cookies.

Wasn't that just freaking peachy? Another damn injury to add to the ones he'd recently acquired.

"What the—?" he slurred, prying open his lids and blinking up into the faces swimming a couple of inches

above him. Faces that looked remarkably like…faeries? He
blinked again and two momentarily became one.

Yep. A freaking crazy-haired faerie. Although what the
hell one was doing almost cross-eyed half an inch from
his face was something he wasn't ready to contemplate.

He narrowed his gaze until his vision cleared, revealing a faerie that was more likely to grace the pages of a
graphic novel than a children's bedtime story book—which
meant he was hallucinating and his mild concussion had
just been bumped up to serious head trauma.

Realizing he was scowling up at her, she gave a startled
squeak and scuttled out of sight—too fast to see if she had
any wings. The sudden move made him dizzy so he closed
his eyes to prevent a brain aneurysm and gave a silent snarl.

Great. Just freaking perfect. His life officially sucked.
He'd escaped an aggressive drunk intent on mowing him
down only to be felled by a pint-sized attacker intent on
splitting his head open like a watermelon.

What the hell had he done to deserve this?

His musings were interrupted by a soft sound of throat-
clearing and a shaky but peremptory, "Hey."

He cracked open an eye and mulled over the fact that
she was still there, and couldn't decide if it was good or
very bad. Good that he wasn't hallucinating and bad because…yep, there was still a wild-haired, wide-eyed faerie
staring at him like he'd crash-landed in her flower patch.

Then he spotted the flashlight raised ready to bean him
if he so much as twitched and he decided that if he *was*
hallucinating she would be dressed in gossamer wisps, not
a huge ratty old USMC T-shirt, looking fierce and crazy
and ready to inflict more pain.

His heavy sigh emerged as a low groan. *So much for that
fantasy.* He'd finally lost his mind if the sight of this wild
exotic creature made him want to smile when he had ab-

solutely nothing to smile about. His surgical career might very well be over thanks to a drunk who'd sideswiped him, leaving him with broken carpals and ulna in his dominant hand, along with damaged ligaments.

Suddenly his well-ordered life had been invaded by a horde of women eager to take care of him and to escape the chaos he'd packed a bag and headed for the one place on the planet he'd been happy—his father's house on the Olympic Peninsula.

It had been an impulsive decision but Ty wanted to be alone. What better place than his childhood getaway in Port St. John's? He'd spent summers here escaping from the rigidly stifling atmosphere of his mother's house until he'd turned eighteen. Maybe he should have called first, but his battery had died and, frankly, it hadn't even occurred to him that Henry Chapman wouldn't be home.

Or that he'd be attacked by a wild faerie commando barely reaching his chin. It was humiliating, *dammit*. He just hoped his friends never found out or he'd never live it down.

And another thing—what the hell was this creature doing in his father's house?

He pushed up with his good arm, intending to demand answers, and promptly froze when pain had him sucking in an agonized breath. Sweat popped out on his forehead and he was forced to sag embarrassingly against the nearest wall to breathe past the nausea.

"Who…are…you?" he gritted out in a voice guaranteed to send hospital staff running. "And what the hell did you throw at me?"

The faerie arched her brow at him as though he was a grumpy adolescent who'd momentarily forgotten his manners. "You first," she said, with only a hint of a quiver in her voice.

It both irritated and earned his reluctant admiration because it took guts to hold off a guy almost a foot taller and a hundred pounds heavier with nothing but a firm little chin, a steely-eyed stare and a flashlight. All while dressed in nothing but a huge, faded T-shirt and a kick-ass attitude.

That mouth—wide, lush and soft—was another matter altogether. A mouth like that gave a man ideas. Ideas that would probably earn him another concussion.

"That way we can get the introductions out of the way before I inflict any more pain on you," her mouth said, completely destroying the fantasy forming in his head.

He squinted at her silently for a couple of beats before looking pointedly at the flashlight. "Thinking of giving me concussion?" He gave a hard laugh. "Hate to rain on your parade, babe, but some idiot already beat you to it."

"No," she said, gesturing to his shoulder with a jerk of her chin. "I'm going to reset your shoulder, *babe*. You dislocated it when you took a header into the floor."

Her tone suggested he was an idiot, which irritated the hell out of him enough that he tersely pointed out, "Which I wouldn't have done if you hadn't tried to split my skull open like a watermelon."

"Which *I* wouldn't have done if you hadn't broken into my house and scared me half to death," she retorted just as shortly, visibly relaxing when they heard a car screeching to a stop outside. Car doors slammed and there was the sound of boots thudding up the stairs, then a brisk knock at the door.

"The cops?" he demanded, outraged. "You called the damn cops?" He knew he was being unfair, but the whole situation was surreal, taking him back to the last time he'd been in this Washington seaside town, beaten up and in trouble with the cops because he and his buddies had thought they had something to prove in a bar filled with local roughnecks.

He'd just turned eighteen and had wanted to flex his I'm-now-officially-cool muscles. He vividly remembered standing in a jail cell while his mother had coldly and furiously berated his father for not keeping Ty on a short leash.

Yeah, right. Henry Chapman had worked all the time and as long as Ty hadn't ended up in his ER, he'd pretty much trusted him to stay out of trouble.

That had been the last time he'd spent summers in Port St. John's because he'd been in med school and then establishing his surgical career, but mostly because he'd been mad at Henry for not standing up to Ty's mother. For not fighting for a relationship with his son.

It had been pretty juvenile but if his recent accident had taught him anything it was that life could be snuffed out in an instant and it was time to mend his relationship with his father.

He was distracted from his inner musings when he caught her over-the-shoulder glance that suggested his IQ was lower than a rock's. It didn't faze him because, let's face it, it wasn't the first time he'd been an idiot. He'd thought he'd outgrown his impulsive tendencies but apparently not or he'd never have hopped on the first flight into SEATAC airport and headed for the Olympic Peninsula.

He didn't know what he'd been thinking because it hadn't even crossed his mind that Henry Chapman would be out of town—or that his childhood sanctuary would have been invaded by a crazy faery wearing an oversized US Marine Corps T-shirt.

"Of course I called the cops," she snorted, backing towards the door and rising onto tiptoe to peer through the stained-glass inset. "*I'm* not an idiot. Besides, you could be a serial killer on the run from the FBI, for all I know."

He found himself staring at her, wondering if he'd face-planted into an alternate universe. "I think you've been watching way too much TV."

"I'm a city girl," she replied, reaching out to unlock the door. "We're taught from the cradle to be suspicious of strangers."

The door opened to reveal two cops, who flashed their badges as they stepped into the entrance hall, identifying themselves only as, "Police Department, ma'am."

She waved the flashlight at Ty, her voice a little wobbly as she hit a light switch and continued to address him. "Especially strange men who break into their homes in the middle of the night."

Ignoring her, Ty squinted up at the cops as light flooded the entrance. There was something familiar about the big guy taking in the situation with cool, assessing cop's eyes but he couldn't think past the headache the crazy woman had inflicted on him.

"The question here should be what the penalties are in St John's for illegal squatting," he growled, scowling at the way the bigger cop was now smiling at GI faerie and asking her gently if she was okay, as though he liked what he saw and wouldn't mind getting her number before hauling Ty off to county lockup.

Yeah, right. Like *that* was happening.

He shifted to get to his feet but his vision swam along with his stomach, so he held up his good hand to get someone's attention. Someone who wasn't so damn busy flirting, that was.

"Hey," he growled irritably, when everyone continued to ignore him. "A hand here." They all turned, surprised by his request. Okay, so it was more of a demand, but what the hell? "When you're done flirting, that is," he ended snidely, hiding a smirk at the big cop's hard look—which he returned. The younger guy grinned and GI faerie huffed out a startled laugh.

She went to shove her hair out of her face and nearly conked herself on the head with the flashlight. Ty watched her face flush as she swung away.

"I was… I was… I was just about to call for an ambulance," she ended on a rush, clearly more than a little rattled.

"No!" he yelled, wincing when the sound echoed through his skull and everyone tensed, the cops turning, hands on weapons. He sucked in a deep breath. "No," he repeated more calmly. "I'm fine."

"You most definitely are not fine," she said decisively, waving the flashlight around again. "Look at you. You're a mess. You need a hospital."

Insulted, he snarled, "I don't need a damn hospital. And will someone take that damn flashlight away before she injures herself?" He waited until she slammed it down on the entrance table and turned to him, hands on her hips and eyes narrowed dangerously.

"Good. Great." He shifted and winced. "I just need a little help, that's all. An explanation would be even better."

"For what?"

"Maybe we'll start with what the hell you're doing in my house and then move on to the unprovoked attack."

"Unprovoked?" she squeaked in outrage. "You looked like the walking dead after my brains. What the heck was I supposed to do?" Three pairs of eyes swung her way and Ty noticed the cops' similar expressions of male confusion. She must have too because she pushed out her lush lower lip, crossed her eyes and huffed out an exasperated breath. "For your information," she continued primly, "this is my house."

"No, it's not." And when no one moved or spoke, "*Dammit*, will someone tell me what the hell is going on?"

She made a tsking sound at his language and turned to the cops. "If he won't go to the hospital, you'll have to hold him down while I do it here." Her voice dropped and she whispered…loudly. "It's going to hurt. We usually strap them to the bed and stick them with a bunch of needles before we try this."

"Hold me—? Needles? Whoa, *you* hold it, lady. Right there." He lifted his good hand in the universal stop gesture and dared them to come any closer. "What do you think you're doing?"

She studied him silently for a couple of seconds before sharing a look with flirty cop. "I'm going to fix your shoulder."

Oh, no. No way in hell.

"No offense, *babe*," he snorted, gritting his teeth against the agony as he struggled to his feet. Where he completely embarrassed himself by swaying as sweat exploded from his pores. His vision swam and it took supreme self-control to stay upright. Fortunately he hadn't eaten since the questionable airline food or he'd be totally humiliating himself. "But I'm not letting a bossy faerie commando anywhere near my shoulder." He jerked his chin behind her. "They can help."

"Oh, for heaven's sake," she snorted, stepping close now that she had two burly cops with guns at her back. "I think the bossy faerie commando is more qualified to do this."

Yeah, right. "I doubt it." He glared at the cop. "Flirty cop here can help me."

"It's Detective Petersen." Flirty cop arched his brows and looked amused but made no move towards him. *Fine.* He turned to the younger cop and got a helpless shrug.

"See," she said smugly. "They know who's in charge

here." She patted his shoulder. "But if it makes you feel better, I'll let Detective Petersen help. And don't worry about it," she soothed, as if she was talking to a frightened kid. "I know what I'm doing. You won't feel a thing."

Ty ground his teeth together and sent her a *touch me and die* glare that she totally disregarded by tugging gently but firmly, clearly wanting him back on the floor.

Which was no way in hell happening. He tried to shrug her off and ended up slapping a hand against the wall when the world spun.

"It'll be much easier this way," she soothed in a soft husky voice that had him blinking and scowling at her again.

"Easier for whom?" he slurred woozily.

Unperturbed, she sent him a smile that was so bright and sweet it distracted him from the crafty gleam in her eyes.

"For you, of course," she murmured, smoothing a hand down his back like he was seven and scared of the dark space under his bed. The move both irritated and pleased him, especially when flirty cop went on hard-eyed alert. Then she added, "This way you won't get any more injuries when you pass out again and crack the floor with your head," and his irritation became outright male insult.

"I am not going to pass…" he began, only to suck in a sharp breath when the world tilted woozily and he slid down the wall to the floor. "Okay…okay, so maybe I do need to, um…lie down."

Clammy and panting, Ty lay on the hard floor, cursing and battling humiliation as the pint-sized tormentor ordered the two cops into position and disappeared upstairs. *Dammit*, this was usually his gig. If word got out he'd never live it down.

Cursing himself for thinking he could just waltz into town and everything would be okay, Ty opened his mouth to order the cops to help him up but she was back with a large towel. "Relax," she soothed. "I can't send you to jail like this."

She slipped the rope towel beneath his back, under his armpit and across his chest. Completely ignoring his gritted curses, she handed the ends to the cops.

Then she planted her knee on his chest and gripped his arm above his cast. Exotic eyes locked with his, she said, "Ready?" and gave it a sharp, hard yank.

Pain exploded through him as his shoulder popped. He let out a ragged groan and lay sweating and groaning while his mini-tormentor sat back on her heels with a loud sigh of relief.

Looking pleased, she gave his chest a comforting rub and rose, affording Ty an unimpeded view of surprisingly long, shapely legs—right up to a pair of teeny boy shorts beneath the baggy T. Boy shorts that were currently hugging world-class curves.

Huh, he thought woozily. Maybe the view from here wasn't so bad. Then from down a long tunnel he heard her instructing them to take him to the hospital and his pain fog miraculously cleared.

"No," he said firmly, sitting up and hugging his arm to his chest, relieved that the excruciating agony was down to an almost bearable throb. "I told you, no hospital."

"But—"

"No hospital," he all but snarled, and was awarded with a huff of exasperation. "Besides," he slurred, "I'm not leaving you in my dad's house."

No way was he telling anyone that the thought of going into a hospital made him break out in a cold sweat. He couldn't do it. Not yet. Not when his future as a trauma surgeon looked so grim.

CHAPTER TWO

"FINE," PETERSEN SAID TIGHTLY, helping a wobbly Ty onto his feet and all but marching him into the living room. "Let's go. But I warn you, your story had better be good because Dr. Carlyle is here legally. You, not so much."

Ty wanted to shrug off the support but his legs refused to obey the directives from his brain. A lamp was switched on and he blinked in the sudden bright light as he sank down onto the sofa with a groan. Then the man's words registered and he stilled. "Hold it. Who the hell is Dr. Carlyle?"

"I am."

Mini-commando appeared at his side with a huge emergency kit and glass of clear liquid, which she offered. He hoped it was neat vodka and opened his mouth to tell her to just bring the bottle but it emerged instead as a snort of disbelief. "Sure you are," he drawled, taking the glass and saluting her. "Because they let adolescents practice medicine now."

Gold flecks hidden in the swirls of her blue and green eyes flashed, reminding him of sunbursts reflecting off water. It distracted him until he realized that he was letting himself be bewitched by a pair of striking eyes.

Annoyed that it was working, he transferred his attention to the contents of the glass and said tersely, "This is water. Don't you have anything stronger?"

"No. Alcohol exacerbates swelling and internal bleeding." He looked up to tell her that if he had any internal bleeding she was responsible for it, and got caught in her gaze again.

"But I can give you a shot for the pain if you like," she announced, wide-eyed innocence totally belied by the laughter in her eyes.

"Yeah, right," he snorted. Okay, so maybe he'd got ahead of himself there for a moment, but the woman was clearly tougher than she looked. "I have my own meds."

"So," Petersen interrupted, impatient with the delay. "Now that you're all cozy and comfortable, maybe we could see some ID?"

Ty considered telling him what he could do with his request but he was exhausted and knew any argument would just delay their departure.

Collapsing against the back of the sofa, he muttered, "Front pocket."

Neither cop made a move towards him. In fact, they shared a stone-faced look until bossy faerie said, "I'll get it," in a voice that suggested they were all idiots.

He stretched out his leg to give her room and sent Petersen a challenging smirk. He couldn't exactly reach into his pocket with an injured arm and the other holding a glass. Besides, if letting her stick her hand in his pants annoyed flirty cop and got him to leave sooner rather than later, then Ty was game.

But it had been a long time since he'd let a woman reach for anything in his pocket and much to his shock—and stunned bemusement—his body stirred.

What the—?

No way, Ty thought with a sharp sideways look. No

way was he attracted to Little Miss Commando. It just wasn't possible.

Was it?

Absolutely not. He didn't like mouthy, bossy women and he didn't like women who attacked defenseless people without provocation.

Her gaze caught his and she flushed, yanking his wallet out and tossing it at Petersen as though it was a live grenade.

Not meeting anyone's eyes, she grabbed the glass out of his hand and downed the contents before shooting off the couch and bolting behind an armchair as if he was contagious.

Amusement vied with insult. *So*, Ty mused, fascinated by the rosy flush creeping up from the gaping neckline of her T, *she handles an intruder without losing her nerve but sticking her hand in a guy's pocket freaks her out?*

She flashed a glare out the corner of her eye when she caught him staring. Her flush deepened and so did her scowl.

Rubbing a hand over his face, Ty wondered what the heck he was thinking. He'd come to Washington to be alone. Yet here he sat—head pounding like a jackhammer—hugely entertained by his attacker while being interrogated by local cops.

Déjà vu.

Paige slid a sideways glare at the man sprawled on her sofa like he belonged and everyone else were intruders. This was all his fault, she decided huffily. He'd broken into her house, scared her into a new blood group and now he was sitting there looking all impenetrable and imposing, pumping off waves of masculine irritation and blast-

ing testosterone and pheromones around the room like a
leaky nuclear reactor.

Silent and deadly.

Especially to unwary females.

Except she was *very* wary. She'd grown up with three
older brothers and knew how the alpha mind worked. Innately confident of their place in the world, they silently
and arrogantly challenged the rest of humanity. Like her
brothers, he seemed to dominate the room completely and
effortlessly. As though he wore an invisible sign that said,
"Badass territory, enter at own risk."

Curious, she took another peek and caught him still
studying her like she was a new species of bug he'd just
discovered and wasn't all that impressed by what he saw.

Her face heated and she shifted nervously because she'd
caught a glimpse of herself in the foyer mirror and just *had*
to look like a wreck the night a hot, rumpled guy broke
into her house.

Paige studied him as light from the nearby lamp cast his
features in bold relief, highlighting his fierce beauty and
illuminating stark blue eyes made bluer by tanned skin.

A shiver snaked through her, promptly tightening her
nipples.

What the—?

Paige quickly crossed her arms over her breasts, rubbing
her arms as if she was cold. *Stop looking at him,* she ordered herself silently. *He broke into your house and scared
you. He is not yummy and he's not harmless.*

No, he wasn't harmless, he was *trouble,* she admitted.
The kind of trouble smart women avoided. Fortunately
Paige was very smart and could spot trouble at a hundred
paces. But even battered and bruised he exuded an almost
tangible authority that was pretty darned hard to ignore.

He was one of those seriously hot men—like a Hollywood action hero women sighed over and men secretly wanted to be—with black silky hair tumbling around his lean angular features like a dark halo, highlighting his ice-blue eyes and the unmistakable gleam of intelligence and mockery.

And yet…also unmistakable was a hollow-eyed weariness that made her chest ache. But he wasn't one of her little patients. More like a hot grumpy warrior angel who'd lost his wings in a recent altercation with dark forces and had found himself stranded on earth.

Paige gave a huge mental eye-roll at the fanciful thoughts and ruthlessly ignored the quiver in her belly. Guys with all that seething testosterone usually didn't give her a second glance. Instead, they buzzed around the tall popular girls—girls with long legs and big boobs—like flies around a carcass.

Fortunately the detective turned, interrupting Paige's unwelcome thoughts. He tossed the wallet on the coffee table. "So. What brings a fancy LA doctor to our modest little town?"

Interest caught by his odd tone—kind of confrontational and mocking—she looked at her intruder a little more closely. "LA? Doctor?"

His mouth curled in a slight smirk as he coolly eyed the detective. "Yeah, and I've been sitting here wondering how the hell you became a cop, Petersen."

Petersen's laugh was more of a snort. "Who'd have thought, huh?" He shoved his hands on his hips, jacket open exposing his gun and shield in a blatantly aggressive move. "Your dad know you're here?"

"No. I didn't get a chance to call."

Bemused by the undercurrents in the room, Paige demanded, "Dad?" Her gaze bounced between the three men, hoping to get some clue about what was going on, but they were all wearing their *let's be macho and inscrutable* faces.

"Phone your father and get this sorted fast, Reese," Petersen said, before turning away and heading for the door. "Oh, and welcome home."

"Not arresting me, Detective?" Ty taunted.

The cop paused at the door, his eyes amused as he took in the scene. "Not today. This is your free pass, Reese. Don't make me regret it."

Thoroughly confused and annoyed by the baffling man-speak, Paige demanded again, "What? What did I miss? Who is he? And, *dammit*, why are you leaving?"

Petersen gave a huge sigh and shook his head. "Ask him."

"What? *No*," Paige said, jumping to her feet. "You can't just leave him here. What am I supposed to do with him? Take him away."

"He's harmless," the cop said with faint mockery. "And it really is his house."

And before Paige could do more than stutter, "B-but," the detectives had disappeared down the passage. Through the roaring in her ears she heard the front door closing behind them.

For several long seconds she stood staring open-mouthed at the doorway, before turning and demanding, "What was that?"

"Nothing," "fancy doc" sighed, rubbing a large hand over his face. "Ancient history. But he's right, I'm harmless." And when she opened her mouth to laugh at that big whopper, he drawled, "Believe me, doing anything more strenuous than breathing is currently beyond my capabilities." He shifted then winced. "I just need a drink and a place to crash. The rest can wait till morning."

Realizing she was still clutching the emergency kit like

her life depended on it, Paige set it down on the coffee table with a little more force than necessary.

"No."

She didn't quite know what she was saying no to, the alcohol, him spending the rest of the night in her house or the fact that her life was spinning out of control...*and just when she'd thought she was finally getting it together.*

"No?"

She caught his expression and nearly laughed at the stunned disbelief on his face. As though people—women most probably—didn't say no to him very often. She gave a silent snort. They probably didn't. Not looking the way he did—all simmering male irritation and dark angel looks. Women probably lined up hoping to tease a smile from that mouth...or something that required mouth-to-mouth resuscitation.

Her spine snapped straight. Well, not *this* woman. She could resus herself just fine, thank you. And all those yummy pheromones flying around like busy little bees looking for the nearest flower to pollinate could...could... well, they could just buzz off.

There would be *no* pollinating.

Not this flower. Nuh-uh. No way.

Not that he looked like he wanted to pollinate her flower, she admitted with brutal honesty. He'd called her an adolescent and a bossy faerie commando—which put a *big* black mark against him as far as she was concerned. He was just like every other alpha guy who thought they were in charge and everyone—women especially—was eager to obey.

"No," she repeated more firmly. "No alcohol." *Right. Let's go with that one.* "And no crashing on the couch until you tell me who you are and why you broke into my house. You can do that while I strap your shoulder. Besides, I know the owner and you are definitely *not* him."

He sighed and rubbed his forehead like *she* was giving *him* a headache when the opposite was actually true.

"Look," he said wearily, "I'm fine. I don't need doctoring. And before you get all bent out of shape," he continued curtly when she opened her mouth to argue, "I can handle my own damn injuries." His ice-blue eyes took a lazy trip from the top of her head to her bare toes. "And as appealing as you are…" his mouth curled up at one corner as though her appearance amused him "… I just want to be alone. I really, *really* need that." He closed his eyes. "So…can you wave your magic faerie wand and disappear?"

"Ha-ha, very funny," she snapped. "If you think I'm about to head off to bed with a stranger on my couch, you can think again."

The look he sent her most probably sent people running for cover. Paige, who had weathered scarier looks and survived, returned it coolly.

Finally he muttered something that sounded like, "Bossy little smartass," and gestured to the emergency kit. "Fine," he said wearily. "Just get a move on so we can both get some sleep before the night is completely shot. And there's my ID." He jerked his chin at his wallet on the coffee table. "Knock yourself out. Call Dr. Henry Chapman too if it'll make you feel better. I might not have seen him in a while but I'm pretty sure he still remembers he has a son."

Paige was halfway down the stairs the next morning when she caught sight of her flashlight on the entrance table and remembered her boss and landlord's grumpy son on her sofa. Or, as she'd dubbed him—after he'd grunted and promptly thrown an arm across his eyes after she'd strapped his shoulder, in a blatant message for her to get lost—Dr. Bad Attitude.

Feeling like a thief in her own house, she tiptoed to the living room and peered around the door to find him still sprawled across her sofa where she'd left him. One long leg hung over the end, the other was foot-planted on the floor, probably to keep him from rolling off the sofa.

The blankets and pillow were halfway across the room as though he'd flung them there in a fit of temper.

The breath she hadn't been aware she was holding escaped in a silent whoosh. So…she hadn't dreamed him up. Neither had she dreamed up what a very fine specimen of manhood he was, she admitted with dismay.

But she didn't need this kind of complication, she told herself firmly. Boss's son or not, she'd send him on his way the instant he opened his sexy blue eyes.

Catching herself drooling at the sight of all that taut tanned skin highlighted by neon pink taping, Paige tried schooling her features into a frown. It didn't work, especially when she recalled his reaction at her liberal application of pink. Instead of making him look ridiculously feminine—which was what she'd intended—all it had done was emphasize his dark smoldering masculinity.

Covering her mouth to stifle her snickers, Paige yawned and retreated to the kitchen. She needed a hefty dose of caffeine if she was going to get him out of her house.

She filled the reservoir and measured out ground coffee then pressed the start button and was in the middle of a jaw-cracking yawn when she heard ringing. The sound galvanized her into action and she shot out of the kitchen, following the sound because she couldn't remember where she'd left her phone.

Muttering frantically, she prayed the ringing would stop before it woke the grizzly camped on her—

"Oops," she said breathlessly, rushing into the living room to find the bear, wearing low-slung jeans, a mile of pink tape and a black scowl, with her shoulder bag in his hand, dumping the contents on the coffee table.

"Hey," she said when he shoved everything out, presumably looking for her cellphone. When he found it he stabbed at the screen with a long tanned finger, heaving a huge sigh as it went silent.

"Hey," she said again, rushing forward to snatch up her phone, glaring at him when she saw that he'd ended the call. But he'd already resumed a horizontal position with one arm slung across his eyes and all she could see of his face was a very nicely sculpted, very grim mouth and a hard jaw covered in a few days' growth.

Her own black scowl was completely wasted. "That could have been an emergency."

He grunted in what he probably thought was a very eloquent reply before adding, "Since when is 'kick-ass grl' an emergency?" in a deep rough voice that might have sent shivers up her spine if she hadn't been annoyed.

"Maybe that's what I call my boss," she shot back heatedly, because she'd totally felt the shivers, darn it. When a ping came from her phone, she stabbed the screen bad-temperedly to access the message.

Hrd abt lst nite. Sid's in 15. I'm buying.

She didn't question how "kick-ass grl" knew about her midnight visitor. St John's wasn't *that* big and everyone—especially emergency personnel—seemed to know everything that happened within minutes of it happening.

Frankie Bryce was an EMT and seemed to know stuff before it happened. Probably because she had friends in high and not-so-high places.

But it'd been a long week and Paige wasn't about to turn down free breakfast, especially at Sid's, which was a hugely popular diner on the boardwalk. It overlooked the harbor where the coastguard did their water training—in skin-tight wetsuits and sometimes jammers—and served the best coffee and pie in town.

That she'd have to cough up details of last night was a given but Frankie had grown up in Port St. John's and might know about Tyler Reese, hot and grumpy son of Port St. John's favorite doctor, and fancy LA doctor of who knew what?

She thumbed a quick reply then bent to scoop up all the purse junk Dr. Cranky had exploded all over the coffee table, turning her head in time to see him eyeing her butt. She squeaked out a protest and straightened so fast she almost gave herself whiplash.

"Hey," she accused, slapping her hands over her bottom. "Eyes off, Mr. Cranky, or I might decide not to offer you any coffee before I toss you out."

Ty snorted, unconcerned that he'd been caught ogling her posterior. "You had your shot." He yawned, eyes as gritty as his temper. "The next one's mine."

She stomped off muttering about rude unwelcome guests and Ty waited until he was alone before pushing to his feet. He followed the smell of coffee to the kitchen, feeling like he'd been run over by a train.

A train named Paige Carlyle, he thought darkly.

He'd already inhaled one mug and was reaching for his second when she bolted down the stairs, looking flustered and sexy in a bright blue tank top tucked into faded jeans. The outfit hugged her sweet curves and clung to surprisingly long, shapely legs.

Dragging his gaze away from her legs was difficult but

he managed, noting absently that her wild hair had been tamed into a shiny inky bob that swung against her delicate jaw. Feathery bangs framed her exotic face, making her eyes appear bigger this morning—if that was possible.

She stopped short when she saw him, no doubt because he was staring at her like she'd just popped through a tear in the space-time continuum. But what was he to do? The transformation from wild faerie commando to…to girl-next-door was startling.

"What?" she demanded, looking down at herself, probably to check for missing fabric, a streak of toothpaste… or a big neon sign that said, "Bite me." Apparently finding nothing amiss, she looked up and with her arms out at her sides in a *what's wrong with my appearance?* gesture she asked, "What?" again, this time with annoyance.

Alarmed to find his tongue stuck to the roof of his mouth, Ty just shook his head. No way was he telling her that she looked good enough to eat and that he suddenly couldn't remember his last meal. Turning away, he poured himself more coffee and decided that Dr. Paige Carlyle was too fresh and sweet, too vulnerable for someone as cynical as him.

She'd probably grown up loved and indulged by her family while he…well, needless to say he didn't believe in love or happily-ever-after. His mother regarded her two children with cool disinterest, unless they disappointed her then it was with cold displeasure; and his father with absent-minded affection. He'd seen Henry Chapman look at his dog that way too.

Better that she think he was rude and obnoxious.

Besides, she was hardly his type anyway. He dated tall sophisticated women; women who knew the score and weren't interested in anything more than dinner and a good time. He was fairly sure Little Miss Medic hadn't even heard there *was* a score. And with *that* mouth, she certainly wouldn't be easy to ignore.

Okay, so the rest of her wasn't easy to ignore either but he was pretty sure it was because she reminded him of a creature from some graphic novel fantasy world.

She appeared in the doorway, wearing a little jacket, shoulder bag slung casually over her shoulder. "You're still here," she said, nibbling on her soft lip and looking adorably self-conscious.

Instead of answering, he lifted the mug in a silent toast, spooked by the abrupt desire to yank her against him and taste her shiny pink mouth. In fact, if she didn't leave soon he might do just that and forgo mainlining caffeine altogether. It would go a long way to waking him up.

"Anyway..." she continued in a way that made Ty think she was rolling her eyes in her head. "I was thinking." She bit her lip uncertainly. "About what Detective Petersen said last night?" He arched his brow, wondering where she was going with this. "Anyway," she sighed impatiently, "I wondered why you came here instead of going to your father's house."

Ah. His mouth twisted wryly as he studied her over the rim of his coffee mug. The last thing he wanted was to discuss his almost non-existent relationship with his father... but...then again he supposed he did owe her an explanation.

"My grandparents built this house. It's where my father grew up and where I spent every summer until I was eighteen." She tilted her head and confusion marred the smooth skin of her forehead.

He sighed. "I would have called my father but my phone died and I thought I'd surprise him. But don't worry, I'll be out of your hair as soon as this caffeine kicks in."

She was silent a long moment before giving a short nod. "Do you need help...um...dressing?"

Immediately an image of her helping him *un*dress flashed into his mind and before he could stop it, his mouth curved. Seeing it, she rolled her eyes and went bright pink.

"You are such a…a *guy*," she accused, turning away. "I have to get going. And since you're my boss's son, I'm not going to throw you out or call the cops. But I *am* going to assume you'll be gone by the time I get back."

He moved to the archway to watch her open the front door. "Lock up behind you," she tossed over her shoulder and closed the door with an almost slam.

He found himself smiling for no reason other than he'd managed to get under her skin and lifted the mug in a cocky salute to the fact that he finally had what he wanted—blessed silence.

He enjoyed it for a few moments until his amusement faded. Turning, he rinsed out his mug and placed it in the dishwasher. Somehow all the air, all the life had been sucked out with her departure. It had never happened before—with *anyone*—which meant he needed to get out of there before she returned.

Before he was tempted to help *her* undress and find out if she was a figment of his overactive imagination or the real deal.

CHAPTER THREE

PAIGE HEADED FOR SID'S, telling herself that she was giving Dr. Bad Attitude exactly what he wanted—space. But the truth was she'd been grateful for the excuse to escape.

It was unnerving to have a man in her living space—especially one who made her want to growl and sigh at the same time. Who made her tingle in places that hadn't tingled in far too long one minute, and stifle the urge to throw something at him the next.

She didn't like it. Not one little bit. She'd learned early on that guys like him weren't attracted to women like her. She was the eternal "cute girl" they treated like a little sister.

Wanting something—or someone—she couldn't have reminded her too much of a past she'd thought she'd long outgrown.

She'd had everything until her mother had died. She lost both parents that day, her mother to ovarian cancer and her father to grief. He'd retreated into his work, leaving a devastated pre-teen to cope with her grief alone because her brothers were much older and didn't do girly things like talk about their feelings.

As if grieving for the loss of the most important person in all their lives was somehow unmanly.

She'd tried and failed to keep the family together, as

she'd promised her mom. One by one her brothers had left, Bryn, the oldest, to accept a position as assistant manager of a football team in San Diego, Eric for the SEALs program, and Quinn to the US Air Force, where he flew classified aircraft on top-secret missions.

Then her father had unexpectedly remarried and it had been like losing everything all over again. Her brothers had rarely visited and she'd suddenly felt like an unwanted reminder of her father's pain.

To be honest, he hadn't known what to do with her and he'd probably thought a new mother and step-siblings would help her cope with grief. But they hadn't, and instead she'd retreated into her school work.

In her senior year salvation had come in the form of a full bursary to med school and everyone had seemed to heave a huge sigh of relief. With Paige gone there had been no need for her father to feel guilty every time he saw her.

She'd thought that by acing her exams she would get his approval, but despite finishing her degree early and at the top of her class, her father hadn't even attended her graduation. Instead, he'd sent a gift and a note with his apologies that the family would be in Aruba.

Dammit, she'd always wanted to go to Aruba.

At least her three brothers had made it—Eric in fatigues on his way home from a mission and Quinn in full US Air Force uniform. They'd made her laugh with their antics and she'd scarcely felt her father's absence.

Fine. She'd been devastated but she'd finally acknowledged that she was on her own. Her brothers had their own busy lives and their father...well, she could totally take care of herself.

Besides, it was safer not to let people close. It hurt too much when they left.

* * *

Francis Abigail Bryce was already in their booth, looking like a movie star in her dark blue paramedic jumpsuit. She'd ordered coffee and was sitting there with a faraway expression on her face. And because she looked just a little bit sad, Paige said the first thing that came to her mind as she slid into the booth opposite her.

"You do know that redheads are supposed to have freckles, don't you?"

"And did *you* know that people who've beaten up late-night intruders with their awesome ninja skills aren't supposed to look so fresh and perky the next day?" Frankie answered smartly, eyeing Paige with sharp green eyes. "Why do you?"

Paige grimaced. "You heard, huh?"

"That's like saying have I heard the coastguard is in town," Frankie snorted, and slid a latte across the table. "I was on duty last night when your call came through. If I hadn't had an emergency I would have helped you bury the body."

Paige grinned and lifted her latte in a toast. "You're the best friend ever. But…" She paused to take a huge gulp, sighing in pleasure when the hot creamy liquid hit her stomach. "As it turned out, he wasn't dead, just concussed. But breakfast first, I'm starving," she said as the waitress approached.

Once the waitress left with their order, Frankie demanded a minute-by-minute account of her midnight adventure, laughing when Paige recounted Ty calling her a bossy little smartass and a faerie commando, and snorting indelicately at his manly reaction to pink tape.

"Men are idiots," Frankie said dryly, "including Ty Reese, so don't go getting any idiotic ideas about saving him."

Paige rolled her eyes and waited as the waitress delivered their food. Tyler Reese needed saving about as much as a prowling mountain lion. But that didn't mean she wasn't curious about him.

Trying for casually offhand, she said, "So…you do know him?"

"Hmm," Frankie murmured, looking amused.

"And?" Paige prompted a little impatiently, when her friend took another bite of omelet without replying. "Spill already before I hurt you."

Frankie nearly choked. "Like you could," she snorted, wiping her mouth with the napkin Paige shoved at her. "Ty's right. With those huge exotic eyes and delicate face, you do look like a faerie. If you weren't my best friend, I'd hate you."

Paige snorted, "Yeah, right," because Frankie was one of those exotically beautiful redheads. Smooth creamy skin, thick lustrous hair *and*…and *darn*…she looked a million dollars in a swimsuit.

"So…what do you know about him?"

Frankie studied Paige for a moment. "You mean other than he has a thing for stacked blonde Malibu beach babes?"

"Yeah." Paige sighed, wondering at the rush of intense disappointment at the news. It was a ridiculous reaction to have about a guy who'd broken into her house and scared the heck out of her. Besides, guys like Tyler Reese had genetically built-in radar for beautiful blondes—or redheads—and having grown up with three brothers who'd dated endless lines of stacked blonde bombshells, it was something she thought she'd accepted.

"Other than that. Which is hardly breaking news, by the way. Guys *always* go for the hot blondes."

Frankie sighed and said again, "Men are idiots," and

looked miserable, but after a couple of beats she seemed to shake off her strange mood. "He's not for you."

That brought Paige up short. Her breakfast abruptly turned to lead in her stomach. "Not that I'm interested or anything," she said shoving her plate aside, "but what's wrong with me?"

"It's not you, it's him." Frankie broke off and studied Paige silently before saying, "Okay, maybe it is you."

Paige didn't know why the idea that Frankie thought she wasn't good enough for Tyler Reese hurt so much. She should be used to being ignored, not pretty, sexy or popular enough, but the truth was, it would be nice to be a kick-ass girl they drooled over. Like Frankie—movie-star beautiful and built like an underwear model, only with attitude.

A *lot* of attitude.

"Oh, don't look at me like that, honey. I only meant that you're too open and generous for someone whose mother is the Wicked Ice Witch of the West. Believe me," she continued when Paige opened her mouth to deny that she was interested in Ty Reese, "I've known him my whole life. At one time he, Nate and Jack were inseparable. They did *everything* together. Including try their stupid moves on everything with breasts. No, jeez," she snorted. "Even *before* girls got breasts they were stealing kisses and breaking hearts." She shook her head. "You don't want to go there." After a moment's silence she said vehemently, "It'd be like stuffing your heart in a mincer and turning it on grind. You don't deserve that. No one deserves that."

Paige knew Frankie's brother Jack had been an army ranger before being KIA a few years ago. She opened her mouth to ask about Nate but was distracted by the odd expression on Frankie's face.

Concerned, she turned and followed her gaze in time to see three guys entering the diner. They were dressed in US coastguard uniforms and the hotness factor was enough to raise the temperature in the diner by a thousand degrees.

"Who's that?" she asked curiously, when Frankie made a little sound of distress. She looked stunned. Kind of like she'd run into a wall.

"Huh?"

Paige jerked her chin at the newcomers. "Who's that?"

Her friend took a deep breath, looking strangely flushed and panicked. "No one," she muttered, lurching abruptly out of the booth. "Look, I gotta go. I'm teaching a first-aid class in twenty minutes."

This was news to Paige. "I thought you were off duty for the next few days." But because Frankie looked so rattled—a look Paige had never seen on her before—she didn't pursue her sudden suspicion that Frankie knew at least one of the coasties.

Or was maybe running scared?

"JT bailed from the senior center program at the last minute so I said I'd take it. Don't worry," she said, when Paige opened her mouth to remind her of their plans. "I haven't forgotten our hiking trip. Meet you at twelve?"

Paige nodded, her fascinated gaze moving beyond Frankie to the tallest and hottest of the trio and… *Oh, wow*… Her eyes widened. The tall dangerous coastie… he must be the one her friend was running from because the guy was staring their way, and the abrupt tension emanating from Frankie told Paige there was definite history there.

She must have made a sound because Frankie's eyes widened and she looked spooked—like she wanted to bolt but was forcing herself to act cool.

"I really have to go," Frankie said abruptly. "But a word of advice here. Stay away from those guys, Paige. They're bad news. In fact, stay away from the whole male gender. They suck."

And with that she spun on her heel and headed for the door.

Fascinated, Paige watched the tall, hot coastie looking granite-faced and dangerous as he contemplated her friend's stiff departing back.

That's one hot BAB, she thought, referring to her and Frankie's name for bad alpha boys. Or was that badass boys? She couldn't remember because they'd both been a little tipsy at the time.

She could feel the simmering testosterone and attitude from clear across the room. Then he turned and their eyes met. *Yikes,* she thought, *a very bad BAB*. And, boy, he had "military" badass written all over him.

Used to dealing with alpha males, Paige narrowed her eyes and mouthed a fierce "I'm watching you", feeling invincible because just last night she had taken out an intruder with nothing but a flashlight and her awesome ninja skills.

After a long moment his mouth kicked up at one corner like he found her cute and amusing, and right there, in Sid's Diner, Paige decided Frankie was right.

Men sucked and Paige was going to have no problem heeding her own as well as Frankie's advice.

She was going to stay away from men—especially the tall dark cranky ones who broke into people's houses as easily as they broke women's hearts.

Ty was trying to dry himself one-handed after a shower when he heard pounding on the front door. Wondering if some of the crazy women he'd left LA to escape had tracked him down, he wrapped a towel around his hips and whipped open the bathroom door…coming face to face with—

"Aaaai-ya!"

He ducked just in time to avoid being beaned with a… frying pan?

Reacting without thinking, he shot out a hand and yanked the pan away before Paige Carlyle could take another swing at him.

"What the hell, woman?"

She let rip with an ear-piercing shriek and scrambled backwards, her expression one of shocked surprise. Before Ty could reassure her that he wasn't a pervert hiding in her shower, the front door crashed open and heavy steps pounded up the stairs.

A large man appeared at the top of the landing in a fighter's crouch, dark eyes hard and cold, ready to take down the enemy. In that instant Ty's towel lost the battle and slid to the floor.

The newcomer instantly took in the scene and after a stunned pause visibly relaxed. His mouth kicked up at one corner as he rose to his full height.

"Well, now," he drawled, hooking the arm of his aviator shades in the neck of his tee-shirt. "Am I missing something, T?"

Ty didn't know who was more surprised by the frozen tableau on the landing, him, Paige or—

"Nate?"

Slapping a hand to her chest, Paige gasped furiously, *"Omigod!* What are you *doing* here?" and collapsed against the banister. She wrapped one arm around the landing rail as though to keep her from sliding to the floor. "I thought you'd left," she squeaked, her tone rising into the stratosphere. "I thought you'd… Who is *he*?" She gestured wildly at Nate, nearly whacking herself in the head. "And what the heck is a m-military B-BAB doing in my h-house?"

He and Nathan Oliver—whom Ty had last seen just before he'd deployed to some hotspot six months ago— shared a confused look. "Military BAB?" Ty asked what was on both their minds.

She finally lost her battle with gravity and plopped onto the floor, breathing as though she'd run up the north face of the Olympic Mountains. "I'm still asleep, aren't I?" she gasped, rubbing the heel of her hand against her chest and clearly on the verge of a coronary. Then she looked up and locked eyes with the part of him at eye level and gave a strangled squeak.

"Omigod!" she gasped, slapping a hand over her eyes. "My eyes."

Nate snickered as Ty whipped the frying pan up to cover himself. He sent his friend a dark look and turned to apologize but Paige had drawn up her legs and dropped her forehead on her knees. She was breathing heavily and muttering to herself.

"This is just a nightmare, Paige," he heard her mutter in a singsong voice. "Wake up and take a *deep* breath." She made a few gasping sounds. "That's it…nice and easy." For several long moments she continued to breathe like she was practicing for the labor ward while he and Nate watched in fascination.

Finally… "There you are. Now you're going to open your eyes and *everything* will be back to normal. Nice… and…normal." Another deep breath, this one less panicked. "No more sexy…*naked*…men." She gave a snorting laugh that he was pretty sure was an insult to his manhood. "Or military BABs anywhere. *Poof.* Gone."

Ty grimaced and bent to scoop up the towel, managing to wrap it clumsily around his waist before Paige looked up.

"You're still here," she accused, taking in the towel clutched at his hips before cutting her eyes to Nate. Arms folded across his chest and leaning casually against the wall, he studied them with a casualness belied by his watchful eyes. "Why are you still here?"

Ty wasn't sure if she was talking to him or Nate and opened his mouth to apologize but, "You think I'm sexy?" slipped out instead.

Nate snorted rudely and Paige rolled her eyes. "Please. You've clearly let yourself go," she said breathlessly, her gaze cutting to his towel and then sliding away. "You're a mess."

Not likely, he thought when Nate laughed with the appreciation of a long-time friend. "You said sexy naked men. And as I'm the only *naked* one here—"

"Don't mind him, sweetheart," Nate interrupted dryly. "He's always been shy about letting girls see him naked." He pushed away from the wall and pulled Paige to her feet. "Hi," he said. "I'm Nate and you must be the cute doctor that took down a dangerous intruder one-handed."

"It was dark," Ty growled, wiping water out of his eyes on his equally damp shoulder. "Don't mind me," he muttered when Paige allowed herself to be steered towards the stairs. "I'll be down as soon as I get dressed."

"Take your time," Nate called over his shoulder. "Dr. Cutie and I are going to get better acquainted."

After a couple of beats Ty turned and returned to the bathroom. By the time he descended the stairs, Nate was shoulder-propped against the arch leading into the kitchen, sipping coffee.

"Still spreading joy and happiness everywhere you go, I see," his friend drawled laconically.

"And you're still trying—and failing, I might add—to look like the coolest kid on the block."

Nathan Oliver chuckled. "I don't have to try any more, T, it just comes naturally. You, on the other hand, look like sh—"

"Yeah, yeah," he interrupted, catching Paige's quick furtive sideways look and the faint flush staining her cheeks. "I know exactly how I look."

"I heard you got beaten up by a girl and just had to see for myself." He chuckled at the exasperated sound Paige made in the back of her throat and reached out to ruffle her hair. "Did a good job on him too."

Ty's eyes cut to Paige, wondering at the casual way his friend had touched her. "I already looked like this before a crazy person jumped me and tried to beat me up with a flashlight."

She heaved a huge sigh and Ty could almost hear her eyes roll around in her head. He moved into the kitchen and purposely crowded her as he went for the coffeepot, biting back a smile when she sucked in a sharp breath and scuttled out of his way, muttering what sounded like, "He's just a stupid BAB, Paige. Get a grip."

"What's a bab?" he asked, after pouring coffee for himself and leaning against the counter. He eyed her over the mug rim and tried not to notice the silky smoothness of her skin.

She started, like he'd caught her doing something indecent. "BAB?"

A frown slowly wrinkled the smooth skin of her forehead and Ty had to restrain himself from reaching out and smoothing it with his thumb. *What the hell?* He wasn't a touchy-feely kind of guy so why the hell did he suddenly want to touch her?

Again refusing to meet his eyes, she muttered something beneath her breath and he had to dip his head to peer into her flushed face.

"What's that, Dr. Cutie? You say something?"

"No." She shoved her way past him. "Excuse me," she said with excruciating politeness, and headed for the stairs, muttering, "And the next person to call me that is dead meat."

"Where are you going?" he asked, watching her take the stairs at a mad dash. He heard her say, "Out," as she disappeared. Thoroughly confused, he turned to Nate. "What the hell did you say to upset her?"

"Me?" Nate drawled. "I didn't do a thing but rush to rescue the damsel in distress. You, on the other hand, were the creepy stalker standing there dressed in nothing but pink tape, and…" he leaned forward and sniffed "…smelling like a spring garden." He chuckled and flashed a look up the stairs where Paige had disappeared. "Maybe I should invite her sailing. Cute and feisty is an irresistible combination."

"And maybe you should back off," Ty growled, feeling unaccountably annoyed. "What are you, seventeen? She's not the kind of woman you take sailing just because you need to get laid. Pick someone who knows the score."

"Oh, yeah?" Nate drawled. "And how would you know? I thought you two only met last night."

"We did," Ty growled. "When she tried to crack my skull open."

"Then what's your prob—? Ah." Nate nodded sagely. "I get it. You want her for yourself."

"What—? Of course not," Ty scoffed, feeling his gut clench. "She's a bossy pain in the ass who decorated me in pink, for God's sake." He jerked his chin at his cast. "I'm here because I need peace and quiet to think about what I'll do if I can't do surgery again. I don't need an annoying distraction, no matter how cute and feisty. Besides, she's not *my* type any more than she's *yours*."

"Oh, I don't know," Nate said, thoughtfully. "I think cute and feisty would be a refreshing change, don't you?"

"No, I don't. It would be suicidal."

Behind them they heard a sound and turned to sec Paige standing at the bottom of the stairs looking like she was considering which of them to maim first.

"Oh, hey," Ty said. "I was just—"

"I'm leaving," she interrupted. "I hope your visit with your father goes well. I left his address on the entrance table. Please lock up when you leave." Her tone, as cool as her expression, suggested she hoped it was soon.

She'd obviously heard.

"Listen, I didn't mean—" he began, but the front door slammed. Hard. He winced. "I think she heard."

"Yep." Nate clamped a hand on Ty's shoulder in brotherly support. "And now you're scum just like the rest of us. Welcome to the club."

CHAPTER FOUR

A FEW DAYS LATER, Paige was still smarting over the fact that Tyler Reese thought she was an annoying distraction he didn't want. She told herself she didn't care that "cute and feisty" wasn't his type because snarly and arrogant certainly wasn't hers.

She still shuddered because, as far as she was concerned, cute was a metaphor for "fun but too ugly to date" or "you're like a sister to me". She wouldn't go there if her hair was on fire and he held the only glass of water left in the universe.

Fortunately, by the time she and Frankie had returned from their hike, her house was empty except for a thank-you note taped to the refrigerator. It had obviously been scrawled by Nate.

Dear Paige,
T says he's sorry for being a bonehead and flash-ing the family jewels—but you've probably already forgotten that. He also wanted to thank you for your hospitality and for not insisting he be incarcerated like a common criminal. He has a thing about jail in this town. Anyway I'd like to thank you for knocking some sense into his thick skull—although it might take time to sink in.

Nate.
P.S. I was serious about taking you sailing.

Right. Like she would actually accept. She was fairly certain it had just been to get a reaction out of Ty. *Why* was something she tortured herself with along with other thoughts of him. Thoughts like, if he'd returned to California. Like if he and Henry Chapman were getting along.

Like if she'd exaggerated his "endowments" in her own mind.

She told herself she had because no one looked that good without being "enhanced" by a photo editor.

But she couldn't stop thinking about something else she'd overheard him say to his friend. Something that explained why he was so grumpy. He was a surgeon who'd injured his dominant hand. She wondered what had happened and had questioned Frankie about it, but her friend didn't know either.

It was six-thirty and the chilly morning wind blowing right off the straits caught Paige when she left the house. She considered going back for a jacket but it was a twenty-minute drive through town on a quiet day and she didn't want to be late for the morning briefing.

Her aged sedan, Old Bertha, sat hunched against the curb looking both familiar and forlorn. Paige gave the roof an affectionate pat and quickly unlocked the door so she could escape the wind. Over the past week they'd had gloriously fine weather and the icy gusts coming off the straits were an unwelcome reminder of the Pacific North West's reputation for unpredictable weather—especially this time of year.

She dumped her shoulder bag on the seat beside her and shoved the key into the ignition. Instead of the engine turning over, all she got was an ominous click.

Used to her car's eccentricities, Paige said a silent prayer and tried again. Nothing.

"No, no, *no!*" she begged, heart skipping a beat as she flicked a glance at the dash clock and calculated the time she had to fiddle with the engine. "Just this once, girl. *Please.*" Bracing herself, she silently urged the car to start, then sucked in a breath, mentally crossed all her fingers *and* toes, and turned the key.

And got a whole lot of…nothing. *Dammit.*

Muttering under her breath, she popped the hood and shoved open the door, grabbing her phone so she could call the hospital. Frankie would also be heading to work soon and could swing by.

Hopefully.

She heaved up the hood and propped it up with the metal thingy, shivering as icy wind sneaked cold fingers down the back of her neck into her snug long-sleeved T.

Having absolutely no idea what she was looking for, she shoved her head under the hood, hoping the problem—like a loose wire or something—would jump out at her.

"Well, Paige," she muttered irritably, "maybe you should have taken motor mechanics at school instead of calculus. Is calculus going to help you fix Bertha? No, and neither is—"

"Problem?"

With a startled squeak, she jerked upright and whacked her head smartly on the hood. For a couple of seconds she saw stars before impatient masculine hands pulled her free.

"What the hell, woman?" Tyler Reese growled in that deep bedroom voice that sent shivers right up her spine only to have them spreading further. Like *everywhere.*

Or maybe it was the heat of his hands on her as he gently probed her head because her body responded—embarrassingly fast.

Her nipples tightened—but that could easily be from the cold—and her knees wobbled. She finally gathered her wits enough to shove at the broad chest blocking her view so she could rub her own damn head. And breathe without getting a lung full of warm masculine scent that made her want to bury her face in his throat.

Oh, boy. Not good.

Lurching out of range, she scowled up at him. "Ouch, *dammit*. What are you doing, sneaking up on me?" she demanded irritably, because he clearly wasn't feeling "it" like she was. Then, realizing he was outside her house— *what the heck?*—she gulped. Her eyes widened. "Are you stalking me?"

One brow rose arrogantly. He said mildly, "Good morning to you too, Dr. Carlyle." And when she just scowled at him, he sighed. "Okay, not a morning person. Good to know and to answer your question; no, I am not stalking you. I saw you pop the hood and pretend you know what you're doing."

"I am too a morning person," she practically snarled. "And how do you know I don't know what I'm doing? Maybe I took a class in motor mechanics."

His eyebrow rose up his forehead in patent disbelief. "You took calculus instead."

"Yes," she sighed. "And even if I did, Bertha is selective about who works on her." She pulled her phone out and began thumbing through her contacts.

"Bertha?"

"Car," she said absently, tapping out an urgent message to the dayshift ER supervisor. By the time she looked up, Ty had stuck his head under the hood and was fiddling around one handed, muttering about "idiots who don't take care of their cars".

Ignoring his comments—because she was still mad at

him—she joined him, hoping he knew what he was doing and would magically get Bertha started. Instead she was assailed by his warm masculine scent.

Damn. She sent him a sideways glance that was filled with rebuke. It should be illegal for a man to smell so good and—despite the fading bruises—*look* so good.

"What?" he asked, attention firmly on some alien engine part she didn't recognize. Busy resenting the hell out of him, she said the first thing that popped into her head.

"Huh?"

"You're staring at me," he said mildly.

"I was just wondering if I was having nightmares about zombie psychos or if you're really standing here, messing with me...uh, with my engine, I mean. My car," she said huffily, when his mouth curled. "Messing with my car."

Instead of answering, his head turned and suddenly his face was an inch from hers. Their gazes locked and for a breathless moment she felt herself sink under his powerful sexual spell, wondering at the heavy liquid sensations taking over her limbs...and the wild kamikaze butterflies dive-bombing her belly.

A little voice in the back of her mind yelled, *Move away from the sexy BAB, Paige. He's trouble, remember.*

"Paige."

She blinked slowly, fighting the pull of him, thinking, *This is bad. This is really, really bad.*

"What's bad?" he asked, and it was a couple of beats before she realized she'd spoken out loud. Pressing her lips together, she shook her head, recalling that he'd already called her a crazy person.

"I'm sorry," he said, the quiet intensity in his gaze echoed in his tone.

Her forehead tightened in confusion. "Sorry?"

"About what you overheard the other day. I didn't mean…well, it."

"Huh." Paige stepped back from the car on wobbly legs and leaned her hip against the fender. She folded her arms beneath her breasts. His eyes dropped from her mouth and, to her horror, her nipples promptly tightened. His mouth curved and she was tempted to punch him because she wasn't one of those voluptuous beach babes he probably dated in droves.

His gaze rose up her neck, past her chin to linger on her mouth before meeting hers. The laser heat in them had her knees wobbling.

No, darn it. No wobbling. You're mad at him, remember.

"Didn't mean for me to hear, you mean?" she drawled coolly.

"No," he said, shaking his head. "I didn't mean it."

"It?" she enquired politely, gritting her teeth against the melting heat taking up residence in her body beneath that hooded gaze. "What exactly are you sorry for? The part where you called me a bossy pain in the ass and an annoying distraction you didn't need or want? Or was it the part that dating me 'would be awful, not to mention suicidal'?"

He sighed and shoved a hand through his hair as though she was being deliberately difficult. "The latter," he explained with more than a hint of exasperation. "Definitely the latter because you're still an annoying, bossy pain in the ass."

And just when she was about to tell him that he needn't worry about her wanting to date him even if he was the very last man in the freaking universe, from directly behind them a gruff voice asked, "Problem?" nearly giving her a coronary.

She spun around with a startled gasp, forgetting that she was perched against the left headlight, and would have fallen into the road if Ty hadn't reached out and yanked her back onto her feet. She immediately growled at him and pulled away, blinking at her neighbor who stood watching them with amused curiosity.

Harry Andersen had been a coastguard for fifty years and now spent his time watering his plants, looking out for Paige, helping the neighborhood seniors and keeping an ear on his ham radio and an eye on the weather. He claimed his bones were better barometers for weather changes than any new-fangled instruments the coastguards used.

In the months she'd been here, Paige had grown to love the old man. His face had that lived-in quality of some-one who'd spent years squinting into the sun and wind that came off the ocean.

His wise brown eyes were often a little bleak and lonely because his wife of fifty years had passed away a year be-fore Paige's arrival in Port St. John's.

"Hi, Mr. Andersen," she greeted him, completely ignor-ing the man at her side because she was in crisis here—and it wasn't because old Bertha was playing up. "What are you doing up so early?"

"I'm always up early, missy. Fifty years of rising at dawn is a hard habit to break." He came forward and peered into the engine. "Know what you're doing there, sonny?"

"Yeah," Ty grunted, "but it's hard, doing it one-handed."

"Why don't you take the girl to work?" the old man sug-gested. "I'll see what I can do about *this* old girl."

"No!" Paige blurted out, freaking out a little at the thought of being stuck in the intimacy of a car with Mr. Bad Attitude for more than five seconds. "I'll just call Frankie. I'm sure she can—"

"That's a great idea, Mr. Andersen," Ty interrupted, sending Paige an inscrutable look as he brushed past her and gave her a rush to rival any she'd ever had for chocolate. "I'll just fetch my keys." And loped up the walk.

Paige shoved her fingers in her hair and considered doing an emergency chocolate run but she was too busy gaping after Tyler Reese...who'd disappeared through the door a few feet from hers.

What the heck was he doing, living right...next...door? How long had he been there and how had she not known? And another thing...why hadn't he told her?

But she knew. He'd wanted to be alone. Besides, his father still owned the building and the adjacent unit *had* been empty for a couple of months. *He* probably also didn't want her getting any ideas about taking care of him. Or worse, that she would think they were a "thing".

As if.

He thought dating her was suicidal, for cripes' sake, and she...well, she *knew* it wasn't going to happen. *Ever.* Besides, the last thing she wanted was to crush on another unattainable guy like she had in the tenth grade. He might be sorry about what he'd said, but he was still a BAB. And BABs were trouble.

Big. Bad. Trouble.

"This old girl deserves better, missy." Harry interrupted her mental meltdown. "Worn pipes, frayed electrics...?" He tutted gruffly. "It's a wonder she hasn't blown up in your face."

Paige sighed. And right there was something else to add to her freak-out list because the news was about as welcome as discovering the sexiest guy in America thought she was an annoying pain in the ass.

Mentally crossing her fingers, she said as calmly as she could, "I know, I know. The question is, can she be saved?"

Please, please, please, say yes.

"Well... I can't say for sure," the old man admitted reluctantly, scratching his head. "The starter will have to be replaced and some other parts too if you really want to know."

Paige *really* didn't want to know but she gulped and asked bravely, "Will...will it be expensive, do you think, Mr. Andersen?" while frantically calculating the balance in her account and wondering if she was going to have to forgo eating for the next couple of weeks or dip into her meager savings.

For a moment Harry said nothing as he tightened a few more bolts. Then he straightened. "Now, don't you worry about a thing," he said, awkwardly giving her shoulder a rough pat just as Ty returned, car keys jingling. "I know Gus at the repair shop. I'll work out a good deal for you." Ty sauntered up, as if he had all the time in the world. "Off you go to work now, missy. You don't want to be late."

"I'll drive," Paige said, reaching out to snag Ty's keys. "You should be resting your shoulder. And don't worry about the car," she interrupted hurriedly when he looked like he might object. "I'll take good care of it and have it back by tonight."

His eyebrows rose up his forehead. "I'd be worried if it wasn't a rental," he drawled as she scurried off to grab her shoulder bag. "Considering the condition of yours."

Paige rolled her eyes and muttered through an interminable few minutes while she adjusted the seat. *Damn long-legged freaks.* And then when she finally turned the key, the SUV jerked forward a couple of yards and promptly stalled.

Snickering at the way Ty leapt out the way, the expression on his face priceless, Paige called out a strangled "Sorry" and managed to restart the car and shove it into gear without further embarrassing herself, giving Ty a coronary, or injuring more than just his pride.

She alternately snickered and moaned with embarrassment all the way to the medical center across town because if Tyler Reese had suspected her of being a crazy woman, he would now be certain.

Unfortunately, the morning shift was quiet, giving Paige way too much time to stew over the fact that he'd been living within feet of her the last few days and she hadn't known.

But then again maybe her subconscious had detected that potent combination of smoldering male pheromones and seething testosterone seeping through the wall because…well, because. Her breath whooshed out audibly, causing a nurse to send her a curious look.

Realizing it was the fifth time she'd sighed, Paige mentally slapped herself. *Okay, fine.* So she'd had a few hot dreams and a couple of bad moments in her shower imagining him—*yikes, her heart rate doubled and heat raced across her skin*—naked and running his hands all over her slick flesh.

She scowled at her body's traitorous response.

Big freaking deal.

It didn't mean a thing because she'd had the same dreams about that black-haired guy who'd starred in a vampire TV series.

And then because she was fantasizing about lying on a warm deck while Ty and the vampire hottie massaged oil into her tingling skin, Paige tore out of Radiology, fanning herself with the report she was supposed to be reading.

And promptly collided with a large frame.

She gave a squeak of surprise and lurched backward, dropping the report. "Omigosh, Dr. Ch-Chapman, I'm s-so sorry," she spluttered in shock, blinking up into familiar blue eyes peering at her with concern. Familiar because just that morning she'd felt herself being drawn unwillingly into eyes that exact color.

She hoped, *really hoped* the medical director couldn't read minds.

"No need to apologize, Dr. Carlyle," the older man said cheerfully as he bent to retrieve her report, "Nothing serious, I hope."

Thinking he was referring to her hot thoughts about his...*gulp*...son, Paige fought the heat of embarrassment creeping into her cheeks. She bit lip and asked warily, "Why do you...um...ask?"

"It isn't every day I get bowled over by a beautiful young woman," he said, chuckling, nodding to the file he handed her.

Realizing he'd been talking about the report, Paige spluttered out a relieved laugh. "Oh, this. Um..." *Holy cow, she had to get a grip—especially in front of the big boss.* "A young patient fell off a trampoline onto his head," she explained breathlessly. "I was just on my way back from Radiology."

"Problem?"

"The X-ray detected an odd shadow. I don't think it's anything to worry about," she explained, "but I'm going to recommend a CT scan just to be safe."

"Excellent decision," he said, shrewd blue eyes twinkling at her. "I'm glad I ran into you." He chuckled a little at his own joke. "I heard you had a break-in the other night."

Paige gulped, fighting the heat of embarrassment creeping into her cheeks because the last thing she wanted to discuss with this man was the one she'd just been imagining naked.

Not that she had to imagine anything, especially as she'd already seen him naked. "Oh...um." She stifled a hysterical giggle and felt her face heat.

"Are you all right, Dr. Carlyle? You're looking a little flushed."

Her flush deepened. "It's… I…um, it's been a hectic day," she began, only to be interrupted by her pager. "Emergency," she explained after a quick look at the screen, hugely relieved to be saved by the pager.

He nodded. "Go see to that. We can talk another time," he said, and Paige bolted, wondering what the heck they had to talk about. That she'd given his son concussion and a dislocated shoulder? Or that she'd called the cops on him?

The ER shift supervisor grabbed Paige the instant she hurried through the doors. "There's been an accident up near Angel Lake Ranger station," he rapped out. "A school bus on the way back from a field trip left the road. Details are sketchy but it sounds like they slid off a sharp incline into a gully. Dispatch said there was a lot of screaming and it was difficult to get information."

Paige's heart clenched with dread. She hated it when little kids were hurt in accidents. "Is medevac on their way?"

"Climbing accident up in the mountains," Chalmers said impatiently. "You're up. They need someone to help with the kids."

"I've got a young patient who—" she said but he grabbed the report and gave her a nudge towards the ambulance bay doors.

"I'll take care of it. You. Go. Miss Bryce is waiting."

Paige took off. The bay doors whooshed open as she approached and she had a split second to register that an ambulance was idling in the bay, passenger door open and Frankie frantically beckoning.

Paige grabbed Frankie's hand and they took off, the momentum slamming the door closed behind her.

It wasn't unheard of for an ER doctor to accompany EMTs to the scene of an accident but it wasn't exactly standard operating procedure either.

Paige prayed they wouldn't find death today.

CHAPTER FIVE

STATE TROOPERS HAD already blocked off the road and were redirecting the sparse mid-afternoon traffic. They waved the ambulance on, and even before the vehicle screamed to a stop Frankie was leaping out.

Paige scrambled after her and headed for the edge of the road, where troopers were in discussion with forest rangers. Intent on getting to the trapped children, she didn't see the single figure not in uniform until she was almost upon him. At the sight of familiar wide shoulders, hard chiseled profile and dark wind-tousled hair she'd seen just that morning, her eyes widened and her step faltered.

What the heck was Tyler Reese doing here?

He must have sensed her scrutiny because he turned his head, his laser-bright gaze instantly locking onto her. If he was surprised to see her, it didn't show. Instead, he broke away from the group and headed towards her.

"You're here," he said briskly, taking her arm and pulling her aside.

"What are you doing here?" Paige asked absently, distracted by the skid marks swerving across the road and disappearing into the gap in the foliage. The bus was nowhere to be seen but from below she could hear the frantic cries of children and the soothing tones of male rescuers. Her heart squeezed.

"We came across the accident and stopped to help."

She made a move forward but Ty tugged her back.

"I need to get to those children, Tyler," she said, yanking on her arm. "They may be hurt."

He tightened his grip. "Nate's down there with a few rangers but we've got a bigger problem," he said in a tone that had Paige's head jerking up. He looked as grim as he sounded and her belly clenched in dread.

"What?"

"Most of the kids are fine. Some need medical attention but the paramedics can handle them."

"Then—"

"The teacher is trapped," he growled. "She was standing when the bus swerved across the road and rolled down into the gully. They managed to get to the children but she's pinned by crumpled metal."

"Can't they get her out?" Paige demanded, looking pointedly at the group milling around instead of acting. "Surely there's enough muscle here to move the obstacle?"

"They can't," he said bluntly, his eyes intent on hers. "Her arm is pinned. The minute they lift it she's going to bleed out."

Paige instantly understood Ty's implications. The metal was providing pressure and was keeping the teacher from bleeding out. The artery would have to be clamped before the weight was removed. There wasn't time to put pressure on the wound and transport her to a hospital. She would die before they got her up to the road.

"Well," she said briskly, "it's a good thing you're a surgeon, then, right?"

Ty's mouth twisted as he held up his casted hand. "Not happening, Dr. Carlyle. That's why I'm glad you're here. EMTs can't handle this procedure. It needs someone with surgical experience and knowledge."

Paige gaped at him then said in a fierce undertone, "Are you insane? I'm a pediatrician, not a surgeon. You, on the other hand, *are* one."

He held up his cast. "I can't use it," he reminded her tightly.

"Why didn't dispatch request a trauma surgeon? There's a very good reason I didn't choose surgery as my specialty."

One dark brow rose arrogantly. "You faint at the sight of blood?"

"Don't be ridiculous," she growled. "I work in ER." Ty's mouth curled very slightly at one corner.

"That's exactly what she's counting on. And they didn't request a trauma surgeon because at the time they didn't know they'd need one."

He let that sink in for a couple of beats, then taunted, "You going to let a fifth grade teacher bleed out, Doc? In front of her students?"

"Of course not," she snapped, furious with him for expecting her to perform something a trauma surgeon should do. Finally her breath escaped in an audible rush. "Fine," she said tightly. Maybe he couldn't actually perform the field surgery but he was going to guide her through it. "I'll do it but I need help."

Immediately his eyes shuttered and he turned away. "I'll get an EMT," he tossed over his shoulder.

But before he could take a couple of steps Paige snapped out, "Hold it right there, buster."

He froze and after a long moment turned his head, his expression a little stunned.

"Are you talking to me?"

Paige refused to back down. "You're the surgeon here, *Dr.* Reese," she reminded him shortly. "The EMTs are busy, remember. Taking care of the children."

His whole body recoiled as if she'd struck him. "No," he said coldly, and turned away.

"Yes," she insisted fiercely, hurrying after him. "You want me to do this then the least *you* can do is talk me through it."

At her words, he stopped abruptly and turned eyes as cold as the North Pacific on her. His entire body vibrated with tension. "I said no."

Paige caught the hollow misery behind the fury but couldn't let it deter her. "Dammit, *Dr.* Reese," she snapped. "You want a fifth grade teacher to die because you're mad at the world?"

"I am not mad—"

"You are. You're hurting and mad at everyone. Are you going to let that stop you from doing what you do best?"

"You don't know what I do best," he rasped, fury in the tight lines of his jaw and mouth. "Especially as I can't *do* a damned thing."

Holding his gaze with difficulty, she gave a casual shrug even as her heart pinched. Now wasn't the time to feel sorry for him. She needed him. The *teacher* needed him. "You've done it before, haven't you?" And when he just stared at her, she exhaled impatiently. "Well, then, we… I mean… you…" She chewed on her bottom lip and admitted in a fierce undertone, "*I've* never done it before."

His eyes blazing a promised retribution, Ty turned without another word and walked off.

"Hey!"

He paused and sent her a dark look over his shoulder. "Get going," he snarled. "I'll bring what you're going to need. And sometime, Dr. Carlyle, you're going to tell me what a pediatrician is doing working in ER."

Relief made her knees weak as she stumbled towards the troopers pulling fifth graders up by ropes. The whole exchange had taken less than a minute and it was another before she was wrapping her arms around a trooper and clinging to him like a monkey as they were lowered to the wreckage, wedged in by trees and rocks about fifty feet down.

Paige scrambled through the broken window and paused to cast an experienced eye over the children still left behind. She murmured encouragement as they clung to her, noting absently that Frankie had already set up triage and was studiously ignoring the man calmly and efficiently organizing the children.

Nate Oliver looked big and capable and just a little dangerous, as though he did this every day. But then again he did. He was a coastie.

"Dr. Cutie," he greeted her, looping the harness around a child before lifting him through the window. His voice, cheerful and upbeat for the children's benefit, dropped to a murmur meant for her ears only. "Glad you're here—she's barely hanging on."

Paige slid on the almost vertical floor and was grateful for his easy strength as he steadied her. He nodded to the front of the bus. "It's real bad," he reported softly. "T was about to turn me into a field surgeon but I don't think Grace Parker wants my version of first aid."

"You're a medic?"

"Nope, but I can get by in a pinch." He shook his head. "This is more like a giant squeeze. Have you seen him?"

"He's bringing med supplies."

Nate's eyes widened then sharpened, amusement and approval gleaming in the dark gaze. "He's coming down… here?"

"Not willingly," she admitted, and headed towards where a park ranger was crouched beside the teacher. Behind her she heard Nate laugh softly and say beneath his breath, "Well, well. This is going to be very interesting."

Yeah, well, she wouldn't exactly use the word "interesting". *Terrifying* would be closer to the mark, especially when she saw Grace Parker pinned to the side of the bus by a twisted mess of metal seats. Her white face was sweat-drenched and she had her teeth clenched against the pain.

"Hi," Paige said, moving as close as she could get, "I'm Paige."

"Yes," the woman rasped, her face tightening as she let slip a little moan. "I remember…you came to the school on health day."

Paige ran her eyes over Grace's pinned arm and estimated that she'd lost about five hundred ccs of blood—probably when rescuers had attempted to free her.

She squeezed the woman's free hand and noted that it was icy. They would have to hurry before she went into shock. "I've never had so many kids ask me about blood and guts before," she said, pressing her finger to the area above the injury site to feel for a pulse. "Or want to show me all their scars."

"They're a handful, all right." Grace breathed through another moan and grabbed Paige with her free hand. Her gaze was fever-bright with a dangerous edge of panic. "They're okay, aren't they? Please tell me they're okay."

"They're going to be fine, Grace. Scared mostly," she soothed. "But it's you we're all concerned about."

Her eyes closed briefly and she gave a short sobbing laugh. "I'm going to lose my arm, aren't I?"

A shadow blocked out the light and even before Ty eased into place beside her, she knew it was him. She had absolutely no idea why her senses were so attuned to him but her entire body went on alert.

Ignoring both it and him, she asked, "Why do you say that?"

"Keith—the ranger—said it was too dangerous to move me," Grace said tightly. Her eyes filled with tears. "B-but I… I have to tell you that I can't feel it. My arm, I mean. Tell them, Paige. Tell them to move this thing off me."

"We can't, Grace," Paige began, sparing a brief glance at Ty's hard, remote expression. He looked a little like he had the night of his attempted B&E, pale, clammy and his mouth set in a tight white line. His posture screamed anger and bad attitude. Whether at the situation or her, Paige couldn't tell. "The bar is stopping the bleeding."

"Try to relax," Ty said, crouching down near Grace's head and handing a bag to Paige. "And to make sure you don't move, even a fraction of an inch, Dr. Carlyle is going to give you a mild sedative."

Grace pressed her lips together and turned her face away. "I… I… It's bad, isn't it?"

Paige nibbled on her lip indecisively. Sometimes people wanted you to tell them everything was going to be okay and others needed to hear the bald truth.

Ty chose the truth.

"Yes, it's bad," he admitted calmly as Paige pulled on surgical gloves and reached for the sedative. "But it could be a lot worse," she heard him say. "I don't want you to worry now. Dr. Carlyle is a specialist and you couldn't be in safer hands."

Paige, swabbing an area on Grace's uninjured arm, glanced up briefly, thinking it was a good thing he'd failed to mention that she wasn't a trauma specialist or Grace would be as terrified as Paige. Instead of looking terrified, Grace's gaze was locked on Ty as though he was her lifeline and she was ready to do anything he asked.

Paige gave a mental eye-roll but then reluctantly admitted that she'd probably do anything he wanted if he spoke to *her* like that.

Which was kind of pathetic if you thought about it.

While she waited for the sedative to take effect, Paige wrapped a pressure cuff around Grace's arm and kept up a calm chatter when Ty took over.

Out the corner of her eye she saw his mouth tighten as he struggled one-handed but when she tried to help, he growled. She backed off, wondering if she'd done the right thing getting him down here, because it was clearly too much so soon after his accident.

But then his gaze—cool and clear—caught hers. He murmured, "You ready?"

And Paige felt her stomach drop and lift at the same time. *Oh, God, she really was going to do this.*

She exhaled slowly and nodded just as coolly. "Yes. You?" *Look at her, all calm and collected.*

Ty's eyebrow rose, as though he knew she was shaking in her sneakers. "I'm not the one about to perform a ligation in less than ideal conditions."

Great. So not the way to instill her with heaps of confidence.

"I can *do* this," she insisted with a lot more confidence than she felt. She wasn't a surgeon but she was the only person standing between her patient and death. She paused then said, "I'm ready."

His gaze searched hers for a long moment before he nodded. "Fine." His voice was brisk, professional. "The broken bar is gouging into the brachial artery midway up the humerus. Her pulse is weak so I want you to use a surgical glove as a tourniquet. Tie it a couple of inches above the injury site. It'll stop the bleeding long enough for you to clamp the artery."

Paige quickly obeyed.

With his left hand he sprayed the area with disinfectant. "Now, you're going to do an arterial cut-down at the point of impact. Using an eleven blade…no, that's a thirteen. The other one. Okay, now make an eight-centimeter longitudinal incision distal to the deep brachial confluence."

Paige positioned the scalpel and noticed her hands were shaking. She sucked in a sharp breath. *Dammit*, this was why she wasn't a surgeon. This was why—

A large warm hand engulfed hers.

"Paige." Ty's deep calm voice interrupted her mental panic. "Dr. Carlyle," he said again when she didn't respond, because she was in full freak-out mode and trying to breathe without passing out.

"Look at me. Good," he said when she lifted her head. "Don't think about it. Just follow the sound of my voice and do exactly what I say. Okay?"

She dropped her gaze and tried to swallow past the growing panic in her throat.

"Hey." He leaned forward to catch her gaze. His eyes were no longer cold and remote but warmly encouraging, full of strength and confidence…in her. *Gulp.* "You'll be fine. Now say, 'I'm okay, Ty, I've got this.'"

She sucked in a shaky breath, licked dry lips and repeated, "I'm okay, Ty. I've got…" *gulp* "…this."

"Good." He gave her a hand a brief squeeze before letting go. "Without overthinking everything, let your training take over. Make the incision. Not too hard, just enough to cut through skin and muscle." Repeating his instructions in her head, Paige filtered out everything but the sound of his voice. "Excellent. Now push your fingers through the muscle until you feel the brachial artery…got it? Okay, gently palpate it to ensure it's not the cephalic vein or the median nerve. For God's sake, don't kink or sever that nerve or—"

"I'll cause paralysis. Yes, I know. Now what?"

His mouth twitched at her impatient tone. "Have you isolated the artery? Push aside the muscle with one hand and clamp the artery with the other." Clamps appeared in her field of vision and she fumbled a little as she took them. "Careful…you don't want it to rip. Have you got it?"

Paige rolled her eyes and looked around. "Yes, I've got it. Can we move her now?"

"No," he said, rising to his feet to beckon Nate and two rangers who'd stayed behind to help. "You can loosen the tourniquet and make sure that arm doesn't move. We haven't finished yet."

Paige twisted her body out of the way and immobilized Grace's arm while the men moved in. For an interminable moment the crumpled seats refused to budge until Ty muttered beneath his breath. Before Paige could open her mouth to tell him to stop, he gripped metal and pulled. There was a lot of grunting and swearing until the mangled metal finally gave way.

Grace Parker cried out as the pressure on her arm eased and Paige scrambled to cover her with her body. Eyes tightly closed, she waited for the entire mess to come snapping back…but after a couple of beats she heard Ty say, "*Dammit,* Paige, that was stupid."

Careful not to jostle the injured teacher, Paige spun around to tell him he was the idiot when she caught his involuntary grimace. Just then Grace gave a low moan and tried to sit up.

"Careful there," Paige soothed, gently applying pressure to keep her still. "Don't move. I'm not finished yet."

The teacher sucked in a sharp breath. "Did…did you have to c-cut it off?" she slurred, more than a little out of it.

"Nope," Paige said promptly. "It's still here." She quickly filled a syringe with pain meds while Nate and

Ty moved Grace to a more accessible area. "I'm giving you something for the pain and I want you to close your eyes and relax. We've got you."

Within seconds the woman had slipped away again and Paige readied herself to perform a ligation. She needed to do it quickly or the tissue would necrotize and Grace would lose her arm after all.

She irrigated the area and prepared the suture kit while Ty awkwardly swabbed the wound one-handed, then she clamped the other end and very carefully sutured the severed artery. When they got Grace back to the hospital the orthos would be waiting to repair the damage properly.

Once she was done, Ty slowly removed the first clamp, testing the integrity of the ligation. After a couple of beats Ty grunted his satisfaction and removed the second clamp so the blood flow could resume.

"Great job, Dr. Cutie," Nate said, giving her shoulder a tight squeeze. "You should have joined the army. You'd have made a kick-ass field surgeon."

Realizing she was still holding her breath, Paige let it go with an audible whoosh. She flashed a look at Ty to gauge his reaction but his face was set in a hard unreadable mask.

Yeah. So much for, "Great job, Paige, I couldn't have done better." Realizing she'd been waiting for his approval, Paige shook her head at herself and inflated the BP cuff. Everyone held their breaths as the needle fell...and fell... finally bobbing at around seventy.

"Better," Ty murmured, and rose, turning away to hide his involuntary wince. But for some reason she was becoming an expert on Ty Reese body language. He'd clearly wrenched his shoulder again.

Men!

Planning to catch him before she went back to the hospital, Paige quickly finished up, but by the time Frankie and Dale moved in to take over, he'd vanished.

Slouched low in his chair, Ty propped his feet on the deck railing, wincing as pain lanced through his shoulder. He needed to get ready for dinner with his father but moving meant using muscles he'd abused earlier today.

Lifting the beer bottle to his mouth, he admitted a little ruefully that maybe he'd been an idiot to help move those seats. But he'd seen Paige do what needed to be done without turning a hair. What else could he do but be a man?

He hated to admit it, but she'd been right about him. He *was* mad at the world. Mad that he'd been forced to rely on the skills of someone else to save his hand. Mad that he was living in a limbo caused by a drunken idiot who'd ploughed into a crowd of theatergoers because Ty looked like someone he had a grudge against. Mad that everything continued as though his world hadn't come crashing down.

But at least he was walking, he thought with self-disgust. One victim of the hit-and-run had died and at least another had a crushed pelvis. He had no right to feel as though he was the only one affected by one man's drunken rage.

Yet Paige hadn't hesitated to put herself between her patient and danger. She'd wanted nothing more than to be there for her young patients but she'd stepped in because... because he was a coward and there'd been no one else.

Then Nate had complimented her and suddenly Ty couldn't get away fast enough. He'd been filled with such self-loathing that he'd snarled at Nate's suggestion that he have his shoulder checked out.

He didn't need anyone to tell him he'd torn something. He was still a doctor, damn it. And no one was going to bully him into anything he didn't want and wasn't ready for—especially a feisty little medic with big eyes, a soft mouth and an even softer heart.

The memory of her stiff spine and huge hazel eyes filled with challenge and reproof as she'd squared off with him made him smile. She might look like a strong wind would blow her away but she was tougher and…he chuckled… meaner than she looked.

A whisper of sound caught his attention a beat before light spilled onto the deck and the person he'd been thinking about opened the French doors and stepped outside.

She looked towards his darkened sitting room and must have noticed that his French door was open because she stomped towards it, muttering about people leaving an "open invitation to the crazies of this world".

"Need something?"

She uttered an ear-piercing shriek and stumbled back a couple of steps, nearly falling over a deckchair. "*Dammit,*" she swore, catching herself. "Stop *doing* that!" For a few moments her heavy breathing filled the darkness, reminding him of things he hadn't had in a while. Things he'd convinced himself this morning that he didn't feel for Paige Carlyle.

Things that should have scared him into escaping back to California but which kept him glued to the lounger because he was tired of running. She stomped closer and demanded, "What the heck are you doing, sitting out here? It's freezing."

He reached out, snagged her hand and pulled.

She gave a startled "Oomph," and tumbled right into his lap. "What—what are you *doing*?" she squeaked, as light from her apartment spilled over her shocked face.

And then Ty did what he'd told himself he didn't want. He swooped down and crushed her soft mouth with his.

He'd meant it as punishment for everything she'd put him through but the instant his mouth touched hers he wanted more.

A lot more.

To prevent her from escaping, he slid his left hand up her back and buried his fingers in her cool, soft hair. She uttered a muffled protest and made to push away but Ty tightened his grip, opening his mouth over hers to snatch her breath, silence her protest.

His sudden intensity must have startled her because she gasped, and he took advantage by thrusting his tongue into her warm, wet mouth.

He tasted surprise and something hot and hungry and suddenly he was desperate for the taste of her in his mouth and the feel of her naked skin against his. And then even if he'd wanted to, he couldn't have stopped because she suddenly straddled him and he was seeing more stars than there were currently in the night sky. The move surprised him and he was abruptly harder than he'd ever been in his life—in less than two seconds flat.

She took advantage of his momentary surprise by fisting both hands in his hair and dragging him closer, as though she was afraid he'd try to escape. But Ty wasn't going anywhere. Instead, he slid both arms around her and responded with a hunger that might have shocked him if he'd been able to do more than growl with the need clawing at his gut.

Things went a little crazy then as Ty kissed her the way he liked it, hot and wet and deep. She made little mewling sounds and responded, closing her teeth around his tongue.

It made him grin and slide his hand up her back to cup her head. When he finally ran out of air, he broke away to graze his lips across her jaw towards the soft skin just below her ear.

She tasted like temptation, soft and delicious…so delicious that he found himself humming in the back of his throat and testing another patch of skin.

She was breathing like she'd just swum across the strait, and since he was too, he punished her by biting down on the tender lobe he'd exposed.

She jolted, her fingers clenching reflexively. Since they were still buried in his hair, the sharp pain made him nip her again until a delicate shudder moved through her. She made little huffing sounds that shouldn't have turned him on but did—and began rolling her hips, the hottest, softest part of her pressing into the hardest part of him.

In no time he was shuddering and huffing because… *Holy cow*, she was the sexiest thing he'd ever kissed and he was suddenly desperate to feel all her softness beneath him, feel her around him as he thrust home.

With one thought—to get them both naked—Ty made to roll her beneath him. The move had him sucking in air as sharp pain tore through his shoulder. He stilled, hoping it would go away because there was no way he was stopping now.

But Paige must have heard that involuntary sound of pain because she froze. "What—?" she gasped, looking as stunned as he felt. "What's wrong?"

"Nothing."

His gaze dropped to her swollen mouth and he tried to pull her back but fire engulfed his shoulder and he couldn't suppress a groan.

"I knew it," she said breathlessly, scrambling off his lap and making his eyes cross because… *Holy cow.* "You're hurting."

He huffed out a laughing curse and grabbed her hand to keep her from escaping, drawing her between his knees.

He grimaced and shifted to adjust his position. "Then why are we stopping?"

She must have seen the direction of his gaze because she uttered a startled snort. "Not that, dummy," she wheezed huffily, and yanked her arm free. "Your shoulder. You hurt it again."

"What? No, it's just a little stiff, that's all."

Paige pressed her lips together but a weird grunting kind of snort escaped. She tried to look innocent but Ty had no trouble following her train of thought because his erection was still pressed against her.

"Okay," he admitted with an unabashed grin. "So 'little' is a gross misrepresentation but I was actually referring to my shoulder, Miz I'm-not-so-sweet-and-innocent."

She rolled her eyes, not looking the least bit offended by the name. "I grew up with three older brothers," she said, pointing an accusing finger at him. "And stop trying to distract me. I was also talking about your shoulder. Not…" She waved her hand at his lap. "Not that."

Chuckling, he tried to roll his shoulder and had to suck in a sharp breath. Okay, so maybe it was a little more than stiff. Not that he would admit it, though.

"You're lying. You tried to be a macho hero today and tore something, didn't you?"

Irritated and hurting in more than one area of his anatomy, Ty rolled off the lounger and rose. "Quit nagging, I'm fine. Now," he growled, moving stiffly towards the open French door, "if you'll excuse me, I'm going out."

"To the hospital, I hope," she huffed, following as he headed inside.

He scoffed, "Don't be ridiculous," and turned to block her path with a big arm across the doorway. "I'm a trauma surgeon. I know how to treat an injury."

She canted her hip and folded her arms beneath her breasts. "Fine, then you won't mind if I see it."

For a moment he was irritated as all hell; then he slowly allowed his mouth to curl, instinctively knowing how to distract her. "Why didn't you just say so?" he drawled, enjoying the play of emotions across her face.

Paige stared at him for a couple of beats, her brow wrinkled in confusion, but Ty knew the instant she caught on because her mouth dropped open and a wild flush bloomed beneath her skin.

"You…you…*guy*," she stuttered, looking as though she didn't know whether to laugh or hit him. Finally, she huffed out an exasperated breath and spun away. "Fine," she snapped, stomping off, muttering, "I hope it falls off."

Before she could slam the door, Ty called out, "My arm or…?"

In a thrice it whipped open and she yelled, "Use your imagination." She was about to disappear but stuck her head out to snap, "And another thing. Wear a damn bell or quit sneaking up on me. Next time I might be holding a carving knife."

Ty was chuckling when her door finally slammed. He waited a couple of seconds, half expecting another insult, but her light was switched off, leaving the deck in darkness.

Leaving Ty alone.

Yeah, he thought as his amusement faded. Exactly how he wanted it.

Wasn't it?

CHAPTER SIX

A WEEK LATER, Paige arrived home and made a beeline for the kitchen. It had been a crazy day and she'd barely had time to think, let alone eat or catch a minute for a break.

She put on coffee and opened the overhead cabinet before remembering that she'd used the last mug that morning.

Muttering about her lax housekeeping skills, she kicked off her shoes and headed for the deck. She vaguely remembered seeing the rest of the mugs scattered there, mostly because she tended to get sidetracked in the morning and kept leaving them either on the deck railing, the steps, or on the wooden patio table.

But when she opened the French doors she found all eight mugs on the table, sparkling clean as though waiting for her to bring out the coffee.

Her eyes widened. And that wasn't all. The beach towels she'd draped over the wooden deck chairs to air out a few days ago were neatly folded beside the mugs.

Eyebrows rising up her forehead, Paige looked around to thank the cleaning fairies and found a half-naked Ty sprawled in the lounger, fast asleep.

Without her permission, her gaze swept over that wide, tanned expanse of awesomely sculpted chest to the eight-pack abs she'd been dreaming about licking...*phew*...and the happy trail that disappeared into a pair of faded low-slung jeans.

To her absolute horror her nipples tightened and her knees wobbled. She grabbed the back of the nearest chair to keep from falling and told herself it was hypoglycemia giving her such a head rush.

He, on the other hand, looked disgustingly healthy—not to mention *really* hot—and relaxed, and the fading bruises were barely visible on his sun-warmed skin. She glared at him and barely resisted the urge to grab the pitcher of water beside him and cool him the heck off.

"Don't even think about it," he warned in a voice rough and deep with sleep.

Pulse bumping up a couple notches, Paige screwed up her face. It was the first time she'd seen him since the night of "The Kiss" and despite trying very hard not to, she'd found herself worrying—and thinking—about him at the most inconvenient times. Worrying about his shoulder, his hand and…and darn it, she worried that he wasn't taking care of himself.

Which was really stupid and girly. Of course he could take care of himself. He was all grown up. She gulped and mentally fanned herself. Especially in nothing but those low-slung faded jeans that drew her eyes like a magnet because they lovingly cupped him in cuppable places.

"Think about what?" she asked in an attempt at innocence, but either Tyler Reese could read minds or she wasn't a very good actress. One arched brow made her suspect the latter.

His mouth curved as he swept his sleepy blue gaze over her. She'd had some pretty hot dreams about that mouth, *dammit,* as well as his broad shoulders…wide chest… washboard abs…lower— Dreams she'd awakened from all sweaty, flustered and extremely frustrated.

"What?" she demanded, conscious of the fact that while he looked rested and relaxed, she was feeling—and probably looking like—the effects of a hectic week.

He yawned and scrubbed a hand down his face. "You try throwing water on me and you won't like my reaction."

"I'm not worried," she said smugly. "Look at you, getting soft with all the lazing around. I took you down once and I can do it a—" Her words ended on a shocked squeak when she found herself beneath him on the lounger. He'd moved so fast she hadn't seen it coming until she was flat on her back with his big, hard body covering hers.

She blinked and found his lean dark face a couple inches above hers. "Wha…?" A delicious heat and lethargy invaded her limbs.

No, darn it. Not delicious, a voice yelled in her head. *Dangerous. And unwelcome.*

Yeah, Paige, unwelcome…because…because… *Oh, boy.* She sucked in a lungful of warm delicious man and couldn't for the life of her recall… What was she supposed to remember again?

"You were saying?" Ty smirked as though he could read her thoughts and all she could do was swallow and say, "Huh?"

At her eloquent response, Ty gave a crooked grin that was far too appealing for her liking.

"Look at you." He snickered, mimicking her. "All flustered and flushed, and my personal favorite…speechless."

"If I'm……speech-less, you big lug," she pretend-wheezed, "it's…because… I…can't…breathe."

He immediately shifted his weight to his uninjured elbow but instead of allowing Paige to breathe easier, it pressed a certain part of his anatomy—a very long, thick, hard part—into a certain corresponding part of her anatomy.

And look at that—she lost her breath, this time for real.

"You're…um…" She broke off and squirmed, her face heating when he just grinned.

"Just ignore it."

"Oh, right." Paige spluttered out a laugh. Like that was even possible with that…yes, *that* jabbing her in the thigh. Or the hard, flat *naked* belly against hers. Or the way his thigh pressed against her— *How the heck had he sneaked a leg between hers?*

"Seriously," he advised as though she wasn't already melting. "Don't give it another thought…unless…"

She stilled, her eyes narrowing suspiciously. "Unless what?"

"Unless you wanna check it out," he said casually, his eyes beginning to crinkle at the corners.

"What? No," she gasped in outrage, giving his shoulders a bad-tempered shove, moving him…nowhere. "Is that how you charm your women, Reese? Play doctor and get them to give you a…a…physical?"

"I was talking about my shoulder," he said dryly, and with one economic move rolled off the lounger and rose to his feet. Huffing like a steam engine—because no way had he meant that—Paige found herself admiring the play of muscles beneath all that smooth warm skin. Flesh that until a second ago had been so close she'd have been able to lean forward and lick it.

"You planning on sleeping, Dr. Cutie?" Ty asked over one wide shoulder.

"Call me that and die," she said sleepily, propping her head on her hand and transferring her gaze to the view the deck afforded of the sea, harbor and marina. "But to answer your last question, I think I might. Not all of us get to nap in the afternoon. But… I see why you like it here. It's beautiful."

"It sure beats watching what passes for daytime television around here," he said dryly, scratching his naked chest and stretching the kinks out of his back. Finding her attention locked on his chest—again—she shifted her gaze and caught sight of the mugs.

That reminded her of food.

"You didn't happen to see any faeries cleaning the deck while you were lazing the day away, did you?" she asked, rolling to her feet with a big yawn. "I'd like to thank them."

"You're welcome."

Surprised and a little confused, she blinked up at him. "Huh?"

"I said you're welcome."

It took Paige a couple seconds to compute. "You?" she said, gaping at him. "You're the—?"

"Cleaning faerie."

Immediately an image of Tyler Reese dressed in a pink tutu, tights, wings and a crown popped front and center in her mind. Before she could stop it, a snort emerged and by the expression on his face—speechless and a little pissy—her reaction was clearly as unwelcome as it was unexpected.

She slapped a hand over her mouth to stifle her amusement but it just grew and grew until it finally burst out of her. In seconds she was howling with laughter.

In fact, she laughed so much she had to sit down, plopping back down on the lounger. After a few minutes she calmed down enough to see through tears of mirth. His expression of annoyed exasperation mixed with reluctant amusement nearly set her off again but she managed to keep it to a couple of strangled chuckles. Finally she sighed and wiped her eyes. She hadn't laughed like that in ages. It felt good. Almost as good as seeing him at a loss for words. She bet that didn't happen very often.

"You about done?" he inquired politely.

She grinned up at him, all her previous fatigue forgotten.

"I bet you look awesome in a pink tutu and tights." She ran her eyes over his wide, sculpted chest and shoulders and had to remind herself that Tyler Reese was the hottest thing she'd seen since she'd been seventeen and her brother Quinn had brought home a SEAL friend for the holidays. She'd stupidly fallen for a pretty face and a hot body, only to have her heart broken when he'd pursued everything with breasts. Everything except her, of course.

She cringed at the memory of practically throwing herself at him, although to be fair she'd been a little young—and a lot inexperienced—for him. But he'd barely noticed when she'd worn her brand-new bikini, ruffling her hair like she'd been six or something. She'd made sure it was the last time she'd been home when one of her brothers brought home a friend.

Fortunately she wasn't seventeen and had had a few—some kind of serious—relationships over the years but she wasn't stupid enough to fall for another BAB because of sexy blue eyes and a warm hard body.

No way...no matter how good a kisser he was.

Good? Try out-of-this-world spectacular. But guys like Ty Reese and Dean Walker barely noticed her beyond the fact that she was Quinn's cute little sister...or...or the annoying neighbor they wanted to ignore.

She sighed. *Yep. Story of her life.*

Because she couldn't take all eight mugs at once, Paige hurried into the house with four and made a beeline for the kitchen. The coffee was finished and a delicious aroma filled the air, reminding her that she'd barely eaten all day. Her stomach growled loudly.

"Caffeine, then I promise to feed you," she muttered to her stomach. Or maybe a cold shower, she thought, rolling her eyes at the blood still pumping through her veins at warp speed. The darned man was potent and the only way to keep her heart safe was to avoid him like mildew.

She poured coffee into her favorite mug, turning to the fridge for milk, and promptly collided with a human wall. She lurched back with a shriek and bumped into the counter, spilling scalding coffee over her hand.

She managed a painful gasp before Ty whisked the mug away and shoved her whole hand and half her arm under the cold tap.

"What—what the heck are you doing?" She gaped up at him as water splashed everywhere.

"That was careless of you," he murmured deeply into her hair, sending an army of goose-bumps marching down her spine. And because it left her backed into the corner of the counter, surrounded by delicious masculine heat, the goose-bumps morphed into arrows of heat pinging in her belly.

Oh, heck, no.

"Me?" she demanded on an outraged squeak as she tried to yank her hand free. *No tingling, pinging or melting allowed, dammit.* "What did I tell you about sneaking up on me?"

He sent her a chiding look that said she should be thanking him, not giving him a hard time. *Yeah, right.*

"Fortunately you're not holding a knife."

"I could always get one," she muttered defensively. "Fortunately for you I'm too hungry to fight with you."

He gave a soft grunt and muttered something that sounded like, "Too bad, I wouldn't mind seeing you try." And reached over to snag a kitchen towel. With her palm gently cradled in his he proceeded to dry her hand and arm. "It's a little red but no permanent damage done. You should be more careful."

"I wouldn't have to be careful if people stopped sneaking up on me," she muttered, her gaze on the dark silky head bent over her hand. Her fingers looked pale and delicate in his, making her feel excruciatingly feminine and, darn it, sending sensation zipping up her arm.

He looked up then and before she knew it, she was drowning in his startling blue eyes.

"Um…" she said, locking her knees against the urge to melt at his feet—wouldn't he just love that? His pupils widened until only a thin ring of blazing blue remained and before she knew it her mind went utterly blank.

Finally he took a step back and shoved a hand through his hair, rumpling the already tousled strands. "Why don't…?" He cleared his throat and tried again. "Why don't you change out of those…um, wet scrubs and I'll take you to dinner?"

Paige's eyes widened at the unexpected invitation. "You mean like a…a *date*?" But when his answer was to turn and stare at her as though she'd suggested something illegal, Paige cringed inside, wishing she could recall her words. *Yeesh*. Was she a sucker for punishment or what?

"No, I mean like dinner…between…" His breath whooshed out and he looked a little panicked. "I mean, you're hungry, I'm hungry and I'd like… I've seen the contents of your refrigerator." And when she continued to stare at him, he growled, "Dammit, you want dinner or not?"

"I want," she said primly, secretly pleased that she'd managed to rattle him because—if she wasn't mistaken—he'd definitely been about to kiss the socks off her. "But I warn you, I'm starving. And I want dessert."

A dark brow rose up his forehead. "Dessert?"

"Yep." She nodded, pushing away from the counter and heading for the door. "And wine. Lots of wine."

Ty took her to a steak house on the waterfront, mostly because he was craving steak and the Surf 'n Turf served the best in town, but also because it had a great view of the harbor.

Okay, and maybe he'd been a little bored and was looking for company. He, Tyler Reese, king of the I-want-to-be-aloners was sick to death of his own company. He needed a distraction and who better to distract him than his very distracting neighbor?

She was sexy and feisty and she made him smile when he hadn't felt like smiling for a long time. There was just something about her that drew him in despite himself. Earlier on the deck he'd wanted to kiss her more than he'd wanted his next breath and the overwhelming impulse to take her there in front of the entire marina had scared him.

Okay, try terrified, because Paige Carlyle didn't strike him as the fling type. His parents should never have married, partly because his father was a workaholic and forgot he had a family but mostly because his mother didn't know the meaning of compromise. She'd grown up wealthy and had expected Henry Chapman to keep her in the style to which she'd been accustomed. And while he'd tried, by working around the clock, she'd resented any time he spent away from her.

For a long time Ty had resented that too because he'd had to live with the fallout when his mother's marriages imploded. As a kid he'd been dragged from one house and stepfather to the next. He'd had no say in any of it and had vowed that once he grew up *he'd* be the one in control.

His accident had made him feel like a kid again, helpless against the whims of others. So he'd take Paige to dinner and when he left her at her door at the end of the evening, that would be that.

He'd stay away—for good this time.

It was still early and the dinner crowd was thin but Paige looked around with interest, giving Ty the impression that she hadn't been there before. Why that idea appealed to him, he had no idea. It wasn't even like this was a real date.

A bouncy teenager dressed in jeans and a Surf 'n Turf golf shirt approached and cheerfully asked where they would like to sit. She took one look at Ty and blushed, fumbled the menus and blushed even more when she dropped them.

Paige bent to help and with a quick laugh rose to her feet, chattering about how she'd love a view of the harbor. The waitress hurried over to a window table and stuttered when she handed Ty a menu and nearly took out his eye.

After she left, Paige said reproachfully, "You scared her."

"Me? What did I do?"

"You're wearing your inscrutable surgeon's face. Some people find it scary."

Clearly she didn't consider herself "some people" because she never hesitated to tell him off. He found it a refreshing change from all the people—women especially—who wanted to appease him.

Paige Carlyle didn't strike him as an appeaser.

"You mentioned something the other day about growing up with three brothers."

"Uh-huh."

After a couple of beats of silence, he reached out a finger and pushed the plastic-coated menu down until he could see her eyes. He raised an eyebrow, surprised by her shuttered expression when she was usually so easy to read.

"What?"

"Mother, father, brothers?"

She tried to tug her menu away but when he held on, she growled at him.

"Fine," she said huffily. "Dad is living with his new wife and family in Tacoma. Bryn is the manager of a San

Diego football team, Eric's a Navy SEAL and Quinn's in the Air Force."

"And your mother? Is she also remarried?"

"No," she said flatly, a faint frown marring the smooth skin of her forehead. "She…um…she died when I was young."

"I'm sorry," he said quietly, dropping his hand. "I can see that it's still painful."

"Yes, well." She gave a ragged laugh. "What was even more painful was that less than two years later my father remarried and I suddenly had another family I didn't need or want." She shook her head. "He didn't even wait two years before…well, never mind," she dismissed quickly, taking a gulp of water the waitress had delivered. "I'm sure you don't want to hear the boring details of my sad and lonely adolescence."

She drew in a shaky breath and he could see her shake off her painful thoughts. When she next looked at him her eyes were huge and liquid in the soft lighting as they met his and he felt himself fall just a little bit. Before he could catch himself, she asked, "What about you?"

Huh? "Me?"

"How bad is it?"

He shook his head to dispel the notion that she was bewitching him and that he was letting her. He stilled, a thread of panic winding its way through his chest. *Not just no way, but no way in hell.* He was letting the atmosphere—and memories of his own sad and lonely childhood—affect him, that's all.

"It?"

She lowered her lashes and the lacy pattern they made on her cheeks drew his fascinated gaze until she murmured, "Your injury," abruptly jolting him out of the sensual haze she was spinning with her eyes.

Cursing himself for behaving like a love-struck adolescent, Ty hitched a shoulder. "Only time will tell," he said casually to hide the churning in his gut. *Dammit*. He needed to get a grip before Little Miss Medic had him rolling over and begging for treats.

Tyler Reese, rising trauma surgeon, didn't beg for anything from anyone…least of all women. He was in control. Like always.

She nibbled on her lip, clearly wanting to say something more. And just when he thought she was going to offer her sympathy—or, worse, get him to talk about his feelings—she said, "So, you really washed my mugs and cleaned the deck?"

He sighed, a mix of relief, gratitude and impatience that she was still an annoying pain in the ass. "Why should that surprise you?"

She shrugged, flashing him a guilty look before retreating behind her menu. "No reason," she said quickly. "No reason at all except…"

"Except what?"

"Well, you're a surgeon," she said impatiently, as though that was reason enough.

Tired of talking to plastic, he whipped the menu away and demanded, "What does being a surgeon have to do with cleaning up after myself?"

"Well, technically it was cleaning up after me," she said primly, and when he just stared at her, Paige continued. "You have to ask? Really?" She sighed. "Fine. Surgeons don't exactly have a reputation for cleaning up messes. They swoop in like demi-gods, save the injured and dying with their mad, awesome skills and then disappear, leaving the grunt work to the rest of us peons."

"*Us* peons? You're a pediatrician. What's peon-ish about that?"

She sniffed and stole his menu out from under his nose. "Surgical rotation," she explained, looking pleased with her sneakiness. She was silent a couple of beats before saying casually, "So did you?"

Confused by her rapid changes of direction, he asked, "Did I what?"

She rolled her eyes like he was being deliberately obtuse. "Wash my mugs and clean my deck."

"Technically the deck is half-mine—okay, fine," he sighed, scrubbing a hand down his face. "The place was a mess. All I did was stick the mugs in the dishwasher and pay a kid ten bucks to clean the deck. No big deal."

She choked and stared at him, her eyes going huge. "T-ten bucks? You paid a kid *ten bucks* to clean the deck? *Yeesh. I* would have done it for ten bucks."

He snorted but before he could point out that she was a specialist and must be earning good money, the waitress arrived to take their order.

He ordered wine and the biggest rare steak on the menu with a side salad while Paige ordered the lady's steak with fries and vegetables. When the food came, Ty watched her face light up as she tucked right in. Clearly she hadn't been kidding about being starved.

After a few seconds she realized he was staring at her and paused with her fork halfway to her mouth.

"What?" she demanded, looking like she'd been caught with her hand in the cookie jar. "I'm hungry, okay?" She grimaced and put down her fork as though realizing she'd been almost inhaling her food. "ER was so busy today I didn't get a chance to eat or drink," she said a little defensively.

"What are you doing in ER if you've already specialized in pediatrics?"

Paige's sigh did amazing things to the simple cut of her

bodice and just about fried a couple of billion brain cells. Brain cells that he would need if he was going to have to make tough decisions about his future…or resist the sensual web she was spinning around him.

Completely oblivious to his burgeoning brain aneurysm, she said, "Money," on a rush of expelled air and a flush of embarrassment.

"Money?" He was surprised. He hadn't pegged her as the kind of woman who'd pursue a career for money. But, then, he'd been wrong about women before, so what the hell did he know? "Surely you can't be earning much here. In fact, I know that working in the city would pay a hell of a lot more."

An odd look clouded her features before she reluctantly admitted, "It's not that." She was silent a moment before shrugging and picking up her fork to poke at her food. "I had a scholarship so…"

"Ah." He nodded in comprehension. "So you have to go where they tell you."

"Yes. Fortunately, I was sent here." She turned to look at the scene outside the restaurant window. Lights lit up the harbor and boardwalk, reflecting off the water and the boats moored there. He knew without looking what she saw. A pretty, picturesque town nestled between the Straits of Juan de Fuca and the Olympic National Park. "I know someone who was sent to a one-horse town in the middle of nowhere where mountain men grunt, spit and scratch themselves in public. Believe me, this is paradise."

She pushed her plate aside and before he knew what she was doing she'd pulled his plate closer and was cutting his steak into bite-size pieces. "I have another year to go and until then I have to put in my time in ER where I'm needed."

A little disconcerted by her actions, he said absently, "I can speak to my father—"

"No," she said firmly, interrupting him before he could finish his sentence. "Thank you, but a contract is a contract. Besides, I've got this."

Amusement and admiration warred with exasperation at her fierce independence. "I'm sure you have," he said mildly. "But it's not a sign of weakness to accept help once in a while."

"It is if it comes with strings," she retorted.

"Strings?" He was confused for a couple of beats and then his jaw dropped at her implication. "You think my father would…?" The idea was shocking and something he'd never, *never* considered. Could Henry Chapman be capable…?

"What? *No!*" She gaped at him, clearly just as shocked by his suggestion. "What a terrible thing to say about your own father."

He was mollified by her angry denial until he thought of something else that made his stomach cramp. "You can't mean that *I* would…?"

"No!" A wild flush of horror and mortification heated her cheeks. "I didn't mean *that* either," she muttered, attacking the steak with renewed vigor. *"Jeez."*

Thoroughly confused, Ty searched Paige's expression for clues about what she meant but she'd hidden behind a swing of silky black hair. "Then what the hell *did* you mean?" he demanded.

Without replying, she shoved his plate back across the table, glaring at him as though he'd suggested something indecent. Which, of course, he had and it had completely freaked him out thinking of his father and— No, not going to think about…that.

Too freaky.

Another thing that was *just* as disturbing was thinking about Paige with someone who'd demand payment for doing a small favor.

It made him wonder what kind of men she knew.

"Only as a general statement, *yeesh*. All I'm saying is that generally if people do someone a favor they expect something in return. Besides…" she waved her fork in the air "…guys don't…" She stopped abruptly. Face flaming, she dropped her gaze to stab bad-temperedly at her steak.

Ty leaned back in the booth, fascinated by the myriad emotions chasing across her delicate features. "Well, don't stop there, Dr. Cutie," he drawled. "Not when this conversation is getting so very interesting." He waited for her reaction and when it came—in the form of a poisonous glare—he prompted, "Guys don't what?"

Her soft mouth firmed. "Nothing."

Leaning across the table, he repeated, "Guys don't what?"

"Think of me that way, okay?" she snapped, pressing her lips together as though to prevent any more secrets from spilling out. "Happy now?"

Baffled, he studied her mutinous expression, searching for clues to her thoughts, and when she stubbornly remained silent, he asked mildly, "And what way is that?"

Her reply was a huge eye–roll, as though he was the dumbest person alive. Hiding a smile, he picked up his fork and speared a succulent piece of steak. "I hate to disagree with you," he said dryly, "but guys most *definitely* think of you that way."

CHAPTER SEVEN

BY THE TIME they left the restaurant, Paige was feeling pleasantly mellow. Whether it was from the excellent wine or the heat of Ty's body as he steered her towards his SUV, she couldn't tell, only that she felt relaxed for the first time in months. Years, maybe.

Okay, maybe not relaxed, she amended, catching sight of his hard profile and sculpted mouth in the dash glow. Buzzed. Like there was some weird energy source humming just beneath her skin.

It might have alarmed her if she'd been thinking clearly but she was still surprised by how much she'd enjoyed their spirited conversation—everything from her favorite toothpaste to the correct procedure for handling difficult patients.

She must have dozed off because the next thing she knew someone was shaking her. Muttering irritably, she tried to turn over but something had her pinned.

She frowned and opened her eyes, blinking in the light shining through the windshield. In the next instant she recognized... "Ty?"

She sat up and looked around, noting that they were parked in the street in front of the house. Her neighbor, looking big and badass, stood beside her open door, his face in darkness.

Her heart gave a funny little flutter that she told herself was alarm but she couldn't quite convince herself.

"Whaddid I miss?" she slurred, shoving a hand through her hair in an attempt to wake up.

"Here I thought my scintillating conversation had left you speechless," he drawled, and reached for her seat belt, "when all the while you were snoring."

She stuck her tongue out at him. "If it makes you feel better," she said, sliding out only to stumble against him, "I don't fall asleep on just anyone, you know."

She was almost certain it wasn't deliberate, but when he steadied her by pulling her against him, she decided to stay there a few moments longer to test her theory. Dropping her forehead against his warm solid chest, she gave a hum of pleasure because she couldn't remember the last time anyone had held her. Or the last time she'd *let* anyone hold her, never mind lean on them.

It was kind of nice.

She shivered. *Fine, so maybe nice wasn't quite the right—*

"You falling asleep there, Dr. Cutie?"

Okay, Paige thought with an inner sigh. *Moment over.*

She gave him a half-hearted punch for his transgression and shoved away. "I hate that name," she muttered, turning to stomp down the path and up the porch stairs. "I *really* hate that name. And the next person to call me that is gonna be sorry."

She stopped in front of her door and reached into her purse for her keys, sparing him an annoyed glance when he joined her. He was mostly in darkness but light from the single wall-sconce illuminated half his face, highlighting one cheekbone, his strong jaw and the deep bow of his top lip.

His mouth was smiling, suggesting he enjoyed baiting her.

She yanked out the front door key and pointed it at him accusingly. "You're lucky you have such a pretty mouth," she announced. "Or I might be tempted to punch it."

He chuckled softly. "Men don't have pretty mouths," he said, snagging the key and inserting it in the lock. The door swung open and when she didn't move, he propped his shoulder against the frame, his gaze amused, patient.

"*You* do," she insisted, stepping close. Reaching out a finger, she traced the sculpted lines she suddenly wanted on hers more than she'd wanted anything, including that last mouthful of decadent chocolate dessert.

It took a moment to realize he'd stilled and when she did she abruptly dropped her hand and spun away, eager to pretend the rejection hadn't stung. Ty caught her hand and used it to tug her around. "That wasn't a rejection," he murmured, lifting her hand to his mouth.

At the move her eyes flew up and he held her gaze as he gently bit down on the soft pad of her finger.

Tingles instantly shot up her arm, and her knees wobbled. "What…?"

"That," he murmured, taking a nip out of another finger, "was surprise you didn't slug me. And just so we're clear here, there is *nothing* pretty about me."

His voice, deep and velvet-soft rasped against her flesh and spread delicious warmth across her flesh. "*You,* on the other hand…" his arm snaked around her and he yanked her against him hard enough to knock a startled gasp from her "…are pretty everywhere." His hot gaze dropped to her mouth. "Especially here."

Then he dipped his head and kissed her, laughing softly when she gasped again. He ignored the invitation, sliding south to gently kiss her throat and the fluttering pulse at the base of her neck.

"You drive me crazy, do you know that?"

Oh, yeah. Crazy, she knew. Crazy she was feeling right now—especially with his warm mouth moving up her throat and sparking a prickly heat in her blood.

"G-good crazy?" she rasped, her hands coming up to clutch at his shoulders. "Or...b-bad?"

He sucked a patch of delicate skin into his mouth, drawing a ragged moan from her throat. "Bad," he murmured. "Very...*very*...bad."

A heavy lassitude invaded her limbs and she was tempted to slide right to the floor in a puddle of pleasure, but she locked her knees and demanded, "Is that good bad...or—"

"Good," he interrupted hoarsely. "Bad...but good. Definitely good." And before Paige could draw in another breath, he whipped her through the front door and backed her up against the interior wall. "So good," he continued as though he hadn't just scrambled her brains, "that I want to find out just...how...bad you...can be."

Breathless at the speed with which he'd moved, Paige gaped up at him, partly because *she* couldn't move—but mostly because he'd shoved a thigh between hers. He moved and the hem of her dress rose another couple of inches, causing the material of his jeans to scrape roughly against her inner thighs.

A good kind of rough—the kind that promptly sent a rush of liquid heat flooding her belly.

"What...what are you doing?" she squeaked, shocked more by the sensations flooding her than the fact that she was letting him manhandle her. Again.

Instead of replying, he nudged the door closed and pressed his muscled thigh closer to ground zero. And then…*oh, boy*…she experienced a rush to rival all rushes. Her head went light and her limbs heavy or she would have objected to what he did next.

Muttering something beneath his breath, his mouth came down on hers as a big warm hand slid up her thigh. The kiss was hot and hungry and just a little bit out of control, but the instant he cupped her bottom, she jolted.

"I…um… Ty?" She felt intoxicated—a little tipsy, a lot off balance—like she'd downed an entire bottle of red wine instead of just two glasses.

"You taste good," he murmured against her throat. "Like fruit…" Another inhalation. "Or…marshmallows."

"Cherries," she blurted out breathlessly. "It's…um… cherries." Maybe. Probably. She couldn't think, couldn't breathe and when his teeth gently raked the tendon in her throat, she lost all feeling in her legs. She would have slid to the floor except for the hard thigh between hers.

"You make me hungry," he growled, moving up her throat to nip at her chin and swipe his tongue along her bottom lip.

His fingers squeezed her bottom and a desperate pulsing began deep in her belly. She shuddered. "I…uh…you've just eaten."

His chuckle was soft and deep. "Not that kind of hunger," he murmured, tracing an invisible line of fire from the corner of her mouth to her ear with his tongue. "The kind that's been driving me crazy since…the night…you… decorated…me in pink." Each word or phrase was accompanied by a nip with his sharp white teeth. "But things are about to change."

She heard a moan. Probably hers. "They…are?"

"Oh, yeah." Ty murmured something that sounded a lot like, "And I'm going to start right here." Then his hand slid beneath her panties to squeeze her naked bottom and Paige

nearly shot through the roof. Suddenly, any thoughts of resisting—*yeah, right*—faded and all she could concentrate
on were the sensations invading her body.

A whimper escaped that might have embarrassed her
if she'd been able to think clearly.

She wasn't. She could only feel.

And, boy, there was suddenly a heck of a lot *to* feel. His
chest, his hands, his mouth…his belly—oh, God—those
rock-hard abs and thighs…*everything* between. Every…
long…thick…hard…inch.

He growled and the sound stuck her as thrilling and
unbearably exciting. Breathing heavily, Ty lifted his head.

"Say it."

"Uh… I… What?"

"Say it."

"This is a b-bad idea?"

"The very worst," he murmured agreeably. So agreeably
that she pulled back and tried to shove him off her but he
simply pressed closer, cupping the back of her head in his
big palm and brushing his mouth across her cheekbone,
her mouth…her chin…her neck. In fact, everywhere he
could reach. Barely-there caresses that made her shudder
and lose her train of thought.

He must have felt it too because his mouth caught hers
and suddenly he was devouring it like he'd been starved of
oxygen and wanted to gulp it all in at once. Fill his lungs…
fill himself with her.

"Paige," he rasped, sucking in air like a drowning victim. "If you're going to stop…do it…now. Before I—"

"Don't," she growled fiercely, arching into his gently
grinding movements. "Don't…you…dare…stop or…or
I'll… *Oh*…" She was unravelling faster than she could
drag air into her lungs. "If you stop, I…promise…" another
breathy moan followed by a growl "… I'll… I'll hurt you."

His chuckle was as rough and ragged as her breathing. "Oh, yeah?" he said, teasing her with sharp little nips to her shoulder. "How bad can it be, Dr. Cutie?"

"Three brothers," she reminded him, turning her head to nip at his jaw in punishment. "They taught me to fight... dirty."

He stilled and after a couple of beats leaned back to look into her face. Eyes, hot and heavy, glittered beneath the slash of his dark brows.

"How dirty?" he demanded, looking dubious and hopeful at the same time.

Her slow smile was filled with reckless mischief. "Very... *very* dirty," she promised, and launched herself at him.

Stunned by the suddenness of her move, Ty stumbled back a few steps, barely catching her before she thudded against him. And before he could draw in his next ragged breath she wrapped her slender legs around his hips, grabbed his hair and yanked his mouth to hers.

Ty staggered backwards under the assault. His knees were as steady as cooked noodles and he felt drunk, as if he'd spent all weekend on a bender. But that was probably because she was sucking the air from his lungs and rubbing against his erection like she couldn't get enough.

"Wait..." he rasped, seeing stars and weaving like a drunken reveler at Mardi Gras. "God...*wait*!" They stumbled into the entrance table, knocking over the flashlight. Paige snorted a laugh against his mouth and clenched her thigh muscles, the move killing off a few more trillion brain cells.

He muttered a curse under his breath and changed direction, heading for the living room, needing to get them horizontal before he lost all feeling in his legs.

Paige refused to co-operate, sliding her tongue against

his and then giggling like a loon when they bumped into the wall, the archway and then a side table. A lamp went crashing to the floor and he lurched sideways. The next instant they tumbled onto the couch in a tangle of limbs.

For long tense moments neither of them moved except for their ragged breathing. It took him a few extra beats to realize that Paige was shaking, her whole body trembling.

Aw, man. Had he hurt her? He'd meant to twist so that she landed on him…not the other way around.

"Paige," he said, gently running a trembling hand down the elegant line of her spine. She was small, delicate and sweet…and gasping like he'd crushed her chest. "Paige…" he rasped, "you…okay?"

Then she gave a muffled snort and tried to bite him and Ty finally caught on. He fisted a hand in her hair and yanked her up and—yep, just as he'd thought.

He stared at her. Okay. Not so sweet.

"You're laughing?"

She gave another strangled snort and he dropped his head back, huffing out a laughing curse that had her giggling even louder. Then she tried to sort out their tangled limbs, managing somehow to shove her elbow in his trachea and knee him in the nuts.

"Holy hell, woman," he growled through the roaring in his head. "Watch where you put that knee."

He tried to grab her leg but his casted hand couldn't get a grip. Finally, with much fumbling and giggling, she got her knees under her and sat up, straddling his hips, all flushed and tousled and glowing with triumph.

He blinked up at her, breath working its way in and out of his lungs like bellows. And then he promptly lost it again when he *really* looked at her—hair tousled, mouth red and slick and swollen from his kisses.

Her eyes sparkled with mirth and…yeah, arousal. No

mistaking that. His heart gave a vicious kick against his ribs and he stilled, gazing up at her because, in that moment—flushed, half-naked and her face alight with laughter—he'd never seen anyone more beautiful.

For long moments they stared at each other. Something about his confused emotions must have shown on his face because her laughter faded and her eyes darkened uncertainly.

"If this is where you tell me that this is temporary and you're leaving soon, I know," she said, suddenly dead serious. "It's okay. In fact, it's great…really great, because…because that's all I'm offering too. This…" she gestured wildly, nearly whacking him in the face "…is it. A one-night-only offer."

Feeling both relieved and irritated, Ty caught her hand before she hurt herself or broke his nose. "That's not what I was going to say," he growled. "But I'm glad you said one night and not one time. Because, Dr. Carlyle, once won't be nearly enough."

Her brow rose. "Sounds like a challenge, Dr. Reese."

Even as his hands slid from her knees to her hips, pulling her in hard, Ty was shaking his head. "Not…a…challenge," he rasped. "A…promise."

Damn…she felt good. Better than good. Especially when she uttered a laughing gasp and placed her lips on his throat. Her tongue flicked out, and fire flashed across his skin, eliciting a deep groan. She lifted her head to gloat and he gently wrapped a hand around her neck, catching her mouth to launch his own assault.

Within seconds she was making those sexy sounds that threatened to blow his mind and she slid her soft palms down his chest to his zipper to press against his erection.

He felt his eyes roll back in his head. Her mouth curved

and with her stormy eyes locked on him, she slowly straightened and…popped the button.

The whirr of his zipper was drowned by her appreciative hum and the next instant her hand slid into his opened jeans to wrap around his length. He gave an involuntary moan.

"You like?" she purred, nipping at his lip and setting off a series of shudders that licked at his spine like fire.

"Oh, yeah," he croaked, wondering if he would be forced to turn in his man-card if he begged. And, *man*, he was close, very close to begging.

It took Ty less than five seconds to get naked, whipping around when she gasped.

"Omigod," she squeaked. "You're huge."

Rolling his eyes, he huffed out a ragged laugh. "I'm not *that* big, Paige." Then, abruptly realizing he'd just insulted himself, he quickly amended, "Okay, I am, but I'll go slowly. I promise."

With a wicked grin and a low appreciative sound, he lifted his hands to her breasts, brushing the backs of his fingers against the tight buds clearly visible through her dress. Her back arched and her head fell back, her eyes slowly drifting closed.

Her sigh sent an unnamed emotion slicing through to his chest to lodge right next to his heart. It felt a bit like heartburn but seemed an awful lot like affection and something much more dangerous…something he didn't dare name.

Desperate to ignore it, he surged up and whipped Paige's dress over her head. Her bra followed and, wrapping an arm around her, he flipped her over so he was kneeling between her splayed thighs.

Then he tugged her panties down her slender legs and tossed them over his shoulder before she could protest. And suddenly he couldn't breathe because she was finally beneath him, naked and flushed, looking like a sensual feast when he had no idea what to sample first.

"Don't…don't look at me like that."

He lifted his head and caught her biting her lip. Okay, so he did know where to start. He'd start at her mouth and work his way down to paradise.

Carefully balancing his weight on one elbow, he lowered his body over hers, groaning when her warm silky skin slid against his.

"Like what?" he murmured against her throat.

She turned her head, silently inviting his mouth to feast on her tender flesh. "Like you…want to, um…" ended on a sigh as though she'd forgotten what she wanted to say.

"Take a couple of hundred greedy bites out of you?"

"Yes…that." She sounded distracted, humming in the back of her throat as her hands explored his shoulders, his back and his butt. As though she needed to touch all of him at once.

He drew back far enough to see her eyes, soft and clouded with desire. Realizing he was studying her; she tried to cover herself.

"Nuh-uh." He laughed softly, catching her hands. "No hiding."

He stroked his hand up her belly to cup her breasts, thumbing her velvety areolas and watching in fascination as they tightened.

"Ty…" she choked out, squirming against him until he bent his head and took one nipple in his mouth, his hand skimming south, between her legs. *"Omigod,"* she whimpered when his thumb bumped against her little knot of nerve endings. It had her undulating into his strokes with growing urgency.

He'd been watching his hands explore her but at her gasp his gaze flew up and he couldn't look away. Her eyes drifted closed as he slid a finger between her tight folds, a flush of arousal staining her lightly tanned skin a deep beguiling rose. It was the hottest thing he'd ever seen.

He must have touched a particularly sensitive spot because her body spasmed and her eyes flew open, dazed and dark with arousal.

"Oh... I..." she breathed, and just when he thought it too much too soon, she moaned and parted her legs. Her hands rose to clutch his biceps as though she was afraid he might stop.

"Tell me."

"I...uh..." She gave an inarticulate little cry, bucking, straining against him when he added another finger.

He could feel her trembling on the edge and again ordered, "Tell me," as his thumb slowly circled the knot of nerves at her center.

Strung as tight as a bow, she breathlessly demanded, "*Omigod*, you want to talk *now*?"

"Tell me you want me and I'll give you what you need."

"I...want... I...*you*," she managed, her head tossing from side to side as she made soft huffing sounds, her face a mask of agonized pleasure.

"Good enough." He chuckled, keeping her balanced on the edge several moments more before finally giving her what she needed—an orgasm that took her apart as completely as it took her by surprise.

Her eyes flew open and locked on his as she shattered and it was the sweetest, most erotic thing he'd witnessed.

Finally, she collapsed beneath him, her eyes drifting shut on a ragged sigh. Quickly retrieving the condom from his jeans pocket, Ty rolled it down his shaft and then, lacing his fingers with hers, he lowered himself between her quivering thighs.

The moment his erection bumped against her damp

flesh, Ty saw stars. He gritted his teeth against the urge to thrust home and find release but he wanted to see her eyes go all misty with pleasure when she climaxed again.

"Again," he rasped.

She gave a ragged, breathless laugh and clutched at him. "I... I can't," she gasped, whimpering and squirming until he pinned her hips, rocking...rocking against her as he stared into her dazed expression.

The sight of her deepening flush was enough to make Ty go a little crazy then. His hand smoothed the length of her thigh, his long-fingered surgeon's hand detecting the fine quivers rippling just beneath her skin. Then he wrapped his hand around the back of her knee and gently lifted.

Positioning himself, he slowly pushed into her, groaning when her tight flesh clamped down on him. She immediately wrapped her legs and arms around him and bucked. Once. Twice.

Gritting his teeth for control, Ty sucked in a ragged breath and began to move. Slowly. He wanted it to build, to savor the incredible sensations, but Paige had other ideas. She gave an impatient growl and reared up, sinking her teeth into his shoulder. The unexpectedness of it jolted him and they fell off the couch, Paige landing on him with a surprised *"Oomph"*.

After a startled pause, she gave a muffled giggle that ended in a long low groan when Ty rolled them across the floor and thrust deep. Then he stilled, dropping his face into her neck to keep from having a brain explosion. Or maybe another kind of explosion. One that threatened to streak up his spine like a bolt of lightning and fry all his neuro-circuits.

Paige's breath hitched and she brought up her knees to hug his hips and score her nails down his spine. It was the impetus his body needed and before he knew it he was pulling out and shoving in deep, over and over again as he raced for the finish.

Gasping out a triumphant laugh, she threw back her head, looking so gorgeous and hot that he lost his legendary control. In seconds her body began to ripple around his and he watched, fascinated, as her eyes went blind. A wild flush rose beneath her skin and in the next instant she arched up and came, a long low moan torn from her throat.

The sight—and sounds—of her pleasure triggered his own and with a hoarse bellow he followed her over the edge.

CHAPTER EIGHT

IT WAS JUST before six when Paige pulled into the hospital staff parking. Her shift didn't start until seven but apparently good—*okay, spectacular*—sex gave her a massive burst of energy that left her tingling all over and raring to start the day.

Or maybe it was the full-blown freak-out she'd been heading for ever since she'd awakened wrapped in delicious heat and Ty's amazing man scent. Just the sight of him, sprawled face down across her bed, gloriously and edibly naked, had given her such a rush that she'd been tempted to jump his bones. Again.

Fortunately the cool bathroom air had cleared her head of all the intoxicating pheromones temporarily rendering her stupid.

Standing on the cold tiles, getting her breathing under control, it had seemed like a good idea to head into work early to avoid any awkward morning-after moments.

She sighed. Okay, so she'd panicked and run. *Big deal.*

It was over; she could finally get on with her life without obsessing about the sexy guy next door: *blah-blah-blah.* Besides, Ty wasn't the kind of man to get stupid over someone like her and wanting more was just…*stupid, okay.* It was stupid. She got that.

Yeesh.

He was just one of those hot temporary flings every woman deserved to experience at least once in her life. At the advanced age of thirty she'd finally done it. *Yay.*

Just then she caught sight of her reflection in the rear-view mirror and did a double take. *Yikes.* She was wearing a sappy grin that just screamed... *Paige Carlyle Got Lucky Last Night.* And that wouldn't do. So she promptly scowled to erase all evidence—along with memories—of the past eight hours.

See, she told her reflection smugly. *Easy as that.*

Mood lifting at the very adult way she was handling things, Paige got out and stretched all those aching muscles she'd forgotten she had. It also made her realize how hungry she was.

In fact, she was starving. So, instead of heading for ER, she walked through the automatic doors and hurried down the passage to the cafeteria. It was still early and the tables were mostly empty.

Grabbing a tray, Paige ordered coffee, a couple of pastries and then, because her breakfast looked unhealthy, added an apple just as her phone buzzed.

It was a text from "kick-ass grl". Turn around, it said, and when Paige turned, she saw Frankie holding up the far wall, booted feet propped on the chair beside her.

Paige quickly paid for her breakfast and headed over.

"How was your date?" Frankie asked casually the instant Paige got close. "The one I had to find out about from the waitress at Surf 'n Turf, by the way, because my *best friend* doesn't tell me anything."

Paige shrugged casually, hoping her expression didn't give her away. "It was more like a...favor."

She mentally rolled her eyes at the lie.

"Right," Frankie drawled. "A favor. Like having dinner with a sexy surgeon on vacation is a favor." She snorted

and waggled her eyebrows. "So did he do *you* any...
um...favors?"

"What? *No!*" Paige spluttered in protest, covering her
pink face by sliding into the opposite chair. She glared
at her friend. "Get your mind out of the gutter, will you?
It was a mutual *dinner* favor. My refrigerator was empty
and he...well, he needed someone to have dinner with so
people wouldn't feel sorry for him."

Frankie snorted her opinion of anyone feeling sorry for
Ty Reese. "And after?"

"After?" Paige asked innocently, reaching for a stick of
sugar. "What after?"

Out the corner of her eye she caught Frankie's narrow-
eyed scrutiny and tried not to look as guilty as she felt.
After a short pause the other woman's eyes widened and
her feet hit the floor with a loud thud. "You did it, didn't
you?" she accused. "You finally did it."

Startled, Paige paused in the process of dumping sugar
in her coffee. "Did what? What did I do?"

"Not what," Frankie snorted, pointing her finger reproachfully at Paige. "Who."

Heat climbed into her face and Paige grabbed the to-go
coffee to hide behind. "I have absolutely no idea what
you're talking about."

Reaching across the table, Frankie nudged Paige's hand
down and snorted. "Oh, yes, you do." Her eyes sparkled
with laughter. "You did Ty."

Gasping, Paige made an attempt to shush her but Frankie
smirked and chortled, "And by the look on your face, spec-
tacularly too."

Paige hissed at her to be quiet and darted a guilty look
around at the other patrons. "Dammit," she muttered, turning back with a scowl only to find Frankie grinning like
a loon.

"So-o-o-o-o," her friend said, drawing out the single word into about a million syllables. "Spill everything, Dr. Cutie. I need details."

Paige scowled. "What are we, twelve?"

"Of course not." Frankie snickered, looking cool and sophisticated even in her paramedic jumpsuit. "Not unless twelve-year-olds are having spectacular sex with hot surgeons. Besides," she continued, clearly enjoying Paige's discomfort, "it's about time you did something stupid."

"What?" *Did Frankie read minds now too?*

"Yep. Because getting involved with Ty?" She shook her head. "Stupid."

"Who said anything about getting involved?" Paige muttered irritably. "Besides, I told you it wasn't a date." Her face grew hot at Frankie's derisive snort. "And how the heck can you tell, anyway?" she demanded huffily. "It's not like I'm wearing a neon sign that says 'Paige Carlyle got some last night'."

Frankie's brow arched. "Maybe it's the hickey on your neck and the deer-in-the-headlights look."

Paige slapped one hand to her neck and the other to her eyes. "I do not!" she gasped, horrified that despite her efforts to appear as though everything was fine…it apparently wasn't even close.

Frankie reached into her shoulder bag and withdrew a compact mirror. "You most certainly do," she drawled, grinning when Paige grabbed for it. "You were also wearing a sappy grin when you walked in and no one smiles at the crack of dawn unless they got lucky."

Horrified, Paige fumbled the compact and finally got it open. Fortunately there was no sappy grin, but there *was* a hickey—no, two *dammit*. And then—*Omigod!*—she saw a third, on the upper curve of her breast when she pulled at the neck of her T-shirt.

"I do," she gasped, trying unsuccessfully to cover the damning evidence. "I totally do. I look like a…" She gulped and snapped her mouth closed.

Frankie leaned closer and prompted, "You look like a what?"

"Like a starved woman," Paige said firmly, grabbing a pastry and shoving it in her mouth. She was absolutely *not* going to discuss how she looked in case she started freaking out again.

"Satisfied and pretty darned smug, you mean." Frankie chortled. "If I wasn't so envious, I'd say good for you." Paige made a sound of distress and after a couple of beats Frankie leaned forward, all signs of amusement gone. "I hope you know what you're doing, Paige," she said quietly. "Ty is…"

She swallowed the pastry without tasting it. "Bad. Yep, got that." *But so* good *at being bad.* She hadn't thought she'd prefer Frankie's teasing but the sudden turn the conversation was taking had turned her stomach to lead because the truth was…she *didn't* know what she was doing.

Oh, boy.

She'd thought she could easily handle a casual fling, but she was beginning to suspect that she wasn't wired that way. It might have something to do with her childhood, but Paige tended to want the impossible. She wanted permanence and Ty…well, he was the last thing in permanence. She knew that.

She really did.

"He'll leave and—"

"Break my heart. Yes I *know.*"

Frankie's expression was a mix of affection, exasperation and concern. "I just don't want to see you hurt," Frankie said quietly.

"I'm not going to get hurt, Frankie," Paige sighed, reaching over to squeeze her friend's hand. "I know what I'm doing. Really."

But Paige didn't know what she was doing and it was all Tyler Reese's fault. *Damn him*. With his deep bedroom voice…and sexy blue eyes…and hot, hard body…

Oh, my lord, Paige thought in dismay. *I'm in trouble. Big, bad, sexy trouble.*

Ty woke to the sound of banging and for several moments he wondered where he was. That was until he'd got a whiff of Paige's seductive scent and went instantly hard when memories of the past eight hours flooded back in a rush of images.

He rolled over but even before his hand slid to the spot where he'd last seen her, he'd known he was alone. And some idiot was banging on the front door.

Grabbing a towel from the bathroom, he stomped down the stairs and yanked open the front door with a snarl on his lips.

Nate leaned against the wall, looking cool and wide awake as he studied Ty over the top of his aviator shades.

"What?" was Ty's surly demand to the other man's arched brow. He hadn't had much sleep but should've been relaxed after all the physical activity of the night before. Waking up alone hadn't been nearly the relief he'd thought it would be. In fact, he was feeling like a one-night stand—only in reverse because he was usually the one to bail before morning.

"Good morning to you too," Nate said holding up a food bag and a tray of to-go coffee.

Ty scrubbed a hand down his face and demanded, "What are you doing here?"

"I'm here to save you from the big bad Navy SEAL that

was waiting on your doorstep, looking like he was ready to use his government-trained assassin skills."

Ty looked around. "What SEAL?"

"Hey," Nate said, sounding insulted. Probably because he thought he was big and bad. "I was actually talking about the one looking for his sister." He offered Ty a large covered disposable coffee cup before adding, "Dr. Paige Carlyle. I can just imagine his reaction at finding some naked dude answering her door."

Nate laughed at the look on Ty's face and Ty folded his arms across his chest and spent the next few moments re-thinking his views on physical violence.

"You should see the look on your face." Nate snickered, clearly enjoying Ty's predicament.

"I'm tempted to wipe that smirk off yours," Ty growled, wiping his hand down his face. "But I've just had surgery."

"Like you could," Nate finally managed. "Relax, T. I sent him to the hospital. To see his sister." He grinned when Ty's eyes widened. "A good thing too or he'd have made mincemeat of you."

Ty wanted to say he could take care of himself, but his hand was in a cast and he didn't think his shoulder would withstand a Navy SEAL attack. Especially after discovering Ty had slept with his sister.

"What are you doing here?" he asked instead. "I thought you were working."

Nate shrugged. "One of the guys wanted to trade days, so I thought we could go sailing. I knocked at your door *and* called your phone but you didn't answer. So I decided to try here." He chuckled. "*After* I sent the SEAL away. Imagine my surprise when you actually opened the door, because the last time I asked, you said she was a pain in the ass. You were here because you needed peace and quiet and didn't need any annoying distractions. No matter how cute they were."

Ignoring him, Ty looked up at the sky. It was clear, but in typical Pacific North West spring fashion, the wind coming off the strait was freezing.

Dressed in only a towel, *he* was freezing.

"You want to go sailing? In this weather?"

Nate looked out at the morning and turned back with a raised brow. "What's the matter? It's a perfect day for sailing. If you're too much of a California wuss to handle a little fresh breeze, I totally understand."

With a growl, Ty pulled Nate inside. "Get in here, *dammit*. Before the neighbors call the cops."

"Yeah," Nate drawled, stepping over the threshold. "I can see why they would."

Pausing in the process of shutting the door, Ty demanded, "What's that supposed to mean?"

"It means there's a naked man in Dr. Cutie's house again." He pulled off his shades. "Why exactly are you in the cute doctor's house instead of next door? Where you have a perfectly good shower of your own?"

Ty slammed the door and turned, almost colliding with Nate, who'd stopped dead. "Never mind." The other man chuckled, catching sight of the bits of clothing scattered across the entrance floor. "I can totally see what happened."

Ty shoved him aside and bent to gather up the discarded clothing. "Yeah?" Ty demanded. "Maybe she had intruders last night who left a mess. Ever think of that?"

Snickering rudely, Nate hooked his shades in the neck of his T. "What I think is that you clearly have a thing for Dr. Cutie. If I'd known, I would have introduced you to her brother. You know, meet the family and all."

"I don't have a 'thing' for anyone and she doesn't like

to be called cute," Ty snarled irritably, beginning to pull on his clothes. And he was *not* meeting Paige's family, for God's sake. *Jeez Louise*, they'd only known each other a few weeks and most of that time he'd managed to avoid her.

He most definitely did not have a "thing" for her. Or anyone else, for that matter.

He found a teeny little pair of baby-blue panties covered with white daisies and shoved them in his pocket because Paige didn't need Nate looking at her underwear.

"We're not a thing." Nate's expression was a mix of pity and amusement. "What?"

His friend shook his head. "You poor stupid sap. Look at you defending your lady and hiding her skivvies from your best friend."

"She's not my lady," Ty denied quickly, and then winced at the knee-jerk response. And because he felt guilty he growled, "And you're no longer my best friend."

Nate looked unconcerned. "Then you won't mind if I ask her out, because word is she's a lot of fun."

It took a couple of beats for Ty to process that but when he did, he rounded on Nate with a protesting snarl.

His ex-friend merely snorted. "Yeah, thought so," he drawled. "You so have a thing for the cute doctor. Relax. The guys say that, as fun as she is, *they* don't get to see her skivvies." Ty's shoulders tensed at the news that the coasties were discussing Paige. He was about to point out that Nate was gossiping like a little girl when his friend added, "Guess they'll be interested to know she wears teeny blue ones covered with little white daisies."

In the process of pulling his shirt over his head, Ty's head snapped up to find his friend looking enormously entertained at his expense. "You do that," he told Nate, "and I'll kick your ass all the way to Canada and back."

Instead of answering, the other man simply grinned and

dumped the bag of food onto the entrance table while Ty finished yanking on his clothes.

It was only when they were on the boat, heading out into open water, that Nate called out as he steered into a large swell, "So, if Dr. Cutie isn't your lady, what is she?"

Ty pretended not to hear. Besides, he didn't know what Paige was other than sweet and sexy…oh, yeah, and hot. She was also smart and funny and surprisingly vulnerable beneath that sassy tough-girl exterior. And just thinking about how she looked when she came had him fumbling the ropes and cursing.

She wasn't his lady, he insisted silently. She'd made that abundantly clear by sneaking out without saying goodbye. Yet *something*—he didn't know what—wanted more than one night. More than— *No, dammit,* he snarled silently. *I don't want or need anything from—*

"Look out!"

He looked up as the boom swung at his head, and ducked just in time to avoid being dumped into the icy ocean. He straightened and a voice in the back of his head warned, *Excellent advice, buddy. You'd be smart to heed it.*

When Paige knocked off work a few days later, clouds, dark and heavy, lashed the seaside town with rain while high seas pounded the shore.

Within seconds she was soaked and had to go scrambling around in the rising water to retrieve her keys, which had slipped from her cold fingers. When she finally got her car open, she sat shivering and dripping all over the interior, wondering if she should stay put or risk the drive home.

As promised, Harry had negotiated a good deal that hadn't resulted in her selling a kidney or wiping out her savings; but the mechanic had warned Paige to be careful about driving in wet conditions until the engine had been completely overhauled.

She rolled her eyes. *Yeah, right.* She'd put it on her list right after the entry that said: *Stop thinking about you know who.*

Deciding to leave the decision up to Bertha, she turned the key and exhaled gustily when the engine turned over.

"Okay," she muttered. "Home it is, then."

The streets were deserted. Water gushed across the roads, turning them into fast-flowing rivers, and she was forced to grip the steering wheel when Bertha abruptly hydroplaned across an intersection. Now, instead of shivering with cold, she was shaking with terror and sucking in air like a vacuum cleaner.

She was halfway home when rain turned to sleet, pinging against her roof like tiny missiles that turned her windshield to slush and the road to an ice rink. By the time she parked in front of her house she was a wreck.

She hurried up the path to her front door on wobbly legs, only to discover that everything was in darkness. Clutching her shoulder bag as ice dripped off her nose, Paige fished out her house keys with stiff fingers…and sneaked a peek at the adjacent unit before she could stop herself.

She hadn't seen Ty since "The Night", as she'd dubbed it, and considering it would take her about a decade, maybe longer, to forget the way she'd thrown herself at him, she was quite happy to keep it that way.

She didn't know what she'd expected but it wasn't seeing the front door standing wide open. *What the heck?* She paused. Surely he hadn't just walked out and forgotten to lock up? Or maybe he couldn't because something bad had happened.

Hurrying across the space separating their front doors, Paige peered around the frame, half expecting someone to leap out and scare the bejesus out of her. When nothing happened, she sucked in an unsteady breath and ventured inside.

Dim light from the marina made its way through the sitting room sliding doors but other than a lot of dark shapes Paige hoped were just pieces of furniture, the place was empty.

Maybe. Hopefully.

"Ty?" she called, moving to the bottom of the stairs that led to the second floor. "Tyler?"

Not wanting to be like the brainless bimbo in a slasher movie, Paige retraced her steps thinking that maybe Ty had gone to check on the connection box. In that moment her worst nightmare—and all those horror movies she'd watched with Frankie—materialized as a huge hulking shadow, backlit by a raging storm, appeared in the doorway.

Paige opened her mouth to scream and a deep familiar voice demanded, "What the—? Paige?"

She gave a strangled gasp and lurched backwards. It was only when her butt hit the floor that she realized her legs had given way.

The next thing Ty was crouched over her. "Paige," he demanded, reaching out to tuck dripping black strands behind her ear, "what the hell happened? Answer me, *dammit*. Where are you hurt?"

No way was she saying her butt. That would be mortifying, especially if he demanded to examine it. "Just p-peachy," she finally gasped, her breath hitching on a giggle that bordered on hysteria. *Great*. Looking like a drowned, terrified rat was so *not* how she'd imagined their next meeting. "Y-you," she babbled, wrapping her arms around her knees because she was suddenly shaking like she had dengue fever.

"Yeah. Me." He frowned and wrapped his fingers around her wrist to check her pulse. When she continued to giggle helplessly he nudged her chin up to peer into her face.

The next instant his searching blue gaze had her trembling for another reason entirely. One that was as unwelcome as it was unsettling. For some reason she sat, frozen by the expression in his eyes, the heat pumping off his body and...and the memory of— *Nope. So not going there.*

"I'm fine," she insisted, shoving his hand away and scrambling to her feet. She wrapped her arms around her body and edged away. "I'll just... I saw your d-door open and thought...uh, never mind." What she'd thought was ridiculous so she headed for the door, her teeth chattering from a combination of cold and reaction.

"Hey, wait up. Where are you going?"

"Since you're okay, I'll... I'll... I need to go." *Far away.* From the delicious heat pumping off his body and the dreams that had plagued her the past couple nights. Just thinking about them gave her a hot flash.

"Don't be ridiculous," he growled, pulling her back around and clearly having no problem facing *her*. But then he probably did this all the time, she thought darkly.

"There's no power. I was trying to fix the problem at the outside box but I can't see what the hell I'm doing." He disappeared for a minute and returned with a couple of towels. "This storm literally came out of nowhere," he continued, running one towel over his hair and holding out the other. She took it and immediately buried her face in the thick terry cloth. "Just before the power went out the radio said the storm's being driven by the collision of a warm front from California and a huge polar cell pushing its way south."

Paige peered out into the icy storm and shivered as the

wind sent sleet angling in under the porch roof. The only way she could make out the houses across the street was from the faint glow of lights through the gloom.

Moving to the end of the porch, she looked around the side of the house. Marina lights swung crazily in the gusting winds, and Paige could scarcely see the boats and yachts lurching around at their slips. What she couldn't see was Harry's lights.

"Are we the only ones without power?"

She leaned out further and would have taken off in the wind if Ty hadn't grabbed the back of her scrubs and hauled her back.

"Get back from there before you get soaked," he growled. "And I think so. Although…now that you mention it I think the Andersen house was in darkness. Is Harry away somewhere? Or is their house also on this circuit?"

Really worried now, Paige nibbled on her thumbnail. "I'm going to check on him," she announced, a bad feeling cramping her belly.

"I'll go," Ty began, but Paige shoved the towel at him and hurried down the stairs. She heard him curse and mutter something about stubborn females as she ran into the street. She barely felt the additional moisture, only swiping irritably at the bits of sleet dripping into her eyes as she raised a hand to knock on Harry's door.

By the time she realized no one was going to answer, Ty was a large comforting presence beside her, trying the handle while she peered in through the panes beside the door.

"Don't panic," he said gruffly. "I'm sure he's okay. Maybe he fell asleep in front of the TV."

"It's not like him," she murmured, her stomach cramping again at the thought of something happening to the old man. In the eight months he'd been her neighbor she'd come to love the retired widower like a grandfather.

She couldn't bear it if anything happened to him.

Shaking now from more than cold, Paige hurried round the house to the stairs leading to the deck. The wood was slick with ice and she nearly took a header into Harry's window box.

Pushing open the sliding door with shaking hands, she was both relieved and frightened when she found it unlocked and the house dark and silent.

"Harry? Mr. Andersen, it's Paige. Are you okay?" Please be okay, she prayed frantically, hoping he'd be sitting in his chair, startled out of sleep.

What she found had her heart squeezing in her chest. "Harry?" She rushed over to where he lay in a heap on the floor, dropping to her knees beside him. "Harry, can you hear me?"

CHAPTER NINE

"Be careful," Ty warned, coming up behind her. "Don't turn him over until you know what you're dealing with. I'll call emergency and unlock the front door."

She nodded, unable to talk past the huge lump in her throat as she slid her fingers beneath Harry's jaw. She found a pulse and went weak with relief. Thank God. He was alive, although his pulse was way too fast and all over the place.

"He's alive," she called out, and heard Ty murmur something. When he reappeared in the doorway, she continued, "I've got a pulse but he's in A fib with brief periods of PSVT. I'm going to turn him over and start compressions. How long till the EMTs get here?"

His face was set in unreadable lines. "We're on our own," he said, dropping to his haunches and helping roll the old man onto his back. "There's been a pile-up on the highway so they may take a while."

Paige's heart squeezed at the news. Even in the torch-light, she could see the ashen tinge to Harry's weather-toughened skin. Her hands shook as she checked his pupil reaction. She'd never had to perform emergency procedures on someone she knew or loved.

She placed the heel of her bottom hand on Harry's sternum and laced her fingers. "How long?"

"Ten…fifteen minutes…an hour…they can't tell." Her heart dropped. Ty must have seen something in her face because he reached out and placed a hand over hers. It was warm and firm and she had to fight against the urge to cling to it. But clinging meant you expected the person to always be there and Paige had learned early that was never the case.

"Just keep doing what you're doing," Ty said. "Where's your emergency kit?"

Without breaking rhythm, she lifted her head and their eyes caught and held. His were steady and calm.

"In the upstairs spare bedroom. My keys are—"

But Ty was already gone and by the time he returned she'd had time to examine Harry more carefully in the torchlight. All the signs pointed to dehydration. Low electrolytes could easily have triggered atrial fibrillation, especially if he had an underlying condition. She wasn't certain what had caused him to lose consciousness but the first order of business was to get a sinus rhythm back.

They could deal with everything else later.

Sucking in a shaky breath, Paige sent up a prayer that the AMTs arrived in time to help him. She couldn't…just couldn't bear to lose him too. Not now.

He'd need a calcium channel blocker and her main worry was blood pooling in his heart. If it began clotting, he could die before they got him to the ER.

Within minutes Ty was back, tossing a package at her.

"Find a vein," he instructed tersely, pulling out a bag of Ringer's lactate. "He needs liquids ASAP. I found some anti-diarrhea meds on the counter. Probably caught the enterovirus going around and tried to treat it himself."

That sounded like Harry, but Paige blamed herself for not keeping closer tabs on him. She'd been so preoccupied with avoiding Ty and pretending her life wasn't unravelling like a pair of cheap pantyhose that she'd barely been home or even thought to check on Harry the past week.

And now he could die.

Hands shaking, she tried to find a vein, finally applying a tourniquet and quickly inserting the needle when one appeared. She attached the cannula and slapped an adhesive dressing over the area to stabilize it while Ty awkwardly hooked the bag one-handed to the back of the chair.

"No CCBs," he said gruffly, rising to his feet to look around the kitchen. "Without channel blockers we need some electrolytes."

"Try the cupboards," Paige suggested, resuming chest compressions. "I know Epsom salts isn't ideal but he uses them for his plants. We need some dextrose too so check the cupboard beside the stove. Maybe there's something there or in the bathroom that we can use."

Ty rummaged around in the cupboards, grunting with disappointment each time he found nothing. He finally headed off to the bathroom, calling out a minute later that he'd found something.

Paige flashed a nervous look at the kitchen clock, wondering how long Harry had been unconscious. They'd been there nearly seven minutes already and still no sign of the EMTs.

Ty reappeared, holding a container, and went straight to the kitchen cupboard. He took out a cup and rinsed it with water from the kettle before dumping contents from the container into the cup. He added a few drops of kettle water and reached into the overhead cabinet for a bottle of honey.

He added a drop to the mixture and gently mixed it.

"Mag chloride and five percent glucose," he growled. "We'll repeat it every half-hour till the EMTs get here." He thrust the cup at her. "I'll take over compressions while you inject this into the line."

"Ty..." With his cast he wouldn't be able to perform CPR properly.

"I can't handle a syringe one-handed," he snapped, and Paige took the cup from him. "I can't do a damn thing one-handed."

She couldn't help noticing that he'd once again retreated behind an invisible wall, just as he had that afternoon on the mountain.

It felt like an age since she'd overheard him telling Nate that he might not be able to resume his surgical career. But even if that was true, he could still consult in other ways... especially with all his medical knowledge and skill. He couldn't just waste it—people needed him.

"You're more than a surgeon," she said abruptly, and when he looked up, she nearly bobbled the cup at his shuttered expression and chilly eyes, as if she was a stranger who'd overstepped her mark. A muscle flexed in his jaw and the tension in the room ratcheted skyward until he turned away.

Okay. Clearly that was an unwelcome subject.

Furious with herself for getting all girly and hurt like they were an item, she turned her back on him and concentrated on getting the solution into a syringe. Harry she could help, Ty, it seemed...not so much.

She injected the solution right into the cannula port and altered the flow rate then dropped to her haunches. She made to take over but Ty brushed her aside with a brusque, "Call again."

Grinding her teeth together, she rose and snatched his cell off the table. "I didn't ask," she reminded him furiously. "You could just as easily have gone on ignoring everyone and everything the way you like. Besides, you came here to be alone, remember? I didn't ask for anything from you."

Without looking at her, he said coolly, "No. You wouldn't, would you?"

Stunned by the accusation, she demanded, "What's that supposed to mean?"

"It means that Paige Carlyle likes everyone to believe she can handle things just fine on her own."

She opened her mouth to tell him that she'd been forced to handle everything from the age of fifteen when she heard a siren. She snapped her mouth closed and rushed to open the front door just as her friend dashed up the stairs.

Frankie's partner, Dale Franklin, followed with a covered stretcher, grunting his thanks when Paige helped him haul it onto the porch. They heard Frankie demanding, "What happened? How bad is it? And— what the hell, Ty?"

Paige had the feeling the last question didn't have a thing to do with Harry and hurried back to stop Frankie from interrogating Ty about "The Night". His murmured response was drowned out by the sound of Dale's footsteps thudding down the passage behind her and by the time they entered, Frankie was checking Harry's BP and ignoring Ty.

He had his hip propped against the counter, arms folded across his wide chest, when Paige returned. His mouth was pressed into a firm, unsmiling line that made her think he hadn't liked Frankie's questions. With his hooded gaze on Paige, he gave a terse report of what they'd done, grabbing Paige when she went to help.

He yanked her hard against his body, his grip tightening when she rammed an elbow into his hard belly.

"Let them do their job," he growled against her ear. She turned to snarl at him but his gaze was oddly gentle. It was then she realized she was shaking from head to toe, barely keeping it together. She held her body rigidly and sucked in an unsteady breath, praying she wouldn't fall apart until she was alone.

Ty's heat finally seeped into her limbs. She didn't know how he did it, considering he was as wet as she was. She forced herself to move away. "I'm f-fine. You don't need to b-baby me. Harry…"

"Will be fine," he murmured, his big body a strong, warm wall at her back. "Thanks to you."

The last words were so soft she almost missed them and then wished she had when tears burned the backs of her eyes. She pressed a hand to her lips to keep them from wobbling.

"What if we're too late?" She bit down on her thumb as Frankie and Dale loaded Harry onto the stretcher. He suddenly looked old and frail and she needed to do something more than stand there and fall apart. "What if—?"

"You got to him, Paige," he interrupted firmly, detaining her when she went to follow the EMTs. "Why don't you go change into dry clothes? I'll drive you to the hospital."

"No," she said, shrugging off his hand. "I'm fine. I'll go in the ambulance. Besides, I know how much the thought of going to the hospital scares you," and hurried from the kitchen.

When he was finally alone, Ty shoved an exasperated hand through his hair and released his breath. "I am not scared," he muttered irritably. And when the silence mocked him, he cursed. Then, because it was more satisfying, he cursed her.

If he was scared, it wasn't of going to a hospital where he might never be able to fulfil his passion.

It was Paige.

She terrified him; with her huge eyes…and her damn open, engaging smile. A smile that he'd missed over the past few days—more than he wanted to admit. A smile that made *him* smile just thinking about it.

And the look in her eyes when she'd watched the EMTs load Harry onto the stretcher had momentarily rendered him stupid and made him forget her fierce independence. She'd been more than clear the other night had been a one-off thing. At the time he'd thought it was what he wanted too, but the past couple of days he'd barely seen her and… He sighed. He'd missed her, *dammit*.

So he'd come to Port St. John's to be alone…big deal. Everyone deserved some alone time without being badgered and called a coward.

Little Miss Medic expected him to carry on as if everything was fine. But *nothing* was fine. Not his damn hand, not his uncertain future and certainly not the way he kept thinking about her when she wasn't around. Thinking about the way her breath hitched an instant before she surrendered…the breathy moans she made when he brushed his fingers over her soft skin and the look on her face when she came.

Cursing up a storm, Ty repacked the emergency kit.

She was just a woman, he reminded himself. A little more annoying and bossy than most, but still…just…a… woman.

So what the hell was his problem with Paige?

"Absolutely no problem at all," he snarled to the empty house. "Besides, why the hell should I care if Miz Independence wants to pretend nothing happened? In fact, I'm relieved." A muscle twitched in his jaw. "No, I'm ecstatic," he muttered through clenched teeth. "Because now I can go home, have a nice long shower and move on without having to worry about bossy, annoying pain-in-the-ass distractions."

Realizing that he was starting to sound like a crazy person, he set his jaw and stomped over to the doors leading to the deck. He locked them with an impatient twist of his wrist and looked around for Harry's house keys because there was no question the old man would be admitted for observation and tests. And to ensure that happened, Ty reached for his phone to call his father. Henry Chapman had been Harry's doctor for thirty-five years and would want to know.

But Ty couldn't find his phone anywhere. After searching the entire house, he remembered that Paige had picked it up to call emergency. She'd most likely shoved it into her pocket without thinking.

Finally, Ty locked the house and stomped back home. When he caught himself *thinking* of it as home, he paused, oblivious to the wind blowing snow into his face and down his wet shirt.

What the—? Oh, no. No way. This freezing, storm-battered town was *not* home and the sooner he returned to his life in balmy Malibu the better.

He'd hit his favorite beach, he decided darkly, and cuddle up to some lithe, tanned beach bunnies who wanted nothing more than a good time.

Yeah. A good time sounded…good. No, it sounded great.

Muttering, he stormed through his front door and promptly fell over something lying just inside. Swearing, he picked himself off the floor and in the light of his torch saw Paige's shoulder bag, its contents spilled across the floor.

Dammit, the woman needed a damn keeper. She was a walking disaster. But he was not—*would* not be—anyone's keeper. Especially a woman who'd blown his mind with her soft mouth and sensual moans then turned around and pretended *he* was the annoying neighbor.

Shaking his head at all the stuff women carried in their handbags, Ty began stuffing everything back. When he came across her keys, wallet, cellphone and lip gloss, he sighed and rose.

Looked like he wouldn't be moving on just yet.

At least not until he made sure she got home okay.

Despite the ugly road conditions, he made it to the hospital without incident and headed straight for ER. It was like a scene from a television medical drama and Ty wished he was a million miles away.

He sucked in air, conscious of his pounding pulse and the constriction in his chest. On a purely intellectual level he realized he was having a mild panic attack. His testosterone scoffed at the idea and he forced himself forward.

Casting a quick glance over the room, he decided that no one appeared in any immediate danger and went looking for Paige. He spotted her bent over a chart, bedraggled and wet. She muttered something and turned abruptly, uttering a little yelp of surprise when she ran into him. He shot out a hand to keep her from falling over a nearby crash cart.

"T-Ty? What are you doing here?"

She was pale and lines of stress pinched the area around her eyes. His gut clenched hard.

"Harry?"

She stared at him for a couple of beats. Her throat worked as though she was having trouble getting the words out and then her eyes abruptly filled. *Aw, man.*

His chest squeezed and with a muttered curse he gently pulled her in, instantly struck by her terrifying fragility.

She was such a tough, feisty woman that her tears sliced at him with sharp claws.

"Dammit, Paige," he murmured into her damp, tousled hair. "I'm sorry. I'm so damn sorry. Harry is….he's special to you, isn't he?" He set his jaw, finding her tears more devastating because she was so determined not to fall apart.

In the course of his job he often had to give people bad

news about their loved ones. It was never easy, but Paige…
dammit, she slayed him. His throat tight with an emotion
he couldn't name, Ty tightened his arms around and murmured soothing words into her hair. He was determined
to be there for her, if only it—like their night—was this
one time.

Finally she sucked in a deep breath and lifted her head.
They were so close Ty could see his reflection in the tears
clinging to her inky lashes. And felt himself fall. Hard.
Right into her huge damp eyes. Right into the swirl of blue
and green and gold.

And for the first time in his life he experienced the air
being sucked from his lungs—heck, from the entire universe—leaving his mind in chaos and his heart and lungs
aching like he'd been kicked in the chest.

Oblivious to his inner turmoil, Paige gave a ragged
laugh and dropped her forehead against his chest. "He's…
I think he's going to be okay," she murmured. "He came to
in the ambulance. Dr. Chapman… I mean your…f-father…
sent him for a bunch of tests but his vitals look promising."
She drew in a shaky breath and stepped away to brush impatiently at the tears on her cheeks. "Anyway…" she grimaced and took the clipboard a nurse thrust at her as she
hurried past "…we're swamped."

"I thought your shift was over," Ty began, but Paige was
already moving away, her attention clearly on a mother
and child nearby.

"Paige?"

She flung over her shoulder, "Look, I'll see you later.
Maybe." She stopped abruptly and turned, her gaze searching. "Are you okay? Being here, I mean?"

"I'm fine," he growled with exasperation, ignoring the
urge to get the hell out so he could feel fresh air on his

face. Paige's gaze was searching and he sighed, holding his arms out at his side. "See. Fine."

Paige expelled an exasperated breath and said in a tone that suggested she was rolling her eyes, "Okay, you're fine," she muttered, and turned away, only to stop and swing around. "In that case, will you look in on Harry? See he's got everything he needs, I mean?"

Ty murmured that he would and was still standing there, embarrassed by his outburst, when his father appeared beside him.

"Tyler," Henry Chapman greeted him with a worried frown. Lines of tension bracketed his eyes and mouth as he took in Ty from head to toe. Upon seeing Ty unharmed his frown eased. "You're okay."

"I'm fine, Dad." He sighed and caught himself rolling *his* eyes because everyone thought he was a wuss. "Harry's skin was grey and clammy when we found him and we have no idea how long he'd been unconscious."

"He's a tough one," Henry mused. "But he admitted to being sick the last few days. It's probably just electrolytes, but we're running a full battery of tests. You made a good call there, son, giving him magnesium and honey."

"It was Paige's idea."

"Paige…?" Henry's expression cleared and he laughed. "Oh, you mean our ER pediatrician." He turned to look around and Ty's gaze followed to where she gave an abashed mountain of a guy a piece of her mind. "She's a little firecracker, isn't she? We were exceptionally lucky to get her. The kids love her."

"Dad, about that. Why don't you put her in Paeds instead of ER?"

Henry shook his head. "We don't have the funds for a children's ward, Tyler, and no specialist to run it. I try to send all the under-twelves to her but my request for a children's wing and a full-time pediatrician is under review. Besides, she's only here to pay back her student loans and we can't offer what those big city hospitals can. I'm hoping to change her mind but until then…" He looked around. "Look, I have to go. Dinner Sunday?"

Ty shocked himself by saying, "Will it be okay with Rhonda?" He'd met his father's new wife—a retired high school science teacher—but had avoided any family dinners because the truth was, somewhere down deep was that kid who wanted to punish his father for not playing a more active role in his life. But he was thirty-five years old, for God's sake, too old to be harboring grudges like an angry adolescent.

Henry sent him a sharp look. "Of course it's okay. It's your home too." He caught sight of someone trying to get his attention. "I'd better go." He started walking off but paused to say across his shoulder, "Oh, and that cute girl?" Amusement gleamed in eyes the exact shade of Ty's. "The one who beat you up?" Henry chuckled at Ty's expression. "Bring her too. You need a little fun in your life. God knows, life with your mother wasn't easy but not all women are like Renée, son." He inclined his head towards Paige. "And that little girl has the biggest heart of anyone I know. Just looking at her makes me smile."

Ty shoved a hand through his hair and sighed. Just looking at her made him smile too. It also made him think about things a son shouldn't be thinking in front of his father. "She's not a little girl, Dad," he reminded Henry mildly. "She's a specialist."

"And a damned good one too," Henry retorted. "But look at her, son. Doesn't she just light up the room?"

Clearly Harry hadn't expected an answer because he immediately headed off, leaving Ty to watch Paige until she disappeared into an exam room. Irritated with himself, he shook off the odd pang of loneliness, because if his childhood had taught him anything, it was that he didn't like leaving things up to chance. He wanted to know his next course of action and he'd learned to ignore things he couldn't control.

Like relationships and feelings.

Because who the hell could control those?

And then there was Paige Carlyle. His father was right. She did light up a room; whether with her smile or her big eyes that sparkled with the same wonder and enthusiasm as the little kids she treated, she tended to draw people to her like a moth to a flame.

And Ty wasn't any different.

He'd come to Washington to be alone and make decisions about his future. Instead he'd spent most of it deliberately avoiding thinking about what he would do if he couldn't be a trauma surgeon and actively seeking out a woman who didn't want anything more from him than he had to offer.

And it was driving him nuts.

Yeah, shocking, he admitted wryly, especially as he'd never wanted anything more from women than brief mutually satisfying affairs. Paige didn't fit into any mold and she was independent to a fault. She'd also turned his ordered existence upside down, leaving him floundering in a sea of frustration and emotional turmoil.

He liked order, dammit, and he liked control; neither of which could be equated with Paige Carlyle, and brought back memories of his childhood he'd rather forget.

When a passing nurse sent him a curious look he realized he'd been standing there scowling like a crazy person. Sighing, Ty turned and headed for the exit, determined to regain control of his life.

He was almost at his car when he realized he hadn't

asked for his phone and that he still had her keys, lip gloss and phone. Sighing, he retraced his steps and approached the nurses' station. He would hand over her keys and wallet and leave.

And that would be that.

On impulse he sent the frazzled nurse a friendly smile and, leaning forward, said, "Can you do me a favor?"

Her eyes widened and she went pink. "Um…sure, what can I do for you?"

"Two things actually." He flashed a quick look at her name tag. "Nurse Tucker, is it?"

"It's Nancy." The woman dimpled with pleasure and fluttered her eyelashes. "And if it gets me another sexy smile, I'll have your babies too."

The other nurse at the station snorted and said, "I'd like to know what your *husband* would say to that, Nance."

"Oh, shoo, Shaz!" Nancy giggled. "A woman's entitled to flirt a little." She winked at Ty. "So what can I do for you, handsome?"

"It's for Paige Carlyle."

"You mean Dr. Cutie?"

His mouth curled at the moniker Paige couldn't seem to shake. "Yep. Can you dig up some dry scrubs for her? Oh, and when she's finished for the night I want you to stall her."

Nancy and the other nurse shared a curious look. "No problem with the scrubs, consider it done. But…she's already put in a full shift and…"

"Long enough to call me," he explained. "She came in the ambulance with Mr. Andersen and needs a lift home."

Nancy looked unsure for a moment and Ty understood that they were protecting Paige from potential crazy stalkers. He dug his wallet out of his pocket and pulled out his ID.

"Henry Chapman will vouch for me," he said, showing her the ID.

"All right, Tyler Reese," Nancy said, her flirtatious smile back in full force. "And what number should I call?"

Ty rattled off his number before realizing that Paige still had his phone. "No wait, call Dr. Carlyle's cell number, she still has mine." He could see Nancy's curiosity bump up a couple of notches but she promised to call him when Paige was finished for the night.

Ty thanked her and left, ignoring the voice in his head demanding to know what the hell he thought he was doing.

He didn't have any answers. He only knew that his life was as out of control as his feelings for one sexy, pain-in-the-ass distraction.

CHAPTER TEN

It was after ten when Ty parked in front of the house and killed the engine. He'd stopped at an all-night burger joint despite Paige's insistence that she wasn't hungry.

"You didn't have to wait for me," she said for the tenth time in as many minutes. "Especially when you're afraid of hospitals."

Ty opened his door with a look of exasperation. "I'm not afraid of damn hospitals. And I didn't wait. I got Nancy to call me. End of story." He got out and shut the door.

Her eyes tracked him, big and capable and a little irritated, as he rounded the hood. *Okay*. She rolled her eyes.

Clearly *that* discussion was over.

Shivering in the freezing air that had invaded the interior, she looked around for her shoulder bag and was just about to freak out when she remembered that she hadn't had it with her in the ambulance.

It reminded her of Harry and her heart squeezed before she remembered that he was fine. She'd already checked on him and he was sleeping comfortably, which was a lot better than the alternative. She paused a moment to wonder what would have happened if Bertha hadn't started that afternoon. No one would have thought to check on him and—

The passenger door opened abruptly and she gave a startled squeak. "*Omigod*, will you stop doing that?" she gasped, glaring up into Ty's dark face. "And shut the door. It's freezing."

He studied her silently for a moment. "You planning on sleeping in the car?" he enquired mildly, easily holding the door open and snagging the bag of food that she'd been hugging to her chest.

"Well, not anymore. *Yeesh*," she grumbled, sliding out to stand shivering on the sidewalk in thin oversized scrubs and a huge jacket Ty had found in the back of his car. "I don't suppose you'll consider doing your breaking and entering thing again?" She hunched into the jacket for warmth. "I have no idea what I did with my purse or keys."

Ty nudged her away from the car and closed the door, locking it with a *beep-beep* of his remote. "I don't suppose," he said mildly, grabbing her hand and practically frog-marching her up the path to his door. She tried to swerve towards her own door, but he simply yanked her after him.

"Dammit," she muttered, having to run to keep up with his long legs. "You'd think with everything that's happened you'd make an exception." When he just snorted, she batted her eyelashes at him and asked sweetly, "What if I asked pretty please and promised not to call the cops? I know they scare you as much as hospitals do."

He made a sound of annoyance and nudged her up the stairs. "Cops and hospitals do not scare me," he said with exaggerated patience.

"But—"

"You do," he interrupted irritably. "You scare me."

That brought her up short. She gaped at him. "Me? I scare you?" She didn't know whether to be pleased or insulted.

Light spilled from overhead, giving the illusion of enclosing them in a cocoon of warmth. Despite being from

California, the icy cold didn't appear to affect him. She didn't know why that surprised her as he was the kind of man that radiated heat and sexuality at a hundred paces. *Darn sexy alphas.*

Half his face was in darkness, the other half all planes and angles that stole her breath. No one should look that good, she thought with dismay, huffing with annoyance when she caught a whiff of his delicious man scent. Who the heck smelled that good after a full hectic day and half the night? She probably smelled like disinfectant and other not-so-pleasant ER smells.

"Yes," he muttered, nudging her inside. "You scare the hell out of me."

His touch, after the stress of the day, had heat and excitement spinning through her so abruptly that she whirled around. "Well, then, maybe I should just go. Clearly you want to be alone— *Hey.*" Her hand jerked up in the universal "stop" gesture when he kept coming.

She didn't know what she was saying stop to but when her palm came into contact with a warm hard chest, alarm signals ran up her arm and into her brain. Signals that urged her to move the hell away.

Her brain might have been on board but her hand tingled with the urge to explore that wide expanse of muscle and sinew. Heat arrowed right up her arm into her chest and her nipples instantly tightened into painful little buds. *Yikes.* It felt like someone had touched a live wire to her skin, sending little pricks of current skating across her flesh.

Maybe she was just coming down with a chill, she thought. She'd been drenched at least four times today and—she mentally rolled her eyes—maybe her body hadn't received the message that she was over him.

She slowly lifted her gaze from where her fingers were stroking him, moving to the hollow of his throat where she really, *really* wanted to put her mouth; up past the hard square jaw that hadn't seen a razor since that morning to his finely sculpted mouth. She waited for him to say something…*anything*…so she could watch his mouth move, finally lifting her gaze when it didn't.

Unmistakable tension radiated from his big brawny body and Paige got caught in his sexy blue eyes.

Wait…*what?* Weren't they supposed to be done with this?

"Ty—" she began, snatching her hand away as though she'd been burned. She thrust it behind her and backed away, swallowing hard because she didn't want him thinking she couldn't keep her hands off him.

When her voice finally emerged it was breathless. "Maybe I should check on Harry, he—"

"You already checked. Five times," Ty interrupted in a deep voice that sent a delicious thrill through her. "He's going to be fine, Paige." He moved towards her, a large hungry cat on the prowl, a dangerous predator with Paige in his sights.

Oh, boy.

"He just needs a couple days on fluids and a change of meds." With his eyes on hers he kicked the door shut behind him, ratcheting Paige's pulse up a couple of hundred notches. "Before you know it he'll be back home, where you can keep an eye on him."

She nodded and nervously licked her lips, wondering what the heck she was thinking by entering his lair…uh, house. It was so much easier taking charge in her own space.

As though he knew what she was thinking, Ty took a couple of steps towards her, his mouth curving when her eyes widened and she sucked in a startled little breath.

Dammit, girl. Stop reacting like he's about to eat you

instead of burgers. Narrowing her eyes, she stiffened her spine and stubbornly held her ground, even when he kept coming, only to stop a bare inch away.

Instantly his heat surrounded her, and she had to tip her head back because everyone knew that you had to face a predator to show you weren't afraid.

And she wasn't afraid…not exactly. She sighed. Okay, she was terrified. Terrified of the feelings turning her jittery and terrified of the hold he had on her, hijacking her dreams and stealing her peace of mind.

Finally, he broke the ratcheting tension by planting a hand against the wall behind her and leaning closer. Paige reacted like he'd shoved her, backing up to escape the heated web of need and want he so easily wove around her.

"What are you doing?" she squeaked breathlessly.

Without replying, he moved closer, then closer still, only pausing when his mouth was a whisper away from her ear. "Do you know what I want?" he breathed, his voice rough and deep and scraping along every exposed nerve ending.

Terrified of what it meant, she locked her knees and shook her head. "B-burgers?"

He stilled as though she'd surprised him and after a couple of beats he chuckled, the gravelly low sound sending hot and cold shivers dancing through her. "No." His lips brushed her throat. "Not burgers."

Paige's hands came up, and though she really intended to push him away, they curled tightly into his sweatshirt.

"Ty…" she began, torn between wanting desperately for him to kiss her and an overwhelming need to protect her heart. She instinctively knew that if he kissed her again, it wouldn't end there. And then she wouldn't be able to pretend that this was just a casual fling that she was totally over.

Her head thunked back against the wall in an attempt

to knock some sense into it but her body had a mind of its own. Her hands did too, releasing their grip on his sweat-shirt to smooth over hard abs and warm skin beneath his shirt.

He gave a laughing groan that drew Paige's attention to his mouth and—oh, God—she suddenly needed it more than she needed her next breath. In fact, she would prob-ably die without it.

Like in the next two seconds.

"Ty," she breathed again, and even to her own ears it sounded like a plea. It momentarily cleared her head enough for her to say, "I thought you didn't want—"

"Oh, I want," he interrupted hoarsely. "I want…another kiss…another night…" He shifted closer and his breath-ing became as ragged as hers. "I'm hoping…this'll finally do it."

Heat pooled low in her belly and her bones began to melt, along with her resistance. "Do…what?"

He closed the half-inch to take a nip out of her mouth. "Get you out of my system," he growled, slanting his mouth over hers and tracing her lips with a line of fire. "Hope-fully…for good, this time." And then he sucked her bot-tom lip into his mouth and brushed aside his jacket to cup her breast through the thin scrubs.

She gave a ragged moan and arched into his touch.

"Dammit," he breathed. "This wasn't supposed to feel so good."

"So…good." And because he felt so good, Paige smoothed her hands up his wide back, marveling at the solid strength beneath her fingers and the way his muscles shifted and bunched.

She couldn't remember ever wanting anyone this badly.

She made a hungry sound in the back of her throat, helpless against the need pounding through her, wanting…

needing more, especially when she canted her hips and found him big and hard and fully aroused.

She slid her hands around and down his chest and abs, curling her fingers into his jeans waistband. Mostly to hang onto and then, when his belly muscles clenched, to torture.

"Paige...*wait*." His breath whooshed out and he grabbed her hands, lifting them away and pinning them to the wall above her head. "Be sure," he warned. "Because if you're not...dammit, say something before...before I lose what little control I'm hanging onto...and take you right here against the wall."

Suddenly Paige wanted to take that control. She wanted wild and fast because it had been that kind of day. Oh, and up against the wall sounded good.

Now even better.

With her hands still locked in his, she lifted her mouth and murmured, "Maybe just one more time—"

Before she could complete the sentence, Ty swooped down and caught her mouth in a hard, hungry kiss—a kiss that instantly turned lethal and had her body responding as though he hadn't satisfied her every sensual fantasy a few nights earlier.

He fed her hot open-mouthed kisses, his hands releasing her to sneak beneath her scrubs and rasp against naked flesh. The sensations rolling through her had her pressing closer, moaning in triumph and anticipation when he swelled and hardened against her belly.

Her breath caught and her core went hot and wet. Just as her knees gave way, Ty uttered something hot and explicit beneath his breath and swept her into his arms.

She squeaked at the abrupt change in elevation, clutching at his shoulders as he headed for the stairs. "Your sh-shoulder," she gasped.

His answer was a low huffing laugh as he took the stairs

like he was in a hurry. And, *oh, boy*, Paige could certainly relate. She was in a hurry too. "What—what about…the wall?"

She'd have been okay with the wall.

Ty turned right when he reached the landing. "I have another wall in mind," he said, kicking open the bathroom door. He let her go, allowing her body to slide down the length of his.

And when her eyes rolled back in her head, he gave her bottom a sharp slap and ordered, "Strip," reaching into the shower to turn on the water.

The position allowed Paige to admire the wide V of his shoulders that tapered to narrow hips and long, muscular legs. Oh, yeah, she thought, drooling. And those tight buns she dreamed about sinking her teeth into—

Ty turned and caught her hungrily eyeing his backside. He uttered the low masculine sound that never failed to send tingles skittering through her and he reached out to wrap his hand in the front of her scrubs top. With his eyes on hers, he slowly pulled her closer and when all that separated them was his hand, he growled, "Were you ogling my backside?"

Paige snickered and backed away, uttering a squeak of surprise as her top went flying over her head.

"Hey… *Oomph*," she muttered against the sudden invasion of his mouth. He kissed her as he did everything else, with single-minded purpose; plundering the depths of her mouth as he pillaged her senses.

With each article of clothing that vanished he pressed hot, open-mouthed kisses against her skin, stealing her breath and making her moan for more. Undressing became a sensual feast of hands and mouths and hungry sounds. By the time they were naked, steam filled the bathroom.

When Ty paused to wrap his cast in a waterproof casing, Paige's hands examined his wide chest and her tongue flicked at his tight male nipples. She hummed her appreciation against his smooth warm skin and scored her nails down his spine to his tight buns, loving the rough laugh and warning growl emerging from deep in his chest.

He caught her hands and with his hot blue gaze on hers drew her into the shower. Breathless with excitement and anticipation, Paige half expected—hoped—he'd shove her up against the wall and have his merry way with her. But his gaze abruptly gentled as it probed hers as though he was searching for something.

"Ty…?"

"No more talking." Then he dipped his head and dropped a kiss on her mouth before firmly turning her away from him.

Confused, she craned her head around to see him reaching for the shampoo and squirting a dollop into his hand. She frowned. "I thought—" she began, only to have him interrupting once more.

"No talking," he growled, smoothing shampoo over her head. "Close your eyes…and just feel." Then he gently washed her hair, slowly massaging her scalp until she sagged against him in a boneless, speechless mass.

"You warm yet?"

Paige could have told him that she was melting but her voice emerged on a low groan of pleasure and she couldn't even drum up the teeniest bit of offense when he laughed.

Once he'd rinsed her hair, he reached for the soap and proceeded to wash her with the same gentle strokes, taking extra care with her breasts, her belly…before moving to legs. And when her body tingled and her heart raced because surely now he would take her against the wall, he turned off the water and reached for a huge fluffy towel.

With his hot cobalt blue eyes locked on hers, Ty wrapped her up and carried her into the master bedroom. He paused beside the bed to drop a light kiss on her mouth and just when she began losing any sense of the world around them he broke the slight suction and tossed her unceremoniously into the middle of the bed.

She instantly bounced up with a laughing protest on her lips, only to be pushed flat when he followed her down.

His hungry mouth silenced her protest.

Surprised by the sudden change in his mood, she shoved at him and rolled them over until she was straddling his hips. "What was that?" she demanded breathlessly.

His answer was to chuckle and grab her hips. He pulled her snug against his erection, making them both groan. He took advantage of her distraction to cover her breasts with his big hands. Instantly she stilled, the sensations so lusciously decadent that her spine flexed and her head fell back in pleasure.

"This is me," he murmured, rearing up to brush his lips against the pulse pounding in her throat. "This is me taking control and getting you out of my system."

Paige clenched her thighs and sucked in a sharp breath at the feel of him, long and thick and hard between her legs. "How is it I'm the one on top, then?"

"This way," he rasped, dipping his head to catch one pebbled nipple between his teeth, "my hands are free." He spent a couple of seconds torturing her nipples before wrapping both arms around her and holding her close as he drew her flesh into his mouth.

She tried to say something but her mind slid away and there was nothing but Ty's mouth and hands sending her tumbling into heat and pleasure.

And when a dangerous thought slid into her mind—that

she was playing with fire and this was as far from a fling as she could get—she pushed it aside because after tonight she'd be over him for good.

Accustomed to sleeping alone, Ty awakened sometime before dawn baffled by the warm soft presence beside him. He turned his head and in the dim light coming from the bathroom saw Paige still sprawled face down a couple of inches away. Her face was half-hidden by a silky curtain of inky hair.

Memories of how she'd got there flooded back and he couldn't have stopped himself from reaching out to smooth back that swing of hair any more than he could resist tracing a hand down the length of her spine to her soft, curvy bottom.

She gave a soft sigh and before he knew what he was doing, Ty had pulled her closer. With her back pressed to his front, he spent a minute enjoying the way her sleep-warmed curves fitted against him—as if she'd been fashioned with him in mind.

Murmuring sleepily, she snuggled closer and he slid one leg between hers, bending his knee as he reached around to palm one plump breast. Realizing that the position would prevent her from slipping away without him knowing, Ty smiled.

Let's see her sneak away from him now.

She stirred and murmured a sleepy, "Ty?"

"Yeah," he growled, pressing his lips to the back of her neck. "Expecting someone else?"

She yawned and stretched, arching against him in one long sinuous move. His body instantly responded until she said, "I dunno… Danny maybe, or…um… Nate?"

He sank his teeth into her shoulder, smiling against her

skin when she made a sound between a snorting laugh and a yelp.

He couldn't remember ever laughing in bed with a woman before and when she asked sleepily if he wanted her to go, he tightened his hold on her and shocked himself by murmuring, "No, stay."

He lay awake for a long time listening to her breathe, wondering—not for the first time—what the hell he thought he was doing. He'd never wanted a woman to stay or wrapped her close to keep her from leaving. And he'd certainly never lain awake wanting more from her than she was willing to give.

Because, let's face it, he wasn't good with more. His life was in California and he'd never—*never*, he reminded himself sternly—considered changing it for a woman.

Still didn't.

Look at what had happened to his parents. They'd met at Stanford and the next thing they'd been married and living in Port St. John's. Henry had had big dreams of building the largest hospital on the Olympic Peninsula, a hospital that would serve the county, the town and the coastguard, as well as the entire length of the Juan de Fuca Strait.

His mother had hated it and when Ty had been two she'd packed him up and returned to California. And though he'd seen his father on the odd visit, he'd had to wait six years to spend summers in Washington. By that time they hadn't even known each other.

He'd once asked Henry why he'd never sued for custody or objected to Ty's change of name, and his father had replied that a child needed his mother.

Yeah, but Ty had needed his father too…away from the stifling expectations of a woman who'd demanded perfection from her son and then frozen him out when he'd disappointed her.

It was no wonder he preferred to remain unattached. His childhood had been an emotional minefield and he'd buried his emotions until...*dammit*, until Paige.

But that didn't mean he was falling for her, he assured himself. It just meant he was bored and needed a distraction. And who better to distract him than his sassy neighbor?

Sometime later he felt movement and was instantly alert. "What's wrong?" he rasped, rolling over to see Paige carefully slipping off the bed. She jolted when he spoke but didn't turn around.

"I...uh...nothing, I just need the...um...bathroom."

Scrubbing a hand over his face, he watched as she snagged one of his T-shirts and pulled it over her head. He wanted to object to her covering all those sweet curves but she was already pulling away from him. And despite what he'd said last night, he wasn't ready to let her go.

Not yet.

Sitting up, he studied her through narrowed lids. "You were sneaking out, weren't you?"

"What? No," she said quickly, and to Ty's mind guiltily. Her eyes slid away. "Of course not. What makes you think that?"

He searched her face for a hint of what she was thinking but for once her expression was unreadable.

"It might have something to do with the way you're avoiding looking at me," he drawled.

She fidgeted nervously, tugging at the hem of his T-shirt, although Ty could have told her not to bother. He'd already seen every inch of her and liked what he'd seen... and touched...and tasted.

His body stirred and his mouth began to water. He also liked seeing her all flustered, especially when she thrust a hand through her hair and began to mutter to herself. She clearly didn't know what to do with her hands because she finally huffed out a breath and stuck them into her armpits.

"It's just… I'm not good…with *this*," she said defensively, edging towards the door and sending him quick nervous looks as though she expected him to pounce and needed a head start.

Beginning to enjoy himself, Ty propped a hand behind his head. "What's 'this' exactly?"

She thrust out her bottom lip and blew out an exasperated breath and although he couldn't see her eyes, he suspected that she was rolling them.

"This…" She gestured wildly, including his entire room. "This…um, after stuff."

"You mean after hot sex?"

A wild flush rose into her cheeks and Ty took pity on her, tossing back the sheet and rising. He paused to stretch and heard a strangled sound catch in Paige's throat. Her eyes widened at the sight of his morning erection and when he said, "Why don't we—?" she whirled and a second later the bathroom door slammed.

Grinning, Ty pulled on a pair of jeans and on his way past the bathroom he called out, "I was about to say let's go out for breakfast. But if you're up for shower sex, I'm game."

Her reply was incomprehensible and in the form of a muffled squeak, making Ty laugh. "Okay, but if you're not out in five minutes, I'm coming in."

CHAPTER ELEVEN

IT WASN'T OFTEN that Paige and Frankie had a day off together but when they did, they liked doing something they wouldn't normally. Last time they'd gone hiking—not Paige's favorite pastime, although the scenery had made up for the unpleasant physical exertion.

It had been Paige's turn to choose and she was eager to explore all the little towns along the coast. Frankie, naturally athletic, had smirked at Paige's choice of outing but with the promise of lunch at the charming Three Orcas Restaurant, overlooking a rocky bay, she'd reluctantly agreed on condition that Paige paid.

They'd managed an early start and headed for the scenic route to an artists' colony nestled in a bay a couple of hours up the coast.

Paige had jumped at the chance to get out of Port St. John's, needing to clear her head of all the intoxicating male pheromones making her crazy.

Although she was enjoying having Ty around, she kept waiting for the other shoe to drop.

He'd been in Washington for nearly six weeks and she knew without being told that he would soon be returning to LA. She'd casually mentioned his check-up a few times but whenever she did he either shut down completely or he'd put his hands and mouth on her and then she not only forgot what they were discussing, she forgot her own name.

She understood that he was worried about how his hand would impact his future but she couldn't help being hurt that he refused to discuss his concerns with her.

But that was okay, she told herself, they were just neighbors. Granted, they were neighbors with benefits, but Ty was hot, she was willing, and they enjoyed each other's company. End. Of. Story.

Besides, ever since the storm they'd fallen into a kind of unspoken routine where Paige would go to work and Ty would spend time with his father, Nate or Harry. When she got home, he'd badger her about her eating habits, and more often than not make her dinner.

Suddenly she was spending more and more nights in his bed and she was afraid that when he left she wouldn't be able to sleep alone. Her mom had been gone more than fifteen years and it was strange having someone around to nag her about eating properly and getting enough rest. Paige couldn't remember anyone else ever making the effort. If she didn't know any better she could almost convince herself that he cared.

But that was dangerous thinking and although she tried not to, she began looking forward to eating home-cooked meals she didn't have to prepare.

Okay, so she enjoyed his company and whatever came after dinner—and sometimes before—was good too. *Big deal*. What woman wouldn't get excited fantasizing about coming home after a long day in ER to a hot sexy guy, a home-cooked meal and great sex?

Well, Paige was no dummy. She was going to enjoy it while it lasted, without getting her feelings hurt or her heart involved. She'd learned early that people didn't stick and when they bailed you got your heart stomped on. But that wasn't going to happen because her heart wasn't involved with Ty.

Nope, it was locked away safe and sound.

But her body…well, that was something else entirely. Her body craved him with an intensity that would have scared her if she let herself think about it.

So she didn't.

She shoved it to the back of her mind and never made the mistake of waking up with him again, having discovered the emotional intimacy of mornings-after made her feel exposed.

And feeling exposed—especially with a man like Ty— would be fatal. Better to slip away and pretend they were just friendly neighbors. Besides, he'd never mentioned her early-morning Houdini acts so he was clearly happy with the way things were.

Well, good. Fine. She was happy too.

Especially as she was about to spend a glorious day with her best friend.

Once on the highway, Paige opened her window, cranked up the volume of the radio and sang along to every song—even when she didn't know the words. After snorting at her creative lyrics, Frankie joined in and pretty soon they were laughing like loons.

It was exactly what Paige needed; a fun day away from all the confusing emotions she didn't know what to do with. Besides, she needed a healthy dose of reality and could always count on Frankie's perceptive smartass-ness to make her laugh.

They stopped for morning tea at a quaint little seaside café so Paige could stuff her face with waffles smothered in fresh berries and cream.

By midmorning they'd pulled into Battle Bay and set

out to explore the quaint little galleries filled with hundreds of paintings depicting life on the Olympic Peninsula.

They headed over to watch craftsmen and -women work. It was fascinating and educational, especially the candle sculpting, but Frankie had been more interested in the artist creating huge metal sea creatures. That the guy had been hot and shirtless hadn't escaped their attention and Frankie had spent an inordinate amount of time photographing... well, his artwork too.

By the time they were headed back to Port St. John's, Paige was feeling mellow for the first time in weeks. Life on an emotional roller-coaster was exhausting and she was looking forward to her life getting back to normal.

Liar.

Ignoring the disgusted voice in her head, she thought instead about the gifts she'd bought for Ty and Harry. She'd chosen an amazingly realistic carving of a coastguard cutter for Harry and a fierce-looking eagle for Ty.

She couldn't wait to see his reaction.

"You know," Frankie said lazily when they were about fifteen minutes from home, "this was actually a fun day. We should do it again. Maybe sleep over somewhere and make a weekend of it."

Paige hummed her agreement. "I knew you'd like it."

"What I liked," Frankie drawled, "was seeing that guy Matt Rolfe with his shirt off." She hummed. "That was the highlight of the day."

Paige giggled. "I thought it was the crab salad and Manhattan iced tea."

Frankie waggled her brows.

"So I guess all those photos you were taking weren't of his artwork?" Paige asked.

When Frankie gave a snorted "Puh-*leeze*", she momentarily took her gaze off the road.

"Shame on you. Is that why you asked him if he ever posed in the nude?"

Her friend rolled her eyes and fanned her face. "Did you see that guy? *He* was the work of art. Boy, I sure learned a whole lot about art appreciation today."

"He was okay, I guess," Paige mused, thinking about another man she wouldn't mind painting in the nude—if she had any talent, that was. But her stick figures could hardly be termed as talent.

She was enjoying the image of painting a naked Ty with chocolate paint—stuff she could lick off—and almost missed Frankie's horrified sideways look.

"Okay? Are you nuts?" Her friend whipped off her sunglasses to gape at Paige. "With all those gleaming muscles and a great butt showcased in faded denim, the man was the embodiment of the statue of David. Holy cow, I nearly swooned at his feet."

"Mmm," Paige said, unimpressed. "Have you looked at David? I mean, *really* looked?"

"Well, not as much as I looked at Matt Rolfe," she confessed. "But what are you getting at?"

"I did a study on David in art class and, well…he's a little small."

"What are you talking about? That statue is huge."

Paige snickered. "Not where it, um…counts it isn't."

Grinning widely, Frankie said in an echo of Paige's previous statement, "Shame on you, Paige Carlyle, but believe me when I say Matt Rolfe filled out his jeans just fine. And just because you're getting some, it doesn't mean the rest of us aren't looking." She glanced at Paige. "Or aren't jealous as hell. Especially with that goofy smile you wear most of the time."

"What?" Paige blinked innocently and made a show of looking at her reflection in the rearview mirror. "What goofy smile?" She hadn't said anything about how she'd been spending her nights, mostly because she'd barely seen Frankie since the night of the storm. Oh, yes, and maybe because she didn't know what the heck to say except... *wow* and...*holy cow.*

"Don't try that with me, Dr. Cutie. With both you and Ty looking all relaxed and mellow, it's obvious what's been going on."

"Nothing's been going on," Paige insisted, her mellow mood vanishing. Nothing *was* happening. Well, except for a lot of amazing orgasms...but nobody needed to know about those. "And when did you see Ty?"

"The other evening when you were on duty. Didn't he tell you?"

"No, um... I guess it didn't come up."

"Well I was at the Seafarers when he and Nate came in and I overheard them discussing his accident."

"His accident?" Paige said, trying to sound casual because Ty certainly hadn't shared much of anything personal with her, especially his accident.

"Yeah, well, after what I heard, I did an internet search on it and apparently some drunk guy thought Ty was someone else and tried to run him over. Fortunately the bumper only clipped him or it would have been a lot worse than a few bruises and a couple of broken bones." She shook her head. "A real pity as he's supposed to be one of the top trauma surgeons at St Augustine's."

Frankie frowned and turned to Paige. "And why didn't you tell me he's leaving next week?"

Paige's mind went blank. "I...um— What?"

Frankie's gaze sharpened and she cursed softly. "You didn't know. Damn, Paige. I'm sorry."

Paige rallied quickly and casually hitched her shoulder. "Don't be," she said, sending her friend a dazzling smile that probably fell way short of its intended brilliance. "Of course I knew he was leaving…just not next… You know it doesn't matter because it's not like we're a thing…or anything," she finished lamely.

Frankie sounded skeptical. "So hot regular sex isn't a thing?"

"Of course not," Paige spluttered out on a strangled laugh. "We barely know each other and—"

"And you're in love with him."

"What? *No*," she squeaked, wrenching the wheel and nearly driving into oncoming traffic. After righting the car, she turned to gape at Frankie like she'd announced something horrifying. Because she had…kind of. Horrifying and *so-o-o* not true. "Of course I'm not in love with Ty." That would be ridiculous and really, really stupid.

"Stupid I give you," Frankie retorted, and it took a couple of seconds for Paige to realize she'd spoken out loud. "But what's so ridiculous about it? Is it because he might never do surgery again? Because if it is—"

"What?" Paige demanded indignantly. "Are you crazy? Of course that's not the reason. He's leaving, so whether or not I'm in love with him—and I'm *not*," she insisted when Frankie rolled her eyes, "is beside the point. He's leaving." Oh, boy, it was finally happening. "Maybe now I can get some sleep." Her heart squeezed and she got a very bad feeling in her stomach. Hopefully it was just the crab she'd had for lunch because the alternative was— *No. Nope. Not happening*. "End of story," she said firmly, although she wasn't sure who she was talking to.

"Sleeping's overrated," Frankie dismissed with a flick of her hand. "You can sleep when you're—" She sat up abruptly and swore. "What the hell is that driver—? Hey, watch out!"

Her warning came too late for Paige to swerve out of

the way and was drowned out by the sound of crunching metal and shattering glass. The last thing she heard was Frankie's curse.

Ty raced through the automatic doors at the JDF Medical Center and headed straight for ER. The nurse at the sign-in desk looked up as he ran past.

"Hey!" She bolted around the counter and grabbed his sleeve. "You can't go through there. Stop!"

Ty whirled on her, breathing fast. He probably looked like a wild man but he didn't care. Only that he—

"Paige Carlyle," he snarled. "Which room?"

The woman's brow wrinkled. "I don't know... Dr. Michaels, I think...she—"

"I'll find her," he growled through clenched teeth, shaking off her hand and heading for the swing doors separating the waiting area from the exam rooms. The door closed on her spluttered, "We're in Code Yellow."

The place was in chaos. Nurses, orderlies and paramedics rushed about and he could hear a furious male voice snap, "Find her, before I have all your asses in a sling."

It was the first time he'd been in the belly of ER since his accident but the fact that his chest was squeezing the life out of him had nothing to do with apprehension about his future, cardiac arrest or even that he was afraid he'd never work in another ER again.

All he could think about was the call he'd received fifteen minutes ago from Nate. Sitting on Harry's deck, playing chess, he'd been enjoying the sun and the old man's stories about his glory days as a coastguard. One minute he'd been chuckling and plotting his move, the next...

"There's been an accident," Nate had said brusquely without his customary greeting, and his next words had sent Ty's world into a tailspin. Nate barely got out, "Paige is…" and Ty had already vaulted off Harry's deck.

"That was Nate," he'd called out, dashing the few yards along the marina walkway and taking the stairs to his deck at a dead run. "There's been an accident." He'd said nothing about Paige in case Harry worried, but the drive to the hospital had been the longest fifteen minutes of his life; even longer than waiting for the orthopedic surgeon to pronounce his diagnosis after his surgery. Even longer than waiting in a jail cell at eighteen for his mother to arrive.

And now, with the current chaos, the worst possible scenarios flashed through his head. At the center was Paige, battered, bruised and the cause of all the panic.

He grabbed the first person he came across, the nurse from the night of the storm. "Nancy—"

"Can't talk now, handsome," she hurriedly called out. "We've misplaced a…something."

He was about to ask her what the hell they'd misplaced when she raced off, leaving Ty to search every ER room himself.

He found her in the last room.

Not on the gurney, hooked up to IVs or machines, as he'd expected, but comforting the middle-aged woman on the bed. "Oh, my gosh, I'm so sorry," the woman sobbed. "I took that bend too fast and when I pumped the brakes there was…nothing. Not a thing." She paused to wipe her eyes. "I didn't see you, I really didn't."

Ty froze in the doorway, his eyes racing over Paige, his heart pounding so hard he was surprised to see his chest intact. He opened his mouth but when nothing emerged he closed it with a snap.

The sight of her clearly in one piece caused something like a brain explosion and it took a few moments before he found his voice. "What the hell are you doing?" he rasped furiously.

Paige jolted like she'd been shot and flashed a startled look over her shoulder. The sight of a bruise blooming along her cheekbone had his anger rising in tandem with relief. Stalking closer, he whipped her around.

"Dammit, Paige," he growled, freezing when she winced and he got a good look at her face. Her eye was swollen, she had a vivid bruise along one side of her face, and a laceration that had yet to be attended to. Blood trickled from the wound and one side of her shirt was covered with blood.

"What the hell?" he rasped. "I thought…" He didn't complete his sentence, mostly because his throat closed; instead, he yanked her into his arms and crushed her close, his relief at seeing her, a little battered but very much alive, so immense that for a moment his knees buckled.

He locked them and tightened his grip on her, needing the feel of her in his arms probably more than she did. She cried out and he immediately let her go. "Damn, I'm sorry," he murmured, carefully stepping back so he could look her over. "Why haven't you been seen and why are you attending to someone else?"

"A patient has gone missing," she explained. "Everyone's busy and I'm not a priority."

"You damn well are," he snapped out, and took her arm before turning to the wide-eyed woman on the bed. "Ma'am, are you okay?"

The woman blinked. "I, um…sure. My son is on his way and your…your wife was kind enough to sit with me while I wait for a scan. But I'm fine. You go ahead."

"Ty—" Paige began, only to stop with a huff when he sent her a look that usually had ER personnel scattering.

He turned to the woman. "Excuse us while I attend to my…*wife*."

He pulled Paige into the opposite room and led her to the bed. "On," he said tersely, and when she made an annoyed sound in the back of her throat he sighed and growled, "Please."

"Ty, I'm fine," she began, gingerly getting onto the bed. "You didn't need to come."

"I came," he gritted out, "because I thought—probably stupidly—that you might need me." He didn't say that the thought of her being seriously injured had scared the living spit out of him. He didn't tell her that his mind had gone utterly blank and that at one point he'd thought he was having a coronary.

Getting madder, he slammed open drawers and cabinets, looking for what he'd need, before turning to find her sitting on the bed, watching him with serious eyes, her soft mouth pressed into a firm line. As though he'd done something reprehensible.

"You didn't have to come," she repeated dully. "As you can see, I'm fine."

"I'll be the judge of that," he growled, wanting more than anything to wrap her close and never let go. Or maybe wrap his fingers around her neck for scaring him.

The latter impulse was less frightening than the former and allowed him to focus. With his jaw clenched, he gently cleaned Paige's head wound, relieved to find it was just a little over an inch long and wouldn't even need stitches.

"What happened?" he asked when he'd calmed down enough to talk without snarling.

"Mrs. Eberhart said her brakes failed."

"I heard that part. What happened, Paige?"

She winced when he touched a particularly tender spot and huffed out a breathy growl like she was irritated. She didn't know the meaning of irritated, he thought furiously.

"I don't know," she said. "We were just up the coast and

Frankie and I were talking about—well, never mind that."
She flashed him an unreadable glance before continuing.
"We were approaching a particularly steep bend and the
next thing this red car came out of nowhere. It swerved
into our lane and— Damn, that stings." She sucked in a
sharp breath when he applied antiseptic but after a couple
of beats she continued, her voice tight. "Anyway, I didn't
swerve in time. She hit the driver's side and we…um…we
spun into a section of rock face."

She was silent while he taped the wound closed. "You
didn't have to do this, you know. Frankie would have—"

"Shut up," he interrupted quietly, and picked up the oph-
thalmoscope. "How bad is the headache?"

"I'm f—all right," she said huffily when he shone the
light into her eyes and pain lanced through her skull. "I
have a headache. Big deal. It happens when you rap your
head against something." She pushed his hand away. "Just
give me a damn aspirin and I'll be good to go." She made
to slide off the bed but Ty put his hand on her chest to keep
her there and she made an odd sound and froze.

"What? What's wrong?" he demanded, his eyes sweep-
ing over her for signs of trauma he hadn't yet picked up. In
the process he caught sight of her bruised wrist. "Dammit,
why the hell didn't you say something?"

"Ty." She caught his hand and wrapped her fingers
around his wrist. "It's just a bruise, I promise."

He flexed his jaw. "What else, Paige? A bruised wrist
doesn't make you go white with pain."

For long moments she just looked at him as though she
expected him to give up. But Ty wasn't anybody's fool.
During his ER rotation he'd treated everything from crush
injuries to impalements and knew when someone wasn't
being straight with him.

Finally, Paige sighed and slowly lifted her T-shirt and

it was Ty's turn to suck in air. He carefully helped her lift her shirt the rest of the way and cursed when he saw the line of bruising across her chest and abdomen from the car's seat belt. "Lie flat for me," he murmured, and when Paige snorted, he chuckled. "This is purely professional, believe me."

He gently probed her ribs, watching her face for a reaction she wouldn't be able to hide from him, and then listened to her chest for internal trauma. Finally he grunted in satisfaction and pulled her shirt down. He helped her sit up.

"Let's wrap that wrist, shall we?"

"Your hand—"

"Is just fine," he interrupted briskly. "A lot better than yours."

He found a crepe bandage and carefully strapped her wrist. He struggled a bit with the clips until she reached out with her good hand to help. Finally there was nothing more to do but Ty didn't move away. Instead, he lifted her chin and with his gaze locked on hers he kissed her carefully on the mouth.

His lips clung to hers, needing the connection more than he'd thought possible. After a long moment of unresponsiveness she uttered a soft sound and her...lips...melted. *Thank God.* He'd been beginning to think that she was deliberately distancing herself from him. He changed the angle of the kiss and—

The door slammed open. "Paige, we have a blue thirt— Oh... Oh, I'm sorry," the nurse said when she took in the scene. She was about to back out of the room when Paige shoved Ty aside with her good hand and eased off the bed.

She looked a little dazed. "What about a b-blue thirteen?" she stuttered, her cheeks blooming with the color she'd been missing a short while ago. It took a moment for the RN's words to register and although not all hospitals used a code blue thirteen, he knew it meant an infant in distress.

"Paige, I'm s-sorry. I wouldn't ask you to do this...not after all you've b-been through." The woman's eyes filled. "Everyone else is busy and I don't know what to do."

"It's okay, Beth," Paige said, turning to snag a lab coat and stethoscope as she hurried from the room. "I'm fine, really. Lead the way."

Concerned, Ty followed. "Paige, don't tell me you're going to treat a patient while you have a possible concussion."

She looked over her shoulder as the nurse handed her a clipboard. "I have a hard head. I'll get over it," she said, and Ty got an odd feeling she wasn't talking about her head. She turned away to scan the hastily scribbled notes before pausing to flash him a look that was curiously closed and devoid of her usual spark. "I know how hard this was for you. But I just want to thank you. For everything."

And the next instant she was gone, leaving Ty to stare at the corner around which she'd disappeared and wonder what the hell had just happened. It had seemed like she was saying goodbye. Like she would never see him again. Like... His chest squeezed.

"What the hell just happened?" he demanded, and though he'd spoken out loud, he certainly didn't expect anyone to reply from directly behind him.

"What happened where?"

He knew it was Frankie even before he turned but the sight of her had him taking a step back. "Jeez, woman, I should be asking you that."

Frankie's one cheekbone was bruised, there was a contusion along the side of her jaw and her arm was in a sling. He gently took her chin in his hand and studied her eyes. "You okay? Has anyone checked you out?"

Her gaze was curious. "Paige did because everyone else was busy. But what about you, T? You don't look so good."

Ty's automatic response was that he was fine, but he wasn't. Not by a long shot. *Not by* any *shot, dammit.* He sighed and shoved a hand through his hair. "I'm just peachy."

Frankie looked like she didn't believe him. Not surprising, considering he felt like he'd been punched in the head.

"Really? Because you look like you just lost your best friend."

He wasn't ready to think about what was really bugging him, let alone talk about it. And certainly not with Frankie. "What I didn't like was getting a call to say that there'd been an accident and that Paige— But you were there too and I'm glad to see you're okay. You are okay, aren't you?"

"Yeah, nothing a hot soak in the tub won't fix." She was silent for a couple of beats. "So who called?"

"Nate," Ty admitted, and as he was looking right at Frankie, he couldn't miss the abrupt change that came over her. Her back stiffened, her eyes instantly cooled and her mouth curled into a sneer.

"Can't believe the big man actually took time off from his busy schedule to care about people he had no problem forgetting when he became a fancy Navy SEAL."

Ty, suitably distracted from his own disturbing thoughts, sighed. "Frankie," he said, slinging an arm across her shoulders and hugging her to his side. He pressed his lips to her temple. "When are you going to get over whatever has you riled up over Nate?"

"When hell freezes over," was her instant reply, but before she shrugged off his arm she laid her head against his shoulder in an affectionate gesture. "And you can tell him that too." She stalked off a few paces before turning. "But I have a piece of advice for you too, T," she said walking backwards. "This place is a madhouse and Paige is hurt-ing more than she's letting on. Go help her."

He wordlessly held up his cast and Frankie sneered for the second time in as many minutes.

"Since when did something like a broken hand ever stop you?" she demanded. "The Tyler Reese I knew climbed down a cliff face with a fractured ankle to rescue me when I was fifteen. Man up, T, and see what's right in front of your nose." And with that piece of baffling advice she spun away and disappeared around the next corner.

CHAPTER TWELVE

Paige paused and scanned the notes in front of her. "Just give me the Cliff Notes version, Beth, and ignore the bruises. That's all they are, bruises."

"All right," the RN said on a sigh, gently bumping shoulders with Paige in unspoken support. "The patient was brought in fifteen minutes ago with tachycardia, tachypnea and a low-grade fever. EMTs had difficulty keeping him conscious and ventilated. We immediately drew bloods and bagged him but we're still waiting for the results."

"Any signs of injury?" Paige asked, hoping they weren't dealing with an abused baby because if that happened it might spark the flood of emotion she was bottling up behind a thin veneer of professionalism. If that dam broke she'd probably cry about everything that had happened over the past twenty years.

"Nothing except a recent spider bite that he was treated for, and, believe me," the RN admitted in a low voice, "we looked."

"Okay, I'll examine him but you might want to get a trolley with a paeds CL insertion and electrodes. Oh, and see if there's an ECHO available," she called out when Beth hurried off, pausing to check the next sheet before pushing open the door to ER 4.

Bryce and Courtney Cavendish hovered close to the bed,

looking terrified as a nursing assistant worked on keeping the toddler ventilated. Dressed in just a disposable diaper, little Joshua looked tiny and fragile on the large ER bed.

Despite having being bagged, Paige could see that his breathing was fast and erratic, and instead of looking flushed, as one would expect in a child running a fever, his skin was pale, almost translucent.

"Good evening," she said, entering the room with a calm professional smile. "I'm Dr. Carlyle."

They turned as one and their reaction instantly reminded Paige of her bruised face. "Just ignore the bruises," she said on a little laugh. "I had a little mishap this afternoon. So," she continued briskly, "when did you first notice Joshua's symptoms?"

Paige listened intently as she gently examined the toddler and was probing his head and shoulders for trauma when he suddenly jerked and opened his eyes, giving her the opportunity to watch his pupil reaction.

She knew the instant he realized that she was someone strange because fear and confusion flashed across his little face. It crumpled and he opened his mouth to cry just as his eyes rolled back in his head.

Courtney rushed to the bed looking like she wanted to gather her son into her arms but her husband wrapped his arms around her and drew her away with a murmured, "Let them do their job, honey."

"Oh, God." Courtney turned and wept quietly into her husband's throat and Paige tried not to feel envious of their obvious love for each other and their child. What must it be like to have that kind of unspoken, unwavering support?

"He's all right," Courtney continued to sob. "Our baby's going to be all right." She turned wet, hopeful eyes on Paige. "He's going to be all right, isn't he?"

Paige winced inwardly. How did you tell a child's distraught mother that you had no idea what was wrong with him and that he might need some invasive procedures to get those answers? Procedures that could be both painful and dangerous.

"I promise that we'll get to the bottom of Joshua's problem," she said gently, knowing she couldn't in all good conscience tell the terrified woman what she wanted to hear. "Before I ask you and your husband to go with Nurse Bremner, I'd like to ask you a few questions."

"Of c-course," the young father said, looking white and shaky as though he understood what Paige wasn't saying. Her heart squeezed and she instinctively knew they weren't dealing with abuse. These parents obviously loved and cared for their son. The trick now was to fix little Joshua as soon as possible so his parents could take him home where he belonged.

Intent on the Cavendishes, Paige was only vaguely aware of a large presence coming up behind her and it was several moments before she realized it was Ty. Studiously ignoring the prickles of awareness marching up and down her spine, she concentrated instead on her questions.

Besides, she had no idea what he was still doing there and couldn't afford to care. Not with the crisis they were facing, and not with her heart. She needed to concentrate and wished he would go away. *Far, far away.* Now instead of next week. Now before she got in any deeper.

He waited until the young couple left with the nurse to take over the bagging.

"I thought you'd left," Paige said briskly, sending him a brief glance as she checked the toddler's pupil reaction again.

"I'll wait around until you're ready to leave."

"It might be late," she warned absently, frowning as

something caught her eye. "In fact, you should go. This is going to take a while. I'll get a taxi."

"I'm not leaving," he growled irritably.

But he was. He was leaving next week and he hadn't told her. In fact, he hadn't said much of anything, let alone the important stuff. Blocking out her thoughts was difficult with a headache but she leaned closer to Joshua and gently pressed her fingers to the boy's neck. "Mmm." She whipped her stethoscope from around her neck and fitted them to her ears as she pressed the disk over Joshua's chest. "Did anyone else notice that?"

"Notice what?" the NA asked, leaning closer. "What did you see, Dr. Carlyle?"

"Where's the blood work?" Paige asked as she gently palpated the boy's chest, ignoring the pain shooting up her arm from her injured wrist because she could hear a dull sound and that was never a good thing. "We need those results." She turned to the NA. "Put a rush on them, Stacey. If it's what I think it is, this little boy's in trouble."

"What—?"

"Results. Please. Here," she said, thrusting the stethoscope at Ty. "If you won't leave then tell me what you hear." After a brief pause, Ty took the scope and moved beside her, silent as he slid the disk over the tiny chest. Paige held her breath.

"Dammit, Ty," she burst out after a long pause. "Tell me you hear it too."

Despite her earlier wish that he'd leave so she could start getting over him, she was abruptly glad he hadn't. All other qualified personnel were occupied and if she was right about her patient, they couldn't afford to wait.

"Heart rate is dropping," she murmured, "but so are blood saturation levels." Paige eyed the monitor with concern. Saturation levels were a lot lower than they'd been ten minutes earlier despite the PPV. And Joshua, who'd again come around, had begun to hiccup and his crying was weak.

"Hmm," Ty murmured. "Lung auscultation reveals coarse crackles while the heart appears…muffled." He removed the stethoscope and looped it around Paige's neck. "I think you're right. What's your take?"

The question put him inches away. "With the slight jugular vein enlargement, decreased saturation levels, brady-cardia and hiccups…dammit, all it can be is a—"

"Tamponade," they said simultaneously, and Paige's shoulders slumped. She'd hoped he would come to a different conclusion but wasn't surprised he hadn't. Little Joshua was in cardiac tamponade, a dangerous condition that oc-curred when the sac around the heart filled with fluid, putting pressure on the organ and preventing normal func-tioning. When that became too much, one or more cham-bers sometimes collapsed.

It was often fatal.

"Okay. What do you want me to do?" Ty asked quietly, his gaze intent on hers and not offering advice she hadn't requested in deference to her official status as the doctor in charge.

The question surprised her. For a trauma surgeon who liked taking charge, he was being remarkably restrained. She didn't have time to wonder why.

Absently rubbing her aching temple, she spied the sonar machine. "I need a better look," she said, hurrying over to the equipment. "And I don't have time to wait for an ECHO."

"Fluoroscope?" Ty asked, referring to a very expensive machine that worked like a real-time X-ray.

Paige snorted. "You're kidding, right? You do remember

that this is the wilds of Washington and not some fancy LA clinic?"

He stared at her for a long moment before sighing. "You're doing it the old-fashioned way, then." And Paige stilled.

Oh, yeah, she reminded herself, *you're the primary on this one. It's up to you to see the Cavendishes get to take their son home.*

"You've done it before?" he asked quietly.

Paige paused before saying, "Not on an infant. Please, tell me you've done this on an infant?"

"Nope, sorry."

"Oh, boy." She looked up and their eyes locked, and just for an instant everything fell away. With difficulty she forced herself to ask, "Can you, um…?" but he held up his injured hand and Paige realized how much she'd hoped he would offer to do it.

"I'm also not registered to practice in Washington, Paige. You know that."

She did. She knew that but they needed someone experienced—preferably with full use of both hands.

"Listen," he said quietly. "With the NA we have two pairs of hands among us. I'll talk you through it."

She paused, knowing that he was right. He had the experience and she had the dominant hand in working order. "Pulse dropping to seventy, Paige," he announced, with a sharp look that said he was waiting for her decision. "And he's showing signs of cyanosis."

Snapping into action, Paige grabbed a tube of gel to squirt a generous amount on her tiny patient's chest.

"Keep bagging him," she urged the NA, noting the definite signs that the toddler wasn't getting enough oxygen as she located his heart with the probe. She sucked in a breath when the organ popped into view on the screen.

"Marked pericardial effusion with evidence of early cardiac tamponade," Paige muttered. "Dammit, it's worse than I thought. Maybe we can get him up to OR—"

"There's no time," Ty interrupted, pointing to the top of the heart where the right chamber appeared to be slightly squashed. "Do it now before he arrests."

Paige sucked in a deep breath. "You're right," she muttered, before saying briskly, "Stacey, we need twenty-five ug per minute of dopamine and one point two mg furosomide, una tantum, while I prep him for a pc. Where the hell is Beth? *Dammit*, I need five mils of two percent lidocaine, a twenty-two-gauge pericardiocentesis needle with guide and dilators, a scalpel, pigtail catheter and a vacuum bag." She sent Ty a quick look. "If you're serious about assisting, I'm going to need pediatric electrodes and an iodine swab."

Working quickly, Paige injected a sedative directly into the drip-line port, and opened the line.

"We need a forty-five-degree angle of elevation," she began, but Ty was already working the levers with his feet. Beth finally returned and Paige instantly directed her to the bed. "Make sure he doesn't move, Beth. I want him absolutely still for this," she said, moving into position with a quick prayer.

So many things could go wrong with such a tiny patient.

"You'll do fine," Ty said calmly, correctly interpreting her hesitation. "Just breathe deeply and focus. I know your wrist hurts. Block it off and… That's good," he said when she'd sucked in a deep breath and let it out. "Now take another and let it out slowly while you decide what you need to do." He held out the large-gauge needle attached to a twenty-ml syringe and a scalpel.

She reminded herself that he was used to taking control, that he was the one usually giving orders. Yet here he was easily letting her take the lead without attempting to influence her.

Paige took the scalpel with her left hand and gave a wince. "You okay?" he asked as she transferred it to her right hand. She nodded, and spared him a look. "Good," he said crisply. "That's good. An incision will make the cannula insertion easier. Make a half-inch incision at the point where the left costal margin meets the xiphisternum. Great," he added after Paige made the cut.

"Now…introduce the needle and dissect the subcutaneous tissue. You'll feel a small pop when you pierce the wall," he murmured calmly, maneuvering the sonar probe to give Paige a clearer image of the heart with its inferior fluid-filled sac.

"Right, now angle it towards the left shoulder at a twenty—no, sharper, Paige, you don't want to damage the internal mammary artery or the neurovascular bundle on the inferior rib surface. There, that's it…perfect. Okay, now gently pull back on the plunger as you aim for the left shoulder tip…*slowly*…there, see on the monitor? The needle tip is about an inch from the sac. Just a fraction more," he breathed into the tense silence that had settled over the ER room, a silence broken only by his murmured words and the slow, irregular beeping of the heart monitor.

Calm had settled over Paige. She'd pushed the pain to the back of her mind and concentrated instead on breathing as Ty had instructed. Her ribs hurt with every inhalation but she soon realized that her breathing had slowed to sync with his.

She didn't know if he'd done it purposely but it felt like they'd entered a vacuum where everything—the room, the world and even her abused body—faded. Her hands seemed to be connected to his mind, already doing his bidding before he could voice his thoughts. It was a strange yet exhilarating experience to be so attuned to another person that you knew, even before they spoke, what they were thinking.

"Excellent…perfect positioning. Now…wait for the… Okay, hold steady for the flashback then carefully fill the syringe."

All eyes watched the monitor as the syringe filled.

"It's cloudy," Ty murmured, and though she wanted to look, she kept her eyes on the screen. Any movement on her part could cause the needle to penetrate the heart and put her patient in cardiac arrest.

Then the monitor stopped beeping.

Paige froze. Had she done something wrong?

Ty murmured for her to wait. It had to be the longest seconds of Paige's life but after a few hair-raising moments, the beeping resumed and she released her breath on a gusty exhalation of relief.

"Cardiac rhythm is already normalizing," Ty murmured. "What's next?"

"Guide wire," she said shakily, trying awkwardly to remove the syringe from the needle. Finally Beth took over, quickly twisting it free. "Thanks. Get it up to the lab, will you? I want a full analysis by morning. Be sure to request a fungal test and I want to check clotting parameters so we can correct any abnormalities while we wait."

With deft movements, she inserted the guide wire through the needle until it entered the pericardium. Once she'd removed the needle, she passed a soft-tipped pigtail catheter over the wire until it too entered the pericardium. She slid the wire free and connected the vacuum bag, finally securing the incision site with a couple of small stitches and tape.

When there was nothing more to do, she stepped back to check the monitor. "Looks promising," she murmured to herself as relief began to flood through her, along with all the myriad aches and pains she'd ignored during the procedure. "Heart and respiration rates rising…sinus rhythm returning…and, wow!" She gusted out a shaky breath as her lips curved involuntarily. "Look at that. His color's better too."

They'd done it and it wouldn't have been possible without Ty and his calming presence—without his firm, quiet instruction. He was too good, too knowledgeable a physician to lose because he was mad at the world.

"Stacey, call upstairs and let them know he's on his way. I want to keep him sedated until we know more. Beth, put a rush on those samples while I talk to mom and dad."

When the nurses had left, the only sound in the room was the quiet beeping of the machine and Paige's heart pounding in her ears. She needed a minute.

No, maybe two, because her head suddenly swam, pounding out of control, along with her heart. Every bruise seemed to have a pulse of its own too and she felt each throb as if for the first time. She must have swayed because Ty was suddenly there, supporting her.

"Dammit, Paige—"

The door opened and, conscious of the picture they made, Paige quickly stepped away and turned to meet Joshua's parents. They were visibly upset by the sight of their son, hooked up to monitors and with a tube sticking out of his chest. Paige drew them aside to explain and by the time her little patient had been whisked away to ICU it was all she could do to walk to the door.

She hurt. All over. Including her heart.

Ty was waiting outside and the instant she stepped into the corridor he gently took her arm. "You're done," he said, slipping the lab coat and stethoscope off her.

She was a little surprised to find him still there. "I

have a patient," she began, only to be interrupted by the shift supervisor.

"He's right, Paige," Marc Wallace said, coming up behind her. Her boss looked as though he'd been through the wringer. "You're done for the day and I don't want to see you till Monday."

"But—"

"Look at you," he said gently but firmly. "You can hardly stay on your feet. I'll get Kara Grant to take over the boy's care but from what I hear you did all the hard stuff." He reached out to squeeze her shoulder, murmuring an apology when she winced. "You saved a little boy's life, Paige, now let your man take you home."

Paige wanted to tell him that Ty wasn't her man but before she could get the words out, Marc was gone and Ty was steering her towards the exit.

Aware of the deep trembling in her core, Paige was silent on the drive home. Other than a few concerned looks, Ty too said nothing. Exhausted and hurting, the last thing she wanted to deal with was his leaving.

He parked and helped her out the SUV but when he tried to steer her towards his unit, Paige shook her head. She wanted to be surrounded by her own stuff and sleep in her own bed tonight. Besides, it was time she got used to being alone again.

Without arguing, Ty let her into her house and switched on the lights. It had been days since she'd actually spent any time there and the place felt empty.

Yep, a little voice drawled in her head. *As empty as your heart is going to be when he leaves.* But Paige wasn't going to think about that now. She just wanted to sleep. Maybe until her life got back to normal or she woke up and realized the past couple of months had been nothing but a pleasant dream.

Besides, talking clearly hadn't got her anywhere so far.

She headed for the stairs and when he came up behind her she turned to stare at him dully. The overhead light cast most of his features in shadow, illuminating only one side of his face. His eyes were dark and unreadable and his mouth unsmiling.

She couldn't stop her gaze from dropping to study its sculpted lines or keep from recalling exactly how it felt on hers. Especially the kiss in ER. It had confused her as much as it had sent her heart skittering because he'd kissed her as if she was delicate and precious to him. But it was a lie. Like his lie of omission.

"I told you I'm not leaving," he growled softly. "And I meant it."

Too tired and heartsick to tell him what she already knew, Paige turned and slowly took the stairs. She concentrated on lifting each foot because her muscles had stiffened and it was an effort to move.

At the landing she headed for the bathroom, vaguely conscious of Ty disappearing into her bedroom. She turned the shower to steaming and had to sit on the bath to remove her shoes. It took a concentrated effort but she'd managed to unlace one sneaker before two masculine hands and a dark head appeared in her vision.

He brushed her hands aside and finished the job of undressing her. Then he stripped and drew her into the shower.

Tears pricked the backs of her eyes and she gulped them down. She couldn't—just couldn't—bear memories of him in here too. "Ty," she began, but he gently soothed her and closed the door.

"Let me, Paige," he murmured against her temple. "Let me take care of you."

And though she surrendered—mostly because she

didn't have the energy to resist—Paige knew he didn't really mean it. But that was okay. She'd had enough experience taking care of herself.

She didn't know how long he let the hot water work on her abused muscles, but resting against his hard warm body she drifted, only to stir when he carefully ran the soapy sponge over her. Once her skin was pink—where she wasn't black and blue—he tugged her from the shower, dried her and pulled a huge T-shirt over her head.

She began floating and it took her a couple of seconds to realize that he was carrying her. The comforter had already been pulled back and within seconds of him gently tucking her in, everything slipped away.

Sometime later she was roused from a disturbing dream where she was standing on the rocky shoreline, watching a figure disappear into the fog. She must have been crying because Ty's hands were soothing and her face was wet.

She pried her eyes open and blinked in the low light. Shirtless and with his hair mussed, he looked big and bad and dangerous in her girly room.

"Hey," he murmured. "You okay?"

"Yeah," she croaked, rolling over and wincing when her body protested. "Ouch. Why?"

He helped her up. "You were crying. Bad dream?"

"Hmm," she said noncommittally, unwilling to recall the devastation she'd felt in her dream or what it might mean. "How's…um… Joshua?"

"He's fine. Vitals stable." He held out his hand. Two small tablets nestled in his palm. "Take these," he said, handing her a glass of water.

Wordlessly she swallowed them, easing her body down into the bed when he took the glass from her. She was just slipping into sleep when she jolted.

"Ty?"

"Right here," he murmured from somewhere close.

The sound of his voice had her body relaxing. "But you won't be," she murmured sadly.

"Won't be what, babe?"

Babe. She knew she should be protesting but she liked it. "Be here."

"I'm right here," he soothed, running a hand down her arm. "I'm not leaving you tonight."

But he would. And soon. "I know, you know," she murmured, feeling her throat close when he smoothed a strand of hair off her face.

"Know what?"

She silently enjoyed the gentle caress for a few moments before admitting, "That you're leaving."

When Paige next woke, the sun was high and the bed was empty. As empty as the house felt. And when she went next door, she found that empty too and tried not to care.

He'd promised he would be there but he'd lied. Just as her mother had fifteen years ago when she'd promised a frightened pre-teen that she would never leave her.

CHAPTER THIRTEEN

TY STARED AT the rolling lawns of his mother's manicured gardens and wished he was a thousand miles away. He lifted the wineglass to his mouth and grimaced. The Chablis was perfectly fine but he'd have preferred whiskey or beer. Always had, despite his mother's efforts to turn him into what she called a "civilized man".

Somehow she'd found out he was back in LA and had issued a dinner invitation. Ty knew a summons when he heard it and hadn't been surprised to find she'd invited the daughter of an acquaintance to dinner. The woman was as perfectly nice as the Chablis but Ty kept comparing her to the one woman he couldn't seem to get out of his head.

What had surprised him was his mother's latest companion. Paul Richmond was well heeled and well educated but, unlike her previous husbands, he could hardly be called polished, sophisticated and smug. And because he wasn't, Ty had liked him instantly. However, he wasn't in the mood for a dinner party and he wasn't in the mood for his mother's brand of matchmaking or interrogation—which the evening was actually a cover for.

The week since his return had been jam-packed with meetings and appointments, mostly to keep him from thinking. It hadn't worked, because all he'd done *was* think. About Paige, about her accident, and about the mind-numbing terror he'd felt when he'd thought she'd been seriously hurt.

He shook off the disturbing images that had constantly been on his mind since that day—images that had followed him even in sleep—because if he thought too much about them he might have to admit that he'd been an idiot.

That leaving Paige had been the biggest mistake of his life.

One minute he'd been watching her sleep, the next...

Okay, so maybe he'd freaked out a little. He'd experienced a crushing feeling in his chest that had had him staggering from the room, thinking he'd been having a heart attack. He'd gone looking for brandy and had found a six-pack of his favorite beer instead. Beer she had to have bought for him because she *was* a wine drinker.

His world had tilted alarmingly and he'd felt as though he'd been rushing towards disaster without a brake. Without a single thought to the consequences.

It was that last notion that had scared him the most. That he knew where this was going and simply didn't care.

So he'd done the one thing he knew would get his life back on track. The one thing he'd gone to Washington to find.

Control of his life.

And while Paige had slept he'd bumped up his flight, packed in record time and left before she could wake because he knew if she looked at him with huge exotic eyes that drew him in against his will, he'd willingly go under for the third time.

A hundred times since then he'd assured himself that escaping from her had saved his life, so why did it feel as though there was a huge empty hole in his soul and that he was slowly suffocating?

A couple of days ago he'd seen his specialist and though

he was still mostly uncertain if his hand would ever withstand the rigors of surgery, he hadn't felt much of anything when Peter Dawson had claimed he'd healed well and with therapy might even get back his former dexterity.

The news should have pleased him but all he could think about was the tentative relationship he'd been forging with his father and about reconnecting with Nate. Relationships he'd left behind.

And in the dark hours of the night he lay awake thinking about Paige and wondering. If she was okay, what she was doing and who she was doing it with. A million times he'd caught himself turning to tell her something or he'd reach for his phone only to realize that she wasn't there and that he'd given up the right to call.

He'd left her curled into her pillows, for God's sake; left her bruised and hurting and needing someone to lean on while he'd slipped out like a thief in the night.

He'd called Frankie, but other than to tell him he was scum she refused to take his calls. But only after telling him that Paige was over him and dating again.

Dating?

His gut clenched for about the trillionth time since he'd heard. *Well, hell.*

And suddenly he could stand it no longer. He had to get away from the stifling atmosphere of his mother's house and the smog and traffic of LA. It had taken him over a week to realize what he hadn't as a kid. He could breathe in Washington and it had nothing—or almost nothing—to do with the fresh air.

It had to do with the people. His father, Jack, Nate and Frankie…and now a sweet, feisty, bossy pain-in-the-ass distraction he couldn't stop thinking about and needed more than his next breath.

With a muttered oath he slammed down the glass on the

nearest surface and headed for the door, only to be stopped
by his mother's peremptory, "Tyler, why don't you tell us
when you're going back to St Augustine's? I hear they've
been horribly short-handed since you buried yourself in
the wilderness."

"I'm not going back, Mother," he said impatiently, because his mother refused to admit that his injury might put
a permanent damper on his meteoric surgical career. A career she liked to tell everyone about. "And Port St. John's
is hardly the wilderness."

"What do you mean, you're not going back?" she demanded, ignoring everything else.

"I resigned." He hadn't but that was his next step.

He was going back to Washington.

He was finally going home.

Renée gasped and paled. "But…but why, for heaven's
sake?" She rose off the couch looking both elegant and
cool, the perfect line of her brow marred by a wrinkle of
displeasure. She might be sixty-two but looked fifty and
was still beautiful. "That's so typically reckless and short-
sighted of you, Tyler. I thought you'd outgrown that juvenile behavior but it seems spending time with that man, in
that Godforsaken place, has turned you against me again."

"Mother—" he began wearily, only to be interrupted
by a cold, "You'll regret it. I certainly did. Besides, I have
it on excellent authority that you'll make a full recovery
and when you do—"

"When I do, Mother, it might not be as a surgeon."

"Of course it will, darling, and St. Augustine's will take
you back. Dr. Hudson assured me of that."

Furious that his mother had been discussing him with
the hospital administrator, he said flatly, "It's done. I've
put my house on the market."

Renée gasped and slapped a hand over her heart as

though he'd stabbed her in the chest. "Oh, my God. You're moving to Washington, aren't you? You're throwing away everything you've worked so hard to achieve. And for what? A rundown harbor town with a second-rate hospital?"

"Yes," Ty said quietly, firmly. "I am. And Port St. John's is hardly run-down. In fact, it's tripled in size in the last twenty years and is a hugely popular tourist resort town. And *that man,* as you call him, is my father." He turned to walk out the door.

"You'll regret this silly decision, Tyler, just as I did."

"No, Mother, I won't," he said quietly over his shoulder. "What I regret is not doing it sooner."

Over his mother's spluttered protest he heard Paul Richmond say, "Let him go, Renée. His mind's clearly made up." And just before he closed the front door he heard Paul add, "Besides, the boy's in love."

His mind instantly rejected being called a boy almost as much as those last words. He actually scoffed as he slammed the front door behind him.

He'd just realized that he belonged in Washington, that's all. Nothing hearts-and-roses about that. Just a hankering for the town of his birth and spending time with his father, with Nate. And with Paige, too, he admitted.

If she ever spoke to him again.

Satisfied that he'd cleared up that misconception in his own mind, he slid behind the wheel of his shiny sports car and froze as everything abruptly fell into place—like the cogs of a safe lock tumbling into place.

It was as if an inner door swung open, revealing... Ty swore, his chest squeezing and his gut churning just like it had the night of Paige's accident. With a blinding flash of insight he realized that all the emotions bombarding him that night, tonight—every moment since—were none other than…

Oh, God, he could barely think the word, let alone say it. But there was no denying his feelings. He was…*yeah, that*, with a woman who'd wormed her way into his heart, first by knocking him out cold and then with every smile, every scowl and every blush since then. A woman who faced her problems head on instead of running from them. A woman he suddenly couldn't see himself living without.

There was no getting away from the truth.

He loved Paige Carlyle and wanted her in his life.

He'd just have to convince her to renegotiate their deal, that's all. A deal that would last the rest of their lives.

Firing up the engine, Ty whipped out of his mother's driveway and headed for the southbound freeway, his mouth curving in a wolfish grin. His little faerie commando had better watch her six because Ty was planning a sneak attack. And he knew exactly how surgically precise and devious it was going to be.

His feisty little medic—aka Dr. Cutie—didn't stand a chance.

Paige heard music as she drifted up through layers of sleep and caught herself smiling before she remembered that her life sucked. Oh, yeah. It was the first time she'd actually managed to fall asleep without tossing and turning because she missed having a big warm body to curl into.

Maybe she should get a dog, she thought sleepily. A huge big shaggy dog. One that she could take for long walks on the beach and curl up with on a cold rainy night. One who would always be happy to see her and wouldn't disappear in the middle of the night and break her freaking heart.

Yep, she yawned, snuggling into the pillow she was wrapped around. A dog sounded great—

Her eyes popped open and she froze as two things registered at once. One, the music was closer than she'd thought and, two—*oh, boy*—her pulse charged ahead of her brain because…because someone was moving around downstairs.

Her eyes widened incredulously.

You have got to be kidding me.

What the heck were the statistics of that happening twice?

Well, she thought furiously, flinging back the covers and grabbing her trusty flashlight off the bedside table. This time there would be no mercy. This time she would not—*not, you hear, Paige Deborah Carlyle?*—let a sexy BAB render her stupid.

Narrowing her eyes, she firmed her lips and tightened her grip. *This* guy was going down and *this* time she would make sure he stayed down. She wouldn't call the cops because Frankie had said she would help her bury the body.

Paige knew *just* the place.

Halfway down the stairs she froze because her heart was pounding so hard she felt a little light-headed and…and there was a warm glow of—she leaned over the banister—candles?…coming from the sitting room.

Music and *candles? What the hell?*

Okay, so clearly her intruder hadn't heard that stealth was a major requirement of "intruding".

Scowling fiercely because she'd taken down the last one with her awesome ninja skills, Paige marched down the stairs prepared to give the guy a piece of her mind. She was the sister of a Navy SEAL, she told herself, *and* a Top Gun. She was—

A huge dark shape materialized beside her and acting on instinct she swung the flashlight with all her strength.

She heard a low oath as it connected and before she

knew it she'd been pinned against the wall and disarmed.
Shocked by the speed with which it had happened, Paige
opened her mouth and…screamed.

Oh, yeah. Killer ninja skills to the rescue.

She thought she heard, "For God's sake, Paige, it's me,"
but it was probably her imagination because Ty was gone.
He'd snuck out when she'd been down and out and she was
never—she thrust a leg between two long muscled ones
and hooked an ankle—*letting anyone*—rammed the heel
of her hand into his gut—*hurt her*—and growled with satisfaction when she heard a grunt of pain as her attacker let
her go—*ever again*!

She shoved hard and the next instant the earth shook.
She uttered a loud *"Haaai ya!"* as he went down hard.

There was a stunned silence, a muttered, "What the—?"
in a voice that was both familiar and as unexpected as the
snort the intruder uttered with his next breath. The snort
turned into a chuckle and soon deep belly laughs filled the
entrance and rattled the panes. It took a couple of dozen
heartbeats to realize that—

"Ty?"

When the man on the floor continued to laugh like a
lunatic, Paige stomped over to the wall and hit the lights.
And there, on the floor where she'd tossed him—okay, it
had been more of a shove—was Tyler Reese, dressed in
nothing but a pair of worn, faded jeans and a wrist brace.
Looking even better than she remembered.

It took another couple of seconds for her brain to compute and when it did, she snapped her mouth closed, narrowed her eyes and stomped closer, snatching the flashlight
off the floor where it had rolled.

"Try anything funny and it's lights out," she snarled,
scowling down at him, one hand on her hip, the other bran-
dishing her trusty flash. She didn't know what the hell was

so damn funny but he took one look at her and whooped with freaking hilarity until, seething with frustration and the remnants of adrenaline, she tried to kick him.

His hand shot out and grabbed her foot and the next thing she knew she'd landed on him hard enough to knock the breath from her lungs. Her bruised ribs protested but before *she* could punch him, he'd rolled and had her pinned beneath him.

She opened her mouth to berate him for manhandling her but Ty swooped down and caught the garbled protest with his mouth. Stunned and a little turned on, Paige tried to shove him away but he grabbed her hands and anchored them beside her head as he continued his assault on her mouth.

And her senses too, *dammit*.

The thought had her nipping his bottom lip hard enough that he broke the kiss and growled, "*Ouch.* What the hell was that for?"

Somehow one of his thighs had sneaked between hers and she could feel how turned on *he* was. The discovery was enough to lend her strength and she punched him once…twice before he grabbed her hands.

Pain shot through her sprained wrist, which had to account for the tears suddenly blurring her vision. It also made her gasp and try to buck him off.

"Dammit," he growled, breathing hard, she was gratified to notice because she was huffing like a geriatric steam engine. "What's got into you?"

"You…" She gulped back a sob and glared at him accusingly. She tried to kick him but he had her legs pinned. "You…you *left.*" Tears blinded her but she furiously blinked them away. No way was she giving him the satisfaction of crying over him. She wasn't. Her wrist hurt, her butt hurt and…and, damn him, her heart hurt too. "Without saying goodbye. Like I was a…a one-night stand, *dammit*."

She must have surprised him because he released her hands and Paige took advantage of his distraction to shove at him, scuttling away when he rolled over to blink at her stupidly.

Her back hit the wall and she instinctively drew her knees up. She recognized it as a defensive pose but she didn't want to be vulnerable to him again. And even though she'd known he was leaving, she'd been as devastated as when her mother had died.

"Hey," he said softly, and Paige realized he'd peeled himself off the floor and was back-to-the wall beside her. His yummy smell enveloped her and she drew in a huge lungful before she could stop herself.

"I'm sorry," he murmured, thrusting a hand through his tousled hair in obvious frustration.

"For what, scaring the hell out of me for the second time?"

His mouth, mostly serious but often sensual—especially when he was contemplating kissing her—curved in amusement.

"No." He grimaced, all amusement gone. "For leaving like that. For being an idiot."

Instead of replying, she gave him a filthy look and *thunked* her head against the wall. After a couple of beats she felt him move and the next moment he was peering into her averted face.

Scowling, she shoved his shoulder.

"Go away, I'm over you."

"Is that why you tried to split my skull open again? Because I have to tell you," he continued when she just growled at him, "for the rest of my life I'll never forget the sight of you standing over me like an avenging faerie commando, ready to whoop my ass."

"I did whoop your ass," she reminded him smartly, secretly pleased with his description. "I wasn't the one knocked on his ass by a girl."

He was silent a moment. "Yeah," he murmured. "I was, wasn't I?"

The tone of his voice aroused her curiosity and when she turned her head and caught him studying her as if he'd never seen her before, a confused frown wrinkled her brow.

"What?"

"You knocked me on my ass."

"I just said that."

"No," he murmured, lifting a hand to cup her jaw, and Paige stilled at the expression in his eyes. Her heart lurched and an entire swarm of locusts invaded her belly. "I mean you *really* knocked me on my ass."

Concerned that he might have hit his head, Paige said, "Ty...?" But he gave a low rough laugh and the next instant she found herself flat on the floor with his hard body covering hers.

Really concerned now, she blinked up into eyes the color of the late summer sky and her breath stuttered to a stop.

With his eyes on hers, he slid his hands into her hair to hold her still and with a soft, "You're awesome," slowly dipped his head to drop a kiss on her startled mouth.

On a muffled oath, he deepened the kiss until they were both breathing heavily and Paige felt just how much the wild mating of mouths had affected him.

Oh, boy. Her too.

He lifted his head long enough to announce, "I can't wait to tell our kids about this," before swooping back to feed her the hottest, hungriest kisses she'd ever experienced.

It was much later when she was sated and draped boneless across Ty's body that she roused herself enough to croak, "Our kids?"

"Hmm?" Ty hummed, smoothing a big hand down her back to her bottom.

"Just before you ravished me you said; 'I can't wait to tell our kids about this.'" She pushed herself up onto her elbow with great effort because she was still trembling from the storm of passion he'd unleashed on her. "Firstly, what the hell? And secondly, *what the hell*?"

He blinked as though waking from a deep sleep and after a long pause, during which his body tensed by degrees, he frowned. "You don't want to marry me?"

Stunned as much by his words as she was by the uncertainty in his tone, Paige gaped at him. After a couple of beats she sat up and reached for the USMC shirt she usually slept in, only to blink when it was whipped out of reach.

"Answer me."

"Well," she said carefully, beginning to get annoyed. "I don't know. You haven't asked me yet."

"But…" He thrust a hand through his hair and after a long pause his breath escaped in a long whoosh. "I'm jobless."

Startled, Paige could only blink.

"And I'm homeless."

Her eyes widened and she was only vaguely aware that her heart had begun a heavy pounding in her chest.

For a long moment he stared at her before reaching out to cup her face with his hands. "And…and you didn't just knock me on my ass, Paige. I fell hard. For you."

"What…?" She swallowed before trying again. "What are you saying, Ty?"

"I'm saying that I'm so in love with you that I'm prepared to beg."

"You…?" She shook her head as if to clear it. "You l-love *me*?"

"Yes," he murmured, kissing her gently on the nose.

"You. The bossy pain-in-the-ass distraction I didn't want but need more than my next breath."

"But…what about your job? Your life?"

"It's here with you, Paige."

She was stunned speechless but after a couple of gasping breaths managed, "I… I—"

Chuckling, Ty pulled her into his arms. "I can't believe the only time I ever see you speechless is when I tell you I love you. Is it that surprising?"

"Well, no," she admitted with a growing smile, because who wouldn't grin knowing that the hottest guy in America had willingly entered her house and declared his love? "I am pretty awesome but—"

With a laugh Ty caught her mouth in a deep wet kiss that seemed to go on forever. Finally he broke away to murmur against her lips, "Yes, you are awesome. But you haven't answered my question."

Breathless, Paige traced his much-loved face and could not help herself from dropping a kiss on his mouth, his jaw and taking a nip out of his ear. "Which one was that?"

He pulled her away to look into her eyes. "Do you love me and will you marry me?"

"That's two—" she began, only to break off with a startled squeak when he dipped his head and nipped her lip.

Curling her fingers in his hair, she yanked his head up so she could see his expression when she said, "Yes. And you'd better not tell our kids what I'm about to do next."

His grin was a mix of relief, joy and blinding love. "And what's that, Dr. Cutie?"

"This," she breathed, shoving him backwards. And when she was straddling him, Paige stared down at him with triumph. "I'm going to turn your world upside down."

* * * * *

*If you enjoyed this story, check out
these other great reads from
Lucy Ryder*

*CAUGHT IN A STORM OF PASSION
FALLING AT THE SURGEON'S FEET
TAMED BY HER ARMY DOC'S TOUCH
RESISTING HER REBEL HERO*

All available now!

MILLS & BOON®

MEDICAL ROMANCE™

THE ULTIMATE IN ROMANTIC MEDICAL DRAMA

A sneak peek at next month's titles...

In stores from 24th August 2017:

- **The Doctor's Forbidden Temptation** *and*
  From Passion to Pregnancy – Tina Beckett

- **The Midwife's Longed-For Baby** – Caroline Anderson
  and **One Night That Changed Her Life** – Emily Forbes

- **The Prince's Cinderella Bride** – Amalie Berlin
  and **Bride for the Single Dad** – Jennifer Taylor

Just can't wait?
Buy our books online before they hit the shops!
www.millsandboon.co.uk

Also available as eBooks.

MILLS & BOON®

EXCLUSIVE EXTRACT

What happens when the forbidden passion between
Dr. Adam Cordeiro and his best friend's sister,
Natália Texeira, becomes irresistible?

Read on for a sneak preview of
THE DOCTOR'S FORBIDDEN TEMPTATION
part of Tina Beckett's sizzling HOT BRAZILIAN DOCS!
miniseries

Adam leaned sideways and kissed her cheek. "See? Painless. That wasn't embarrassing, was it?"

"No, I guess not." She smiled.

"Your turn, since the fortune was for both of us." He presented his cheek to her.

The second she touched her lips to his skin, though, he knew he'd made a huge mistake in asking her to reciprocate. The kiss hit him just beside his mouth, the pressure warm, soft and lingering just a touch too long. Long enough for his hand to slide to the back of her head, his fingers tunneling into her hair. Then before he could stop himself, his head slowly turned toward the source of that sweet heat until he found it. Leaned in tight.

Instead of her pulling away, he could have sworn the lightest sigh breathed against his mouth. And that was when he kissed her back. Face to face. Mouth to mouth.

It was good. Too good. He tilted his head to the side, the need to fit against her singing through his veins. He captured a hint of the coffee she'd drunk, and the wine, his tongue reaching for more of the same.

He forgot about the meal, the fortune cookie…everything, as the kiss went on far beyond the realm of the words platonic and friend and into the hazy kingdom where lovers dwelt.

Every moment from this morning until now seemed to be spiraling toward this event.

A soft sound came from her throat and the fingers in her hair tightened into a fist, whether to tug free or pull her closer, he had no idea. Then her mouth separated from his and she bit the tip of his chin, the sharp sting jerking at regions below his belt, a familiar pulsing beginning to take over his thoughts. If he didn't bring this to a halt now…

Somehow he managed to let go of her hair and place both of his palms on her shoulders, using the momentum to edge her back a few inches. Then a few more.

"Nata…we can't do this." The words didn't seem all that convincing. "Sebastian would kill us."